Where Thy Dark Eye Glances

"In *Where Thy Dark Eye Glances*, Steve Berman ably takes on the challenge [of queering Poe], collecting stories and poetry that critically and lovingly engage with Poe's life, work, and readership...."

"All in all, a beautiful collection, and one to be savoured, especially for a reader who knows and loves Poe — and if you are not such a reader, I recommend becoming one."
— Claire Humphrey for *Ideomancer*

"Berman wisely takes a broad-brush approach, covering not only re-imaginings of Poe's tales but also Poe the man and the act of reading Poe's fiction. This allows a wider variety of pieces, poetic as well as prose, and rescues the book from being overwhelmed by its source material."
— *Publishers Weekly*

Where

THY DARK EYE

Glances

Where
THY DARK EYE
Glances

QUEERING EDGAR ALLAN POE

✳ EDITED BY STEVE BERMAN ✳

LETHE PRESS
MAPLE SHADE, NEW JERSEY

Published in 2013 by Lethe Press, Inc.
118 Heritage Avenue • Maple Shade, NJ 08052-3018
www.lethepressbooks.com • lethepress@aol.com
ISBN: 978-1-59021-334-6 / 1-59021-334-3
e-ISBN: 978-1-59021-428-2 / 1-59021-428-5

These stories and poems are works of original fiction. Names, characters,
places, and incidents are products of the authors' imaginations or are used
fictitiously.

Set in Agmena and Goudy Old Style.
Interior design: Alex Jeffers.
Frontispiece and illustration on page 264: Harry Clarke, from *Tales of Mystery
and Imagination* by Edgar Allan Poe (London: Harrap, 1916).
Cover artwork and design: Niki Smith.
Back cover portrait: Sandy Sandy/Spiritartist.

LIBRARY OF CONGRESS CATALOGING-IN-PUBLICATION DATA

Where thy dark eye glances : queering Edgar Allan Poe / edited by Steve
Berman.
    pages cm
ISBN 978-1-59021-334-6 (pbk. : alk. paper) -- ISBN 978-1-59021-428-2 (e-book)
1. Gay men--Fiction. 2. Poe, Edgar Allan, 1809-1849--Influence. 3. Short
stories, American. I. Berman, Steve, 1968- editor of compilation. II. Poe, Edgar
Allan, 1809-1849.
PS648.H57W49 2013
813'.0108358086642--dc23

2013014291

Table of Contents

READING POE

INTRODUCTION

THERE have been countless studies of Edgar Allan Poe's life, as well as critical essays, papers, and theses on his poetry, his prose, and journalism, so I need not venture into biographical details. Most readers do seem to share a fascination with the more lurid aspects of Poe's life: his obsessions, his excesses, and failings. As one of America's foremost authors, his influence on high and low culture, even centuries past his lifespan, is arguably more important than his body of work.

Examination of his writing and its influence has thankfully not been confined to the straight and narrow path of heterosexual readers: Graham Robb has a marvelous piece on Dupin and his nameless associate (and lover?) in *Strangers: Homosexual Love in Nineteenth Century* that rivals his discussion of Holmes and Watson. Gender and queer theorists have scrutinized "The Fall of the House of Usher" and "The Murders in the Rue Morgue" (the latter quite well analyzed by Jennifer Lui, who remarks on the ill-fated L'Espanaye women as lovers concealing their affair under the guise of mother and daughter in the article "Strange Love in *Frankenstein* and *The Murders in the Rue Morgue*").

Like many late twentieth-century readers, I was originally exposed to Poe's work in one high school English class after another. My adolescence welcomed the works of H.P. Lovecraft and Fritz Leiber. These two gentlemen offered welcome escape into the lands of genetic strangers and homosocial sword & sorcery. Poe, however, suffered the usual fate of acknowledged classics: vapid examination by bored children. An appreciation for Poe would take me a few more years, when I began collecting horror anthologies, the ones that reprinted classic works from the pulps and earlier terror tales — each volume bound to feature a different story by Poe. Away from the different horror of assigned high-school reading, I was ready to appreciate and enjoy them, dwell on the Gothic imagination of his loners and lost souls at my leisure.

Yet there were limitations to what I read; Leiber's womanizing Fafhrd and the Gray Mouser or Poe's various narrators who outdo Bluebeard in their obssession with the death of a beautiful woman could never fulfill my deepest want: passion between men. In high school — pre-Internet, pre-exposure to the vast majority of queer writing and thus ignorant of Arthur Rimbaud or Jean Genet — I force fed my baby-Goth, baby-gay inclinations with crude pastiches of Poe or Lovecraft. The latter, less interested in beauty than Nameless Horror and a pathological fear of oozing fluids, proved a poor model for homoerotic whim while struggling at the typewriter. Poe, though, with his obsession with beauty, often ephemeral and toxic, was ideal for a young man trapped in the closet and pained by handsome high school (and later university) boys. So, like nearly every alienated, "sensitive" teen discovering the powerful metaphors of horror fiction, I tried my hand at writing it myself. Still, any homoeroticism in my own work — while inherent — was downplayed as I had yet to encounter its true expression in speculative fiction. Then, in my freshman year of college, I discovered Clive Barker's infamous story "In the Hills, the Cities" — it forced a paradigm shift in my imagination that allowed me to accept that the fantastical welcomes the blatantly gay.

I have always imagined that Poe's canon, his effect on readers, even the strange life and death he led, deserved "queering." Thus *Where Thy Dark Eye Glances*, a garland of queer *fleurs de mal* inspired by the man himself, by specific works of his prose and verse, and by the experience of reading (discovering, rediscovering) Poe — all bent to the light of a queer mirror for the delight and disquiet of gay and lesbian readers.

Authors already celebrated and still little known answered the call. Their approaches to queering Mr. Poe often differed from my preconceived notions of what I would receive. Nevertheless, the grim revelry with which Poe tied together love and death made him irresistible to writers who have feared (or faced) violence as a result of expressing their affections openly, who lost cherished Prosperos to the Plague Years — who embrace the essential queerness (not necessarily sexual or affectional) of the man and his work. I find a constancy in these authors' stories and poems that makes *Where Thy Dark*

Eye Glances far more than a hodge-podge gallimaufry of pastiche and slashed fan-fic.

I am honored by the caliber of stories and storytellers that have helped make my vision reality. *Where Thy Dark Eye Glances* is no mere dream within a dream but a collective journey into imagination along oft-dark streets and landscapes where the only comfort may be the fleeting touch of another man's, another woman's fingers, before the maelstrom appears and we are lost once again to darkness.

Steve Berman
March 2013

POE THE MAN

THE CITY
AND
THE STRANGER

Seth Cadin

WHAT pulled him first was not the song itself, but that he could not comprehend the language used by its singer. Then as he moved toward it, the strangeness of the melody and the beauty of the voice rose to his attention. The intensity of his fascination with the sound increased with its proximity. Next came the scent of something burning, sweet and spicy, a perfumed charcoal of some kind. He could smell the tang of scorched bronze, and was disappointed when he saw the censer, as it was not uniquely ornate but rough and merely functional.

West Point had become useless to him, and so he'd made his way to New York. Now he felt the city around him as if it were carrying him along in a thin glass sphere. He was the victim of a dereliction which at times stirred him into a frenzy of memories, including many of himself shouting foolishly at John Allan, driven by seething hatred of his guardian's expression of drunken, lopsided disdain. Nevertheless he could see this abandonment left him unfettered by any expectations but his own.

Not to leave aside the machinations of Fate, who clearly had purposes in mind for him. What these might be were tortuously enigmatic to him, except when he was gripped by euphoria or despair. At those times he felt he *understood*, though his conclusions were opposite each other depending on which way his mind had tilted.

On first arriving in the city, he was greeted only by fierce February winds. He used all the funds he had to rent a small room, and fell into a fever, certain he would wheeze and ooze his way to death in his rough bed. When he had enough strength and clarity of mind, he wrote letters. He imagined they would be his last messages to a world that had been determined to either perfect or destroy him since his birth. Otherwise, when awake he stared at the plush velvet curtain hanging from brass rings over the single window, watching an icy light seep around its edges and become a diffuse glow, as if emanating from a portal to an ineffable planet spinning around a colder star.

Time passed in strange stretches and bursts, until he became aware that he was hungry, though at first he decided the sensation was his flesh signaling its final descent into total systemic failure. Yet as the hours went on, the fever receded, and he realized the ache in his stomach represented Fate's dreadful intentions spinning him out, forcing him to rise from near-death and step forth into near-life.

The clothes he wore, his newest work, and a single copy of the volume of poetry he had written as a cadet were all he owned. He also had the name of a man he might persuade to publish his next collection — though how he would ever find the will to sustain his own life until then he did not know. It might be that he would perish as an impoverished stranger in the city, his lofty ambitions pathetically unrealized. He sometimes thought his awareness of his own brilliance was the very weapon Fate relied on most, stringing him between two paths — leading him to become a tremendous success or a dreadful wretch. Yet surely someone in this city could be persuaded to publish his latest work, if not Harpers.

Recognizing that he was now a wanderer, he thought of what John Allan would make of it, this following in the footsteps of his parents — which led his mind into images of their bodies underground, decomposed, skeletons which he imagined faced each other in their calcified slumber. *Follow us here,* they seemed to say. These sudden images were familiar, simply part of his perception of the world, and when expressed to others seemed to alarm them much more than they did him.

Once again he would become "Henri." If someone asked his surname, he would look seriously at them and change the subject. That would give an air of mystery, a sense of nobility displaced, perhaps. He needed to assume a persona, a way of attracting interest in order to induce strangers to pay him for his poetry.

⁍

HE ALSO NEEDED a defense against the weather, but he hesitated not at all to unhook the curtain and make a cloak of it. He folded the fabric over his shoulders, attempting to conceal the grommets by fashioning a twisted collar. The length was too short, coming to just above his knees, but the width made it possible to wrap the dark purple velvet material snugly around his thin cotton shirt up to the neck. There was not even a hand-mirror in the room, but he would have used it if there had been.

"Henri," he said to the room. *Certainly,* two skeletons underground told him, moving their arms around each other.

And then he wandered, following his senses through the city until they encountered the busker's appealingly exotic call, and led him to hover at the edge of the small crowd taking in the performance. His disappointment with the metalwork quickly turned to a new feeling of tingling expectation. The man, only a few years older than himself, had light brown skin and long, twisting curls of shining black hair, and he was playing a stringed instrument which Poe — *Henri,* he reminded himself — could not name. The busker's long fingers stroked and plucked it sensually. His sweet tenor soared along with the music, and Henri could see it affecting the rest of those gathered as well.

It was hypnotic, this performer unfolding what were surely to *him* tunes familiar from the cradle, which the listeners might never otherwise have heard before the grave. As always with art, money was the thing, and when finished the man modestly bowed, directing the sweep of his torso towards a small rough cap on the ground before him. Henri watched as a few hands dropped coins into it like fresh corpses reaching out of their graves. For a moment he would have knifed them all to pieces just to have for himself such excess, the luxury to give instead of need.

Quickly the busker extinguished the incense, preparing to seek a fresh audience with fuller purses to entice. The blurry faces vanished in ones and twos until just Henri remained, transfixed and dizzily transformed. His body's rhythms felt so disturbed, he thought the fever must have returned, or else had left him so weak he would soon collapse at the feet of a man with whom conversation might be linguistically impossible.

5

Then he recognized the feeling from memory, and for a moment his breath stopped entirely. There was a thrill moving from the top of his head down his spine, and only when it reached his stomach did he exhale forcefully. He knew this response, unexpected as it was, because for months he'd experienced it whenever he encountered a certain fellow cadet who had been charmingly enamored of his poetry. That young man had been possessed of an unearthly quality shared by this unknown busker, and had a similar, seemingly permanent expression of half-dreaming in his large, dark eyes.

This sensation now captivating Henri was identical to that which had come over him when the cadet at West Point had looked up from a handful of his poetry and given a sigh of satisfaction. This was almost as gratifying as the subscription payments obtained from him without comment or complaint — and without the smirking condescension many of his other peers expressed upon becoming patrons of an art they surely appreciated only superficially, if at all. He'd soon found himself dreaming of the other boy sharing his narrow cot, their bodies entangled — still in their uniforms, as if his mind could not summon up more compelling imagery even in the innocence of sleep — and felt crushing disappointment when he reached to pull his friend closer and, waking, clutched a handful of thin wool blanket instead.

I want to touch him, he'd thought then, with wonder but little fear. His mind had always taken him to places that were questionable in their morality, and he'd always allowed it do so, knowing that restraining it would only leave him miserable and incapable of writing anything worth the parchment. He'd tried to have the dream while awake, and let himself caress his most secret beloved in his imagination — picturing his hands moving over skin instead of fabric, enjoying his own blossoming arousal and wondering how it would feel to create the same response for the other boy. It had been wonderful to envision, though not quite as pleasant as what settled over him when a piece of work was completed and exchanged for money. Nothing in his life could compare to that, but it was in a category unto itself, separate from this discovery about his own romantic inclinations.

Now the thought came to him again: *I want to touch this stranger, and discover if his hands on my body would be as deft as they are on those strings.* There was no doubt — only the need to determine how to cross from the thought to the act, if it was possible, or whether to walk away now before inviting yet more trouble into his already difficult life.

Again the skeletons of his parents regarded him, eyeless in their shared grave, but he summoned a black cloth dropped over them to block their view. For once he would like to be unhaunted, as he stood on the pavement, staring shamelessly, knowing any moment the busker might vanish into the city.

"I do speak your language," the man said. He had what sounded like a nearly royal British accent, so posh were its long vowels and extraneous syllables. He gave Henri a long look, and the thrill came again, even stronger — could it be that Fate had for once pushed him towards someone so beautiful whose body and mind were meant to be aligned with his own?

"What do you call that instrument?" he heard himself asking. It seemed a reasonably blameless way to pick up the clear offer of conversation.

"Miranda." There was a hint of mirth in his tone. "However if it were less personally known to me, I would simply call it a *buzuq*."

"It is not unlike a lute," Henri said, "though music is not amongst the arts I know well. But 'Miranda' — " He drew a breath to give his next words proper gravity, intoning them without falsetto. "'*O, wonder! How many goodly creatures are there here! How beauteous — '*"

"'*— mankind is! O brave new world, that has such people in't!'*" the stranger concluded in a convincingly girlish voice. He was smiling now, lighting up his face in a way that sent another twisting sensation through Henri's chest and stomach. "Yes, she who must be admired. Encountering disaster, she finds joyous novelty." He touched the instrument gently, almost with love.

Henri felt a swirling combination of envy and approval. "I've always thought that moment was meant as something of a dark and cynical jest," he admitted.

The stranger laughed, a little song unto itself, with what seemed like pleasure at the observation. "That as well," he said, and packing Miranda gently in a soft-lined case, he offered a hand to shake. "I think we are friends. Yes. Let us say we are, and then who can tell us otherwise? I am called Rafael, and you...?"

"Henri." The handshake was merely a quick clasp, but was it his imagination that Rafael's fingers traced just a moment too slowly along his palm as they released? Was it his own hand that lingered? "I wish I had anything to spare," he continued, glancing helplessly at the cap, which Rafael had discreetly emptied into his pockets before settling onto his head.

"But you don't." Rafael sounded almost cheerful about this. "And now I do, so we will share a meal, since it does no good for one man to starve while another dines alone."

"You're an unusual performer, to be so generous." The words again emerged before he could edit them. "That is, not to impugn your trade, but I'd think every penny — "

" — would be precious, and so it is, but what use is treasure hoarded? I am not a dragon, unless I have been enchanted. Do you think that might be so?"

Henri's sense that Fate had brought them together became even stronger. The question seemed sincere, and as Rafael began to walk, carrying Miranda in her case under one arm, Henri followed without a thought for where he might be led.

"If the enchantment were strong enough, I'd have no way of knowing. But in the lore there is always some sign, so I will observe you carefully in case — "

Again he was interrupted, this time by Rafael pulling him to stand against a wall where passers-by would be unlikely to notice them as the evening shadows grew longer. Henri found himself face-to-face with the other man, his arm gripped at the elbow, and the distance between them much less than mere conversation required.

"Look closely," Rafael said, making his voice low and melodious again. "You might see some spark, some fire-sign of the bewitched dragon in my eyes."

For a long moment Henri did as instructed, unable to resist the steady command, unwilling to disturb the moment. He could feel the city around both of them now, its busy population and rising towers of wood and stone seeming like the emanations of a conscious entity — perhaps a manifestation of Fate Herself pushing him into this new adventure.

The sweet anticipation of unknown pleasures stuck him again. Henri made a pretense of searching for the dragon, and was surprised when he saw what could indeed be the mark of a legendary creature. "Something burns, though whether a dragon's fire transformed or your own spirit, I can't say. It could be you are a dragon's cousin, made flesh by some entanglement of gods and myths."

"Yet I see the same signs in you…Henri." The other man's tone made it clear he knew this was a pseudonym, but there was no hint of condemnation, only a playful acknowledgement that they were both taking on roles. "Perhaps we are reflecting at each other a combustion created by our meeting." Rafael's grip on his elbow loosened, and his hand slid down Henri's arm all the way to the hand again, where their fingers briefly entangled like a promise, a giddy confirmation of what this meeting could offer them both.

Then the grip changed again, closing around his wrist to lead him back into the crowd, toward a small café, where Henri allowed Rafael to direct the production of scones and coffee, paid for with a few of his recently earned coins.

They sat across from each other at a tiny table with an uneven leg, so that now and then it tilted slightly like a boat in a calm ocean. Henri kept his makeshift cloak in place, sure that the poverty of its design was apparent, but still unwilling to humiliate himself by revealing the grommets from which it had recently hung. Still, he knew the time would come to remove it, for surely they had to find somewhere to be alone together, and soon.

After a few moments more of silence, Rafael said, "You have the soul of an artist, I think…?"

Henri was grateful for both the keen observation of something he felt defined him so completely, and the opportunity to hold forth on the subject of poetry and story-writing. He explained his attempts at building a base of private subscribers, as well as his hopes to sell his newest work for publication in the city. He did not mention West Point, or *Tamerlane* by name, simply noting that he had a collection already printed, but he suspected his reticence was obvious to the clearly intelligent man who was quickly becoming something other than an increasingly well-regarded new friend.

They worked through the plate of pastries and cups of coffee without too much haste but also without dallying, and Henri observed that Rafael was as hungry as himself, which made his generosity all the more impressive. When he attempted to express this, Rafael stopped him: "No, you are most welcome, and indeed it's a favor to me that you've joined me, as I've taken every meal alone since my arrival here."

"From where did you arrive, and how did you come to choose — " Henri began to ask, but Rafael was already shaking his head, his lovely dark locks swaying as he did.

"All stories begin with a meeting," he said. "Where I came from is not significant. Where I am now — and what company I'm keeping — is all that matters."

"I must say, your manner of thought and speech is a relief from what I have become accustomed to." Henri attempted to leave the last segment of scone out of politeness, but Rafael waved at it, insisting, until he capitulated and cleared the plate between them with a final bite.

"Deep thought is a holy obligation," the busker said, with a hint of a smile. "But without conversation, it's an empty prayer." Glancing around quickly to see that no one was paying them any mind, he reached across the table and let his fingertips brush the back of Henri's hand on the table, just a moment too long to be anything other than a hint at the chance for further, more private physical connection.

Nevertheless, Henri almost stayed in place, frightened by doubt, as Rafael rose and looked toward the exit. Had he mistaken all these little touches, all the long enticing looks Rafael sent his way? But no:

"I have the use of some rooms, the home of an old friend who is traveling," Rafael said. "Let's go there together and I will read your poetry, since you've heard my music, and it would only be fair, after all."

Alone. They would be alone, in privacy, in a place which Poe — Henri, he had to remind himself, as his resolve to remain anonymous eroded — could only assume would have curtains not made into cloaks, and (he could hardly allow himself to think of it) a bed, where he might find himself inside a waking dream, one in which he would embrace more than a blanket and at last act upon his unnatural but irresistible desires.

As before, he followed, still somewhat unsure if he was headed for the pleasures of sharing his work and then returning to his own cold room alone, or to some other ecstasy he could barely name, let alone envision. Perhaps even a gruesome death — all these apparently benign invitations the designs of a deranged street performer who could easily slaughter him and vanish, a new kind of murderous fiend who would erupt with rage once his prey was captive. He felt curiously unafraid even contemplating this possibility, as he felt sure Fate would direct his progress regardless of the choices he believed he was making, in his mortal ignorance.

They were silent, as Henri walked behind by a few steps, taking Rafael's quick movements as a sign that it would be better if they were not seen walking in companionship any longer. Too late, he realized he had left his poems in his room, but he could recite many of them from memory. Could that be all he wanted — merely the intimate exchange of art, a way for Henri to pay for his portion of their meager meal? Were all the little moments, the long touches and inviting looks, just a product of Henri's vivid imagination? This doubt, this tension of the unknown was not unpleasant. If nothing more than such an exchange occurred, he would be satisfied enough, though at the same time he would feel the same bitter disappointment as when waking from his dream of the young man at West Point.

His sense of the city as an entity faded as they walked. He decided to let himself believe that soon, somehow, the two of them would join together in a beautiful novelty of an experience. It was all the more wonderful for the fact that it was forbidden — how repulsed, how utterly speechless at the perception of such a foul and evil deed John Allan would be, though Henri still hoped sincerely that his adoptive father would never know. This was not just because of the scandal of it. He felt that whatever happened next with Rafael was for the two of them alone — even if it were no more than a sharing of their mutual passions in a chaste and civilized form.

As soon as he had been led up a narrow staircase and into the rooms of Rafael's absent friend, just as the door closed, Rafael pulled him close, seizing his elbows and moving his hands from there to Henri's wrists.

I can't move, I can't speak, Henri thought. Yet after a moment he discovered this was not quite true, for he found himself saying:

"Please..."

That seemed to be enough invitation for Rafael. He released his grip and moved one hand to Henri's face, tracing a line down the curve of his cheek and then over the bow of his lips, and with his other hand guided Henri to do the same, so that they stood stroking each other's skin at last.

"Yes." Rafael answered his plea, dropping his hand to entwine with Henri's and lead him to a small, fraying sofa, set against crumbling wallpaper — a floral design that must once have been cheerful and was now faded, giving the room a disreputable atmosphere which Henri was more comfortable with than he would have been in more glorified surroundings. "But first, I was promised poetry, and I intend to hear some." His tone was playful and promising. When they sat their knees touched, keeping the anticipation of what might follow alive like one of Miranda's strings plucked and vibrating with a high, sweet note.

As for the instrument, Rafael had set the case gently on a side-table when they arrived, and it felt like a third occupant, a witness to their strange association, which would remain hidden between the notes of the next song plucked out upon it by those elegant hands. Hands which had left what felt like indelible but invisible markings, like the man he had once seen in a traveling circus whose entire head and neck were covered with Polynesian swirls of ink, needled on in what must have been a terribly painful process. At the time, Henri had wondered what could cause a man to sacrifice so much in order to transform himself into a freak, but now he understood.

Instead of reciting from his new work, he chose a piece from *Tamerlane*. "'In visions of the dark night/I have dreamed of joy departed — '" he began, and Rafael listened with gratifying interest. When he reached the verse which began "That holy dream — that holy dream," he felt for the first time a masculine hand stroking his knee and leg, not salaciously, but tenderly, as if the naturally tactile musician could not listen without manifesting physically some sign of his response.

Which would not be an incorrect description of the reaction Poe — finally, he forgot completely he was "Henri" or ever had been, becoming himself again with the self-possession that always accompanied his work — felt in his own body, at that. He was glad to have chosen a short poem, because his makeshift cloak was far too warm now, and his clothes under it felt ill-fitting, scratching at his skin.

"Beautiful," Rafael pronounced, though he was looking so intently at Poe's face that it was not entirely clear whether he meant just the poem or also its creator. He stood, pulling Poe up by one hand, and drew him closer still, closer than in the alley or past the doorframe, close enough that their bodies almost touched — almost, but not quite. He met Poe's eyes with just the hint of a question, and Poe felt himself giving a clear, affirmative response without speaking.

Rafael gripped his hand and pulled him quickly into another small room where there was, indeed, a bed, just barely big enough for two men, if they were entangled tightly together, for example. In Poe's mind, the black veil over his parents' grave lifted briefly, and he caught a glimpse of a long finger of bone waving at him in warning or condemnation. "No," he said aloud, and Rafael stopped, having just begun to unwrap the velvet cloak, but: "I mean yes," Poe corrected, and smiled at himself, at the unreal animated dead chiding him like schoolteachers, at the wonder of how he had met this man and come to be in this place, and smiled even more brightly when Rafael reflected his expression.

He thought Rafael might laugh when he saw the grommets, but before he could fear the moment of revelation, that musical voice came again: "Get you out of that lovely curtain, shall we?" And all was well about it, and Poe knew it was, and he reached out with no fear to touch Rafael's hair and neck and shoulders as the curtain was unwound and cast onto the bed.

The next several minutes were silent, because when they kissed, the city blinked out of existence. They began to press and touch in ways that made Poe's previous thrills of anticipation seem as dim as a candle in bright daylight. Even when the world around them returned, the quiet remained, aside from the sound of fabric sliding off skin, as Poe unbuttoned and tugged and let himself briefly collide with Rafael's body while undressing its upper half. Those perfect hands, the work of which had called him into this — he had no doubt now that Fate's mischief was behind the encounter — were busy as well, until they stood chest to chest, still with the echo of their shared smile ghosting at the corners of their mouths, though overshadowed by similarly mutual expressions of fierce desire.

They touched and touched, stroking each other's backs and arms and chests, moving together for another kiss as they did, and Poe delighted in the feeling of skin on skin. However he felt hesitation, uncertainty, and finally admitted: "I'm afraid I've no idea — "

"Oh, I have ideas enough for the both of us," Rafael answered easily. He seemed to have the line prepared, and Poe chided himself for letting his inexperience show so plainly, but there was no sense of disappointment or condemnation from the lover who had been a stranger barely more than an hour or two before.

Instead, he simply led Poe to the bed and gently urged him to lie upon it, removing first his shoes and then working upward — with a rustling that matched the sound in Poe's mind of the black veil shielding all this from the skeletons of his parents starting to slide out of place. *Away, look away,* he told the eyeless remains, and forced his mind to obey the order instead, wanting this bed to have no hint of the gravedigger's trade about it.

As if sensing his shyness, though surely not understanding its true source, Rafael playfully dragged the curtain-cloak over Poe's body as he began to tug and pull away Poe's trousers and undergarments.

"I would like to see a painting of you this way." Rafael stroked a hand from Poe's throat to his belly to his thighs, following the line of the fabric half-draped over his form. He was himself still half-dressed, but now, without removing his hand from where it now rested on the inside of Poe's naked thigh, divested himself of his remaining garments with no fumbling despite having only one hand free. Then he stood, allowing Poe to see his naked body in full, and even turned slowly, as if to say *See, there is nothing to fear, only to rejoice in and explore.*

"I'd like to meet the painter who would take such a commission," Poe heard himself half-joking, and again they shared a smile.

"I may have encountered one or two," Rafael answered lightly, and for the first time Poe fully realized that the knowledge his new friend was now putting to work with him came from entanglements with other men, and felt a different kind of jolt, a terrible longing envy of all who had seen what he was seeing, felt what he was feeling as Rafael's hand slipped up higher from its place on his leg to stroke him most intimately. The pleasure of this pushed the dark thoughts away, and besides, this was not a man who could be jealously kept from all others, clearly. It was his innate freedom of spirit and clear intention to live only for the *now* which was part of his appeal, after all, though the beauty of his face and body did nothing to detract from the intense sensations his touch inspired.

At some point soon after, the curtain-cloak fell to the floor as Rafael pushed it aside impatiently, joining Poe on the bed and entwining with him in a sweet embrace. Poe ran his hands over the other man's dark locks, down his bare back, and felt in return those skilled hands exploring his own flesh. He lost himself in what felt like one long suspended moment as he found that he did, in fact, have more ideas about how to approach the situation than he'd thought, that Rafael was a muse of sensuality inspiring him to bravely reach and touch and stroke. His dream was real, the world was breathing life into his body through the breath of his lover's body, and the fever that had him bound to a different bed in what felt like a distant past life now returned in the form of heat and sweat that promised to heal rather than threatened to destroy him.

They murmured together, a quiet sequence of *yes* and *oh* and *ahh*, and Poe wondered what poetry could capture the essence of communion between them. He knew he would try, and could feel the lines naturally beginning to assemble even as they reached the heights of pleasure. The phantoms of the unknown parental grave lingered somewhere in the back of his mind, and in one dreadful moment he imagined that he and Rafael were themselves skeletons decaying unto eternity together, that this exchange of flesh and wonder was perhaps a kind of madness descending over him on the brink of his own death after all.

Yet just then Rafael's raven-colored locks began to tickle the insides of his thighs and all thought vanished as far away as it ever could, replaced by bliss and amazement. Each time he thought no passionate expression could ever topple the last, he found himself reaching a new height of pleasure and daring, until finally the wave broke and collapsed them, legs and arms and chests wound up together as if they were one body with two persons occupying it, or two halves of one new person, perhaps.

Exhaustion replaced enthusiasm, and Poe felt himself almost immediately beginning to drift into sleep, when he heard again the extraordinary voice that had earlier been directed at any and all now singing quietly, just for him, just for them, just for the strange and beautiful ways in which they had shared with each other the dragon's fire that flared when their bodies joined together. Again the words were in a language he couldn't name, but now he felt he understood them all, though he could never, then or later, offer any translation. Rafael sang him into sleep, and only when he tipped over into slumber did the black veil lift and the imagined sound of bones clicking underground — in shock or in approval of his joy, he would never know — begin to provide distant percussion for the tune.

When he woke, he was alone. The curtain-cloak had been neatly folded along with his other clothes and left on the side-table. He dressed quickly, tucking the grommets into a collar again, and explored the crumbling outer room, but Miranda in her case was gone — no sign of Rafael remained. A terrible fear filled him, and soon it became an immovable sadness, as he ran from the unfamiliar rooms and tried to trace his path back to the corner where he had first found the busker, only to discover it as empty as the bed had been.

He could wander, listening for that unmistakable voice, and he did, but the glass sphere which had held him seemed to have broken, and he discovered no sign at all, not even a lingering whiff of scented charcoal. For hours he explored the city, feeling his search was the pale opposite of the explorations of each other's bodies he and Rafael had made just hours before. Finally he retreated to his own room, which was smaller and even more empty than before, and sat on the bed stroking his clothing over the places where the other man's hands had so recently been, as if searching for some lasting mark.

After several days more of searching he found it, not in his flesh but in his spirit. Surely, he decided, his vanished lover had been an angel wearing the guise of a man, and had blessed him with a shield against falling into the nameless, forgotten state of his missing parents, which he'd once despaired might capture him as well. He decided that his final exhalation would not mean his true demise — that somehow, he would live on and on, and no matter what other lovers Fate had in mind for him — perhaps even those who would dream of him when he took his place in that haunted grave — he would always be searching for the man whose heart-strings were a kind of lute, and whose song would echo in his body evermore.

He read through his new collection several times, and then returned to the café — still with the faintest hope that perhaps Rafael would return there as well, but knowing now that this was just another bitter dream — to sit at the uneven table and begin the only work he could do to bring himself back to the path of life, which he now believed Fate had allowed him to briefly escape only so that he would return to it, fortified and broken all at once.

He began to write, and when he reached the lines "But the skies that angel trod,/Where deep thoughts are a duty — /Where Love's a grown-up God — " he thought he felt that elegant hand on his knee again, approving, under-standing. He almost smiled, thinking of the secret encoded in the verses, and knew that the editors at Harpers — or whatever entity saw fit to publish these works, as he was even more certain now this triumph awaited him — would never guess that such an outrage, such a deviant encounter was etched be-tween the lines.

"Our flowers are merely flowers," he told the skeletons of the actors who had left him an orphan, and their gleaming white skulls nodded, the minds inside long since flown up and away towards the same Heaven where the shadow of Israfel's perfect bliss had made sunshine of his own. There were many stories to tell, many poems to write, much business of publishing and acquiring both fortune and reputation to which he must attend. New York had given him all it had for him already, and his mind was already escaping it again for Baltimore and the spring, even as his body ached for one more moment of passion shared.

All he could do was allow the ghost of a half-man, half-angel to shadow him, and now when the image came of standing over that grave, he was no longer alone, but joined by his invisible beloved, their hands entwined. "Israfeli, who despisest/an unimpassioned song" would be watching, disal-lowing him from cheating Fate with even a scrap of sincerity in his work, just as their entanglement had not one moment that was not perfect in its truthful beauty. No matter how grotesque or egregious, whatever he wrote hereafter would be real, in honor of the gift given and then cruelly taken away. Eighteen long years later, he would stumble to the mortal end of Fate's intentions for his life, and down through the darkness he would mumble and shout many lines penned and impressions gathered, but none so fiercely as the sixth verse of his new poem.

> *The ecstasies above*
> *With thy burning measures suit —*
> *Thy grief, thy joy, thy hate, thy love,*
> *With the fervor of thy lute —*
> *Well may the stars be mute!*

"Well may the stars be mute," he echoed to the skeletons, but like those cold gems strewn across the city skyline he now longed to leave behind, they were also silent and still, and if their new torpor had significance he would never decipher its purpose. He only knew that he would always remember the feeling of that delicate but masculine hand in his own. He would never be completely free from the haunted state that followed him all his life. Yet he knew he would now also always be blessed by a joyfulness, and cursed by a bitterness, without each of which the other would have no meaning, and which together gave his body its own secret place to occupy, outside of the destiny that otherwise consumed him until he died.

⚜

> *Poe's letters indicate that he did indeed spend a brief, impoverished time in New York, around February, between leaving West Point and returning to Baltimore, and the poem "Israfel" dates from 1831, the year he was there.*

MATHEW BRADY,
THE GALLERY OF ILLUSTRIOUS AMERICANS

Daniel Nathan Terry

"Why preyest thou thus upon the poet's heart,
Vulture, whose wings are dull realities?"
— FROM "SONNET TO SCIENCE," EDGAR ALLAN POE

I have charged myself with daguerreotyping
the greatest men of the age, while other
photographers make a business of family
portraits or dally with the ridiculous *spirit*

photography. I have heard that Whipple
has even challenged the heavens, that with aid
of the great Harvard telescope, he has captured the face
of the moon, garnered the praise of scientists and artists

alike. I have no such lofty aspirations, nor will I
trifle with charlatans for the acquisition
of wealth. I mean to serve posterity,
to record the faces of those men

who shape our destiny. When Mr. Wallace entered
the studio with his silent companion — I held my tongue.
I was gracious and took the best images

I could of the lesser, but paying, poet. Then

I beseeched his companion, Mr. Poe,
to sit for me. He wordlessly declined. His eyes
were dark and shadowed with too much drink,
his cheap suit tattered and worn, his necktie

swathed about his throat like a tourniquet.
He was a hollow and penniless man, darkness made
beautiful. It took great diplomacy to convince him to pose
for me, for the nation, free of charge.

A few weeks later, upon hearing of Poe's death,
I held his image in my hand — haunted, love-torn,
desolate — his gaze fixed on me. I knew I had
captured a poet's heart. Let Whipple boast

of holding the moon in his hand.

POETASTER

Steve Berman

NEITHER midnight nor dreary but late on a cold October evening, Atherton James sat before a fire reading a book on legumes. He could not sleep and was relying on both the glass of port and the propensity of Latin within the names and mottoes to lull him. The chair was old, comfortable, cracked leather and would be preferable to tumbled, cold sheets.

A knock on the door roused him just as he began nodding off to the illustrations of wisteria — blurs of lavender on the page seeping into darkness. But he stirred at the repeated, redoubled rapping at his front door.

He adjusted his robe and his night cap. Secured his slippers. Then, when at the door, he pressed his ear against the dark wood. "Who's there?"

"Teacher!" he heard cry though the grain, the planks, the nails. Only one man referred to James with such a moniker, not altogether untrue, but a career decidedly well past him.

He unbolted the lock and allowed the unkempt youth inside his home. It had been…what, months since he had met Thomas in a tavern and encouraged him to come back to James's quaint Hamilton Street abode?

The firelight confined to the hearth barely illuminated any of Thomas; the young man had his overcoat collar drawn high, clutched its edges with white knuckles, and stood hunched in the doorway before stumbling inside.

James gestured towards the warmth and light. His own chair, even. "By the fire —"

"No," muttered Thomas. Rather, he shuffled to stand by the dusty bookshelves at the edge of the room and remained in thick shadow. Dampness, either a touch of rain or perhaps sweat, left his thick hair unruly — reminiscent of that striking woodblock print by that Japanese artist whose name James could not recall at present. Oh, it would be found in a volume behind the boy.

"Teacher, somethin' has... I ain't well."

James retrieved his port, held out the glass to Thomas despite the many steps separating them. He did not *want* to approach closer. Yet. This was all so disturbing, so much more fanciful and fearsome than even the first time he had accepted the handsome young man's offer. Not thirty pieces of silver, no souls were damned — James believed more in illustration than iconography, in the sanctity of the pen over the pulpit. But he had paid, had worried he would be cheated, had been assuaged of all dread when Thomas stripped both of them bare. The sheets had not been cold that night. James had no trouble sleeping that night.

"A drink?" He raised the glass a little higher, so it would catch the light and the boy's attention — James could not be sure where Thomas stared, not while in silhouette — but the boy made no reply.

"No? A doctor then? I could send word. The hospital is not far."

"I heard he went there. Died there."

"Who, my boy. At least come closer. This distance —"

"That author. Poe."

James blinked. Thomas surprised him. They had shared many secrets, much chatter of their pasts, while resting on soft pillows. Thomas had abandoned schooling as soon as he could run fast enough to elude not only instructor but father. This boy should not know the name of any author, least of all a disturbed scribbler who shared his own nightmares with the impressionable public.

"Yes," James said. "I saw the obituary."

Thomas took a tentative step closer. He held out one trembling hand, showing a palm wrapped with a stained handkerchief. "That man bit me 'fore he died."

"What?" Did James not detect a slur to the boy's speech? He put down the port, then approached the boy as a hunter might a wounded boar. "Listen, Thomas. This all sounds like a bad dream. Or a bad bottle of gin. Either way, sleeping it off will do you good."

When he put an arm around the boy's coat, James felt the temblor of shivering reach his own bones. "By the fire at least."

And Thomas let himself be led to the chair and sat down.

In the flickering light, as James prodded the dying log with the poker, its stern metal a comfort to his grasp, Thomas's face looked wan, as if he might faint at any moment. The sole fragments of contrast were bits of ebony: sunken eyes, the rash of hair, and the early growth of a mustache above thin lips.

The boy seemed to become aware of the port finally and downed it in one swallow. He wiped his lips with the same hand that dangled the fragile glass. "Needed a theriac."

"Pardon?"

"What?"

"Just that — that word." James dragged over another chair and then took the glass from the boy's weak fingers. "Not something I expect you to know."

Thomas brought his wrapped hand — James saw that the rag was soiled with ruddy brown blotches, which brought bile up his throat — to his chest. "I was there with my...my *fidus Achates*. No. No, chums. They are chums." Thomas shook his head with the vehemence of a terrier who snatched a rat. "Monday. And we were buying rounds. When he came — walked over to us."

"Who?"

"Poe. Might as well have been H-Hades. No. I don't know who that is. Arghh, Poe. He moved like he was well into his cups already. Drool at the...at the sides of his mouth. Salivatin' like a mad dog as he asked if he could join us for a drink."

Thomas pulled at his hair. The gesture made his forehead look larger than before in the weak light.

"He had coin, plenty of it, so we agreed. What's one more, if he pays, we always say. I thought I might go blind that night, I drank so much. How did he stay upright? He should have been carried out. To the morgue, for all he drank.

"And then, he starts cursin' and it's words none of us has ever heard. Not even you, Teacher, talked to me like that when I'm fuckin' the hell out of your chute. 'Maggot-pie!' 'Reeky death-token!' 'Withered brabbler on some Plutonian shore!'"

James chuckled. Thomas stopped him by pushing that wounded hand against James's lips.

"No. I-I know what they mean now but I cannot find the humor. Melancholia…black bile. His bite spread black bile."

"You say he bit you?"

Thomas nodded. "When he became violent, started throwing fists, snapping his great jaws. Bit me on the hand, my chum Willy on the shoulder right down to the bone, nicked the tip of the bartender's thumb in one snap. We let him run off then."

"Perhaps the wound is infected."

"Black bile. I told you." Thomas's other hand pulled at the dark hairs growing on his upper lip. The late hour, the lack of sleep, gave James the impression that those inky strands had become thicker in the short span they had been sitting there.

James cried out when the bell rang and knocking began anew at his door.

"Who is it?" Thomas asked and eyed the door with trepidation. "I feel that something grim stands at the threshold."

"I'd best see." The knocking grew more violent. James glanced over his shoulder at Thomas before reaching for the latch. A nephew, he would say — the youth was his nephew. He looked old enough, certainly from across the room he might even resemble a man in his late thirties. The poor thing even had bags under his eyes from whatever troubled him so.

James confronted his caller, a corpulent man in uniform who steamed from a black-bearded chimney above the chin strap of his official cap.

"Constable Wiggins?"

"Evening, Mister James, sir. Sorry for the intrusion at this hour." The ruddy-faced constable peered past James into the room a moment, then shuffled about as if anxious. A stout man uneasy at so close to midnight made James all the more tense. He might never sleep this night.

"I was just…well, my nephew is in town and we are up late trading stories — "

"I have stories to tell," shouted Thomas in a pained voice.

"What did he say?"

"Nothing." James stepped closer to the constable and lowered his voice though the chill night air threatened to petrify his tongue. "I-I fear my nephew's had too much drink tonight. You understand…"

"Of course, sir. That's why I'm calling on you at this hour." He tugged at his beard with a gloved hand. "Seems like much of Baltimore's been hob and nobbing a bit too much tonight — wife won't allow *me* a glass, even the medicinal, as her father was a drunk. And a dago, but still, I married her."

"Constable…"

"Yes…well, there's been reports. We've enough burden after that incident at the Chemical Works… Now, these men. Running through the streets." Constable Wiggins glanced in either direction. The street was empty but a sound, perhaps human, did sound out. Perhaps a night bird. "Not niggers or micks, mind you. But good folk have been accosted. Would you believe in Green Mount Cemetery one of these fellows — "

"Well, thank you for the warning," James said and began to shut the door. "It's a queer night."

"Right you are," said the officer.

"Downright grim," yelled Thomas, who pried the door from James's grip and stepped out into the street. "No, not Grimm. Give me Coleridge's *Rime*. I want Hoffmann's *Doppeltgänger*." He turned around slowly, his deep set eyes mournful. "Where am I?"

"Seems a bit off, your nephew."

Teeth almost achatter, James stepped in front of Thomas. "He's…despondent over a woman."

"Lenore," bemoaned Thomas.

"Odd name."

"She's…from New Orleans."

"But we loved with a love that was more than love — I and my Annabel Lee."

Officer Wiggins blinked. "I thought his miss was named Lenore."

James offered a weak chuckle. He was freezing in his thin robe, the slippers did little to help, and he only wanted for the policeman — and Thomas — to let him return to comfort of the hearth and his books. "Heh, well, he does find himself in a quandary…"

The constable raised a hand. "Say no more. Women are the roots of all men's woes. Father would quote scripture on that. 'Ask me never for a dowry or gift, as according to ye the damsel to wife gives unto…'" He tugged again at his beard. "'Unto…' Well, they're nothing but trouble."

James pressed upon Thomas to head off into the other direction, away from his chamber door. "Uh, that was Genesis?"

"*Batrachomyomachia!*" Thomas yelled. The sound echoed. Or perhaps in the distance it was repeated by other manic male voices.

"I don't remember that book o' the Bible," said Constable Wiggins. "Are you sure he's all right?" The policeman grabbed hold of Thomas by one shoulder. "Messing about with two women. I might think you're crazy."

Thomas turned his eyes to the constable's florid face. Quite without savagery, he leaned to bite off much of the constable's nose.

"Fuckin' basta'd," screamed Constable Wiggins as he brought up both hands to stanch the blood. It coursed between the fingers of his gloves, down into his beard.

"Teacher," said Thomas. His chin shone slick with strands of drool as he chewed some, then spoke with a full cheek. "Would you have a pipe of Amontillado?" He chewed some more but could not swallow, spitting out the masticated nose tip on to the dank cobblestones. "I feel a need to rinse my mouth." He turned toward the steps to James's abode.

"Ii 'ose!" When the constable moved his hands away, tufts of his beard came free, collapsing to the ground like clumps of filthy snow. Glimpses of pallid chin were as disturbing as the ravaged beak in the center of the man's face.

With a shaking hand, the constable lifted a pistol.

"Thomas," James called.

But Thomas seemed not to hear.

"Edgar," shouted out James in a fit of insight.

"Yes?" The youth, who had unwrapped the handkerchief around his hand to clean his cheeks and chin, appeared twice as old as when he had stepped through James's chamber door. He regarded the unsteady aim of the constable.

"Ahh, if I may be so bold. At West Point they taught us the proper handling of firearms. You are likely to injure one of us tonight, but not necessarily my person."

"Iim bwinen you to 'ail."

Thomas glanced at James, who mouthed "jail."

Thomas sighed. Not a sigh of resignation. "Impossible. With Nyx smiling down on this city tonight — see, her glowing grin hangs above us mortals — well, I am to explore every crevice, every nook, every cache. What would you know of the beauty of a dying woman? Baltimore knows tonight! What would you say to days of reckoning giving way to nights of vengeance? You know nothing.

"Teacher, come with me."

Distant howls unraveled on the wind. Voices made mad by the wind if they were not mad to begin with.

"Teacher, come with us." Thomas wiped the saliva and blood that glistened on his lips. His eyes were heavy lidded like those of a devotee of Mesmer. "A kiss, a nip on the tongue, let me share this new found appreciation for words, for suffering, and even the most morbid of tastes…all in a kiss, as once we often shared."

James had not realized how close Thomas was. Then, one of those dark eyes exploded as thunder from a storm held by a fat, bleeding, molting man tore apart much of the right side of Thomas's face.

James shrieked at the sight, at the droplets of blood that stained the cuffs of his robe.

The constable squeezed shut what remained of his nose and bellowed through his jaws, his voice horribly distorted, "Mister James. Bandages, sir. No. A balm. Like those of Gilead. That will set me right. He was never worth Lenore."

James shook his head and ran back into his house. He pushed the door shut, turned the lock, stared at it. He could hear through windows, the spaces where door met lintel, the merry mad shouts of the others afflicted with this ravenous disorder.

Though not a young man, he struggled and pushed all the furniture he could against the doors and bare windows. He glimpsed figures running down the street. Dark and pale figures, clutching their high foreheads, gnashing their mouths.

Oh, what he would give for some strong, heavy bricks and mortar. That would keep him safe and them out. He needed to seal himself away.

He collapsed back in his chair by the fire. Clasped his hands together to keep them from shaking.

Atherton James was afraid to utter a word. He did not wish to be a man of that crowd.

POE'S WRITING

THE HOUSE

Ed Madden

> *...sympathies of a scarcely intelligible nature*
> *had always existed between them.*
> — EDGAR ALLAN POE, "THE FALL OF THE HOUSE OF USHER"

He does not speak her name for several days
at a time. Unnamed, she cannot enter his songs,
his paintings. But her body, there is always

her body walking through the room, this body
with its staring breasts, its suspicious smile.
Nameless, a body can enter a room, nameless,

it daubs the palette, nameless it slides along
the guitar strings with his fingers. He sits quiet
in the vaulted room, cool and dark, its walls

blurred in tapestries of war or harvest or some other
boring public spectacle. Is it her — or *him*
that he would paint? Which taboo is worse?

Which awakens this quiver in him, leaves him
broken, riven, split to the core? Daylight

pains him now; the light is violation.

He prefers the dim air that blurs the family
portraits, the sofa, tapestries, all the images
around him that hurt him with specificity, the names

that shame him, fix him here.
He longs for low rooms, dark, or smooth
white vaults without interruption or device:

his paintings approach abstraction, blunt desire
without a name — dim tunnels, coppered
archways. He did not speak her name for days

at a time. Instead he lingered over the guitar
with his only personal friend, speaking to him
with greater and greater intimacy, wild improvisations

on the guitar, attempts to say all
the things that could not be said. Her perfume,
like the scent of all flowers, or women,

irritates — lilacs, violets, the fragrant meadows
of her hair, the bruised buds of her lips — the odors
of all flowers are oppressive. He avoids with fear

certain rough fabrics, spices, chambers.
The only sounds he finds tolerable are the brush
of fingers on the guitar, the songs, the sigh

of pages turning as in his friend's hands.
There were no words for their occupations,
those long hours, the two men, alone,

or that night when, drunk with wine,
he could wait no longer, pressed himself
against a rain of blows, the frail hermit

of the House of Usher overcome, his garments
torn, the noise of it, the door flung open, his sister
there — and the two of them in the dark, her shriek

unbearable. Now, he presses his hands to his ears
at the sound of doors opening, the thunder of hairpins
at night, the roar of her brush, the disturbing murmur

of her skirts, an insect scraping its way through the wall.
When she enters the room, it strains to bear them both,
the woman at the door, the man who left.

⊷

Roderick thinks, *I am my father, and I am*
my mother: my dead father, which is my name,
and my dead mother, this fissured house.

He's always startled by his sister's face: his own,
though her body is not. She hums softly as she
paces the room, a hymn their mother had hummed,

long ago, to his ears a clattering, scraping.
He looks up to the great dragon-gash of her smile.
He turns away, to the books scattered

on the low table beside his couch, the guitar
untouched since his dear friend fled.
He does not speak his name. He picks up a book,

perhaps the one of Belphegor, from whom
he learned that women damn men to hell, or perhaps
a Latin vigil for the dead, remembering the dark

vault of the closet in his bedroom, his friend
gathering his things, cursing, the candle's light
casting a sulphurous luster on his skin,

glistening with sweat. He looked at his sister lifting
the candle, her face impassive, like a carving
on a crypt. He looks at her now, tries

to ignore the stiffening of memory, tries not to think
of the wine, the story, the door forced open,
his friend's rough hands, the fissure that opened

and opened and still opens within him, the rough
textures of his skin, the crushed blossoms
of his lips, the acrid burn of his kiss.

He does not speak his name.

THE HOUSE
OF THE
RESONATE HEART

L. A. Fields

UNDER the bleak gaze of the House of Usher, Madeline and Roderick grew up, but they did not flourish. At the long, withering end of the Usher line, the already insufficient material for producing richly propagating offspring had diminished itself to the point of suicide in bringing forth twins. Lineage, much like a human hair once strong at the root, will sometimes fade and thin at length until at last: it splits.

They were twins, but not identical. They were complimentary. A man, a woman. An intellect, a sensitivity. In being born together, what one gained the other lost, or else they shared in equal measure. In health they were both only partially equipped, in nerves the same. Their color was dampened as if there were not enough of the blush of life to cause them both to be rosy. Their hair was often thin, their nails brittle. Their teeth hung loose in their mouths. Their breaths were shallow, unable to draw in deeply.

There were no two people closer, not among husbands and wives, not among parents and children. They shared all alone for so long, with few companions on the edge of their gloomy tarn. The occasional governess or tutor only remained as long as it took to arrange their departure. Roderick and Madeline lived in each other, leaned on each other, understood each other's aches and illnesses where their father — with his relatively superior health — could not. Their mother had died in childbirth; even the infusion of her entire life's energy could not bequeath her children with a complete fortification. They spent as much of their childhood quarantined in their moldering mansion as they did roaming listlessly without.

There came a time however when Roderick was meant to rally every resource he could and take on the responsibility of the Usher legacy. A daughter was not unacceptable, and if she managed to branch the bloodline and begin a wellspring of potential inheritors, all the better...but it was unlikely. The Usher stock was disintegrating as quickly as the family manse, and the cost of producing the next generation tolls against the female far more than the male.

Roderick was to be traditionally schooled, to meet the sisters and cousins of his social strata, to marry a hopefully hale and hearty young woman, and to continue the bloodline. He was not a winning young man in his boarding school, however. He was too ephemeral, his family too remote and without influence, to earn any real friends but one: another young man, with no female relations, not that Roderick craved their company. His sister was the only woman in his life, and the only one he cared to have. This was another symptom of their time spent commingling in the womb.

"It must have been some mixing before we were born," Roderick said over one summer holiday, after drawing Madeline into a window alcove, holding her hands gently as if they were bundles of feathers, speaking quickly and nervously. "I know that if anyone will understand, it is you. I find myself in love with another boy, feeling soft towards him, feeling girlish around him. I feel towards him as perhaps you might feel towards a young man, unless you find yourself wanting softer company? Have we exchanged desires, Madeline? Do you find yourself wanting the wife I should have, as I would prefer your husband?"

"I feel no such desire, Roderick. I rather prefer to stay devoted to you. Women must divide their loyalties so terribly if they marry, suddenly being part of two families."

Roderick smiled upon her, so wan in the feeble light that came through the window, and their hands still so much alike even after a year apart. He touched his chest on his own starched ascot, and then pointed to Madeline's laced bosom, indicating their resonate, if weak-threaded, hearts.

"We will never not be Ushers I'm afraid," Roderick told her.

"You fear that as well, my brother." She smiled, squeezed his hands in parting, and took herself into the depths of the house.

Roderick returned to school and to the company of his boon companion in the spring. He'd met Allan while the boy was malingering in the hospital wing, where Roderick was often to be found, suffering as he did from several peculiar and chronic illnesses. He might have thought very little of someone faking poor health, but Allan did it with the singular purpose of gaining himself more time to read, and this he did with Roderick, back and forth, for hours. It was the beginning of a very brief time in his life when Roderick felt himself to be budding, improving.

Within the year however, his father's death would call him home again, and from that time on, to home he stayed confined. The bloom that never fully touched this rose fell from it all the same.

Likewise Madeline, who had experienced her own such period of independence and its invigorating symptoms when Roderick was away and she the only child in the house, lapsed back into a soporific existence with his return. To have known her father alive and then to become aware of his presence in death only served to highlight the vast generations of Ushers that had gone before them, and who outnumbered the living residences of the grounds in greater numbers with each generation.

The siblings took comfort in each other. They had no other choice; holding onto the sense of resentment they each felt in some measure would have meant a life of spiritual sickness as well as physical bad health. They each found a way to look optimistically on the situation. They did not represent a burden to one another, but a solace: their one remaining family member was not holding them back from a life of freedom, but rather saving them from utter loneliness and despair. How lucky it is to be a twin! To be part of a family!

Roderick hired tutors for them, a new one every year. Certainly education was important, but he also hoped that one of these men might be someone of note. Perhaps one would desire Madeline and marry her away. Perhaps one would desire Roderick and they would become close companions, masters of the house, renowned men of arts and letters.

But each year it was a disappointment, until Roderick and Madeline were both far too old and far too knowledgeable to justify the presence of tutors. Roderick next considered doing repairs on the estate, but his initial inquiries into men of work and stone revealed that they were not the sort suitable for the companionship of himself or his sister. University had spoiled him, it seemed, for a very specific sort of person. He missed his friend very much, but knew he would never pull Allan out of his own life to come waste away in this cavernous place without some true need of him, which would not come for years.

Roderick and Madeline worsened at the same rate of time, each one's symptoms increasing in equal steps. Madeline would experience a longer moment of catatonia, and Roderick would find that another food had begun to disgust him. Madeline would turn a shade paler, and Roderick would lose his ability to tolerate strong light. Wherever their youth and vitality was being taken to, it appeared in nothing surrounding them. Perhaps their lives were drawing from the same well, which would mean the more one took, the less there was for the other to draw forth; perhaps they were each, alone, altogether deficient.

But at last: after years of slow, simultaneous moldering, Madeline's health came crumbling down. Roderick could feel himself worsening still, but not so quickly as his sister, and at last he was sure that he would outlive her. He started to plan accordingly.

I write to you, Allan, as my best and indeed my only personal friend, with a view of attempting, by the cheerfulness of your society, some alleviation of my malady. Roderick described his ailments, beseeched his friend to come to him, to possibly save his life. He poured himself into this entreaty, bared his soul, reached out the tenuous sinews of his heart…there was only so much time left to touch the one thing that could ever redeem a life, and that is love and human connection. Romantic love: the kind that begins families, the kind that revitalizes, and feeds its own self like the Ouroboros. This is what Roderick was reaching for.

He did not consider what Madeline would be reaching for, how she would stretch, how she would claw to get what she wanted out of life. Her brother became all too anxious to put her underground, to see that chapter of his life ended so he could begin the next, but he did not consider how alike they were in the end, how they were born together and would at last die together.

When he heard stirrings within Madeline's crypt, he preferred to think he was insane rather than believe he had entombed her just to further his own desires.

They tortured each other for days in the end, ruining whatever Roderick might have received from his friend, ruining what might have been a peaceful death for Madeline. Her struggle, his denial; they tormented each other inexorably.

They were family, after all.

THE RAVEN AND HER VICTORY

Tansy Rayner Roberts

I RECOGNISED the woman in the poem. Perhaps no one else would have done. My name (for once) was not present, carefully couched in floral language or complex metaphor. There was no Victory or raven-haired Viceroy, no grey-eyed Victoire in russet skirts, not even a sly dig at Victoriana.

Still, I knew that the woman in the poem was me. The woman in the poem is always me.

++

I FIRST MET Ida May at a charity dance benefit for war widows and children. My aunt, Mrs Grayson, introduced us, as young ladies with something in common. "Victoria, my dear, have you met Miss Midas of Baltimore? She's a writer, like yourself."

Miss Ida May Midas was an intense sort of woman, not pretty, with a pronounced brow and twitchy fingers. She wore brown, a striking gown if rather out of fashion, and she spoke in bursts, not used to polite company.

"Mrs Grayson exaggerates," I apologised. "I pen the social pages in our local paper. Hardly a celebrated poet like yourself."

Miss Midas gave me a dark, almost angry stare. "But you want to write. Real words. Real stories. You have a passion for the craft?"

I was unaccustomed for young unmarried ladies like myself to talk about passion, or indeed much of anything. "I have a great desire to write history," I found myself confessing. "But no one will let me do that, will they? I suppose I'll teach."

"You can do better than that," said Miss Midas, and something inside me unfolded like a crêpe-paper rose.

++

IT WAS A mistake, I know that now. A scandalous, ridiculous mistake. And yet I hardly noticed it at the time, hardly thought about anything except the light in Ida May's eyes as she explained a particular story of genius, or took apart some lesser work with scathing, critical words.

We went about together for weeks, arm in arm. Visiting museums and tea houses, talking of history and politics and all manner of grand things. Words, all words. We filled the world with them. And then, in my aunt's garden at the end of a long and vibrant day, we dropped the pretence that we were merely girls being chummy with each other, and I let her kiss me.

Her mouth on mine was warmth and sunshine, even as the light faded in the garden. We clung to each other like trembling leaves, and then parted. I wanted nothing else in the world so much as her, that night, in my arms.

I opened my eyes for a moment and saw the lawn behind us flare up for a moment in so many colours that I was dazzled, and afraid. The world was all of a sudden a daunting and overwhelming place. So I ran from her.

It has been many years now, and I am still afraid.

++

IDA MAY SENT me letters at first, scolding me for cowardice and scorching me with all manner of rebukes. Sometimes she enclosed downy white feathers in accusation, or dried flowers that fell to powder in my hands.

Every letter made my skin prickle with fear, for with it would come a dreadful portent of some kind. Draughts might blow suddenly behind my neck, or water might drip through the ceiling to wet my hair. Once, the fine Persian rug beneath my feet unaccountably burst into flames, and smouldered for hours no matter now much we soaked it with water.

After that, I left my mother's house for college, determined to train as a teacher and to leave my fears and Miss Midas long behind me.

She found my address soon enough, and though she no longer bothered to write whole letters to taunt me with, she continued to send feathers and flowers and occasional locks of her hair, each of which tormented me anew with small but impossible horrors.

If this was love, I wanted none of it.

⁘

EVENTUALLY, THE LETTERS stopped arriving. I learned to breathe again in a world without magic. There was a gentleman who courted me for a short time, though we parted as friends before our names were joined upon the tongues of our acquaintances. He was not for me, nor I for him.

Then in the third year of my studies, before we were released as qualified women of the world, there was Amy.

We were both so coy and bashful that I am sure no one knew that our friendship had turned to romance — even we were slow to admit that to ourselves. But we both loved poetry, and read it to each other in the spare hours, blushing all the while.

She read me one that she had cut from the newspaper, of a raven-haired princess in a magical land of many-coloured grass, and was surprised that it made my hands shake.

"Why, I thought of you when I read it," said Amy, so startled at my reaction that she forgot to blush. "Because of the title, see? And your hair is so lovely and dark."

The poem was "Victory," by I.M. Midas. It was the first of many. I should have known that nothing would quiet her pen. She would never release me from the burden of that single, fleeting kiss.

I could never kiss Amy. I did not fear society's condemnation so much as a woman in my position should, perhaps. My fear was wilder, that again I might ignite that dreadful power that had sparked between myself and Miss Ida May Midas.

My love for Amy was so much more than what I had felt so briefly for Ida May. Surely our kisses would set whole forests aflame. It could not be risked, and I could never tell her why.

⁘

THE YEARS PASSED. My friendship with Amy turned into a long and heartfelt correspondence as we taught in different schools, in different towns. Her letters soon became more friendly than passionate, and eventually I learned that she had chosen a conventional path, accepting the hand of an earnest young gentleman called Edward. I had never expected otherwise. She was too pretty to be a spinster.

Meanwhile, I.M. Midas grew in reputation, her dark and threatening mode of poetry capturing the imagination of the time. She moved to Boston and then New York, taking up with a bohemian set that only added to her literary stature.

One poem, about the ill omen of a raven, was published in over twenty newspapers across the country and for one brief season made Miss Midas a household name.

I found myself in that poem, as I always did. The raven croaked its chilly message to a woman who searched for victory in dusty old books, who craved a career as a historian (something I myself had ceased to yearn for years before now). A woman who desired to be forgiven by her lover.

Nevermore indeed.

After that, I.M. Midas was often referred to as "the Raven," even in my small circles. There were a few poets and book enthusiasts in my little town, and we met sometimes to read to each other while taking tea. Mr Oswald, who ran the library and the post office, took a particular delight in the words of "Mr Midas," and would regularly clip poems out of the newspapers to share with us.

"Ah, listen to this one, Miss Grayson," he said one afternoon as our little group sat in my schoolroom with cups of tea and slices of fruit cake. "You will appreciate it, I think."

It was not a poem, but a very short story, about a poet dying for lack of beauty, and the lost love who had broken his heart.

"Why is Mr Midas always so sad?" complained Lucille Woodvine, who was an excellent seamstress and quite pretty, but not especially bright.

I closed my eyes, and listened to the end of the story. The poet died, and only then was allowed to return to the land of many-coloured grass he had visited once in his youth, the single time in his life that he had ever been happy.

I would not crack. I would not. This was no more seductive than the letters or the feathers. Ida May had found another way to torture me for the choices of my past, and I would not go to her.

❊

As Christmas approached, our little reading group received word of a new literary journal, *The Stylus*, edited by none other than I.M. Midas. I rejoiced in this news for I truly believed (I wanted to believe) that if Ida May received the acclaim due to her for her best and most powerful work,

44

she might finally let go of the idea that our never-was love was such a great tragedy in her life.

I did not have to subscribe to the periodical, because Mr Oswald had already done so, and was delighted to go over the contents with the group. I did examine the crisp pages with great curiosity, I must admit.

There was a poem by Midas herself, and many other pieces she had chosen from favourite writers and friends — some were beautiful, some banal, and all quite wretchedly bleak.

Ida's poem was about me. Of course it was. The poems are always about me. This one for once made no playful pun about my name, not even a discreet letter 'v' placed somewhere noticeable, and yet it contained all of the elements I knew to recognise. The woman, this woman whom the poet loved, had a "classic" face, "queenly" stature, bright eyes, a musical voice, a pallid brow and curly dark hair.

Even when she did not name me, the Raven was still writing about her mythical Victoria, a woman she had constructed upon a few dim memories.

It was the article published at the back which made me tremble. It was a biography of I.M. Midas, poet-editor of *The Stylus*. A short piece, certainly, but one that was utterly false and scurrilous. No longer was Miss Midas merely writing under a name that implied she was male. Now she had actually allowed a piece to be written which stated her male identity as a fact. Ignatius Melville Midas had a Harvard degree, parents, enjoyed shooting and fishing, all artifice. A wife, by God, "his" helpmeet and muse, the raven-haired Mrs Victoria Midas.

Ida May had claimed me after all, woven me into her imaginary history of a celebrated male poet with a devoted wife.

As I consumed this news, smoke began to pour from the pages of *The Stylus*, and the journal burst into flames. Mr Oswald shouted, and Miss Woodvine screamed, and there was a great to-do with water and blankets.

I was not burnt, which they all claimed was a miracle. But I was indeed broken.

The very next day, I bought a train ticket to New York.

✢✢

"Mr and Mrs Midas" lived in a tall, narrow house in a tree-lined avenue of a wealthy district. I had bought another copy of *The Stylus* at the train station, so as to neatly copy the address on to a slip of paper I could keep in my pocketbook, though I was careful not to read anything else of the journal lest I cause further conflagration.

I stood upon their steps for a very long time before I gathered my courage enough to march up and ring their bell.

A maid answered, a shy girl in a crisp uniform with a cap pulled down upon her face. She bobbed and ma'amed and led me to a drawing room so full of books that I had no doubt I was in the right place.

"I should like to see," I said, and hesitated on the words, for no, I was not yet ready for the confrontation with Ida May. "The lady of the house. Mrs Midas."

The maid stared at me, quite startled, and I was equally startled to see her face. She had such bright eyes, and a brow that could only be described as pallid. It was like looking into the mirror I had owned ten years ago. She could have been me. "Yes, Mrs Midas," she said quickly, and fled.

What was I to make of that? For as I waited, I had a creeping suspicion that she had not been agreeing with me readily that she would fetch her mistress, but instead she had addressed me as her mistress.

No, that could not be.

A housekeeper came next, a stout and comforting woman, though again I had that quiet shock of recognition. She looked so like my aunt, or perhaps myself once I reached the age of my aunt.

"Mrs Midas, welcome home," she said in a voice that was certainly not my own, though I struggled at first to recognise it. "May I bring tea? Or would you prefer sherry at this hour? Mr Midas was sorry not to meet you at the station, but he will be along for supper directly."

"I am not," I said, and there was something wrong with my voice, too. It was deeper, more sardonic, and yet dreadfully familiar. "I am…" But what could I say? I was Victoria Grayson, unmarried, a schoolteacher, a lover of women? Mrs Midas was a Victoria too. "I am afraid…"

That, at least, was the truth.

The door rang, and the maid answered it again. I heard her speaking to the master of the house in the hallway, and he answering her, both in that same voice, the one I heard in the mouth of the housekeeper and of myself.

"Hello, darling," said Ida May, as she entered the drawing room. I had half expected her to be dressed as a man, all frock coat and tails, but she was dressed as she always had been when I knew her, in a respectable brown linen dress and jacket.

"Where are we?" I demanded. Her voice spilled out of me, that rich sound. I was not myself any more. My clothes had changed, and my corset was tighter. I could feel myself stretching to fill her vision of me. She thought I was taller, more slender, and thus I became. "What is this house?"

Ida May Midas smiled at me with that angular face of hers, and took my hand. Gently, she led me to the window and drew back the curtains. The trees that lined the avenue outside were glowing gold with a sunlight that came from nowhere. As my hand shuddered in hers, I saw threads of bright and many-coloured grass spring up in the middle of the street.

"It's not a house," she said serenely, her fingers encircling my wrist like a trap, sprung. "It's a poem."

CORVIDÆ

Peter Dubé

À Edgar Poe et Angela Carter, hommage et reconnaissance.

It's midnight. It's raining and cool and all I can think is strange. Strange, how so many things begin or end with a single word. "Hello." "Goodbye." "Congratulations" and "Condolences." Yes. Or no. Simple things bound on either side with an abyss of noise — or of silence. Complex things find their origins in the slightest, the simplest actions. Light a candle. Lay out a saucer of milk. Go to the corner store or answer the phone to an unknown caller. Unlock something shut up for far too long. Tell someone what you feel; how you feel. Bring home something new and beautiful and make place for it. It all seems so simple; but then isn't. The most baroque ornament must start with a single stroke. This black mark. This violet one. Say "welcome." Say "surrender." Whole worlds open up from tiny things, and we get lost in them. Or perhaps this, these thoughts, are all me, projections of my own needs, my own obsessions. It is likely; after all, I fell out of the womb and into a world of magnified gestures, hypertrophied significations. The back of a hand on the forehead. The fainting spell. The withering glance. The low moan of longing and the sound of black wings, beating near.

Black wings, beating near. How true, that. How often the black bird that haunts my shoulder has cried out, disturbed the air. How often it has changed shapes, changed minds: mine among them.

But let me be clearer; artifice has been my home since the beginning. Mother was an actress and I — a toddler — played among painted palaces and particleboard dooms. Dungeons of tarpaper and crêpe. No child had more bountiful options for concealment and none less sense of the line between work and play, appearances and what they are meant to do, and this would only grow. For me the universe was continuous, every division fluid, debatable, accommodating. One needed only start and see where something led. Say "hello." Say "goodbye." Say "forever."

Beyond "actress," my mother was beautiful. She was tall and well-proportioned; her hair was dark and her eyes darker. She was thick with mystery and she liked it that way. When I was six she performed a summer as Ophelia. Though she was old for the role, she managed to appear (oh, appearance you will be the end of me) all pink-cheeked nervousness and meaningful stares into a poorly defined distance, somewhere past the lobby doors. I remember my games that summer: crawling among the sets, the painted battlements of Elsinore, crawling beneath a chipped throne. One of my favourite games consisted of trying to draw an identical stone pattern on the back of the scrims standing in for the fortress' walls; trying with an aching care to replicate the arrangement. Attempting to make both sides of the panels match precisely. I rarely succeeded and the design team were less than amused with my attempts. In retrospect I have questions too: about what my efforts really meant. About what I was after; perhaps I was less interested in symmetry than in covering up blank spaces.

During that summer, Mother pavaned across the stage in a red, high-waisted gown, stage-whispering a desire she could not possibly understand, given how her own appetites courted recognition more than they did obsession. Still, she commanded attention, every phrase stoking the fires that would burst into blaze during the big moment: the madness and the flowers. Dead violets, underfoot, and fennel, sharp as a slap, she loved it. Like columbine. Like rue. Pansies and pansies and pansies, stirring the mind, all trouble for her then, all trouble for me now. Like rosemary, of course. And not a daisy to be found; I'll drop my eyes before I say a word on this.

None of those flowers, however, were ever as open as Mother's eyes, swimming through the swamp of her affected folly, swaying back and forth, lurching forward for the lip of the stage and pulling back just before she stumbled over. Always, always staring out into the darkness, seeking its contours and its limits, divining its imponderable shape. Those eyes, open, poisonous blossoms, unblinking in the footlights.

I've only ever seen a gaze as focussed one other time. The day I met Val. He was hunched over a laptop, his avian profile — pointed, intelligent — concentrated, his gaze fixed with a predatory attentiveness on the screen. Something perched on a cliff and aware of the motion below. His focus felt intimidating, but I can't resist temptation; I walked by him so I could look over his shoulder. So I could see what absorbed him. It was nothing, or more precisely: a void. An empty space. There on the screen was a long corridor. No one walked in it. No figures moved and no furniture occupied its length, which seemed all but infinite; it stretched on and on, and was punctuated on either side by doors and paintings, alternating regularly. Pendulous light fixtures hung from the ceiling. That was all. Bare otherwise, it was a narrow space that seemed free of any end. This is what trapped Val.

Tapping away at the laptop, the camera eye that stood in for him moved carefully along the tiled floor for a while, then slid rapidly back. He paused now and again. Then he would repeat the process. And again. Though I had no idea what held his attention, I found myself completely absorbed by this fixation. I must have watched him for too long a time, because after a while he turned towards me and said, "yes?"

That was all. That was how it began.

In response to his "yes," I apologized. He told me no apology was necessary, I could just sit down if I was interested in what he was doing. I was.

From one word, we passed on; he told me he worked in the game industry, helping to piece together imaginary worlds in which millions of anonymous people could become lost, in which they would forget the tawdry, bland facts of their actual lives. As he spoke, I felt something like a tide pulling me towards a distant shore. He standing on it. He laughed, saying that of course the details of his daily life were less no tawdry. He spent hours, whole days, labouring on some minor detail, some visual accident no player would ever notice. He shook his angular head muttering to the effect that if any of the gamers who bought these products knew of the tedium that went into their making they would flee from their devices in droves. Days spent squinting at bits of images under bad lighting. Then, pointing at the virtual corridor, he told me that *this* was different. The corridor was part of a personal project, something he was doing purely for himself; his eyes widened and grew wet.

Widened like the damp petals of Ophelia, once. Broad, deep and threatening tears.

A "yes." A venomous flower and an empty hall. Hello.

My mother greeted people with a similar enthusiasm. One that was as unexpected. She would smile broadly, tilt her chin up, look directly at her interlocutor. She had an uncanny ability to match another person's tone and rhythm, creating an unconscious sympathy: a sense of conspiracy between them that passed for intimacy. She smiled like that even in the face of disaster, of failure, of the end of things. As she did shortly after I turned twelve, when she realized her style of performance could never transfer to the screen, when she saw herself receiving less work. The months she stumbled during auditions. The months she saw the intensity of her face failed by photography. She could not speak to a machine, could not reach out to anything but another human being. She could not fake feeling in the absence of it, in the absence of some sort of genuine and responsive presence. Her life — her craft at least — lay in exchange, in dialogue. So she had a drink or three while she cast about for some other route. There was still work in the theatre, of course, but less of it. And even there she had begun to feel a subtle constraint. I saw it grow in her. Saw a refusal swell at the end of the night, night after night as I waited for her in her dressing room. I found it visible in the slow deliberate gestures with which she removed her makeup. Dissatisfaction with the gulf created by the forms and traditions of the theatre. The ocean that spread from stage-front to the first seats. For months I saw her thinking in an uncommon silence. Saw her wiping away the resentment she put on with the greasepaint. I watched as she fought with herself and took to stealing little trophies; saw her build a collection out of anger and of spite. She amassed an armada of artificial flowers and paste jewels. I watched good humour shrink in her as our front room shrank before the assault of her accumulation. The floor swept with wire and felt petals. I watched her searching for some new self in the light-girded mirror on her dressing table and in the bed she covered with her trophies too. Until one day I saw her smile again; she had found that new self. Or she had found a way to create one.

Val looked that way constantly; after all, he was creating whole new worlds seated at his keyboard. He elaborated his long corridor, added turns and twists, side passages and unexpected branchings. I saw the fireworks in his head when he added detail to one of the countless paintings, or called up the room that lay behind a door. His secondary world was all possibilities, and though our relationship deepened, I always knew he responded to me as deeply as he did because he felt I understood his compulsion to create this strange new space. He sensed that I had an enthusiasm for the project of my own. And I did. I loved his passion and his hunger; it drove me to love him.

Over the course of a spring and a summer, we grew closer. I recall the heat of that summer well: the long, longing exploration of each other's body. The nights and mornings filled with touch and tongue. How his hands would travel — with a tense tentativeness at first — up my legs. Touching lightly, but with determination, like someone making their way through a darkened room. Touch: a cool wall at the ankle. Touch again: the thigh, an unexpected turning point. And touch again: there the opening, the entrance. My hands on his back outlining — a chair rail, or a doorjamb. Exploring, searching out the limits of this new dark thing. Until his eyes meet mine, open. The lights going on in a new space, beautiful and waiting to be occupied. Lips now, parting draperies letting the fragrance of a garden in. Tracing the chambers we could inhabit together. Long nights of sweat, laughter, spilled drinks and tangled sheets. But of talk too. Wandering conversations that seemed to go nowhere but in their movement laid the foundations of what I dreamed could be a life together.

We talked about everything: our pasts, in my case the curious story of my mother, in his a family breakdown not uncommon but no less devastating for that; the secrets of our desires, of what we longed to do to one another, and have done to us; our beliefs and values, the things on which we could not compromise; the places in the world that we valued above all others — a small bookstore in Paris, a beach on an island off of Nova Scotia, someplace in the Seychelles I had never heard of, the courtyard at the Cloisters. We talked of food and wine, the despair we felt when faced with governments, the hunger to escape and the need to be alone — together. We talked about ourselves and grew to know the other heard us. Heard us and understood. It was the first time I had ever felt anything like that and it was extraordinary. I drank it up, revelled in the growing intimacy that burrowed further into us each day but never seemed to lessen the rich, black mystery that made a new discovery so exhilarating.

As she worked her way through the knots of her disillusionment with the theatre, untangling her discontent and growing sense of failure and point-lessness, to be heard and understood was something my mother wanted deeply. That suddenly seen smile was a sign she had seized on a first loose thread. Mistrustful of the constraints of plays and dramaturgy and direction, unhappy with the framework of the camera, she was faced with finding a new form in which to meet an audience, a new way of speaking to the world; she found it in a curious hybrid of monologue, performance art and classical theatre. She prepared the project carefully, wrote it herself, commissioned costumes, raised funds and booked it into small festivals at first. It was a terrible gamble, a hazarding of everything. A symbolist roll of the dice. The show was a labyrinthine construct melding a dozen female characters, each doomed in some way; Mimi, Emma Bovary, Cleopatra, Joan, the Ophelia I remembered from my childhood. Each of their stories sliced and reassembled, each of their voices blended with the next and operating in a dizzying chorale. Mother took the tales of suffering and madness, as once she hoarded the remnant blossoms and junk jewels, and transmuted them. She turned the defeats into acts of fierce resistance, the folly into a visionary regime. Where the original versions crushed these characters, Mother had them transcend any reductive reading, made them unseizable, impossible to fix in place, not less tragic but somehow different and, beyond that, magnificent. Though the piece was vertiginously non-linear and utterly ambiguous, it was absolutely compelling; an indefinable through line pulled the viewer in and guided him. But perhaps I should say "listener," because on that stage, so radically bare, containing only a gilded chair, a half screen suggesting — once again, almost forever — a stone wall, a pool of blue light, the barest pole standing in for a tree and at one point a brief snowfall of sequins, it was Mother herself, clad in a black gown trimmed with blacker feathers, and her voice, feeding on the crowd before her, that commanded. Standing there, between the chair and the rudimentary tree, she would open her mouth, speak and call silent wonder into the room. She would fill it with longing and sadness and rage. With love and fear and ambition. Flames taking a town. The last breath of an empress. The hunger of a child before a shop window. Lesions blossoming on skin. A love that died of silence or of fear. A bird circling in a twilit sky. A black, sounding bird once more. Feathers as inky as her own. The audience, nervous in its jackets and its shirtsleeves, its dresses and slacks, would shift uncomfortably at first, fretfully adjusting its garments and then settle down, quickly but not suddenly, caught up in that peripatetic, fascinating account. Trapped, as if never to escape, and breathing life back to her.

The reviews were laudatory: every one glowing. Mother was thrilled. She toured the show; the show grew. It gathered funding and played larger theatres. She appeared in major rooms and spoke at universities. At first, while still a minor, I travelled with her. I saw her in the first rush of her triumph; saw her as she turned fear and rejection into a brighter thing through a sorcerous transmutation that blended drive and labour. Watched for a year or two as her success became real. Saw her in other productions and other moments too, when, as the curtains long since come down, she continued to speak her magical words in the corridors, in her dressing room. Continued to speak because at last she believed herself. I surrendered to it as it grew.

As I yielded to Val. To his eagerness and all the eccentricity that was so apparent the first time I went to his apartment. It was shortly after we'd begun seeing each other and he'd spent more than a few nights at my place. At first this failed to strike me, but as the days went on it was odd. All sorts of ideas stirred: he was a bad enough housekeeper to want to hide it; he lived in some weird sort of communal situation; a criminal enterprise; a boyfriend, perhaps. Scenarios of all kinds, none happy. None ending well. At last, he did bring me home. I shook as he fumbled with the key. I nearly gasped when I entered.

The apartment was small, but — unexpectedly — orderly and clean. The room was uncluttered, almost Spartan, contained only what was necessary, with one exception. Hovering above the sofa, low table, one armchair and the desk in the corner, was a shelf a meter or so below the ceiling, and on that shelf a series of dolls and mannequins, statuettes, busts and what seemed like taxidermy, a smattering of stuffed and mounted animals. The shelf ran all the way around the room and held a score of the things. I saw a bust of a Greek deity, an Eastern European iteration of the devil, a large chess knight, a nineteenth-century belle, a wild cat in frozen aggression, a fully armoured Japanese samurai, and — most striking — a great inky bird with wings half spread. I would learn later that all of these things were automatons. They moved and made sounds: little artificial lives. But on entering all Val told me was that they were his collection. He was a collector: a serious one, in fact. Many of the presiding creatures looking down on us were old, some very rare. However, on entering they managed to impress by sheer presence, without the need for any knowledge of their possible value. If anything, I was more curious without the provenance. I was so taken by this impulse that, in time, we would add to our lovemaking and conversation, the building of a new collection we could share: smaller things and delicate too. We began to assemble the best examples we could afford of an old line of lustrous ceram-

ics depicting an elaborate fairy world. All lavish blues and greens and minia-
turized magical bowers peopled with dragonfly-winged wonders. On one, a
winding path opens up. In the foreground a pair of lavender faeries beckon
to the viewer with one hand and point towards the horizon with the other.
In the midground: a bend in the road with a fountain nearby where a lizard
makes ready to drink. Gazing into that minute and infinite distance, one
imagines the sound of flutes and mandolins. A gathering perhaps, friends
and suitors await the serving of some feast, the unfolding of some tale. At
the edge of the crowd, a tall fey noblewoman glances across the crowd to a
satyr lover. Her merest gaze pregnant with unspoken things and memory.
Above the path, the crowd, the fountain and the thirsty lizard, magnificently
rendered trees in emerald and scarlet spread the silent branches that will say
nothing of this. Absurd, but it enchanted us; these tiny things we kept at my
apartment, in a newly purchased cabinet so no matter where we spent our
time, we were surrounded by our obsessions. We had many, Val more than I.
None were more powerful than his game. His endless, involuting game.

He would spend hours on it. Two or three nights a week he would not see
me, choosing to spend his evenings at home refining twists in the floor plan,
the gilt on a frame, adding a candle to the dining table that lay behind one
door. More glitter. More glitter. More glitter. Sometimes he would seal himself up for the weekend to dig the world deeper, to add some unknowable
texture. Occasionally on one of these weekends he would meet me for lunch
and talk only of the manipulation of pixels, the cheating of reality. I would
listen for a time, then quiet him with hand slid under the back of his shirt, or
with a lascivious smile. Val lived in two worlds, or three: the one we all know,
the one he shared with me and the one that coiled and spread inside his mind.
Between them, he could get lost.

Mother, contrarily, lived in one world, but it was vast, fluid, all change and
all hers. In it she was never lost. But any visitor was at real risk. Nightly, she
would work magic from the stage, pulling her listeners across time and space,
whole epochs, entire continents. Though it might be truer to say she bent
time and space around her listeners, showing them refracted moments and
lives. She would confound custom, conjure away any notion of individual
identity until all experience was one experience — that of her magical account of struggle and resistance, glamour and doom. The faces in the audience would surge from the darkness as the lighting cues changed. One after
another, slightly different, but the look of wonderment and nervousness the

same. One: a pale man, mouth half open. Two: an olive-skinned woman: eyes wide, but shaken, twin windows just about to shatter. Three: a college student, barely out of girlhood, holding her breath, the scarf around her neck loosely knotted and somehow feeling tight. Every night she would tilt up her chin, shrouded in black velvet and black feathers, and live out her imaginary lives. Mad love and mere madness. Murder and despair. Once I was at university there were many evenings when she performed in the city in which I was studying that I sat there listening: riveted. Caught in the narratives she spun. So trapped that the distinction between those elements taken from her actual life became indistinguishable from those taken from literature. It was she, that crying, cackling corvine woman who had lived it all. It was she who loved a handsome, powerful young man too much. Who saw that love tear a family apart, and drive one of them to murder. She who mourned, sank into mania and rose again. She who struck back; slew a patriarch. She walked the stage speaking truths. Suffered. Said "goodbye." She who took a serpent to her bed. She who led an army against the empire of men. She who vanished. Who sank into the shadows once again. She was anger. Wonder. Worry. And escape. Most truly escape, because in the end that is what she did. Over time, Mother altered and revised the piece, tightening the seams, manipulating the pace; she created other shows that emerged from its complexity. She returned to the West Coast for a long run of what would prove to be its final version. The reviews were still more ecstatic. A few days after the show closed, I received a call from Mother's agent asking if I had heard from her. I hadn't and was surprised that he had not. Two days later I learned there had been a substantial deposit to my bank account. And the day after that, another call from the agent. It sank in; I called the police, her friends, an ex-lover of hers. No news. No news for months. The police continued their investigations, but I knew they would find nothing. No trace of a body, no requests for ransom. It was as I expected.

I remembered a long speech from her show, one near the end, in which my mother told those listening that the key to liberation lay in being invisible to jailers. She was gone, disappeared, just as she had always intended to: she had dissolved into her stories and into a world she had re-imagined.

A month later, I received a clipping: a review of the show dated from its final week. A single word was written on it: "congratulations." I knew whom it was from and I knew what she was congratulating me for; in claiming her freedom, she had given me mine. I had more than enough money to finish my education and begin my adult life. She was happy for me, and for herself. She wasn't the kind of person to conceive of anything strong enough to cloud the brilliance of freedom. It would never occur to her that being alone in the world might lessen the joy of anything. But she had set me free; I could study what I pleased, do what I had to, what I wanted to. She had bought me the time to *begin*. The time I needed to establish a career in something as impractical as writing — a notoriously difficult way to keep body and soul together. Though it was part of what held Val and me so electrically together.

When he learned I was a writer he was fascinated. He would introduce questions about my work into our long conversations, ask me about writers whose work I admired, seek out explanations concerning the way narratives are constructed, characters limned, made real. He interrogated me about voice and presence. Then he would nod, eyes closed, as he received his answers. Shortly thereafter he would kiss me and flee to his laptop to burrow away into the game, its endless, intangible possibilities. Often long into the night. With every new piece of information, whether he had heard it from me or tracked it down online, read it in a book or seen it in a dream, the game had to be fed. The world had to move.

Compulsion joined obsession and I can recall waking in the middle of the night to find Val gone. Waking to the sound of the tap, tap, tap coming from the living room, the creep of the ghoulish yellow light through the crack under the door. I reached for his ghost beside me, resisted the urge to get up, seek out the sight of him hunched before the screen, oblivious to me, the room, the whole actual, warm world. Lost in an irrational somewhere else, he would seek to stuff it with all of that actuality, that warmth.

Sometimes, he asked me to join him there, to enter the doppelgänger world by his side. He would show me a handful of its secrets. Corridors that loop around so you can follow yourself and learn from your progress. An unexpected balcony at the end of one hall that overlooks a ballroom on the level below. A room that contained nothing but a mirror and basin filled with water. He smiled at that. Once, while he laid out these immaterial wonders for me, one of our guardian creatures sprang to life. For a half-hour before the eruption I had felt myself observed, as if cool, crystalline eyes I could not see were taking my measure. Carefully considering my weaknesses. It was a terrible feeling that ended only when the thing sprang to uncanny life. The bird on the Western wall began to flap shadowy wings and shriek. A display of anger or of joy? Who knows. It was the first time the creature shattered my peace. And though it was an irregular thing, it was not to be the last. On another, quieter, evening Val drew my attention to a tall portrait of a veiled sitter whose features were always that of someone you loved. At this he teared up. He told me something of the narrative underlying his creation; it involved a quest. The protagonist-player was to wander the labyrinthine space in an attempt to understand his own needs, to learn his own nature, at which point the game universe itself would transform.

"Into what?" I asked him. He only lowered his eyes and turned his head from me.

We moved into our future; he spent more and more time on this project-world. When I protested, he told me he was close to finishing and did not want to slow his progress. When I told him I was concerned with his growing fascination, he said I oughtn't worry. I didn't know what to say to that. It was too flat a declaration. So I watched as he went on, sinking into his perfectible new universe. Observed as day after day his physical presence seemed to grow slighter and his virtual one more real. Even when he moved across the living room taking two right turns as if a corner I could not see obstructed him I said nothing. Or when he pointed at a blank wall and spoke to an image of my face he claimed was there. I observed. I watched as my fear raced to meet my fascination.

I remember what triggered my response at last; Val was seated in front of the computer, tiny images moving before him. He was quiet and motionless, had not so much as clicked in twenty minutes. He just sat there. Suddenly, he closed his eyes, but kept his face directed towards the screen. His attention was total and given to nothing. There was a terrible quality in his motionless vacuity: horror, real absolute horror. The sense of a final emptiness, the total precipitation of his life, his vitality into an indescribable void. My whole body tightened as I watched him, as if an invisible weight, the hand of an indifferent titan grasped and pulled me away. Like it struck at us blindly. I shouted. Told him it had to stop. I cried, sobbed in a way I hadn't since — as a child — I saw my mother emerge from her dressing room in full makeup, wearing a face I thought was not hers. My voice quavered as I told him to open his eyes, to get up. As I told him this whole thing had to come to an end. It could not go on. He answered with a nod. Not a word.

He got up, hugged me, held me for a long time. We went to bed. I actually slept. But I woke in the night to find Val gone again, only this time there was no tap, tap, tap and the light slithering under the door was blue: a cool, thick, melancholy blue.

I went into the living room. Val was not there, but the game was on the screen. A trio of characters roamed the sealed, palatial environment. More detailed, more lavish than I had ever seen it. Torchlight glittered and the shadows grew and shrank with every spectral movement. Stuck to the keyboard was a note in Val's hand bearing only one word: "surrender." On reading it, everything I'd failed to put together fell on me. I sat in Val's chair and stared ahead. I realized that I too had been living in an imaginary world – one of possibility – playing a game and seeing only what I desired, able to ignore an inconvenient actuality. It was what I needed. What I longed for. Like a comfortable blanket, the scent of rain, the taste of water on a long, hot day, the touch of an animal one has lived with for a decade or more, a smile from a beautiful child, a promise from a friend, a place to sleep without worry. I was eager for some certainty, any certainty; more than that, I was desperate.

This happened last night and I have scarcely left the computer since. I watch the three figures track the labyrinth of their endless need, unquenchable: a broad shouldered avatar of Val himself; one that looks like me; and a woman in a black feather-trimmed gown who can only be Mother. They wander the halls; from time to time they move a blunt stone into position, slowly building a wall. Are they keeping something out? Sealing themselves in? A mystery. Once in a while, idly, I hit a button, prompt one of these, my lost loves, to take some different action, to see what happens. To open a door, perhaps. Who knows what lies behind them?

I wait to see if Val will return. I wait to see if any world can be changed. If our desires do await us. And I wonder if I'll ever know what's really happened in all of this. If I'll ever understand.

On the screen some great black winged creature sweeps by and behind me the stuffed raven fills with artificial life and cries out: "Nevermore."

"Nevermore."

Nevermore.

THE MAN WHO WAS

Ray Cluley

I STAND upon a bank of sand in the middle of a sea that is entirely shore. I'm in the dark desert again, alone, and I know that I am dreaming not just because I'm in my pyjamas but because I've dreamt this many times before. My fists are clenched and grains of sand slip between my fingers, though I clench them tight. *Because* I clench them tight. Before me, the smoking ruins of tanks lie smouldering in the sand. It's night; I know they're smouldering because I can feel the heat, and smell the hot metal. It's a familiar scene. Not because of any experience I had there: I did not fight in the Gulf War, not for a single minute of its one hundred hours. It's familiar because of John.

The nearest wreckage is Iraqi. Almost all of the ruined vehicles are Iraqi. Still clutching the sand in my fists, I make my way to a turret that has become separated from the main body of the vehicle it once belonged to. Each ruined chassis is a dark footprint of war, walking away into the Arabian Desert only to stop suddenly, a route like an instructive dance map that starts and stops within itself, and the turrets protrude in bent and twisted shapes from the ground around them like dark growths. War flowers, budding. I know, because John told me, that the Americans called these tanks "pop-tops" due to the way they broke apart when hit, turrets flung clean into the air. They lie scattered before me, a field of blackened metal blossoms cast aside to wilt by some dancing warmonger giant.

I hear him call out from one of the wrecks. John. Man of my dreams, to make a cliché literal. His voice is deep and clear and familiar at first. Then it fills with pain. I try to go to him. I run. I know he's in one of the American vehicles, a Bradley, and I let go of the sand to run faster. As the last of the sand is taken by the wind, so his screaming stops.

And that's when I wake up.

Usually, that's when I wake up.

+

GENERAL JOHN SMITH; a name so plain, you'd think him made up.

I first saw him across a crowd of people at some charity event or dinner, the sort of occasion I usually hate to attend but find, as an occupational hazard, that I often must. It's my job to plan such events and I do it well; give me the internet and a phone and I can arrange anything. I can even mingle and make polite conversation and though I'm reluctant to talk much about myself, I can feign an interest in others. The general, though, aroused my full genuine interest, and did so immediately.

The event was black tie of course, and he cut a striking figure even amongst so many men dressed identically. *Because* of it, probably. He certainly wore his suit better than I mine. He stood at about six feet with the rigid bearing of a man who has served in the military, though his hair was much longer and glossier than military regulation probably allowed. Similarly, he had a very non-regulation beard. Neatly trimmed, lining his jaw in such a precise way as to emphasise the strength of it rather than hide any weakness of it, as many men with facial hair are inclined to do. When he smiled, which I saw him do frequently in his conversation, he flashed teeth that were movie-star straight and white, all the brighter for their appearance within his dark beard.

I fear my description doesn't reveal him accurately at all.

"I see you've noticed the general."

My companion took a sip from his champagne but the glass did little to hide his smile. He knew me better than most.

"The general?"

He'd said it like I was supposed to know who. I didn't. My companion had scored a point in the trivial game of gossip that thrives in such environments. I had guessed already, though, that the man I was drawn to had a military background. It was in his bearing, not only the straight way in which he

62

held himself but in the confidence with which he moved between groups of people. He was not the host of the event but he commanded the crowd as if he was.

"General John Smith," my companion explained, and rolled his eyes either because I hadn't known or because the name sounded so phony. Perhaps for both reasons. I didn't care; I was happy enough staring.

"You'll never guess how old he is," he added, admiring the man. "Served in the Gulf. Served after that, too, from what I've heard. Bloody hell, he looks good for it. Bet he's had some work done."

I disagreed, but kept my opinion to myself. Or maybe I simply hoped otherwise, seeing it as a vanity I hoped the man did not possess.

"Now he's set for politics."

"Swapping one battlefield for another?"

He smiled politely at my joke. "Ferocious man, by all accounts. In a good way, I mean." Here my companion widened his eyes at me. "Imagine."

I disguised my thoughts at that by turning to a passing waiter, swapping my empty glass for a full one.

"Women love him, of course," my companion went on, "On account of his tremendous bravery."

"His bravery?"

"Well, obviously not *only* on account of that. He's a man of calibre, if you'll excuse the military pun."

I excused it by ignoring it. "Did he see much of the war?" I asked. I knew little of the Gulf War except that it was brief.

"See much of it? You really haven't heard of General Smith?"

I admitted as much, caring little for the man's petty persistence in embarrassing me.

He pressed the advantage.

"Christ, really? Nothing of what he did in Kuwait?"

Again, I shook my head no.

"I tell you, to look at him is to become infatuated, but to hear something of his character? What he did in the desert? Doomed." He said this last theatrically, tapping my glass as if to toast the prospect. "To a life of love and longing."

We drank to that, and I surprised myself by doing so with enthusiasm.

"So what *did* happen out there?"

He raised an eyebrow, delighting in my ignorance. "Okay, quick version; he's the man who — "

But my companion had no time to explain, for the man who was the topic of our conversation was fast approaching.

The term statuesque is the staple of old fiction, terrible romances, but the proportions of him did indeed seem carved, solid; something the Greeks would marvel at and try to imitate in their art. His poise was perfect, his movements smooth as if choreographed.

"Gentlemen."

One word, and I felt something of the doom I'd been warned against. The general's voice was strong and clear, with the clipped assuredness of breeding but not too Ivy League. I found my own voice lacking, and so it fell to my friend to make the introductions.

"Good to meet you," the general said, shaking my hand. Holding it just a moment longer than necessary.

"Likewise," was all I could manage.

"And you organised all of this, did you?"

I nodded.

He released a breath as if it must have been an ordeal and said, "Bet that took some planning. We could have used someone like you in the Middle East." He smiled.

His smile was as dazzling close up as I had imagined when seeing it from afar, but it was his eyes that drew me. They were deep hazel and met your own gaze with such intensity it was difficult to not look away.

"By all accounts," I said, recovering enough to respond to his compliment, "it wasn't much of a party out there."

He laughed. I felt myself smile with the pleasure of having caused it and he clasped my upper arm, laughing still, and said, "It wasn't." I tensed, suddenly self conscious about how my body might feel in the suit, but he released me quickly enough, with a friendly pat afterwards.

We talked for a short time about the party, though I barely heard the words. I was too focussed on the musicality of his voice, the rise and fall of its timbre. It wasn't difficult to believe he'd once yelled orders but already he had the orator's skill he'd need in politics and I even wondered how he might sound singing. How his voice would sound when hushed into a whisper.

"This must feel like work," the general noted, "all this talk of the party."

I disagreed politely, but he wasn't fooled, and so we talked of other things. It was some time before I noticed my previous companion had gone. I didn't care. The general was charming and well informed on a number of subjects, all of which he spoke of in a way that seemed to promise he could say more if only the two of you had a private moment elsewhere. His opinions felt like confidences and he heard my own with a seriousness that encouraged my honesty about a great many things. He seemed genuinely interested in anything and everything I had to say; if there was anything false about him, he was good at hiding it. He would do well in politics.

I tried to steer the conversation to his own exploits overseas, and he humoured the attempts with stories that held my attention while remaining modest. Indeed, his brave charge into enemy fire, his actions in the field, seemed all the more courageous for his reluctance to talk about them; he would always turn the conversation away again as soon as it was polite to do so. Where he became most particularly passionate was when talk turned to technology and advances in modern invention.

"It's wonderful, isn't it?" he concluded. "The things we can do today. The march of progress, the devices designed to make our lives easier. I mean, take our cell phones for example. Look at what they can do these days."

It was a wonderful way into exchanging details. Smoothly done, and innocent enough to avoid any potential embarrassment.

"I may need to plan a huge party some day," he said, filing my number away then looking around at all the guests mingling. I worried he was searching for a way out of our conversation, that I had kept him too long from other friends or obligations, but he was merely observing the size and nature of the group assembled. "Or perhaps not a party. Maybe a military operation, eh, Thompson?"

My name is not Thompson, but I didn't correct him. Indeed, I felt he'd made the error on purpose. Not as a slight, but as if to see how it would fit, or how I might respond to it. I tried to give him nothing outwardly, but he saw something that made him smile and that was how our conversation ended that first night.

⊹⊹

SOME NIGHTS I sleep through a thunder of gunfire, standing in a desert that is green and black, a foreign land of night-vision colours. A flare of white — bright, brief, dazzling — and the heavy concussion of a fired shell as dark shapes rush towards each other in the open plains. I call for John, but

my voice is torn from me by a wind that carries the desert from one place
to another; his name is taken from me in a gust of dust and sand. The air I
breathe is full of it so I pull my pyjama shirt over my nose to filter the breaths
I take. It does little to block the smell of burning metal, the stench of hot fires,
or the acrid chemical odour of cannon blast. Later, when it is over, there will
be the stench of roasting flesh, the lingering smell of fear and defeat. The
victors will be suddenly gone and only a graveyard of machinery will remain
behind. This is when the green light of goggles I do not wear disappears and
I am alone in the night desert with torn vehicles and split lengths of track
and huge discarded pop-top flowers. Black poppies in a field of sand. My fists
are full of grains slipping between my fingers and I wait for John's voice to
answer my call. When it comes I'll run to him. I will spread my hands open
for speed, wind taking the sand from my palms, hurrying because his voice
is so full of pain. So full.

I never manage to reach him.

＋＋

THOUGH JOHN AND I exchanged some messages after that first occasion
of our meeting, it was some time before I saw him again, and even then it was
a public and solemn affair. It was a memorial service, a formal event beginning at the grand cathedral for which our city is rather famous. I had arranged much of the event, was responsible for a couple of the speakers, and
my presence was required to ensure it all went smoothly. Attending church
is not a regular part of my life, except for such special functions, and I do
not belong to an organised religion of any kind. I have my own relationship
with God. The Reverend Drummond knows this, and accepts it, even if he
doesn't fully understand my reasons and probably wouldn't accept them if
he did. Still, we are friends, or close enough that I would often coordinate
such ceremonies, especially if the city's wealthier residents were to attend
and donations were to be encouraged.

As the Reverend spoke at length about the futility of war, a hushed voice
beside me said, "I hear you set this up?"

I turned to see who addressed me though there was little need; she's worn
the same perfume for all the years I've known her.

"Miss Arabella," I greeted her. Our little joke.

"*Mrs*," she corrected as usual, waving her wedding ring at me as she always
did. She had made a pass at me once and we'd agreed ever since to blame
her marriage for her lack of success. Easier than to think my tastes would

not extend to her, though she was boyish enough in build. There was still something of flirtation on her part whenever we spoke, as if she thought trying hard enough could one day "turn" me, but it was done in fun rather than frustration.

"Mrs," I said, "Of course. And how is your husband?"

She waved the question away because neither of us really cared. "So tell me about the general."

I was rather taken aback. The general and I had exchanged a few texts, a few phone calls, had even spoke via webcam a few times (technology really is a wonderful thing) but I had not told anybody. My discretion is partly what makes me such a valued member of certain circles and plays no small part in the success of my business; I know who should receive invites to what and, more importantly, who should not, and I understand the subtleties of seating arrangements and the like. That Arabella should know something of my business with the general was almost as startling as my having no knowledge of him at all.

"Don't look so surprised," she said. "He's quite taken with you."

She laughed, for whatever surprise she had seen in me must have increased tenfold with such news.

"How sweet," she said, "You're blushing."

"What do you know about — "

The Reverend raised his voice over our whispered conversation and presented us with a look that was not lost on myself, Arabella, or indeed any of the people gathered close by. We spent the next few minutes in quiet and I used the time to wonder at this turn in events.

Conversations between the general and me had been long and interesting but often circled anything that might be construed as personal, an exercise in caution on his part that I was happy to entertain, enjoying as I do the thrill of the chase, the flirtatious hesitancy that precedes any new relationship worth having. I understood how any relationship we might have could compromise him, even in this apparently more tolerant day and age. He had only recently become a public figure, with an interest in political progress, not to mention a military background that would permit little by way of sexual scandal. I was surprised he might have mentioned any of our communications. It did not surprise me, though, that having done so, Arabella would hear of it. Oh, not from him, certainly, but she knew people who knew people.

"Such a handsome man," she said, whispering her opinion but not taking too much care as to how quietly. "Such a waste." Her tone left her exact meaning ambiguous as to which man she meant; flirtation, to her, was breath.

By this point I had neither confirmed nor denied any of her suspicions, save to redden in the face. But I saw it as a positive sign that he had mentioned me at all, and I enjoyed entertaining the idea of a romantic connection.

"I hear he served in the Gulf," I offered, steering the conversation away but keeping within the topic of her interest.

"Yes," she said. "Tanks."

"Saw a bit of action."

We received another glance from the Reverend who was still delivering a suitably sombre speech. It was rude of me to ignore it, disrespectful even, but I couldn't help pursuing this line of conversation. John was so reticent about the wars he'd served in.

"A *bit* of action," Arabella said, smiling with sarcasm, but seeing the tilt of my head and inquisitive frown she covered her mouth and widened her eyes and said, "Really? You don't know?"

"Don't know what?"

"Jesus," she said, though she knew full well where she was when she said it, at once appalled at the story she had and delighted that she could be the one to tell me. "Horrible. Tragic. The things that happened over there."

I nodded my agreement, perhaps hurrying her along quicker than was politely appropriate. "I tried Google but there was nothing."

"Well, there wouldn't be," she said. Technology might have been bounding forward, but the internet had nothing on Arabella. "He was one of the ones who — "

"'Man hath but a short time to live!'" the Reverend announced with more fervour than the solemn occasion called for, our chatter not unnoticed. He maintained eye contact. "'He cometh up and is cut down like a flower.'"

I nodded at him, not in agreement but to acknowledge my fault and as a promise of quiet. I would ask Arabella about the general later.

Or, I decided, I would ask General John Smith himself. Man has a short time indeed, I thought, resolving to speak to him directly, honestly, and while I was being honest I would tell him how I felt. I would make the most of my life by offering to share some of it with him.

When the Reverend was finished, we filed out from our pews to a cenotaph in the churchyard where several servicemen made speeches about lost brothers in arms, remembering all who had sacrificed before them in wars we seemed to learn nothing from. The general was one of the speakers.

What a speech he made!

He was wearing full dress uniform and stood tall, proud, as he delivered a moving account of time spent on the battlefield, and of a more harrowing time spent with men in various military hospitals. He spoke eloquently, yet refrained from any poetics that might have added an unnecessary gloss to his words. At one point, speaking of lost friends, his voice, usually so strong and so clear, caught in his throat. He massaged the area for a moment, as if the fault lay in his larynx, and continued, not once referring to any prepared text. It seemed he had one, for he clutched a paper in one hand, but for most of the speech his hands were clasped behind his back. I admired the honesty with which he spoke and wondered if perhaps he had deviated from the prepared script. I could imagine something drafted by someone else, crafted to further the general's political aspirations while offering sentiment and condolences, just as I could imagine him ignoring it.

I kept a close eye on him as he spoke, and afterwards tried to find a moment to talk with him, but he was always in the company of others, mostly soldiers, and I did not want to mingle with a crowd so fully his own. What did I know of war? So I looked for Arabella to perhaps pick up from where we'd left off, a poor substitute for the general's company even as pleasant as she can be, but it appeared she'd already left. Many had, once the speeches were over; respects had been paid, and that was all that had been required.

The general noted my presence in the crowd, at least. He nodded to me, and smiled, though it was a smile somewhat lacking in its usual mirth. My nod in return was both a hello and a goodbye and I left him with his fellow servicemen.

It was as I settled into my car that I saw him finally snatch a moment to himself. He deposited what I had thought was his speech at the foot of the cenotaph and rejoined his friends as they were leaving. I watched them pile into a minibus I'd organised for the occasion, knowing it would take them to where a procession would move slowly through the park.

I sat in my vehicle for some moments, debating with myself. Eventually I pulled out into traffic and drove home.

✛

THAT NIGHT I did not sleep. I lay awake, contemplating the events of the day, and the cruelties of war. I considered, too, the cruelties of love. I had a letter from John and I read it over and over, wishing it had been addressed to me. Just as I'm sure John wished he had given it to Thompson when he'd had the chance.

⊹⊹

SEVERAL DAYS PASSED before I spoke to the general again. It began with a text message, a polite enquiry as to my health and happiness, and proceeded to a webcam conversation. I did not confess my feeling to him as I had planned because the distance between us felt too great when each of us was little more than a disembodied head on a fold-up screen. I longed to see more of him than this. But we exchanged some banter that finally crossed the line into undeniable flirtation and he spoke of arranging a meeting, something public but not too intimate. I told him of a coming performance I'd planned with the intention of garnering interest in a new acting company. The launch would offer just the right amount of excitement and frivolity together with the restraint of a public relations event.

"It won't be difficult to get you an invite," I told him.

"Not Shakespeare is it?" he asked.

"Er..."

He sighed, and we laughed. I told him there would be various acts to showcase individual talent, and a short play that presented the whole ensemble and he accepted the offer.

"'In visions of the dark night I have dreamed of joy departed,'" he said.

"Is *that* Shakespeare?" I didn't think it was, but I was hardly Patrick Stewart.

On screen, John shrugged. The buffering made the action awkward, like something automated, and I realised how much I longed to see him in the flesh. The meeting we'd planned could not come soon enough, and I told him as much; the bravest of my flirtations. To my surprise and delight, he reciprocated.

Of course, the days until then passed slowly.

I was to meet John at the launch, which was taking place at a reputable hotel. I had reserved two of their function rooms together with the exclusive use of the bar, and I had invited all those who could benefit, or would benefit from, a theatrical association. For myself, I had taken the liberty of reserving a room. Partly it was to save me the bother of returning home the same evening, but it was a double room; the hotel was one that could be counted on for discretion, and I had my hopes.

He was late. For half an hour I was forced to mingle, smiling my pleasant-ries, which was when I met an old acquaintance I had once assisted with an art installation. I'd found him difficult company then, and he quickly proved he hadn't changed.

"Very modern, all this, isn't it," he said, "the actors mixing with the audi-ence, all of that."

I agreed, but without the same expression of disdain. The performances were to occur amongst the guests rather than on a stage, an intimate and far more lively approach to theatre, I thought. It meant the people here were not all as they seemed, but apparently not everybody enjoyed the frisson of uncertainty.

"I could be chatting to some young thing only for her to suddenly take on some role," he complained. "She'd start bellowing poetry, or worse, and all my efforts would have been wasted."

I thought that to listen to him a woman must already be an accomplished actress in order to feign interest, but I did not make the remark.

"Who are *you* with, then?" he asked me. "Or do you have your sights set on someone here? Come on, who's your target?"

He was eagerly eying up the women. He did not know me well at all.

"I thought the general was to be here this evening," I said, answering his question indirectly but seeming, to him at least, to change the subject.

"Smith?"

I nodded, looking elsewhere as I sipped my drink. Acting the role of indif-ference.

"I hope so," my companion said, "Good man. Terrible what happened. Cruel lot over there, aren't they? Can't do this, can't do that. Hide their women under those Godawful sheets with eye slits. You see that film? You can't even fly a kite in those countries."

And so on. I tolerated as much as I could, hoping he might touch on some-thing more personal about the general, but all I learned was how ignorant this man was, and how racist. He muddled countries throughout his solilo-quy, or rather he lumped them all together as the Middle East or, honestly, "The Land of Tyrants and Terror."

"T and T," he said, "Tyrants and Terror. What they *deserve* is some TNT." He mumbled an explosion and mimed it with his hands before laughing at his own pathetic joke. When he saw I was not amused he at least had the good grace to adapt his topic.

"Soldiers coming back in boxes," he said, "Or with bits missing, or just plain used up, you know? Used up and *messed* up." Here he twirled a finger around the side of his head, and though I was sure there was someone else I could say hello to, I decided to endure more in the hope of a snatch of gossip about General John Smith.

"Injured, was he?"

The man looked at me as if he'd forgotten I was there, or I'd startled him. "Who?" he said, downing what remained in his glass. "The general?"

I nodded.

At this, the man began to laugh. It was an absurd response to such a question, but my scowl only made him laugh harder. When he'd recovered, he said, "You serious?"

Which, of course, was when the show began.

The moment it began I realised how amateur it was and little time passed before I decided to leave, though in truth it wasn't as bad as that. I simply didn't want to admit to being stood up.

One of the performers, painted bronze to play Talos in some Greek story I barely followed, delivered his lines with enthusiasm if not skill. Created to protect his island, he pretended to throw food and drink at "invaders" who were merely bemused guests. I gave him a tight smile and continued past, though it meant shouldering a path quite forcefully through the other guests gathered to watch.

"Excuse me," I said, "Pardon me. Coming through. Ex —"

My exit met the general's entrance and we faced each other, close in the crowd.

"I'm late," he said. "Sorry." Some of his confidence was gone. He stood a little less straight than previously and I realised he was nervous.

"That's okay," I said.

"I booked a room."

I was surprised by such a forward admission and at once thankful that a performance was taking place around us, distracting others from the one we were making a mess of.

I laughed and blurted, "Me too."

We went to my room. I didn't know whether that was a gracious allowance on his part, or simply a willingness to be led in this, and I wondered if it was a first time for him. I took no delight in the idea. In fact, it rather worried me. Perhaps, though, with being a sudden public figure, it was merely the anxiety of being discovered. He was a man of many parts, military and political amongst others, but it only made managing his private life more awkward.

However, my fears of first time nerves were, I think, more accurate. I won't divulge the details of what happened in that hotel room, except to say that although I was pleased enough, I was allowed less physical contact with him than he with me. He dictated what little grappling there was and removed nothing of his clothing, though I longed to see the body I supposed was perfect underneath. Much of the pleasure came as a release of tension rather than anything as intimate as I'd hoped. And there was another problem.

"Who's Thompson?" I asked him afterwards. I was fastening my tie at the mirror but glanced at him in the reflection to gauge the honesty of his response.

John, already sitting ramrod straight on the edge of the bed, seemed to stiffen even more, but said nothing.

"You called me Thompson," I said.

"I did not."

I tugged the knot into place and straightened my collar.

"I *didn't*," he said again, standing this time.

I turned to face him. "Not just now. Earlier. The first time we met."

I stepped aside to pick up my jacket and left him facing his own reflection. When I turned back he was staring at himself with such an expression of regret that I felt terrible for my pettiness and pressed the matter no further, despite the letter I had found that day at the cemetery. The letter I had gone back for, and taken, and read, though it was no business of mine.

"People say I'm brave," John said. He scowled at his reflection. "They're wrong. I'm not brave." He turned away from the mirror and looked at me. "I spent the first half of my life doing as I was told, and all it did was ruin the second half."

"I'm sorry."

He grabbed his jacket from the bed, suddenly in a hurry. "I better go."

"No, John, wait. Please — "

"I'm going home." He tugged his jacket on, rather clumsy in his haste. I tried to stop him but I think I've remarked already on the man's build, his stature. He's built solid. When he barged past my outstretched arm there was little I could do. He was polite enough at the door to face me for a good-bye, but he said it in such a stern way that I knew it stood for more than just this evening.

I gave him a few minutes to make his exit before making my own.

++

SITTING IN THE car outside his place, I tried to clear my mind enough to go home and leave him be. He lived in a reputable part of the city, in a house far beyond my means, but admiring the property did little to distract me.

I'd fully intended to let our tryst be the brief encounter it seemed destined to be, but in moving through the lobby I bumped into the guest with whom I'd shared a few words earlier that evening. The performers were enjoying something of an interval, though mingling with the crowd it was difficult to tell, and many of the audience members were flitting between function rooms and the bar. I spoke a few hellos and a few goodbyes to some of them, including Mr TNT.

"Ah," he said, "Wonderful show." It was a different opinion to the one he'd begun the evening with, but then I knew how that felt. In his case I believe the way the actresses were dressed played a great part in his new view of things.

"I'm glad," I said, with a terse nod that should have bid him a good night, but he chose not to see it.

"Your friend's here," he said.

"My friend?"

"The general. At least, he was." The man glanced around. "I saw him."

"Thank you. I'll catch up with him some other time."

"Brave man." He slurped from his glass in a way that revealed it was only the last so far in a long line of many.

"So I've heard."

"Lives with one of *them*, you know."

"Excuse me?"

"Of course," he said, and I realised with a humourless laugh that now he thought I was bidding him goodnight.

So I made my way to the car, but all the way to it I wondered at his meaning. One of them? Lived with? And instead of driving home I found myself on the streets leading to John's side of town.

I waited and I watched.

Before long I saw John at a window, looking out into the street. He was focussed on his thoughts rather than anything he saw and seemed to be on his own. He removed his jacket and began unbuttoning his shirt.

"Goodnight, John."

But as I was reaching to start the car I saw another man at the window. He was behind John, reaching around him to help him with his shirt buttons. I watched, and their two shapes merged as one undressed the other, and though they turned, then, from the window, and drew curtains closed behind them, it was very clear that this man was seeing more of John than I had been allowed.

I'm usually a calm and considered man, but the sight of them at the window combined with the evening's events sparked a sudden impulse in me that had me out of the car and striding to the house. I beat at the door rather than push at the bell and when it eventually opened I put my hand to it and pushed it open further, forcing my way past the startled man who asked what it was I wanted. He was dusky-skinned, Middle Eastern, and his English was heavily accented. Clear enough, though, for me to know he was demanding I leave. I ignored him, save to spare a disdainful glance, and made my way up the stairs calling for John.

The man pursued me up the stairs.

"John!" I cried, more upset than I had supposed, less angry than I had intended.

"Please," called the man behind me, "He is not decent."

"No, he's not," I threw back.

The man pursued me but I was quicker.

"Let him get himself together," the man tried.

It was too late. I was in the room.

"Where is he?" I demanded of the man who followed me inside. I gave him no chance to answer but instead picked up the heap of clothes that had been discarded onto a chair. I had intended to sling them at the man, jealous and already embarrassed but unable to stop. The clothes were heavy. I'd picked something else up with them.

The bundle shifted in my arms and a face peered at me from the crumpled clothes. I let out a cry of alarm and horror at what I held and cast it aside. Something of the face had been John's. But not much of it.

The other man cried out as well, though his was one of concern as he rushed forward to catch what I had thrown. He was too late; a groan that was all John — had I not heard it only an hour ago? — issued from the floor. The face I had briefly seen contorted momentarily in pain. Then it rolled with the tumble of garments and heavier items.

The other man knelt by the bundle and rummaged amongst it, casting foul looks my way as he righted the pile into something...squat. It smiled a grin that was all lips and blackness, no teeth, and said my name with a harsh rasp of breath.

The Middle Eastern man hushed him. "Quiet, Mr Smith. Wait a moment. Let me help you."

I backed towards the wall with both hands covering my mouth, a child disturbed by a nightmare, but the nightmare I saw took a more certain shape before me at the hands of this foreign man.

What I saw was a torso, a very stunted one, with a face that peered from a shirt that had gathered around it in the chaos of my tantrum. The Middle Eastern man pulled this down and John's head emerged from the collar. It was stripped of hair, all pink skin on scalp and jaw. One eye was missing. He had a nose but it had slipped to reveal the cavity behind. John spoke too quietly for me to hear, but the man with him nodded, absently but efficiently fixing the nose before going to a nearby dresser. In a moment he was settling a wig in place and then pressing something into the vacant socket of John's eye. Then he put his fingers into John's mouth, prised it open, and inserted something not unlike a denture plate, only with more substance. It gave John's face a more defined chin which settled left and right with a serious of clicks as John worked his jaw.

"Better," he said. His voice still had something of a croak but the other massaged the throat and suddenly John was coughing. There was a resounding thrum for a moment and then when next he spoke he had the same strong, clear voice I knew.

"Not much to look at, am I?" he said, and laughed. It wasn't a pleasant sound.

I could only shake my head, dismissing what I saw rather than agreeing.

"This good man here is Hakim."

The good Hakim was inserting something into John's trouser leg, turning it once, twice, three times, and then fussing with the cuff so it settled over a foot that was entirely shoe. He repeated the procedure with the other side, screwing apparatus into place and then leaning John up into a standing position. He kept his arms around John's waist and looked around the floor. I could see the piece he wanted but could only point.

"There," said John for me. "Go on, I'll be all right."

His companion stepped away from him and John took an experimental step without him, finding his balance. His shirt sleeves hung empty by his sides and I wondered, if he fell, could I find the strength to catch him?

"My Bradley took a hit in '91," he said.

I nodded, and tried to keep eye contact.

"It's a tank, not a person. I thought I'd better explain, in case you became jealous."

The foolishness I'd feel for my behaviour would not come until later. Right then I stared with wonder that was, I'm ashamed to say, something like horror. My gaze was drawn to this or that part of his body, and the places where his body used to be. Now Hakim was attaching another prosthetic, an arm, connecting valves and screwing slim cables into place. He went about his business like a tailor who had known Smith's custom for years. Perhaps he had.

"The Gulf War?" I managed.

"Sort of. Part of that, anyway. The Hundred Hour War they call it, as if it was a play. But it was very real."

The story he told had the sound of practice about it, though I can't imagine who he might have told it to. Perhaps, judging from how his friend nodded at intervals, it was part of the dressing process. His…assembly.

"The Iraqis had these Godawful tanks Hussein had bought from the Soviet Union. Piece of shit hand-me-down heaps that were slow and inaccurate and popped their tops when they took a hit. Literally fell to pieces." He countered something in my expression with, "Ha! Like I can talk." It was too bitter to be part of any rehearsed speech, and his companion slowed in what he was doing at John's other sleeve.

"You can leave us, Hakim."

"Your hands, sir."

John looked at his blunt wrists then put them in his pockets, dismissing his assistant with, "Problem solved."

When the man was gone, I tried to explain my presence but John cut me off before I could get any further than his name.

"We waited in the night through a heavy storm. Middle of the fucking desert and it was raining. Wind howling, battering us with wet sand. That's a sound you don't forget in a hurry. Sounds like the night is hissing laughter at you. Maybe it was. Maybe it knew what was coming."

It was a sound I couldn't imagine at the time, but I've dreamt it many nights since.

"They came at us, and we expected that, but there were more of them than anticipated. I was forced to take evasive action, breaking out of formation, cutting ahead at the right flank as the Iraqi numbers tripled right before our eyes."

Here he touched the eye I'd seen Hakim insert.

"I have seen such terrible things," he said. His fingers pressed against the pupil, an accident that shifted it slightly in the socket so that he seemed to stare beyond my right shoulder with one eye when he added, "I've done such terrible things."

"It was war," I said, rather pointlessly. He ignored the comment, as he had every right to. He was still there.

"Round after round," he said. "Twenty-five cal slamming into hard packed sand. Blasting the desert and tossing tanks into torn shreds of metal."

John closed his eyes at the memory. I was selfishly thankful to be rid of that skewed gaze.

Eventually he spoke again. His voice was soft. "We wiped them out." When he opened his eyes the crooked one had somehow righted itself. He met my gaze with a fierce stare, but his anger was clearly aimed at someone or something other than me. "*Of course* we wiped them out. We were better armed, better equipped. I mean, isn't technology wonderful?"

He lifted the stumps of his wrists to me before realising his hands were elsewhere. He compensated by rubbing appallingly at his crotch, "They think of everything!"

I was disgusted, and then ashamed of my disgust, and then I didn't have to think of it because he continued his story. The one I had so wanted to hear until I was hearing it.

"Like I said, we were out of position. Sand was flying, bursts of metal flying in the night. Explosions rocked us, but we targeted tank after tank.

"One of them was ours."

He wiped at one of his eyes — the one that worked — and was silent for so long that I thought he'd finished. Before I could say anything, something that would no doubt make it worse even as I tried to make it better, he said, "Friendly fire. That's what they call it."

"John, you don't need to — "

"Yes I do."

He moved to where I'd seen him at the window. The curtains were drawn but he stared anyway.

"Thompson was the name of one of the men in the tank we hit."

"I'm sorry."

"He died."

Thompson was more than an accidental casualty. I knew, because I had read the letter John had left at the cenotaph. John could not have known, but he knew that I understood. Thompson was the line in the sand neither of us would cross, but we both knew he was there.

"I can't remember who fired first, but it doesn't matter. It doesn't change what happened."

John cleared his throat, a sound most of us make when overcome with emotion but in his case it sounded like a mechanical necessity. I imagined him gargling lubricant to allow his strong smooth speech and I hated myself for it.

"We've got laser-guided sensors that can identify vehicles by their heat signatures. We've got satellite pictures. We've got fucking night vision, for Christ's sake. But it makes no difference if your men are tired. And we were tired. Hundreds of hours of combat experience and simulations, but no amount of training can counter sleep deprivation. Took a while for them to learn from it, too, because twelve years later you've got Operation Iraqi fucking Freedom and tanks are veering off course and — "

By this point I was finally able to go to him.

"Now I don't even *want* to sleep," he said.

I put my arm around his shoulders and tried not to think about how hard they felt. The strength I had admired in him earlier had become something…else, and I'm loath to describe my feelings to you because of how I would seem. I did my best, let me leave it at that, and he must've taken some comfort from it because he settled against me. I put a hand to his hair to stroke it, remembered it was not his, and stopped.

He said something I didn't hear.

"Pardon?"

"It was hell. Fire. Metal. Shells exploding. I was burning in hell, just as I knew I would. You know, our suits can withstand temperatures of two thousand degrees. Two *thousand*."

"You're alive," was all I could think to say. "And you're a good man."

At this he nudged me aside.

"A man?" He laughed a hard sound. "A man? Look at me; I left most of myself over there. I'm not a man. I'm barely anything." And then he looked at me, an up and down that remembered how I looked beneath my clothes, how I felt, and he said again, "I'm not a man."

At first I thought he simply meant by comparison, a comment of self-pity, but the way he reddened afterwards told me he regretted the words and I realised he'd meant something else. He was not a man, not a real one, not because of what had happened to him years ago on the battlefield but because of what had happened only recently. His embarrassment, or his anger — whatever it was that made his skin flush — highlighted the parts of him that were still human. There wasn't much.

"Goodnight, John."

He at least had the decency to call out, to try to stop me from leaving. But he called the wrong name. He called the man he'd have preferred beside him.

He called the man I'd liked to have been.

❉

I HAVE NOT seen General John Smith since that evening, though I keep up with his progress in the papers and the gossip keeps me informed as to his private life. At least, it speculates. I doubt anybody knows much about him really. Brave man, I hear. Terrible business. Some of that I can agree with.

I may not have seen him since then, but I hear him almost every night. I dream of a desert I have never been to, thunder-blasted beneath an ashen sky and a cool horned moon, and I see machines destroyed by what they carry. Metal corpses litter the sands, empty shells that smoulder with a fading heat, and it's John's voice I hear calling from them, screaming out his pain between echoes of artillery as I squeeze my fists around handfuls of sand. Sometimes he gives it a name, this pain. It's not mine. Even so, I run to find him and the sand falls away quicker than in any hourglass. Time runs out, and all the cannons erupt my way, belching flame, raging with fires that roast those caught inside, and I'm hit with thousands upon thousands of letters. A barrage of folded envelopes bearing the same name in his neat cursive script. And I'm buried beneath them feeling a deep pain of my own.

Sometimes, when I wake, it's like the nightmare has just begun and all I had worth keeping, all that was real, I left behind in my dream. These are the days when my hands seem filled with sand, slipping through my fingers however I try to hold it. These are the days when I cannot pull myself togeth-

80

er, dwelling instead on all that was said and unsaid. Dreams within dreams. Things that were, and things that could have been. I think of John, a haunted man in pieces, and I think of the range of friendly fire.

Even awake, I hear his voice, calling from a broken machine.

GWENDOLYN

Máiréad Casey

LONG and baleful are nights when I struggle in vain to suppress the memories of my misfortunate Gwendolyn. I stalk the rooms and dim corridors of this vast estate like a spectre, only taking respite in another perfunctory taste of some infirm relative's spirits or dose of ether. However, try as I may, nothing can deliver me from the resilient and haunting thoughts of my time as governess in the provincial abode of Mr Hastings and his tragic, bewitching adolescent, Gwendolyn.

Etched in my mind are the winding road and bare trees rising like bones from the unforgiving earth on which the house resided. Obstinate and commanding it stood against the backdrop of overcast skies and the tumultuous undulations of the sea; like the canny castles of old, Hastings House was built by a cliffside with the waves writhing like snakes below. I recall the morn I set foot inside Hastings' atrium door as the single most disappointing of my nascent womanhood. The devilishly handsome and well-spoken widow I had been assured to expect in Mr Hastings was revealed to be a rather cantankerous, ill-tempered man who appeared antiquated and decrepit far beyond his maturity. Indeed I still shiver at the remembrance of the film of flaked, translucent skin that clung to his colourless lips, bringing to mind the tactile repulsion of death, like the discarded shredding of a snake or the dehydration of the grave.

Of course, neighbours and relatives that were acquainted with me before and since my migration to the Hastings estate would accuse me of a similar degradation of mind and body. But I can declare with confidence that I surely could not compare to the madness and physiological decay that characterised Mr Edmund Hastings.

At first I was struck by how he spoke of his beloved only child, Gwendolyn; how he did adore, idolise and deify that endearing urchin, swearing upon all he held sacred that she was the image of her departed mother. Although when I was introduced to the girl myself I admit I could not see any resemblance between this singular being and the multitude of portraits of the late Mrs Hastings that lined the walls like the spectators to a stage. I can say however that I fully understood how a man such as Edmund Hastings could regard the young woman with such awe, such conviction of purity and goodness. Certainly there was something preternatural to Gwendolyn's divine beauty that made me blush with a sense of unworthiness. My fingers longed to touch the soft silken dark hair that shone so brilliantly against her awful white flesh and for a poor substitute I caressed one of the woolen curls pulled tight above my ear, only frustrating the knowledge of my own physical inferiority.

Truly it was a hateful, unattainable desirability of Gwendolyn's, so alien yet so enrapturing. It was often commented upon that I was a solitary and pondersome child. I was noted to muse upon the reflective elegance of my toy marbles instead of simply playing the game as other children would. Gwendolyn's inky, ultramarine eyes fixated me in the same manner; they bespoke a similar opaqueness, an impenetrability. These iridescent orbs of hers were set far apart, granting her countenance a strange, becoming felinity. Her skin was of the purest porcelain hue, making her small mouth of such luscious natural pigmentation appear as a perfect rosebud dropped in snow.

Among the endless hours we would spend in her father's cold, dilapidated study, so pungent with the smell of stale ink and rotting words, I could not resist marvelling at the girl's divine attraction. Her face and narrow frame were so enchanting, she appeared a beacon of warmth and light in the desolate landscape I had been reluctant to call my new home.

So fixedly would I gaze upon her that on nights when sleep evaded me I would rise from my bed and stare at the faint reflection in my chamber windowpane only to see Gwendolyn's own features for a brief moment imposed over my own. The maddening brilliance of her dark eyes and the smoothness of her décolletage would steady my frenetic nerves and soothe my beating heart through every gale and tempest in a way that I can now only enjoy through chemical pleasures. Later I would be accused of possessing a deep-seated — even perverse jealousy towards the lovely Gwendolyn. But I ask you, dear reader, how could a being hold any resentment or envy towards a beauty that they themselves took pleasure in? I loved the dear, frail creature from the first moment of our meeting to our fateful last utterance and beyond...

As this was my first employment as a governess, only a few years separated myself and Gwendolyn in age, and indeed the two of us became fast friends as much as tutor and pupil. Unlike the peers of my forlorn childhood and tortuous adolescence, Gwendolyn never retreated from my eccentric musings or wild fascinations but returned my affections with an ardour and an earnestness that to this day I cite as the greatest affirmation of my character. Yet there was a queerness to her, an opaqueness that betrayed little at all as to what machinations dwelt beneath that pleasing veneer. I felt almost if one were to rap their knuckles on the white, poreless flesh of her collarbone they would hear the hollow din of a porcelain doll, utterly empty inside.

I am perhaps being unkind, withholding in the same oxymoronic manner of her dearly devoted father. He would interrupt our lessons more than a dozen times by noon to check on his cherished progeny and ask how she enjoyed her study. By evening he would grow belligerent to the dear child, not speaking a word nor even venturing a glance lest from the corner of his eye. Not that one would desire to share his company on these occasions when he would pace the halls and mutter under his breath words which were indecipherable in content but crystal clear in tone, brimming with gall.

At these times I would take the servants' stairs to reach my bedchamber in order to avoid the sway of his temper. I maintain he resented my presence in the manor and in particular the ardent friendship I had established with Gwendolyn. In truth his possessive jealousy of our intimacy only served to unite us as confidantes. Although I was never privy to how Gwendolyn herself regarded her dominant father's humours, I sensed in my bones that she was pleased to have another young lady in the house to bear witness to

Hastings' oppressive temper. I knew it in moments we were sure to be quite unperturbed under the shade of a nearby grove with my head on her heart and my hand on her tender breast.

But the trees were not the only witnesses to our amour. Oftentimes we would stroll upward to the cliffs to observe the awesome power of the waves in winter and the jagged rocks that remained constant as headstones. We returned to the site with increasing regularity as Hastings grew ever more dependent on Gwendolyn's gentle manner yet continued to be wicked company. Gwendolyn would sit precariously at the edge of the cliff, peering over the precipice with an absorption that chilled me. I declare in those moments she was not the precious doll I knew but an impostor. Her eyes fervent and a grin spread across her face unlike any I had known her show before. One who did not know her would be tempted to mistake her for a woman ten years older and quite taken leave of her senses. I was hesitant to approach her in this trance for fear I should startle the poor girl and unwittingly send her to her doom. Yet in this trance she would remain, arms bolted forthright, fingers gripping the limestone, palms bleeding and back arched like a reanimated maidenhead, voluntarily devoted to the sea.

During one of these episodes, she became uncharacteristically candid, confessing that not once had she approached a precipice without fighting the overwhelming urge to take a running leap and fling herself into the oblivion that waited for her below. She went on to suggest that a similar thrill tempted her imagination to reach out and attack another in a sudden moment of mad, unfettered violence.

To hear these words from one so petite and ostensibly pure made me hate the poor wretch in a way that I still cannot articulate. I think it was the bleak loneliness it awakened in me, realising that this beautiful creature was so vastly, unspeakably unknowable. Whilst I was so rapt in thoughts of my lady's shortcomings, I could see her waiting anxiously on my reply. Taking this as a sign of her returning lucidity, I gently walked toward her and rested my hands on her delicate shoulders. With my head on her neck and my mouth at her ear I told her that these thoughts were taboo, and unbecoming of a cherishable vessel such as herself. Misunderstanding my chiding words entirely, Gwendolyn turned to meet my lips with her own tantalizing orifice, so warm and wanting. I must confess I yielded to the nymphet's advances but that union proved to be the kiss of death for my beloved.

86

In tasting her, in finally experiencing the girl's material body, she was no more an abstract ideal but a person, one who desired as much of me as I of her and sadly, no longer interesting. The silly thing looked so hurt, so confused as she made move to coax her way back into my favour. However, when an idol ceases to be unattainable and transcendent, it can only be mortal, fleeting and trivial. Such are my standards. And so when she tried to brush my pale cheek with her gentle fingertips I slapped them aside as though they carried the pathogens of the plague.

It was not for me to know that she would lose her balance.

I looked on numbly as the object of my affections tumbled frivolous as a rag doll, white legs swinging above her torso in her descent to meet the sea. Sometimes I believe she did it to reclaim my affection. In death my paramour was recreated as the perfect mermaid; legs shattered on the rock, dark hair sailing on the water, eyes open and fathomless as the sea. I became like the god Narcissus when he discovered himself, only able to experience love truly when it is elusive, intangible.

From what felt like a world away I heard a cry. Hastings had spied the ordeal from the corner window. His face contorted into an uncanny grimace; with a fierce, purposeful wrath he continued to stare. I had but a brief window of opportunity to make my escape from his obvious blame and untold rage and proceeded to race downhill until I reached a road and oncoming carriage. Later, of course, when Mr Hastings was in a clearer but more conniving form, he would claim that my flight only further evidenced my culpability in Gwendolyn's fall. Mercifully, the ravings of a mad fool could not incriminate me in that humiliating trial. Despite the disparity in our social stations I was still after all a young woman, boasting a solid background and an unsullied reputation. Afterwards that reputation had changed considerably. Not a soul would commit to proclaiming that it was indeed I who had prompted the cherub to her death but I was never again to gain employment as a governess.

If I escaped the hangman's noose or the prisoner's cell, I did not evade retribution. It is apt perhaps that for all my fatal loathing of mortality and decay, my prime occupation hence has been caring for far-flung elderly relatives in the depths of their degradation and senility. At times I feel myself joining them in their fancies, wholly submitting my consciousness to the tide of memories ridden with both sweetness and horror. I believe I can hear Gwendolyn's musical laughter echoing anon, beckoning me to where I fear to tread. I feel her in every bitter gust of wind that threatens to catch my step; I see her treacherous reflection in every still pool of water. The look in her dark eyes is hateful, but the day is not so far away I fear, that when my vengeful siren calls I will follow.

TELLTALE

Clare London

T HEY say that I am mad.

The doctors grimace and shake their heads, yet few come near enough for me to discuss my situation. The spy window into my room is so small, I wonder how they can make any assessment of my mental state.

Sometimes the shutter slides back and an eye peers in at me as if I were a rare specimen, an exhibit. I'm not expected to look back at them, and I rarely choose to, because all I see is their disgust. Not because of what I have done, but because of what they know I am.

I'm distressed that they are so deaf to reasoned explanations. I will talk about it with anyone — what I think, what I feel, what hurts me. What I did. But I will not excuse what I am.

"Lunatic," the officers mutter through the spy hole, then laugh. Their boots clatter heavily on the floor, the sound mocking the difference between my incarceration and their freedom to move around at will. *Lunatic.* Is that not better than awareness of this cheerless room, the hostility and revulsion? This *pain*? I try not to cry, for that gives substance to their prejudice, but so often, my frustration makes me angry.

Yet I never thought I was a violent man.

I never thought I could kill.

✢✢

ALLOW ME THIS indulgence. I must not tell my story from the ending, but from its inauspicious start.

My parents did not want me. Understand this, I am not offering it as any kind of defence for my behaviour — not now, not then. I did not love them particularly well, and I was like grit in the tender oyster bed of their complacent life. Father had devoted his life as rector to the local church, and my parents were both law-abiding and God-fearing, a combination that made my adolescence a heady brew of emotional confusion and physical pain.

I was sent down from school more than once, and not only for poor studying. My passions were making themselves known to me, without allowing me time to learn either discretion or discrimination. I was startled by my response to men: an awareness of them far in excess of mere sexuality. I could smell their skin, hear the vibration of a breath in their throat, taste their sweat upon the air. This excited rather than disturbed me, for I assumed everyone was attuned in the same way. Eventually, however, I noticed my classmates avoiding me, and the staff uneasy in my company. I was punished more often than my peers, for far less transgression. But my reactions were not anything I could control. I was continually alert to others, my nerves alight with the ripple of their emotions, my own body aching with need for them.

It was not long before I acted upon that need; I was found with a young master in his rooms, and another time with the gardener's son. Both times I discovered the youth beneath the uniform much the same — though, the first time, my explorations were painful and the excited shock was like stepping from a cliff edge. The second education was much easier, and more enjoyable.

The school finally reported me to my parents, and I discovered for the first time just how repulsive my interest was to others. I credit my naïvety to being very young. At home, Father tried to beat something out of me that he did not even dare acknowledge, only knowing that I was different from my brothers in a discomfiting and irreligious way. Nursing bruises, I never imagined how I might break free of such rule.

Then Father sold me.

Oh, such a melodramatic telling, I know! I was not a horse or a sack of grain to be sold, but the result was similar. I was indentured into employment with one of Father's rich parishioners, one who had contributed funds to the church and who held a position of responsibility in the district. He had need of a secretary, and as the only skills I had at that time were reading aloud and penmanship, Father persuaded him I would be useful. Mr. Simeon Allan appeared the embodiment of success and stability, with his own law practice, an independent fortune, and a well-appointed house in a respectable district of the city.

On the appropriate day, Mr. Allan's carriage arrived to collect me and my case. But I had never imagined he would come in person. When he was announced at the rectory door, there was instant panic. Father sent the cook's help to fetch me, the young girl red-faced and rushed, insisting that I come to the parlour immediately. I barely had time to comb my hair and don my jacket.

As I entered the room, Mr. Allan turned from the window to face me. I felt breathless, and not from running down the stairs. He was not as tall as Father but was more imposing. His hair was shot with silver: his eyes were dark and heavy-lidded. He looked older than I had imagined. I was taken by the rich tone of his voice as he interviewed me.

"You are sober and respectful, Mr. Spencer? Hard-working? Eager to learn new skills?"

"I am, Mr. Allan." I nodded, emphasising the commitment I knew Father expected of me. Mr. Allan never took his eyes from me in all the time I stood there in front of him. By the time his questions were finished and he turned away, he'd perused every part of me, from my lips as I gave my answers, to my hand where I clutched the cloth of my shirt, and finally to my feet where I shuffled awkwardly on the worn carpet. My body was responsive towards him as it had often been with other men, but this time was different: this time, I imagined that Simeon Allan seemed equally aware of me. A shiver of pleasure ran through me, as if tasting freedom at last. My heartbeat tripped quickly in my breast as I realised how excited I was by his attention.

"He will do," Mr. Allan said to Father. "Please have his bags put in the carriage. I will brief him on the duties of his job during the journey."

⋇

I WAS, UNFORTUNATELY, an appalling secretary. My concentration was inadequate when Mr. Allan ran through his appointments with me, and my memory fitful. My handwriting was shaky from lack of formal use, and I had no idea how to organise official papers. I wondered how long it would be before he tired of paying for me. He had given me a generous allowance and introduced me to his tailor and shoemaker, though I could not afford anything beyond clothing appropriate for work, and only one item of each. I had some free time, but it was so rare that I did not return home for visits. My parents seemed to prefer to cut all ties with me. That was acceptable to me, too, but it meant my entertainment was non-existent, an irksome situation for a young man barely into adulthood.

Yet I enjoyed living in Mr. Allan's house. I had the smallest single room on the guest corridor, but it was stylishly furnished and I had use of the household staff for my meals and housekeeping. There were other benefits, too. Occasionally I pocketed a stray banknote from his bureau that had not been addressed to any particular invoice, considering it part of my remuneration. And he employed several good-looking young men, particularly his valet. I'd been warned against spending too much time with the rest of the staff, but the valet was often in the hallway when I took papers between Mr. Allan's office and my own small room, where I had been given a desk and chair to work on my own initiative.

I liked to watch the valet, and I especially liked it when he watched me in return. When we smiled at each other, my heart would beat faster with the anticipation of some personal fun. I knew the meaning behind that kind of smile, and I'm sure he did too. I started to invite him into my room, ostensibly to collect my afternoon tray of tea or to remove scrap paper for use on the fires, but really so that we could touch each other and murmur promises of after-hours assignations. It seemed a trivial enough game to me.

One hushed night in the middle of the week, I crept out of my bedroom after dark. Mr. Allan was staying away overnight on business, and I had an appointment of a different kind with his valet. He didn't want to come to my room — the risk of the other servants spying on him was apparently too great — but I was sure my office would provide the warm, private niche that was needed for a young man to play with another one's prick. I was eager to try it for size — both the room and the young man's member.

The corridor ahead of me was shadowed, but the heavy footsteps approaching me were familiar. My heartbeat stuttered and then sped up. I drew quickly to the side, but I knew it was too late to hide from sight. Mr. Allan was not expected back tonight! Yet, to my horror, it was he who paused in front of me. My mouth went dry and a bead of sweat sprang up on my forehead.

"Mr. Spencer? Are you looking for me?"

"I.… No, Mr. Allan."

His gaze flickered quickly over me, the intelligent eyes half-hidden in the dim light. "It's late, but you are still dressed. When I decided to return to-night rather than tomorrow, I hoped not to disturb anyone."

"You didn't." I spoke too quickly, and his eyes narrowed. "I'm…meeting someone." There was a long silence. I could hear his breath — steady, deep. Whereas I was holding mine as tightly as I could, and trying to stop my hand from shaking. Even so, the flame from my candle stuttered in front of my face.

"Your behaviour is not acceptable," he said, slowly but firmly.

"Mr. Allan?"

"I do not wish you to consort with the staff." He took a step nearer, so that he was only a foot's length away, and his hot breath brushed my forehead. I leaned involuntarily towards him: I was suddenly, vividly aware of his body, as if the muscles of his limbs moved in tandem with mine, as if his pulse coursed through my own veins. "Why do you think I insisted on that when you came here? Despite your looks and manner, you are no telegraph boy, Mr. Spencer, nor will you become one here. I will not allow plying or picking up sexual trade in this house."

I gasped.

He laughed softly, not at all embarrassed. "You've never heard a man refer to these things aloud? Are you distressed by my bluntness?"

The throbbing pulse between us had eased, and now warmth flooded me, even though I stood in the same, cool corridor without any coat. "No, Mr. Allan."

He stepped even closer. His skin was lined around the eyes, but his throat was strong and sinewy. The hair over his ears was shot with more silver than on the rest of his head. "What is your name, Mr. Spencer? Your given name?"

I flushed, both at the intimacy but also in pique that he had never known it. "Nicholas."

Long, thick fingers brushed against my shirt sleeve. "Are you afraid of me?"

Nowadays, they say that I am mad. When I think back to that moment in the corridor, I think that Mr. Simeon Allan may have made me so. My whole body came alive, as if it were inhabited by far more than one, simple youth. My head swam, yet my vision grew brighter. It was as if I had been lit from within, but with heat as well as light. I didn't know if I shook from fear, tension or delight, but my voice would not work, and I knew I couldn't reply. With shock, I imagined dismissal, shame, disgust. Mr. Allan's respect seemed suddenly very precious: the potential loss of his daily company, of monumental regret. I heard the word "trade" echoing in my ears, with the sharp edge of his tongue giving it extra, harsh vibration.

"You are shaking. Did you hear me, Nicholas?" My name seemed soft on his tongue.

"Yes," I whispered. "Yes," I whispered again, in reply to his previous question.

"Go to my office." His voice maintained its firm tone, though I imagined I heard a tremor of emotion behind it. "Go *now*."

⁜

HE LIT ANOTHER candle on his desk, sat in his leather-upholstered chair and gestured for me to sit on the other, far less comfortable chair. His face was stern. During the working day he often turned this look on me, but the eyes were always lightened by the reflection of daylight, or interest in his correspondence, or even amused irritation at my inability to keep up with his business. But now his eyes were dark, the expression hard and cold. At least, they made *me* shiver.

I stared at him across the desk top, feeling as if I were a recalcitrant servant awaiting punishment, or at another interview for a position that I knew was far above me. It was strange to be sitting here in the night, rather than the working day, and the candle flame cast shadows over the dark room. Only part of his face was illuminated at a time, making it difficult for me to gauge his mood.

"Nicholas." It was not said questioningly, though I lifted my face to look him in the eyes. "How long have you been in my employ?"

I blinked hard. "Three months, Mr. Allan."

He nodded. "Three months."

Another non-question. I was at a loss what to do or say. The room smelled of parchment, leather and the smoke of his cigars. Everything around me was to do with him. There was residual comfort from the hearth behind his desk, where the evening fire had reduced to warm ash, but my body was still shaking. I felt oddly claustrophobic.

"Nicholas, do you wish to leave?"

I swallowed hard, staring at him like an imbecile. "Leave?"

He steepled his hands under his chin, and the signet ring on his finger glinted against the unshaven skin of his jaw. "You steal my money. You disobey my orders. You encourage corruption of my servants."

"I—"

"I will tell you when, or if, you may speak. Your behaviour leads me to believe that you are unsuited to be here. That you should, in fact, be sent back to your home."

"No!" It was just one word, and not one I intended to speak aloud, but it burst from me with shock. Ashamed, I hung my head.

"Do not look away, Nicholas." He continued to use my given name with an easy familiarity. Was I to be offended or flattered? "Look at me."

I looked up again, my eyes now full of stinging tears. "I do not wish to leave the house. To leave you."

The silence was long and pregnant. I considered how it would be to leave the luxury and comfort I'd grown accustomed to and return to the frugal, stultifying life of my unsympathetic parents. Not only would I be judged a failure, I'd return to scorn and beatings. I couldn't help the shudder that ran through me.

Mr. Allan sucked in a breath. Had he seen my reaction? "I don't want you to leave, either, boy. I have grown used to your company. You are a damned useless secretary, but I enjoy your wit and youth." He watched as one of my tears spilled free and ran a ragged path down my cheek. "I admire your sensitivity. I…am excited by it."

The tension between us had subtly changed. "My sensitivity?"

His smile was grudging. "You are attuned to the human condition. You feel the emotion between us, don't you? It is a rare gift."

"I have no gifts," I protested.

Mr. Allan was still smiling. "With my help, you can learn to develop it…if you wish to."

"I do!" The words burst from me again. I didn't understand why his brooding watch of me inspired this passion, but it was true. I did wish to learn! "Let me stay. Please."

He stood, left his chair and came to stand beside me. He brushed his hand over my head, his palm grazing my temple. "You like men, Nicholas. You want men."

I didn't know whether I should reply to that so I kept silent.

"But in truth, you need just one," he murmured.

"You, Mr. Allan?" I knew I had been too insolent when his hand tightened painfully in my hair.

"You are very foolish and very careless. But you are the prettiest molly I have ever seen. I knew as soon as I saw you that you belonged here. But if you wish to stay, you must be more respectful. More obedient."

I gazed up at him. "I will, Mr. Allan. I will…sir."

"You do not need to call me that, boy."

He had never asked me to show the subservience of his domestic staff: we had always been Mr. to each other. Yet I knew what was meant by the drop of sweat upon his upper lip, and I had seen his knuckles whiten when I called him *sir*. "Please, sir," I whispered, "but I wish to." And, slowly, I slid off my chair and sank to my knees on the rug before him.

His breath caught, and I did not mistake his soft sigh of satisfaction. I had judged him well. That night changed my life and Simeon Allan's, also. He laid his hand on my shoulder, and instructed me on ways to bring him pleasure, with firm words and guiding gestures. I had never known a man like him, not assertive in this way. I knelt there until my jaw ached and my legs started to cramp. I felt the growing tension in him until he reached completion, and then I wriggled, thinking he would release me. Instead, his hand gripped my head in place.

"No, Nicholas." His voice was hoarse and breathless, but still strong. "I say when and how you can move."

"Sir."

He was still thick between my lips, nudging the back of my throat so that I feared I would gag. But he withdrew in his own time, and so I waited for that. "Do you like it, Nicholas? Do you like this?"

I took a chance and acted instinctively. Deliberately, I drew both my arms behind me, and clasped my hands at the small of my back.

"*Oh yes. My boy.*" It was only a whisper. Awed; thrilled. He stroked my throat as if in caress, but to my horror, I felt it tighten. I couldn't seem to draw a deep enough breath. I began to wheeze with panic.

"Nicholas?" Mr. Allan's hand gripped my chin, turning my face to look at him. "Nicholas, breathe deeply. Listen to me. You're safe. Do you hear me?"

His features swam dizzily in front of my face. His other hand rested at the back of my neck, not in capture now, but in comfort. Gradually, my heartbeat slowed and my breath steadied.

"Nicholas, listen to my voice. You're calm now. You are very empathetic."
His concern was mixed with excitement, I could hear it. More than that, I
could *sense* it. "You wish to please me? You want more?"

My head was still full of confusion and thrill, my ballocks so tight with need
that they felt like lead between my legs, but I managed to nod. He helped
me to my feet and then reached for me with an eager grip that shocked me.
For a second my head swam as before. My breath shortened and my pulse
thudded hard: for a brilliant, white-hot moment we were joined as one body,
one heart. He was clumsy, caught up in his own jerked movements, but it
was enough. I'd never been witness to such intense pleasure. I knew this was
only the first time.

⧺

AS HE HAD promised, Simeon Allan helped me to develop myself in many
ways. By day, he helped me improve my penmanship and showed me the ru-
diments of bookkeeping. At night, he'd call me to his room and would play
with me, sometimes for hours. He would allow me to undress him, to peel
each layer of the working day away from him. And then he would teach me
far more than how to avoid ink-blots or to balance a ledger. I was Nicholas
to him – his boy – and in those private times, he became Simeon to me. I
would drop to my knees, even before his command, my hands crossed behind my back and my forehead dipped to the floor, displaying my arse for
him. Embarrassment or protest was never an option. He controlled me with
far more than his hands when I showed challenge or delay in obeying. His
angry gaze could frighten me, and I learned the tone of his voice as a measure of whether I was in favour or not.

Yet in the kinder moments, he gave me gifts and shared other intimate
things with me. One night, he opened the lowest drawer of his desk, removing the set of razors that had been his father's, and were now his. "Shave me,
Nicholas. Make it a close touch."

I had never shaved another man before. Simeon's skin was warm, the bris-
tles rough, even from a single day's growth. The blade was horribly sharp,
but I kept my hand as steady as I could. As I slid it over his cheek, he grit his
teeth, and I felt the stimulation that rippled through his body. I could smell
his arousal over the lemon fragrance of the shaving soap, and taste his growing enthusiasm as a flavour on my tongue.

After I towelled him dry, he took hold of my hand. There were smudges of
soap on my palm and he wiped them away with his handkerchief. It smelled

of his skin; of clean linen; the scent of citrus. I closed my eyes briefly, the sensations overwhelming me.

"Tell me how it is for you, Nicholas. Tell me what your senses tell you." His voice was hoarse, his words more urgent.

And so I told him what excited him so much, but was merely the truth. "I hear your need, sir. I feel your desire." I lifted my head as if sniffing the air. "I sense your power, sir. I know that you want me."

Over time, my perception of him heightened. Not only did I smell the lingering tobacco on his clothes, or the sweat of his body that grew familiar to me. These things were the easy clues found in any true crime penny dreadful. No, I did genuinely *feel* Simeon. His breath — even from the other side of the room — would be on my cheek. His heartbeat would be in my ears, separate from my own, dipping and soaring as I responded to him.

"You're very special, Nicholas."

It was easy to play his game but I came to like it, too. In the night, I would do anything — not just for the gifts, though they were very welcome, but for the sensual pleasure he gave me. I had no idea if he realised his effect on me: I couldn't believe he cared for anything but his own craving. I knew that's how I would be, in his place.

"You're beautiful when you obey."

He was always the master, I was not to forget it. He spoke to me as if I were one of his possessions, a prize. Love was never mentioned. I was just an employee, of course, a minion. And men of his position didn't love other men, let alone admit it. I gave him what he needed, spent my *gift* on enhancing his pleasure. This was the bargain, though sometimes I wondered whether he saw it the same way as I did.

And the other times? When he wished to punish me?

The pain was an integral part of it all.

⁙

SIMEON WAS WORKING at his bureau in his shirtsleeves, his back to me when he told me his nephew would be visiting for a while. I could see the way that his shoulders tensed when he mentioned Benedict.

"It's a comfort for you to have a successor for the business."

Simeon gave a short, mirthless laugh. "The boy is arrogant and halfway stupid. I would fear to leave even the simplest matters in his hands. Until he's learned more lessons, I will continue to hold control of both purse and client ledger."

I excused myself from the room to fetch more ink, but Simeon's call stopped me at the door.

"Put it back, Nicholas."

"Mr. Allan?" Yet I knew what he meant. In my pocket, I had one of Simeon's many rings that had been left out during the previous night's entertainment. I thought I'd been both clever and stealthy to finger it for myself. Either I'd underestimated Simeon's powers of perception, or I'd been clumsy.

He turned to stare at me, a strange mix of anger and sadness in his eyes. "Are the tokens I give you not enough, Nicholas? I won't leave you without proper payment for your work, whatever happens. I cannot name you in my legacies, of course, but your life here is unquestionably more comfortable than it would be otherwise."

I don't know whether I was shocked at his use of the word "work," or resentful at the cruel reminder that I would only ever be his servant — and of so many, secret duties. I placed the ring back on a table, bobbed my head in sullen obeisance, and left the room.

Benedict arrived late afternoon with a flurry of chaos, his cases hauled into the hallway from his coach, his voice loud with imperious orders to his uncle's staff. Simeon was away at his office, but Benedict demanded immediate attention, regardless. He was barely older than I was, but of much finer appearance. A tall young man, wavy hair, expressive hands. His clothes were far richer than Simeon's, even though I'd believed him to be a poor relative. Maybe it was the way he wore them, as if on show to an audience. His hat was placed at a jaunty angle, and his coat was fitted to his shape, unlike Simeon's which hung from his shoulders like a cape.

"You are…?"

"Nicholas Spencer." I held out my hand. "I am your uncle's secretary. May I welcome you to your uncle's house?"

Benedict took my hand, briefly. His silent gaze ran over me from top to toe, and it was more eloquent than any reference I'd ever received. I saw his eyelids grow heavy and a flush of pink appear on his cheeks. This familiar reaction was well-known to me by now. It had taken less than a year of my pubescent youth to realise how many men found pleasure in my looks, even sometimes against their will. Yet Benedict was a very different matter from Simeon's theatre cronies who would run a hand over my arse when they thought he wasn't watching, or even cup my prick through the lap of my trousers. They offered nothing but a leer, rolls of sweaty, obese flesh, and clammy hands. I knew how it'd be with them and had no desire to share myself, not even for their veiled promises of gifts. Simeon had taught me to appreciate many things, including all carnal pleasures.

But Benedict? Could I say he was as different from them as the sun from the sodden soil beneath? It was startlingly true. He was handsome, his stature lean and his hips narrow. His skin was pale, his lips full. This close to him, I could smell the cologne on his skin, feel the soft brush of clean hairs on his hand.

"Nicholas Spencer," he repeated, as if dazed. "A pleasure to meet you."

"May I fetch you some tea?"

"If you'll share a cup with me. I wish to know how well my uncle is administering my inheritance, and I'm sure you can help me." He had dark eyes that matched Simeon's, but Benedict's held youth. We moved into the drawing room and I rang through to the kitchen for some tea and cake.

"And so, Mr. Spencer, will you help me persuade my uncle to consider my plans?"

"Your plans, Mr. Allan?"

He smiled, and the sparkle was directed solely at me. "To reach a much wider range of clients, not just his own peers. To offer financial advice — accounting services. I have *many* such ideas. We must speculate, we must take risks for the prize!" His enthusiasm was enchanting, though he didn't elucidate further. Maybe it was because I was only the secretary. "And you must call me Benedict."

Not "may" but "must." In that moment I tuned into the beat of his heart, a steady pace though slightly quicker than my own. His blood felt pure and hot, and my prick began to swell with excitement. I had not responded in this way to any man since I'd been in the house with Simeon.

We ate together that evening, as Simeon had not returned, and Benedict said he didn't want to eat alone. I could tell the kitchen staff thought I was acting above my station, even though I was often invited to eat with their master. Benedict told me more of his plans for the business — and for his own personal future, successful and brilliant as it would be. I was discreet with my questions, but even so, it didn't seem he had the discretion or evenhanded approach necessary for the law. I was sure he was just unpractised — Simeon would be teaching him his trade to be worthy of his role as heir.

When I said I must retire for the night to finish some of Mr. Simeon Allan's papers, Benedict pushed back his chair and walked with me to the hallway. We paused there: no one was around.

"Nicholas?" He put his hand lightly on my shoulder. His use of my name seemed the most natural thing. "You appear distracted tonight. Perhaps my company is tedious."

"No, of course not."

"Does my uncle work you too hard?"

I started. I'd been daydreaming of Simeon, of his rough hands on me the previous night, of the way he had pushed me to the floor of his room. The taste of him still in my mouth, the pain of his nails digging into my flesh. My excitement mingled with harsh discomfort: the humiliating surrender to him. His groan of satisfaction in my ear as he thrust into me one last time. My own gasp and the rush of wet pleasure beneath me.

Benedict moved his hand to rest on my neck. "You're handsome when you flush like that." He sounded surprised.

I had turned my head to protest when we kissed. It was more of a clumsy, accidental brush than a deliberate caress, but I didn't complain. I lifted up on my toes to bridge the inches in our differing heights and leaned in against him. His breath was cool, his lips much softer than Simeon's.

"Oh God," he whispered. His breath hitched and his body shuddered as if he'd been plunged into cold water: the shock shuddered through me, also. I drew away, terrified of discovery but thrilled beyond belief.

Benedict's cheeks were now as flushed as mine, and he fisted his hands by his sides, as if fighting the desire to touch me. "I…I don't know what came over me," he said. I was silent, knowing very well what had. I smiled gently at him in reassurance, but he moved a few, shaky steps back. "I must finish unpacking my luggage." Even before I nodded, he had turned for the stairs.

I stood in the hallway for a few more moments, my mind in a whirl. For once, my responses were mine alone to savour, and I revelled in them. I had felt Benedict's warmth; he had not pushed me away in horror. My mouth was dry and my skin prickled. I could hardly bear to wait to see him again.

This was how love felt.

⊹⊹

BUT BENEDICT'S VISIT didn't go well. From the first day, he and Simeon argued whenever they were together. It did not make for an easy household. I tried to leave the room whenever I saw one or other of them bent on confrontation, but I was often caught up as an unwilling spectator — even if any view of Benedict was a joy to me. We'd never been alone again, or in a position to kiss, but my desire was undimmed. I didn't worry that Simeon would notice my fascination, for during our time together, his attention was purely selfish. Of course: I was merely the boy.

But cruelly, any chance of time with Benedict was soon to be snatched away.

"My allowance is so small, you embarrass me!" Benedict snapped at Simeon. Today, I had closed the office door when they started to argue, so that the servants in the hall wouldn't hear the details, but that had trapped me in the room with them. "I cannot promote the business on a pittance."

"If you spent less time *promoting* at your clubs, you would live well within the allowance. I do not support idleness and gambling." Simeon's voice was steady but I knew well the edge of anger beneath the words.

"You do not support me in any way at all!" Benedict's tone had shifted to a whine. "I am working for our benefit, trying to make you see that your methods are old-fashioned and suffocating the growth of the firm. Why won't you listen to my ideas for change?"

Simeon stepped towards his nephew, but it was I who cowered back against the door frame. "Because your ideas are ill-considered, and the risks too dangerous. You seek quantity over quality, and your greed blinds you, encouraging those who can never afford us — who will never pay. Our watchword is integrity and quality, not free advice on how to waste money. You do not offer true value."

Benedict flushed hotly. "And is that how you see me as a man?"

Simeon merely glared back at him.

I glanced at Benedict's aggrieved, stricken expression. I ached to help him. I wanted to cry, Do not be defensive! Even in Simeon's dominant moments, he wants to know there is challenge, not just cowardice.

But Benedict turned on his heel. "I will leave as soon as convenient, and return to my rooms in the city," he said. "You won't have to see me again except on the firm's business." He brushed roughly past me as he left the room.

I knew I shouldn't, but I went to Benedict's room as soon as I could leave my work. It was two hours after the confrontation with Simeon. I knocked gently and he opened the door. He had removed his jacket and cravat, and my eyes were drawn to the V-shape of pale skin at his throat. "You're leaving?"

He blinked at my rather abrupt greeting. "At the end of the week. I cannot stay here without Simeon's support."

"There are ways..." I cleared my throat before continuing. "Maybe there are ways you can temper your ambitions to meet with his."

"Never," he snapped, and began to turn away.

"Benedict, please.... I can ask to be released from my contract. I can come with you."

He twisted back around, as startled as if seeing me for the first time. "Why on earth would you do that? I can't afford any staff beyond a shared house-keeper, let alone a secretary. And your life is good here, isn't it? You have a lot to be thankful for. My uncle thinks of you as.... I mean, I can see my uncle admires your skills."

Skills? I stood there, trembling, imagining how dreary the house would be when Benedict had gone. "But how much more thankful I would be if..." I paused.

"What, Nicholas?"

"If your life was here, too. If this were your house."

"Mine?" He seemed confused but I had seen a sly glimmer in his eyes.

"One day it will be. You are your uncle's heir, whatever he feels for you now. He will never leave his property to anyone except family." I had always known that. I was his boy, not his son or partner or — even if such a thing could ever could be — his spouse. My comfort — my life — depended totally on him. "You'll be free to do what you want, then. The life here will be good, and ours to share."

There was a long, shocked silence. Had I dared too far? I did not wish to compromise us both, yet the promise of Benedict's future touch made me shiver with need.

"That cannot be," Benedict said. There was an odd, stilted tone to his voice. "That will not happen for many years."

"Maybe I can speak to Mr. Allan — "

"You will say nothing!" Benedict had never turned his anger on me before. "I can see you're in thrall to Simeon. When he calls, you respond at once, as if afraid of punishment."

"It's not like that." My throat was tight again.

Benedict continued, regardless. "You're the one who needs intercession, Nicholas. Who needs to be freed."

I never heard what Benedict might suggest to rescue me. His gaze slid over my shoulder and his eyes narrowed. Simeon was behind me in the hallway, watching us. I had already sensed him, his heartbeat heavy and ponderous against the startled skitter of Benedict's.

"Benedict, I believe you are finished for the day. And Mr. Spencer? I wish to talk to you in the office. Alone." In the way he spoke, and also the way his pulse vibrated through me, I knew he was furious. His hostility towards his nephew was palpable. And there was something more — a strange, rather shocking pain behind his anger. What could have damaged him so? Simeon was not a man to be hurt by other men.

As Benedict stepped back into his room and closed the door on us, I turned slowly to face Simeon. He was stock still, a sombre, dark-suited, brooding presence. Only his glinting eyes hinted at his emotion.

"Nicholas?" His voice softened, and his gaze ran over me with a censure that barely masked his anticipation of pleasure. No, Simeon was not scared of anything. He was strong and powerful.

And I was his.

"I will go to the office now," I murmured. "I'll await you there."

※

THEY SAY THAT I gave way to obsession.

Yet what *was* my obsession? My total infatuation with Benedict? Or my strange relationship with Simeon, somewhere between submission and desire? I was a fish upon a hook that was at once both painful and poignant.

That week became the longest of my life. I knew it was the last time I had any chance of being with Benedict. During the day, I only caught glimpses of him. He ate and slept at Simeon's house, and worked on business cases with his uncle, but otherwise they were strangers to each other. The alienation was complete.

The depressive atmosphere seeped into me like a disease. I became a wraith at night, unable to sleep, wandering the corridors. I wished, but didn't dare to call on Benedict in his room. Instead, I usually found myself at Simeon's bedroom. I was not allowed in except with his invitation, I knew. Even if we had shared an exhausting time in bed, he would always send me away to sleep. Some nights I lay on my belly for hours, waiting for my sore arse to feel comfortable again, or the stinging slaps on my buttocks to cool. Yet this week, I began to slip back into his bedroom, practising the art of opening and closing the heavy wooden door with nary a squeak. Then I would stand in the shadows of his velvet curtains, watching him sleep: the heavy lids, the deep snores from his throat. The way his hand twitched on the covers as he dreamed.

One night, I swear he whispered my name. He could have had no inkling that I was in the room, yet his mind was on me. I breathed slowly, opening my senses to him. His smell was a rich perfume, his heartbeat a steady thrumming within my own breast. My spying was a terrible disobedience — a terrible risk — yet I took it rashly and regardless. As I stared at the unsuspecting Simeon, I longed for Benedict with a sore ache, deep in my breast, when he had not even physically left the house. How much worse would it be when he'd gone for good?

"I can see you are in thrall to Simeon. When he calls, you respond at once."

Simeon demanded my attention every day he spent at the house, even if he did not want to use me at night. That was how I'd begun to think of it — that he used me.

"You're the one who needs intercession, Nicholas. Who needs to be freed."

I would never be free of Simeon while he kept me here, and he gave no sign of ever tiring of me. If I ran away, where would I go? My family had cast me out, and I couldn't live on the streets. I had no prospects or friends of my own, and no hope of intimacy with others. In my heart, I knew my only escape would be death — either mine or his.

His.

And it had to be before Benedict left me for ever.

⊹⊹

THE NEXT NIGHT, I drank freely at my solitary supper. Simeon had been in town on business all day and, on his return, had ordered a light meal in his room. Benedict was staying at a friend's. The food was served to me almost cold and with none of the respectful finesse the servants showed for Simeon, but I cared not. Both my head and heart ached. I left the supper table without anyone's notice, my senses blurred from Simeon's rich red wine.

The hours until midnight passed slowly. I lay on my bed, still dressed, and listened to the servants retiring to their quarters; a dog barking outside in the street; a late night cab passing the house with a rattle of bit and bridle. Then…silence. I rose from my rest and stepped out into the corridor. No one was about. I closed my door carefully, and walked on stockinged feet to Simeon's room. He never heard me enter, nor stirred as I approached the bed. I had practised well.

I can't tell you now exactly what was in my mind as I looked down on him. His sleeping breath tangled with the whisper of my own; the blood in his veins pulsed with mine, the wet heat of life running through us both. His jaw was darker than his cheeks in the dim light: he had not called for me to shave him tonight. I reached into the drawer beside his bed and slowly withdrew the razor case.

I stood over him, my position giving me, for once, the advantage. My mind was in turmoil. I purged my senses of any stimuli except those I chose — I absorbed the quiet darkness of the room; the aroma of waxed wood; the fresh smell of clean linen. All signs of a rich, privileged life — of all the goods a man could want, of every comfort a man may wish for. But what did *I* want? What was *my* wish?

I wished Benedict to be free of debt to his uncle; free to indulge himself; free to love me.

I wished for my own life to be free.

My first step was hesitant, but then determination took over. I climbed onto the bed and straddled Simeon, trapping his covers around him. He lay on his left side, facing away from me. It was a perfect position for submission: I had often assumed it. I lowered my body onto his, my weight pinning him inside his linen cocoon. Then I drew out the razor and snapped it open against his cheek.

It had taken only a moment, but he'd been alerted. He jerked beneath me, trying to rise, and sudden fear washed over me. I leaned more heavily, forcing his head into the pillow with one hand, then stretched the blade in my other across his face and under his chin — and cut.

I knew I must not falter. The razor sliced into the flesh, and I dragged it back towards me as deeply as I could, wrenching through skin and sinew. Blood spilled immediately, purplish in the half-light, glistening over my wrist. I was fast, but Simeon's body reacted on an instinctive level, fighting me for his life. His mouth opened in a jagged roar, the sound ceasing abruptly as I cut into his throat. His fingers clawed at my arms. I held him tight but it took all my strength. I thrust my forearm across his mouth, afraid that he would make enough noise to wake the household, then dropped the razor and scrabbled for one of his thick down pillows. The blood was slippery and soaked my arm to the elbow. I could smell it, coppery and rank, and I was scared I'd be sick. I fumbled with the pillow, and his head turned slightly so that we were almost face-to-face. His eyes were wide open and he stared at me, his gaze clear and knowing. And then — astonishingly — he let go of my arms and ceased to struggle. It was not in reflex, but a deliberate move.

He surrendered to me.

I bit my lip, mortally afraid of what I saw in his eyes. *Do what you will*, it seemed to say. *I'm sorry for it. But if that is what you want, I will not stop you.* As I watched, his pupils glazed over, and his expression changed to one of great sadness. His mouth sagged open, no longer able to form words. But what was left of his life force gave a ghastly bubble of sound — a wet gargle, a stutter of evacuation. The sound was of such dreadfulness that I was frozen in place for seconds. Then I pressed down the pillow, hiding his anguished face, muffling the final hiss from his gaping throat.

And then he was still.

Tears rolled down my cheeks though I wasn't aware of sorrow or distress, only a surge of relief that it was done. I am the master now, I thought. See? I'm no longer indentured to anyone!

There was no answer to my internal cry. There was no answer to anything. I could hear only my own racing heart, taste only the bile in my throat, smell only the awful, saturating blood. It was the equivalent to me of utter silence.

I stared with disgust at the bed clothes, soaked through under Simeon's body, and ripped in several places from his struggles. Slowly, I climbed back off the bed, careful not to bring any of the stained sheets with me. My legs were shaking and nausea bubbled in my throat.

But I could not leave yet. I had more work to do. I dared leave no trace.

♣

THEY SAY THAT in my madness, I lied and misled. Yet who was interested in me, in those first few days of Simeon's disappearance? It was still my home, even without his presence, but no one cared to notice me without his patronage. His staff was confused, lost without a master's instruction. The young valet returned to smiling at me, but I never responded. For several days, I walked the corridors, following my own initiative on office matters that needed attending to.

Benedict agreed to stay in the house until any message was received from his uncle, and he took eagerly to the role of manager of Simeon's business. I bided my time, hoping to work closely with him and share in that enthusiasm. At last I'd be able to sit by him without Simeon's ominous look! I could touch his hand in passing; share my meals and my conversation with him. Look forward to the night he would call me to his room.

And yet the dreadful silence still hung around my senses like an autumn evening's fog. People came and went, footsteps on the stairs, tradesmen at the back entrance, messengers arriving from Simeon's impatient clients almost every day. It was all background noise to me.

I didn't know who reported Simeon missing to the police, but I suspect it was a client, dissatisfied with Benedict as caretaker of their case. A couple of days later, a young inspector and his older sergeant arrived at the house, respectful yet determined to find information.

"I have no reason to believe my uncle is in any kind of trouble or distress," Benedict said. When had he started to sound so pompous? "He will be in town or with friends, and has forgotten to inform us."

"For over a week, sir, when he has outstanding business issues to attend to?"

"I am handling them for him," Benedict said tersely.

I excused myself from the interview, but the sergeant followed me, a polite distance away until we both reached my small office. "May I trouble you, Mr. Spencer, to ask if you know anything of Mr. Simeon Allan's absence?"

"I'm only the secretary."

"But you're privy to his business affairs."

I looked at him sharply, but there was no accusation in his tone. "Mr. Allan is a powerful man," I said. "He doesn't share his private matters with employees."

The policeman had a pencil and notebook in his hand. His face was lined with age, his hair speckled with silver, but there was intelligence in his eyes, as well as a more incongruous compassion. "Do you think this is a private matter, then?"

"I have no idea."

His gaze ran over me as so many other men's had but, surprisingly, his look was neither scornful nor hungry. "Do you have any reason to be concerned, Mr. Spencer?"

"Concerned?"

"About the fact that Mr. Allan is missing with no trace of his whereabouts. Excuse my boldness, but I assume you see him most days, and spend much time in his company. Is this natural behaviour for him?"

My heart skipped several beats. "Yes," I said. "He does what he wishes at all times."

The sergeant nodded, as if satisfied. "I'm sure you're right, and Mr. Allan will arrive home soon, unconcerned and unharmed. I'm sorry to have bothered you in your work."

As he turned to leave the room, I rose from my chair. I don't know what possessed me to speak further. "Mr. Allan has been very good to me."

"I can see that. You have a good job, a home. Fine clothes." He nodded again, almost kindly. "You must miss him."

"Yes," I blurted out. It was not a lie. My forehead ached. A pulse throbbed behind my eyes. There was a soft percussion in the room that I could not identify. "Yes, I miss him."

⊹

THE PERCUSSION RETURNED in the night. Rhythmic and deeply-felt, perhaps not so much a sound as a sensation, as potent as a voice crying out in the dark. It rumbled beneath my narrow bed until I thought the floor shook. My body resonated with it, my head throbbing, sweat springing up on my skin.

I could not sleep. I dressed and told myself I would fetch a glass of hot milk from the kitchen, but I found myself walking the other way along the corridor, to Simeon's room. Without thinking, I knocked gently. Of course he would not answer it.

The sound followed me—a pulse, a heartbeat that was not mine, yet marched alongside. My legs trembled as I opened the door to his room and stepped inside. A rush of fear and anticipation swamped me, but there was nothing to see. New linen, a swept floor, undisturbed curtains.

The sound thudded against my ribs and I gasped for breath.

You must miss him.

I sank to my knees in the doorway and wept.

⊹

THE POLICEMEN RETURNED a few days later. I was with Benedict in the office when they were shown through, and Benedict confirmed he had still not heard from his uncle. There was an uneasy air in the room, as if suspicions were formed but couldn't yet be voiced aloud.

"You should know, Mr. Allan, that we've received a request to search the house."

"That is outrageous," Benedict snapped. "I have confidential papers here, this is my private house—"

"It's actually your uncle's, though, isn't it?" The inspector was unimpressed with Benedict's bluster. His antipathy was hidden, but I felt the scratch of it on my senses.

"I'll show them around the house," I said.

The inspector nodded thanks. "When your uncle returns," he told Benedict, "I'm sure he'll understand the need to do our job. We have only his interests at heart."

Benedict scowled. He caught my arm as I walked past him, and hissed in my ear, "Nicholas, remember you have nothing except what my uncle gave you out of misplaced charity. If he's not here, you must consider what kindness *I* would offer you, and make sure you do your duty by me. Keep them away from the private rooms."

I looked into his face, and saw his mean, shrivelled heart exposed to me. With a shock, I realised he'd guessed his uncle was gone for good. I could see it in the anticipatory tension across his shoulders, smell it on his greedy breath. He might have no idea how or where, but he did not *want* to know. After the requisite time, he would declare his uncle presumed dead and inherit the estate, and he didn't want a police investigation to interfere with his plans. Whatever he said about continuing kindness to me, I knew, bone-deep, that he would not keep me here. I had been part of Simeon's world, not his. This man did not want me. The kiss had been a foolish aberration, not true attraction.

How had I ever persuaded myself otherwise? Benedict had his uncle's dark, expressive eyes, but not the strength of character behind them. Benedict was handsome in a youthful, pretty way, but not imposing like Simeon. Benedict's voice was too weak, his orders tentative, his decisions flawed. The harsh grip on my arm today was proof of nothing but a selfish fear of discovery.

I felt as if my eyes had been opened most cruelly. The percussive noise returned I shuddered. I almost gagged.

"Mr. Spencer?" The sergeant moved beside me. "Are you ill?"

"He will not return." My voice sounded high and strange. Benedict froze in place and the inspector frowned. He stepped towards me, but the sergeant gestured him back and moved closer, with an oddly protective air.

"You've heard from him, Mr. Spencer?"

"No."

"You know where he is?"

"Yes."

"Nicholas," Benedict snapped. "Stop this foolishness."

I didn't acknowledge him. The sound was increasing, accompanied by a ringing in my ears. Underlying it, a slow beat, a tug to my pulse, a slow heat through my veins.

You're very special, Nicholas.

"Are you frightened of something, Mr. Spencer? Are you worried about your position here?"

I would have laughed, if there'd been a scrap of joy to be found. "No, I'm not. My position is well established. I'm Mr. Simeon Allan's secretary. I'm his boy."

Boy. My boy.

My eyes were misted and stinging. It was difficult to make out the other men in the room. Benedict looked very white, and the inspector moved slowly to block the exit from the room. Did they think I would run for it, to escape my fate? Did they think I *could*?

"Nicholas, don't say any more." Benedict's voice sounded strained.

"Don't you hear it?" I asked.

"Hear what?" The sergeant peered at me with concern. "The carriage outside? The kitchen staff at work?"

"No. No!" I was impatient now. *Of course* they couldn't hear it. It was for me, for my attention — for my communication alone.

"What do you hear, Mr. Spencer?"

The sergeant had a silken voice, as if he tried to tempt me to share my secrets. Simeon had never used seduction on me, yet I'd gone to him willingly. The thudding sank into my flesh, running along my muscles, vibrating against my palate as I tried to speak.

"Where is Mr. Allan? Tell us, now."

"He's still with me," I whispered. "I am with him."

Benedict may have been shouting. I could see his mouth opening angrily, the inspector restraining him. I heard nothing except the pulsation within me and the policeman's voice at my ear.

"What do you mean, son?"

I'd thought I was in servitude. I'd wanted escape. I wanted to find a new life, a new love, one of my own choosing. My throat ached, the beat hammered within my skull. The men around me were blurred, as if moving in and out of my line of vision. "Oh, would that you could hear it," I cried. I stumbled through the doorway as they all stood aside. I made for the stairs to the bed-rooms. "It won't leave me alone."

I didn't care if they followed. I was drawn back to Simeon's room, the throbbing running through me like a thread of blood, tugging me on, reel-ing me in. I flung the door open, ran to the side of the bed, and dropped to my knees on the floor. Dust motes lifted from the surfaces around me. The blankets smelled musty.

"I'm here, sir," I whispered, my head bowed, my eyes on the underside of the bed. "At your call. As always." I reached underneath and pulled up a loose board. Someone in the room behind me gave a choked gasp. I ignored it and tugged out a cloth wrapped into a bundle.

The sergeant's voice was muffled, as if hidden behind his hand. "What's there?"

A foul smell hung in the air. The room should have been cleaned every day, I thought, ready for the master's return, but obviously the staff had become lazy. I didn't care, not now. The aroma of his lemon soap lingered, but it couldn't mask the cloying thickness of blood. The floorboards were scrubbed clean, and soiled linens disposed of, but I could still see the crimson flood of that night.

"I hid it all." My words were not directed to anyone in particular: I had eyes for none of them. I opened the cloth clumsily, revealing a claw hammer first. "I took this from the gardener's shed, to raise the boards. He'll need it back." The razor case was second. I had cleaned everything very carefully before hiding it beneath the floor. Simeon always liked his belongings to be clean.

"Where is the...where is he, son?"

"Here," I replied, softly, affectionately, my hand patting the floorboards beneath me. "I hid him, too. I wasn't strong enough to take him farther. And...this is his home."

There was a groan in the background and the sound of heavy, stumbling footsteps. It seemed Benedict had left. I could hear the inspector talking about sending for assistance.

The sergeant looked both horrified and pitying. "Why are you still here? You could have escaped. We wouldn't have found him for days. No one would have known."

"I would have," I said. "I *did*."

"You have a defence, Mr. Spencer. You're very young, everything about you cries innocence. If the judge believes that Simeon Allan abused you...."

"He never abused me. He loved me!" Simeon's heartbeat still ebbed and flowed like a tide skimming down my nerves. He was warm and live and holding me tight. Wanting me; needing me. It wasn't commanding, it wasn't bullying. How could people be so blind?

"You're in shock. You're in pain."

Yes, I am in pain, I wanted to cry. But it was not the pain of a wound. "I miss him," I said. Now there were other men in the room, hauling me up, binding my hands. I didn't struggle. "I betrayed him."

The heartbeat inside me stuttered, as if feeling the same anguish. I tried to stay with it, but they were taking me from the room, from my house, my home. *His* home.

"I loved him," I said. How could I have ever doubted it? I mistook his care and guidance for capture. His possessiveness was a mentorship I needed, that helped me to find my way.

I could still feel his heartbeat, but so very, very quiet now. I concentrated hard, and mine slipped into rhythm with it.

"I loved you," I whispered to his heart.

Then the sound stopped.

＋＋

THEY SAY I'M mad—a professional opinion. What I am, is totally alone.

No one has come to see me, apart from the sergeant, who spoke haltingly but with kindness. My parents sent a priest with blankets and Bible, and I sent him away. All I have is a handkerchief that was one of Simeon's. Sometimes I hold it to my face, as if he's blindfolded me, but his smell has almost faded from it now.

They say that I'm mad but they've found no evidence except that one fearsome, shocking act when I destroyed everything I held dear — when I destroyed my own salvation. I know that many of them find me despicable for other reasons, for the love I'm not afraid to own. Some would say it's amusing, that I'll defend a socially unacceptable love at the very moment I've lost it. Why make the attempt? Why not distance myself from what I did, what I was? There may be a chance for clemency — to offer up my story as victim, rather than perpetrator, and rebuild a life.

No. Whether it's madness or not, I will pay the price. I took the life that I should have treasured. That I *did* treasure, if only I had realised in time.

I agree with them at last, for I believe that I *am* mad. Isn't that better than living with this endlessly beating, agonisingly broken heart?

THE LORD'S GREAT JEST

Satyros Phil Brucato

EVERY lord must have his cruelties, and my Lord was no exception. The horses strained against their ropes as if in horror of their pending chore. Being but poor brutes, they had no true comprehension of the depth of our king's humour. Still, God's creatures are imbued with some measure of His grace…save, perhaps, we poor fallen specimens, made in our Lord's image and yet born, it would seem, to defile it.

The men cowered in their chains, some begging for mercy, a few soiling themselves. The men-at-arms grumbled at the turn of their task, yet none dared to offend the king's honour by questioning his commands. The stink of terror and vile waste offended my nostrils and compounded the dank atmosphere of the day. Clouds piled up in solemn sky-veils, as if to shield Almighty God's view from the pending deed.

Would that such mercies had been allowed to us.

It is our state to live in fear
Our poor knees to mercies bent
And fair to tremble at the threat
Of some well-pointed argument.

My liege lord availed himself of wine — fine red stuff purged from Tuscan vineyards and carried by main force through the hills. I am familiar with such techniques, as I myself was procured through such adventures. In the carpeted pavilion where my lord took his shade, noble men and women gossiped, distracting their attentions from the activities underway. He gestured to me, and I attended. It was by his grace alone that I was not within that queue, or else long gone to the crypts or shattered like some discarded plaything somehow flawed by its maker's hands.

"Hop-Frog," he said, his fingers twitching with excitement, "It is a marvellous jest, don't you agree?"

"It is," I avowed, nodding my capacious, and rather overlarge, head, "the very toll of Irony's bell."

The king was fond of jests, which is why he sought my company. He regarded himself as quite the humorist, and if in truth his humours favoured a brutish, scatological bent, none within his court would dare make protest them. His ministers and courtiers roared at the king's japes like cruel boys with some rocks and a frog pond. It fell to me to instil some measure of refinement in that court, however poor my efforts may have been.

"The day is hot, my hopping prophet — *drink!*" My master pressed the wine cup to my hands. I took its measure, then downed it without protest. I fear, however, that I am not much fond of drinking. Brews and so forth skew my wits, and my lord knew this. My sardonic wit had amused him from the day I'd first set foot within his presence. Though I must confess I found his manner quite appalling, I could not argue with the favour of his office. I was one of many celestial pranks gathered into our king's court as entertainers for the noble kind. Yet it was *my* wit (if not my humour) that most pleased our gracious lord. And so, here I was, a partner in his latest jest.

The first team of horses found themselves hitched to the first man drawn from the line. He howled as if the pain had already begun. Like a kitten dangled over fire, he shrieked and clawed and struggled but to no purchase or relief. The men-at-arms hitched his legs to the team — one half of the team to the right leg, one half to the left.

Our good king gave the gesture, and the horses were loosed.

Arms pinioned to his sides, the man was drawn to the stake in awful mockery of the carnal act as was practised in the halls of Sodom, damned yet sacred in appeal. For truly, what else could rouse such divine reproach but that which is, by some man's measure, sacred?

God cares not for petty things
To gain His favour, man's deeds must be
Keen of edge and iron-rich
Splendid in depravity.

And so the deeds of my king were, for his appetites were as capacious as his humours…which is to say (like his belly), vast.

Delicacy forbids me to describe in detail the king's foul spectacle. Let us simply say it was an excessive jest. By evening-fall, three score men were writhing in dances of excruciation, dancing a pine-jig of dim theatricality.

"Let it be known," said our king for the third or fourth time that day, "that such is the punishment in my realm for Sodomy."

And this too, may I say, dear reader, was *also* the very toll of Irony's bell.

For in all the kingdom, I knew of no more prolific a buggerer than our good king himself.

✢

GIVEN MY CLOSE (might I say pointed?) acquaintance with our king's true predilections, I remained wary as we watched that spectacle. Not a one of those so terribly speared had *not* been a member of the King's inner secret circle — those men most tenderly taken in our lord's awful favour. Given the normal instinct for self-preserving acts, you would be forgiven for thinking that such men might avoid our lord's attentions. But just as birds often dash themselves against inviting windowpanes, so we men find ourselves drawn (if I may say so) to morbid fascinations in the hopes that some catharsis might be found. We are creatures of pity and terror by inclination, and our tastes seem sharpened by the risk of some fell thing.

In this case, that fell thing was the king himself — a magnificent hallmark of God's handiwork, I must confess, yet tinged with a Saturnian glare. His opulence — grand foods, grand drinks, clothing fit for Papal lords — was well-known, even if his bedchamber pursuits were not. The finest musicians, acrobats and courtesans were summoned to his palace every fortnight, to entertain men and women elevated to grand opulence by God.

And *I*?

I had the fortune to be master of his revels (both public and discreet), my chambers as capacious as my skull. I was well-barbered by a host of concubines purchased at fine price for the purpose of gilding one of God's mistakes. For just as our good king was charming and well-formed by the Craftsman's hand, so I had been tumbled off the lathe at some imperfect juncture, my wits full-formed and my body, sadly, not.

> *This, too, I take and gather*
> *As sure sign of my King's wit:*
> *To employ a half-formed Hop-Frog*
> *In service of his etiquette.*

Nor was I alone among my countrymen in being granted such an office. One other — a sweet-faced boy named by our liege Triptolemus — had been taken from my distant village. We forged a kinship, he and I, in shared captivity. For be assured, dear friend, royal captives is what we were — well-favoured slaves, most certainly, but beaten or worse when the king's humours darkened toward night-black.

Triptolemus and I had good reason to fear our king's attentions. For by some gracious blessing of celestial wit, this young man and I shared a common secret with the king. Had truth prevailed in that forest of lies, all three of us would have been hoist upon the spikes intended to punish buggery. But while the king's appetites were as gentle as his cruelties, Triptolemus and I held common comfort in the touch of a secret angel's wings.

I cannot in good conscience claim he loved me. How could *any* man desire in his heart an accident of flesh such as I? It speaks of strange devotions that so beautiful a young Adonis could cradle my misshapen head, stroke a perfect finger down my cheek, suffer slights and rantings from our king when petitioning on my behalf. Triptolemus kneaded my bent shoulders, rubbed balm on my frequent whip-burns. He held me at night when the torments took me, whispering that he would never leave my side. What inspired such dedication I cannot say. He never told me then, and he cannot tell me now.

Unlike the coarse blunderers who peopled our king's court, Triptolemus moved like air across a flame. So delicate that he could cross a rope across a gorge, yet strong enough to lift me without drawing a hard breath, Triptolemus shared my acrobatic skills. For though my legs force me to a perpetual half-hop along the ground (hence my name — all hail my master's wit!), my arms are strong as cables on a carpenter's high scaffold. With such ropes and scaffolds we entertained our king, swinging like apes through torch-lit halls in defiance of death and common sense. I may have been the stronger man (or *half* man, if you will), but Triptolemus was our Orpheus, so delicate in art that he could look Hell in the face and return to the living world unscathed.

Perhaps our bond grew from that kinship to our distant home, or from the brutal method of conveyance we shared between that home and the good king's court. The trust of wrists and well-timed leaps may well have united us. But perhaps it was our *stature* that struck such affection from our souls. For like me, Triptolemus was judged half a man — well-formed as any artist's statute, but far shorter than even a common girl.

What jesting Maker shapes such men? What heavenly laughter shook the clouds on the nights when we were born?

> When His wits are up
> And His humours sing
> The Lord of Hosts
> Is cruel as a king.

As our good king laughed at Triptolemus and myself, so the King of Kings must have laughed at us all.

And yet, Triptolemus showed no defect. His small height could be judged his only deformity. Diminutive in stature he may have been, but in form? Generosity? Intellect? Grace? He was as perfect as any man I have ever seen...and far more so than our noble lord.

I miss him. Curse me for a fool, I miss him still.

Our king, of course, shared no such sentiments. We were prize foals in fools' motley beneath his royal gaze. And as we sat together, my king and I and his seven man-sized crows, drinking ourselves toward happy oblivion, the stench from our lord's jest filled the air.

I confess I was not in good humour then myself.

⊹⊹

DRINK IS MY Golgotha. If my cup could have been taken from me, I would gladly have wished it so. But my lord bade me drink, and so I did, my head growing heavier than usual with the mixture of thick wine and thicker smells. The men on stakes (still living, and what cruel jest was that?) writhed and spilled their entrails most pitifully. I stared down at my boots, uneasily aware that they had not escaped the legacy of humours spread out around us. I wished for Triptolemus' arms about me then, his soft words soothing my pulsating skull, but was glad to see him spared this spectacle. Back at the palace, our king had decreed a feast to be held in honour of his own wit. Triptolemus had remained behind to oversee the preparations, while I followed the king's train to witness his glorious jest firsthand.

"Dance for us," my king commanded. "Raise that heavy head of yours and amuse our company."

My stomach roiled with revulsion and wine. "I fear, my lord, that I've had far too much to drink."

"Nonsense," replied Bartholomew, the most demanding of my lord's advisors. His sour moustache twitched with disapproval. "Our *king* bids you dance, Hop-Frog. Do so."

I glared at him with all the venom a slave dares display. Behind him, a man I'd known as Antony shrieked for mercy. I could not look up without seeing the forest of violated limbs and trees. Squinting, I could render them into shadows, but nothing stopped that *smell*, that *sound*. "What sort of dance," I asked our king, "would you see me do, my lord?"

"A jig of spring, my toad. As graceful as you can be."

Grace was never, I fear, an attribute of mine.

Bowing, I rose to my feet. My head swirled and throbbed. I tilted as if the world itself had tugged the carpet from beneath me. The king and his advisors laughed. I spread my arms out in pale imitation of a swan.

"*No,* my fool," the king said.

My heavy skull bobbed at the end of my neck. "My lord?"

"Not here," he said, gesturing to the carpet rolled out across the mud by his servants. "You'll soil the carpets."

"Where, then, do you wish me to dance, my king?"

He pointed, not to my surprise, to the forest of budding corpses. "Out there."

The courtiers barked flatteries at my king's command. Bartholomew cackled as he took a sliver of lamb from an ill-looking servant's tray. Caught between two pointed logics — the wall of courtiers and men-at-arms before me, the wall of staked men and men-with-stakes behind me — I bowed again and took my leave of the carpet, stumbled into the reddening mud with as much dignity as I could muster. Once there, I raised my gaze to the skies. A trio of musicians began to play beneath the pavilion, and I danced.

I wish I could say that my eyes remained closed, but that would not be true. Thankfully, tears soon blurred what my will alone could not.

⊁⊱

"IT WAS TERRIBLE," he said.

"It was," I affirmed. It had been my intention to shield him from the truth, to dismiss the king's jest with a few words and a shrug. I could not. Triptolemus' grasp gave me a vessel for my shudders, and so I placed them there. He himself felt shaken too, as if he'd heard more about the pageant than I would have told him myself. His sweat held a sharper edge than usual, and though I could smell the drift of garlic and meat from the kitchens, I had no stomach for a feast.

"I should have been there," he said.

"I'm glad you were not."

"We should not speak of it." He was not being kind. The king learned gossip from the roaches in the walls, it seemed, and if he wanted to add two of his favourite clowns to his next spectacle no one would raise a word against it. Best, then, to speak of nothing and pretend that nothing was amiss.

"We will not." I gave Triptolemus a brief but firm embrace and then stepped back away from his arms. "How go the revels' preparation?"

His mouth bent in silent dismay. "Well enough," he lied. "By an hour past dinner, all will be ready for His Majesty's pleasure."

Such was our discourse: a forest of mirrors casting false reflections. Aware that any wrong word would bring the weight of our lord's wit and humour upon us, we chose our words like grapes among a half-ruined harvest. I nodded to him. "Surely the feast will provide welcome relief for such grand hungers."

"I hope," said Triptolemus, "that it will satisfy him." We both knew, of course, that it would not. Our lord's blood ran hot for amusement, and when it was up no simple foods could appease it.

"I should sleep while I can," I told him, my head still spinning from the afternoon's wine.

"Will you be well alone? " he asked, his face searching my own.

It was my turn to lie. "I will."

My dreams ran wild with sharpened trees.

✥

HUMOUR HAS THE breath of cruelty. Any jester knows this, and I more than most. By the time the servants tendered up their feast, the king's halls rang with noble laughter. Though I had no belly for food that night, I accepted the plate Triptolemus brought me. Starving jesters tender ill jests.

As I ate, I watched Triptolemus fly. His agile limbs cast him in an angel's role, too high and graceful to be bound by earthly weight. He danced in the ropes above our heads, shining with the glow of his exertions. Despite the swamp in my belly, I felt my heart fly with him.

Soar, my young blind Icarus,
Shame Heaven with your grace
Unbound by the dull chains of man
Gone to touch our Master's face...

And then I saw the courtier Bartholomew whispering in the king's ear, his face like the countenance of a late-winter wolf.

The two men laughed. Our lord nodded.

Though Triptolemus still flew, I felt my stomach fall.

And when the angel descended, the devils caught him and brought him to the throne.

I hobbled over to where they stood, but Triptolemus warned me off with a glance. His expression closed tight, like men-at-arms in war formation. He nodded to our king, but I saw his shoulders shake.

Bartholomew nodded to one door, and Triptolemus bowed, then strode toward that portal. I looked to him. He closed his eyes and walked away.

"*Hop-Frog!*" The king's voice cracked through the chamber.

"My lord?" I knew better than to delay. Bowing, I felt my knees shudder. My thick skull blackened with the thoughts locked inside.

"To the ropes with you," he said. "We would see who flies best: the angel or the ape."

The courtiers laughed, of course. It was their nature to obey and their pleasure to observe.

Though I'm sure I fancied it, I would swear that Triptolemus' sweat lingered in the ropes, drifting over the smell of food, wine and candle lard.

In the arc of angels, I dreamed a demon's plans.

❋

THERE ARE BARBARITIES which no man nor woman should accept. And yet we bear them with silent shrugs and empty eyes. In such a state Triptolemus returned, stumbling to his cot with unaccustomed frailty. I rose to greet him but he shook his head. Some novel iniquity had cut him in places my smile could not reach. "We will not speak of it," he said.

I nodded.

Our clowns' court was silent and cold that night.

⊹⊹

"A MASQUERADE?" OUR lord asked.

"Indeed," I nodded. "Like those of the Venetian courts." With words, I painted frescos of delight that should have shamed great Michelangelo had he beheld my art. "All the kingdom will speak of it," I said. "Word of your cleverness will spread from the cold pagan reaches to the sand-courts of the infidels!"

"*What* cleverness would they speak of, Hop-Frog," he said. There was no question in his voice. For all my art, our king was no fool.

But I, of course, am a *great* fool. And though it took all my art, so I fooled him in turn.

We laid plans for the masquerade, Triptolemus still rigid from his secret pain. He embraced me while we felt ourselves unwatched, but his arms felt stiff as paving stones. I tried to will some heat back into him, but whatever had chilled Triptolemus lingered there beyond my grasp.

It took time and no little effort, but soon all things were arranged. The night our of king's masquerade arrived, dressed out in devilish finery.

The costumes I'd prepared arrived as well.

"Apes?" Our king seemed dubious. His advisors eyed the fur suits with unnerved curiosity. I had taken pains to ensure that the costumes would radiate a grotesque potency. Great teeth gleamed white in the shaggy masks and jewels glittered against night-black fur. I had coated that fur with sweet-smelling musk, oils ripe with seductive masculinity. Best of all were the claws — scimitar talons carved from bone. Such props appeal to predatory men. True apes, of course, have no such claws...but each artist must have his liberties.

I had taken mine. And in Triptolemus' distance, I had taken to drinking, too.

My head whirled and my tongue danced. Flatteries spilled from my lips like wine. "It will terrify them all," I said. "Imagine the ladies fainting with horror. Imagine the brave men trembling in the face of your ferocity! *All* will fear you — and then applaud when you remove the masks and reveal the handsome men beneath the image of fierce apes."

"It would be," the king remarked, "a most *poetic* jest." His face tightened to a grin. "And should any man flee the court, we'll know him for his cowardice.

123

A fine jest, my Hop-Frog…and perhaps a useful one as well." Behind his eyes, I saw trees dancing with the bodies of men.

When all were attired, I produced the chains. The king's eyes narrowed behind his mask. Though I had made certain that the men would be refreshed with strong spirits as they dressed, my king's wits had managed to peek through the clouds. "*Chains*, my servant? Do you forget yourself?"

"Not at all, my king." My wits glistened with the spirits' taste. "It is an essential element of the masquerade. Who would believe that mere *apes* could be loose within the palace? You are to be *demon*-apes, my lords, straining against the very chains of Heaven. Look here," I added, opening the door. "I have even brought an angel to hold you all."

Triptolemus stood waiting, his face stern as Heaven's messenger. A pale wrap girded tight across his loins. His muscles gleamed with oil and candlelight.

It was no great task to get them into the chains after that.

※

IT'S SMALL WONDER that folk crave masquerades. Our passions chase us from God's sight, warding us from Eden by flaming swords we carry in our grasp. To admit to our hearts' desires is to fall from grace like the poor acrobats we are. And so we bar the gates to our inner natures, dressing them in costumes that hide honesty behind façade. In masquerades, of course, one's true face is revealed beneath a stylish confection. We may excuse its presence with cobbled finery, but we all know (though few will admit as much) that only in such deceptions may we be free.

And do we not have excellent teachers in such masques: the Lord, our cruelest jester, and His clergy on this earth? The God of sacramental tortures, the men who bless the engines of our pain — they speak of gentleness, yet show none of it themselves. The silky kitten is tormentor to the mouse, and the laws that speak of justice give free rein to the cruel. We hide our truths from the face of the Lord, and yet it is that Lord that makes us what we are. Such ironies bind our earthly lives, and so I found rich irony in binding our lord with chains.

In the grand hall, vast candelabra shed smoky light across the ballroom. Bright-clad apparitions spun and glided on polished stone. Musicians kept a heavenly reverie, their art echoing through stone chambers to each corner of the hall. Outside, darkness swelled with the rustle of bat wings and the skitter of vermin beyond the candlelight. Hungry servants, huddled against the cold, shivered in their rags or slapped cards and flesh and pitiful wagers in vain efforts to keep warm. Horses snorted gusts of foul-breathed mist. Dogs gnawed on bones cast there once the best part of the meat had been consumed by the revellers inside. Like a body on the verge of rot, the palace swarmed inside with pale-skinned maggots of ravenous degree. Not far off, the scraps of our king's jests still hung suspended on sharpened posts, their crow-tattered corpses rich with grubs. The masquerade continued apace, trading truth for falsehood with ever-present glee.

Our king and his man-crows clanked their chains. Through hidden corridors, Triptolemus and I led them towards the hall. "Wait here, my lords," I whispered as I handed the full rein off to my companion. "I will shout alarms to the masquerade, priming them for your infernal appearance."

"And what then?" asked Bartholomew, his glance skipping between myself, our king, and the angel holding his chains.

"I have prepared a shot of brimstone to herald your arrival — a fierce but harmless fire-burst. When you hear it, and the screams begin, crash through those doors and howl like the fiends of Hell."

By this time, the king and his retinue were (as goes the saying) drunk as lords. I had made certain that wine was close at hand, well-sweetened with concoctions to muddle one's wits. Truth be told, my king and his advisors stumbled like veritable *Hop-Frogs* in their chains, their normal grace hobbled by dizzied limbs.

The king's guards, too, had been plied with wine. We all laughed with liquid cheer. Only Triptolemus did not laugh. His face held implacable angelic calm. My chest hurt when I looked at him. Still, my office was to play the fool, and so I did, jigging like a frog on the end of a rough boy's noose.

"We are prepared?" I asked the company, but it was Triptolemus I looked to. He nodded. We had never, he and I, held much need for words between us.

In shadow, I loped up the stairs to a balcony where the brimstone cannon waited. I aimed it near the ceiling, then lit the fuse.

The hall shook with the thunder of its blaze.

Into the smoke-filled hall, I cried: "*My lords and ladies! Flee! The devil has burst the gates of Hell and set his minions loose! Save yourselves! Pray to God! The demons are free! Fly, my friends — fly!*"

I took some small satisfaction in the ensuing pandemonium.

On cue, the king and his advisors charged into the room, their claws gleaming wicked in the candlelight. Bared fangs flashed in their fur-clad heads. Poor Triptolemus clung tightly to their chains, a gorgeous coachman with a furious team. The brimstone singed my throat and nose as I howled theatricalities to the room below. *"See them, my lords and ladies! See the angel wrestling with their chains! Fear the hot breath of their corruption, gentle souls!"* I made it clear that this spectacle was part of the masquerade. Soon, terror turned to hilarity.

The guests and men-at-arms joined the play. Ladies swooned with exaggerated flair. Men-at-arms brandished their weapons with obvious caution, wary of any true threat to the king. The demon-apes raged about the room, tearing dresses and scattering furniture. Servants fled their approach, their faces pale with genuine fear.

The king and his advisors were clearly having the time of their lives.

Leaping from the balcony, I caught one chandelier and swung out in an arc. My hand clutched the torch with which I'd lit the brimstone. *"My lords and ladies,"* I cried, *"let us have an end to this! Let the devils stand revealed!"*

Our wise king caught my cue. He stopped and roared with infernal majesty. Reaching up, he shook free his demonic ape-mask, pulled it off, and roared again.

The crowd roared in approving response.

I glanced down to Triptolemus. He glanced back to me.

And tossed the chain in my direction.

It was, by my design, long enough to reach the hook I had hung from the chandelier.

Never harm an acrobatic fool.

I swung the hook to catch the chain, caught it, and pulled. The arcing chandelier snapped the chain tight around the men below. With a heave that near tore my arms from their sockets, I pulled the chain to anchor it on the chandelier.

The king and his men were yanked high in the air.

We swung back and forth as I drew the cursing men toward me. Years of bitter exercise gave me the strength of an angry god. *"Good people,"* I shouted, my lungs tight with exertion and brimstone smoke, *"Who is this I here behold?"*

"It's the KING!" some woman shouted.

"Indeed?" I yelled. *"Let me get a closer look!"*

And I shoved the torch in his face.

The musk-oiled fur flared. My noble lord screamed.

Indeed, I *had* prepared this jest — had crafted the costumes with an eye towards vanity and ignition. Within instants, the king, Bartholomew and the other courtiers shrieked in their prisons of burning fur.

Atop the chandelier, I cried:

> *The lord is my jester, I shall not want.*
> *He maketh me to cry near still waters.*
> *He lieth down with innocents and turns them to bawds.*
> *I am Hop-Frog, and this is* **my last jest**!

With that, I leapt to the balcony and ran for my life.

＋＋

IT HAS BEEN said that Triptolemus and I fled the kingdom together that night; this much was true. Some tales even cast him as a woman...and this much was *not*. In a merciful world, I could say that we lived a blissful life from then on outward — and to some degree, we *did*. Through cleverness and luck, we secured a home near the edges of those lands, far from the wars and searches that combed the countryside. A wiser king soon rose to claim the throne, and the hunt for us ended with nothing to show but legends of my infamy.

And yet my angel had flown. His haunted eyes looked out toward some horizon that neither of us dared to speak of. Though his arms wound close about me at night, they held an ever-bitter chill. He trembled from the lash of some dire whip inside. No jests, no tears, no endearments could soothe him. Triptolemus lived like a walking corpse. Not long afterward, he stopped walking and simply died.

If this were a kinder tale, I would have passed on with him then, going to whatever Hells or Heavens await creatures such as us. Yet the vitality that guided my hand that night has kept me strong through all these years. The seasons have fled. My life has not. Of all the souls alive that night, I may be the last one drawing breath today.

My vibrant strength has faded, though. What little grace I had is gone. Yet the heart beating in my chest pounds like a blacksmith's favourite hammer on the anvil of each night and dawn. I crave release, but cling to life.

It's justice, I suppose. To recall sweetness in such sour age. To smell the brimstone even when I sleep, its scent lightened by the sweat of love.

I thought myself clever…and so I was. Clever enough to see the cruel wit of our Lord. And even in my solitude, I have to laugh.

We are as frogs before our God
Tumbling through our graceless fall
Mortal men might play at jests
But time's the cruelest jest of all.

HIS HIDEOUS HEART

Kyle S. Johnson

E——,
This will be our final correspondence, for by the time you read this I will be no more. Should it find its mark, this letter will reach you under the guise of being sent to an estranged brother in Frederick, but this is close enough to the truth. You have been, in so many ways, my closest of kin and my only ally in life. Though I feel that I have spent so much of our friendship in your debt, I must call upon you in these final hours to once more provide a lee from rampaging tempests. Though I cannot know for certain that this will reach you and can only hope that it may find you in good health and spirits, I maintain my adamantine faith in your generosity and in the infrequent occasion for small fortune in an overwhelmingly unpleasant universe. It is very nearly all I have left.

My captors will see me hanged by the coming dawn, and to this I have no objections. It is a fate that I have earned in both thought and deed; a death fitting for the monster I have become. The old man is dead, and still I mourn him when the dawn bids me to wake and the night draws me down into sleep. I will mourn him with every waking moment and in every sprawling, delirious nightmare until I arrive at my appointment with the rising sun and the unforgiving noose. But it is an ineffable truth that the old man's demise fell upon him with no less than the very hands that write you this last, solemn confession.

This letter, though the paper may be thin and the ink insubstantial, carries a great weight. In my waning days, I have grown weak and frail, and that weight has grown too great for me alone to carry. Thus, I have chosen to share my burden with you, my greatest confidant and oldest friend, for you are the only soul who truly knows who I am.

Just today, I stopped in front of the mirror in the sanitarium's capacious latrine and caught a glimpse of the husk I have become, and I found nothing recognizable to behold therein. This is the mask that I must wear: an aspect of the ruse I have perpetrated upon them all. It is but a mere inconvenience, a pittance in the parade of my prolonged suffering, a necessary means to the end of my deception. As you well know, I have become comfortable beneath masks that hide greater truths. This final disguise, for all its jaundiced flesh and its sunken features, for all its gaunt and bone-revealing travesty, is still a more welcome attire than the duplicity under which I have labored for the last forty-seven years.

They think me mad, yes, but it is by design. I have presented myself with both violent lunacy and cool detachment. I have recounted the details of my gruesome chore with utter indifference and touted my cunning in the act, for it will serve to convince them that I am little more than a simple maniac, driven by an absolute lack of reason. I have provided them with exactly what they would come to expect of a madman because they must never know the truth of what transpired on that night or in the nights that led up to it. I allow them to take solace beneath the impression that I am no more than a fiend whose mind is given over to some unnatural malady, some devilish madness. They have not earned this right, but I am nothing if not pragmatic. The truth would only serve as a catalyst to the great witch hunt that I fear will someday root out those like me, and it would only lend credence to their claims that my nature is little more than some maddening condition of a depraved mind. It is a means to hide the true depths of my supposed illness, of the suggested disease that I embrace as an aspect of my true self hidden away beneath the masks.

Of the lies I provided to my captors in the deposition, the most grievous was this: the crime was one without object, without passion. The fact is that I desired that which I could never truly have, tantamount to the focus of my wanting. My crime, at its essence, was solely committed to obtain a treasure that I found out too late I could never truly possess, to slake a thirst that could not be quenched.

Of the truths I told, the clearest and most certain: I loved the old man. I feel that I am finally able to admit this to myself.

When I first arrived in the city of Baltimore, I had so very little to my tainted, hidden name. I came to this place with a cautious brand of optimism; the streets would lead to a new beginning where I could live in secret as an altogether new person, autonomous from that damned circumstance that drove me from Virginia. I had no desire to teach again, though I had so loved the profession, for I knew it to be far too dangerous a position in which to place myself. Those who teach are men with names and faces, and those gaudy things lead inexorably to esteem, which could only lead to the horrible discovery of all that I am. I would have happily settled for the most menial of labor, would have even preferred it, so long as I could perform my work in quiet anonymity and not live under the censuring eye of the city itself.

But it did not take long at all before that new, shining city became as dull and doomed as the former, for the streets of opportunity were quickly blocked by the staid hands of my oppressors. It was as though rumor had followed at my heels, padding behind me unseen with matching steps. The citizenry observed me almost immediately from a cautious distance. Their tongues waggled and their skepticism conquered me quickly. From all opportunities for labor I was summarily dismissed, roundly told that there was not yet new work to be found in the still-rebuilding city.

Where I had at first considered that it may have been nothing more than my status as an outsider, I resolved at last that they knew everything that I was. Somehow, they saw through the veneer that I presented them and into the deviant heart of my desire. I feared that they would soon descend upon me as they had in Virginia to drag me into the streets and endure their stones and slurs. They would no doubt have me committed to the great house upon the hill where the frenzied screams of the mad echoed through the walls at all hours. That I now compose this letter within those very same walls is an irony not at all lost on me. I know now that I was as fated for this place as I was fated to have been both saved and doomed by the old man.

The old man had spied me slumping through his neighborhood in my first weeks and observed with his one keen eye the gradual decline of my humor. When I would pass him sitting upon the stoop of his home, he would great

me with an unwavering warmth. On a not particularly memorable afternoon, as if he sensed the emptiness of my pockets and my spirits, taking me
not for a vagrant but simply for a soul down on his luck and waiting for it to
turn, he let me into his home.

What he could not provide in wealth he made up for in shelter and care.
He took me in as his hand out of necessity, of course, for the old man was
left without the use of half of his battle-ruined frame. But it had moreover
been a gesture of his kindness, for it was the only sentiment that the old man
had in what was left of his heart. Truly, he was as righteous a soul as any fair
G-d could ever hope to spawn. His manner was warm and jovial, his charity
boundless. I took the old man for everything I could, and he was all too will-
ing to give of himself, but I inevitably could not obtain that which I sought
the most until the very end.

I could sense that likeness to myself as easily as the draft that wandered
through that rickety old house, as well as I could hear the creaking of the
floorboards beneath his feet wherever he trod. It was in the way he held himself so quietly, so very quietly, as though pinned beneath the great girth of
a secret. I recognized it with absolute certainty, for it was the way in which
I carried myself, no different. Though I sensed it, though I knew, I never
broached the subject with him. The work was easy, and life moved forward
in quaintness and without complication. We went on pretending that way
for a long time, for we had both grown so comfortable beneath our masks.

It was over countless glasses of wine on a moonless night that we first
stumbled, rather gracelessly, into our brief routine. In the guttering candlelight, he caught me looking at his eye. I had done this often, for it was a
horrible, bulbous gem that protruded from his scarred features. I had never
intended it, you see, but it was unavoidable, for it was such a hideous thing,
like that of a vulture. I felt shame when he recognized my leering, but he was
quick to calm my embarrassment. He told me that night how it had come
to such a condition, of his service in the detachment of Captain Maynard
at Bladensburg. His story bled from old wounds that had never closed, and
I listened intently as he recounted at great pains the colors of the burning
city, the shadow of the invading armies, the last breaths of a particular com-
rade — a New Hampshire lad called Sullivan. How he had knelt down in the
filth with the dying man and cradled him in his arms, how he had worked to
prepare him for the darkness that dimmed his vision when the concussion
of a mortar shell sent metal screaming through the sky, tearing into his face

and robbing him of his sight. How when he awoke, he was in an infirmary miles away, robbed of half of his body, half of his vision, and, indeed, half of his heart. I think it was only then that I reached out and placed my hand upon his, when I looked into his wounded face with a confidence I had never known. It was then that the understanding passed between us. We were at last united in our shared moment of melancholy, and it had been the heaviness of our sadness that stirred us to assemble in his chamber that night.

It was as natural as drawing breath and it was everything that I had imagined it to be. My senses were heightened to a level I had never dreamed possible. I could taste the heat on the air and the low, stifled groans that rose into it, could feel the imperceptible rustling of the deathwatches in the walls, and could see through the pitch darkness of the room around us. Foremost among these sensations was the sound, the beating of the old man's heart, stirred from a great slumber, healing from an old injury, louder, louder, louder, until I was certain that all the world could hear, until I was gripped by the dread of certainty that all of the cruel denizens of that city would be awakened by it and drawn to the shaded windows of the old man's chamber, that I would be subjected to a similarly hasty and terrifying exile, another fearful flight.

The world never came knocking at his chamber door, and we fell into sleep easily. The dream that followed was a most horrible portent of my blooming madness: I was wandering through the smoldering ruins of the battered capital and calling out to him, trying so desperately to be louder than bombs, and when I finally found him, he was holding ever so gently the dying man who had in his hands the red thing that I recognized to be a still-beating heart. When I awoke from the dream to his labored breath, my crazed obsession had already been cemented in my brain. I had to retrieve what he had given so carelessly to that man long dead, had to have it all for myself.

Our encounters continued for seven days thereafter, and in each passing day, the old man grew more withdrawn. In the daylight hours, he was increasingly more sullen, impossibly quieter. I feared that it was shame for what had developed between us, what continued in the thick darkness of his room by night, but I knew the truth. I knew that what he felt was the betrayal of a promise he had made foolishly and selfishly. I was consumed by such a confusion of sensations, but it was the anger that became most prominent of all, all directed at that hideous eye, at that infernal badge of valor, that constant reminder of what he had given away so carelessly.

On the seventh day, I resolved to take what I felt he had owed me. Had I not been dutiful in my services? Had I not done all that I could for him and more? Had I not given everything I had? I offered over to the old man the one thing I could not give to anyone else and could never give to another. That he could not offer me the same filled me with such a rage that I felt I had no choice but to take it without permission.

The task was done in the throes of our final endeavor with a pillow that I pressed roughly over his mouth. I know that he must have heard my final words to him, but I shall not recount them here. Those words I will take with me to the grave that is even now being dug for me. Beneath my straining, I could feel the drumming build, hammering against his chest and vibrating into mine, feeling at last the connection for which I had so desperately longed. It would not be enough, and I pressed down harder, spurred by his shrieks, until I could feel its pulse waning, until I felt him go rigid as stone, until I could feel the rhythm of that forbidden prize no longer.

When I was certain he was dead, when I had at last gathered myself from the bedside floor, I hefted his corpse to the bathtub in the adjoining room and began to dig for the treasure waiting within him. I found the physical aspect of the task to be surprisingly easy, though I cannot say the same for the havoc it wreaked on my mind. I cannot describe adequately how I wailed. Oh, how I cried. It did not take long, however, before I felt my fingers upon its slick mass. It had required little more than a few strong tugs, and then it was free. Mine at last. I withdrew my rust-colored hands and the warm object within them. The clock in his parlor struck two, and it had chimed in the hour of three before I realized that my efforts to renew its beat were in vain. So quickly it cooled, its control over me draining, and I awoke from my delirium to find what I had done.

Yes, I think I can say that I was mad then, but only temporarily. When the gravity of what I had done crashed down upon me, I collected my senses and set about dismembering the old man's body. The work was ghastly, but I was fortunate to be in possession of a surprising, natural strength. When it was completed, I wrapped the old man's remains in wax paper from the kitchen, removed three floorboards in the parlor, and placed him among the scantlings below. Before I replaced the beams, I placed the false boon neatly atop the pile.

I had no intention of being caught, true. I thought in those nervous and sad hours before the mocking officers arrived that I might have committed a perfect crime. I would send a missive to the one friend I had, the one loyal soul who possesses this altogether different narrative, and I would craft a tale of the old man's travel to some faraway place where he would rather unfortunately fall victim to some natural cause. Perhaps a broken heart would do him in, for it would only be too fitting.

When the police arrived to investigate complaints of a commotion, I was equally horrified and enraged by their manner. They treated me with condescension, with thinly veiled revulsion, that I could scarce believe I hadn't accidentally left some conspicuous trace of gore on my nightshirt. It had been so long since I had left that property that I had nearly forgotten why I had hated the world outside, why I had so quickly been swept up in the fantasy of safety the old man and his home provided.

I will admit that I acted with such cunning, such calculation, for the raving madness with which I revealed my crime was the earliest conception of the ruse that I cling to now. I would let them think that I was a senseless monster and nothing more. I would tell them that it had been the eye that had so horrified me, and that it had been the phantom beating of that dead man's heart that drove me to confess. There is certainly truth in the former, but the latter is quite the opposite. What ultimately drove me to reveal what I left to rest beneath the boards was not what I heard, but rather what I didn't. My madness was caused by the beating of a heart that was never mine to have.

They are vermin and scavengers all: the arresting officers, the badgering interrogators, the crude jailers, the slovenly judge. Pillars of their wretched institution, shining examples of their communal cruelty. The jury of twelve who delivered their verdict and my condemnation, they told me, had been a selection of my peers. My peers! As though I had ever been a part of their sinister brotherhood. They rave outside my window at all hours, spitting their curses and sharpening their knives. They have all fed so well on the carrion that remains where the man you once knew stood. Their hunger knows no bounds, for they have glutted themselves on my soul for as long as I can remember without even the faintest suggestion of their satisfaction.

At the very least, I have at last earned their leering eyes and their whispered words. At least now they can apply certainty to their longstanding suspicions of my incongruity. I am no longer some implied boogeyman, no longer a menace cloistered beneath their sons' beds or hiding in their closets. I am hideous embodiment of their deepest fears, and I am no longer afraid.

The truth, which I entrust at last to you, is that they are as responsible in conducting me to that ghastly crime as I am for wielding the ax that carried out the deed. They drove me to the old man's steps and into the warmth of his home. I will let them think me mad, for it is truth. For as different as it may be from theirs, my madness is not at all unlike theirs at its core. The only difference is that mine is a madness that must be held in the secret of night while theirs can be worn freely in the light of day. My asylum is small, damp, and dark, but they have their own madhouse, and it hides among the buildings of their ever-expanding cities. From separate worlds, but all mad nonetheless, and our shared psychosis is the most basic and yet indescribable lunacy of all. That madness, the true murderer of men, is love. Let the gallows hurry to claim me, and may the rope carry me to a place where my illness too can see the light and where a heart still beats strongly and only for me.

Yours,
R____

VARIATIONS
OF
FIGURES
UPON THE WALL

Silvia Moreno-Garcia

T HE maid slowly buttoned the dress, her hands inching along Rowena's back. Rowena looked out the sole window in the room — a great sheet of unbroken, tinted Venetian glass — and across the desolate green fields.

"What was the Lady Ligeia like?" Rowena asked.

The maid's fingers stilled against Rowena's back.

"She was a harsh mistress," the girl said.

"How so?"

But the girl did not reply.

After she had finished dressing, Rowena went outside to explore the grounds of the abbey, this bleak jumble of ancient stones her husband called a home. The building was stifling, crammed with odd trinkets, filled with heavy oak furniture, overflowing with tapestries, wall-hangings and the like. It was not the abode for a new bride, but then she did not think Quentin wanted a bride. Not that Rowena had desired a husband, though she bowed to her father's wishes, but she had hoped for a gentle word, a friendly smile.

Quentin had no smiles, his lips pressed into a firm line. He reeked; the sweet, pungent stench of opium clung to his clothes. He stared at her across the table, his eyes following the motion of her hands as she ate.

Married only three days and Rowena already dabbled in misery.

She walked south of the abbey and reached a square patch of shrubs and beds of thorns. A rose garden, but it was autumn and all the roses were gone. She wondered what it might be like come spring and in her fancy she imagined a woman tending to the flowers. Raven-haired, tall. Ligeia.

She'd seen a small portrait of her in Quentin's study. It was a poor portrait, the artist having little skill, though he'd captured the eyes. The eyes were the one element that burned, that truly lived, gazing deeply at the viewer.

The Lady Ligeia. Her passing had left her husband in gloom.

Anne left me, too, she thought. *They all leave me.*

She found comfort in this thought, that Quentin and she might have something in common after all.

Rowena paced around the garden, venturing back into the abbey when it began to rain, tiny droplets of water catching in her hair.

⊹

THE BRIDAL CHAMBER was decorated with massive tapestries of cloth of gold, spotted with arabesque figures, which produced a curious optical illusion. They seemed to shift and change, an effect probably aided by the current of wind blowing behind the draperies. Shadows danced, one in particular moving slowly, undulating, and seeming to move closer and closer to Rowena's bed.

Figures upon the walls crept towards her, then retreated. Crept and retreated. Like a tide.

Rowena turned her head and closed her eyes.

⊹

SHE AWOKE LATE, a scent of almonds catching her by surprise, though it quickly dissipated. Rowena shoved the covers away and paused before the window, examining the slate-coloured sky.

It had rained that morning and her shoes sank in the mud as she went round and round the abbey, looking at the aged vines extending up the grey stone walls, sliding past the high Gothic windows. The window upon the left was the one to her husband's study, where he spent most of his nights in a dream of poppies.

I and you, she thought.

There was no *I*, nor *you*. It was Quentin and Rowena. No. Quentin. Rowena. Separated, bracketed, at a distance. He in his study. She in her tower.

Like a princess, from a fairy tale, with no lover to ask her to throw down her hair.

A tune, which she used to sing with Anne, returned to her.

> *An outlandish knight came from the northlands;*
> *And he came wooing to me;*
> *He said he would take me to foreign lands*
> *And he would marry me —*

Rowena walked around the abbey one more time, her right hand brushing against the ivy.

⁜

ROWENA MISSED THE piano, most of all. She missed the ivory keys beneath her fingers, the melodies she ripped from the instrument, echoing across the room. Anne, standing by the window, listening to the music.

Her fingers upon Anne, ripping a different kind of music from the flesh…

The piano. The songs. Had she been able to drag the piano into this place…

But not the piano. Nor Anne.

You and I are no more, she thought. Bitter, so bitter, this abandonment.

⁜

SHE COULD NOT fathom why Quentin had married her, why his eyes had paused upon her at a small gathering a few months before. She played the piano — this was her talent, her art — and when the piece was done she noticed him staring at her. At her hands. Then his eyes drifted up, towards her face and he regarded her with…curiosity?

His courtship was brief; his gifts extravagant.

She wanted little of him, yet her parents insisted. Demanded.

And Anne was gone, wasn't she? And this was what she was supposed to do, wasn't it? To meet a man of stature, to wed, to birth children.

To be uprooted from home and transplanted — like a rose — into a different bed of earth.

⁜

ROWENA DREAMT ABOUT phantasmagorical shadows dancing around her room. A shadow horse detached from the window's curtains and neighed, a shadow rider slipping from its back.

139

The tapestries shifted and someone leaned down next to Rowena's ear, mumbling a word.

A caress upon her brow, the cold imprint of two fingers brushing her cheek.

Shadows upon the walls.

ROWENA'S FINGERS PRESSED against the table sometimes, at dinner time, trying to trace phantom notes across its surface.

The piano, her piano. Left behind in her parents' home, lid closed. All white and quiet.

Quentin watched her when they dined, a smirk upon his face. He watched her, his eyes half-lidded.

Rowena went still under his gaze, her fingers closing and resting on her lap.

And then he laughed — his laughter like a bark — and she sat still, under the flickering light of the candelabra.

THE WINDOW IN her bridal chamber could not be opened and all Rowena could do was to stare outside, to press her hands against the glass. To count the stars at night; to count nothing if mist veiled them. Or else, to run down the steps, to seek solace outside the walls of the abbey.

In dreams she also ran, dashing across a checkered landscape of black and white. The shadows drifted up, uncoiling from the ground, stretching their arms and catching her in a loving embrace.

Rowena tasted blackness in her mouth; the scent of almonds upon her tongue.

SHE'D BEEN ABED with a fever for several days, writhing and pulling at the sheets, her body burning like an ember. Quentin walked in at different intervals and watched her with detachment, his eyes showing little concern.

"This room is full of whispers," she told him.

"What do you mean?" he asked, his voice loud and gruff to her ears.

"I keep hearing noises. And there, in the corner, that tapestry, that shadow."

Quentin turned his head and shrugged. He turned to look at her again. His eyes were dull and pitiless. Rowena rubbed a hand against her forehead, sighing and shifting to give her back to him.

He cared not. He despised her.

They all did.

Anne too.

There is no *you*.

Rowena slept.

✢

THE HANDS FASTENED each button on her gown one by one, fingertips whispering against her bare skin, sliding up her spine, resting at her nape. A kiss, upon her shoulder blades.

Rowena whirled around only to find the maid on the other side of the room, busy making her bed.

The maid glanced at her.

"Lady? Are you well? Do you still want to go out today?"

Rowena had been sick for nearly ten days, the fever breaking only two nights before, leaving her weak and disoriented. Going out might be a folly, but she could not remain in that chamber a second longer.

"I am well," she said.

✢

SHE GRABBED A stick and scratched words in the mud, by the dead rose garden. She was thinking of Anne, faithless and long gone, but instead of tracing her name she wrote LIGEIA upon the dirt.

Rowena looked at the letters for a good long while before she scrawled them away. Then she drew a tracery of flowers upon the dark earth, though the rain would erase her work soon enough.

It always rained in this place. Always rain and cold, and the gloom of the abbey.

Thunder crackled.

Rowena raised her head, staring at the clouds and then, at the abbey. She glimpsed someone standing at a window, looking down at her. She thought it might be her husband, but the thick glass veiled the observer, making the silhouette anything and anyone.

✢

ROWENA STARED AT the container of incense dangling from the ceiling, its light burning arabesque patterns onto the walls. The light shifted like a snake uncoiling. A snake shedding its skin.

A kiss upon her brow, so light the lips barely brushed her skin.

Rowena blinked. Her husband, who was sitting across from her, frowned.

"What?" he asked.

"Did you feel that?"

"Feel what?"

"I could have sworn..."

Her voice trailed into silence. He grumbled something under his breath. The rain pelted the dull windows of the tower. It sounded like fingers tapping upon the glass.

Fingers upon keys. Black upon white.

✥

ROWENA STARED INTO the mirror, pressing a hand against her pale neck. A swan's neck, Anne said. Her golden hair, like the hair of princesses in fairy tales. Anne had made a crown of roses for her, set it upon Rowena's head.

But that had been two springs ago.

There was *no you and I*. There had never been. Rowena had imagined it.

A piano, the music. Anne's hands falling upon her hands. Roses in a vase, upon the piano.

She was not sure she'd ever have roses again. Perhaps roses could not grow in this quiet, dark place. The roses had died and would never bloom again.

And, as she looked at herself she wondered what Ligeia might have thought of her, the white swan to the dark one.

Rowena brushed her hair.

Outside, it rained. Inside, in another room, her husband lay in an opium haze.

And here, here in the semi-darkness of her chambers, Rowena sat alone before her mirror counting the strokes of the brush.

Herself. Alone. *I.*

✥

If I must doff off my silken things,
Pray turn thy back unto me;
For it is not fitting that such a ruffian
A naked woman should see.

ROWENA PAUSED, FROWNING. She had forgotten the rest. It would come back to her later, no doubt. Her skirts were speckled with mud, her hair was wet. She'd been out for...how long, she did not know. Round and round the dead rose garden. Round and round the abbey.

She climbed the stairs to the tower, undoing the laces of her gown and slipping out of her dirty clothes, leaving a trail of droplets upon the floor.

She stood before the mirror, naked, but it was not a full-length mirror and it cut her off at her mid-section.

Halves, she thought.

Rowena fell upon the bed. She dreamt that a shadow drifted from the walls, drifted under the covers, long, lazy fingers tracing the curve of her breasts and the line of her thighs. The shadow kissed her upon the mouth and it tasted sweet. Like almonds.

✛

JET BLACK. THE tapestry upon the walls was etched with figures of the blackest black. Jet black. If she closed her eyes, Rowena could see the shapes dancing behind her eyelids. Reversed. White upon black.

"Did you sleep in the study last night?" she asked, half-rising from the ebony ottoman.

"Yes," Quentin said.

He came in and out of their chamber, slunk back to his study and returned to her. What for, she did not know. What was the point?

"I thought you might have come in. I heard voices…and a noise."

He shook his head. "You always *hear* things," he muttered.

It was fruitless to speak to him. He thought her excitable and irritating. She'd gleaned as much and more, from the whispers of the servants. From his eyes, which accused her of silent crimes.

"There is something in this house," she said and added nothing.

Nothing more could be added.

✛

HER HANDS WERE so pale. If any roses ever bloomed in the garden, they would be white. Like her skin. Like the ivory keys of a piano, a dash of black upon them. Rowena shifted and glanced at the maid, who was tending to her.

"I must go for a walk."

"My lady, it is raining."

"I must go."

Rowena, though ill, stood quickly and before the maid could bar her way, she was already down the stairs. Barefoot she dashed outside the abbey, her feet sinking into the muck.

It was raining very hard and the wind wailed frightfully. But it did not matter. Oh, no.

143

She stood by the patch of roses, staring at the thorns. Hands fell upon her shoulders, fingers gentle and soft.

"Lady, please!" the maid yelled.

Rowena turned and saw the maid, pitifully trying to shield herself from the rain, standing under the shade of the abbey.

She chuckled, for there was something amusing about the spectacle.

⧾⧾

THE FEVER WAS upon Rowena again.

They bade her change her clothes and put her to bed.

Quentin watched over her, though he did not really watch — half-dozing, half-gone.

It did not matter to her. She did not care for him. She never had.

A gentle hand pressed against her throat. A gentle caress. Like silk.

I and you. You and I.

As Rowena lay under the canopy of the great bed and heard the voice whisper, she understood. *Us, together.* She'd never be alone again.

She twisted and turned. Ligeia's lips fell upon her lips, kissing her, embracing her. Like breathing mist and moonlight.

At last.

I and you. You and I.

Forever.

Something bloomed beneath her skin, blackness traveling inside her veins. She felt it bursting forth, like a rose opening its petals.

The white ivory key and the ebony key. One nestled upon the other. Never be apart.

The taste of almonds upon her tongue.

The taste of you and me, my love.

FOR THE APPLAUSE
OF SHADOWS

Christopher Barzak

I T is true that my voice could not be raised above the sound of a whisper, and that I was not the sort of person who received attention or applause for anything I might say or do, but that is where my Other's ability to tell the truth began and ended. I would call him the prince of lies, if only that title did not seem so crowned with a certain glory and purpose. And purpose was one thing my Other's deceitful behavior lacked. He could only have enjoyed ruining the lives of innocent people. He could only have taken pleasure from the believed lies he told. From where I stand now, though, speculating on his reasoning does not matter. In the world below, I pass my endless hours climbing the shaft of a cavern that leads up to the blue-aired realm; and when one finds oneself thrown into Death's oubliette, cast off from the world, the motivations of the Other William Wilson are neither here nor there.

Or, if his motivations do matter, it is only when I chance to see his face in the swirling mists that fill the cavern entrance, where I am able to stand and observe the world's continuous spinning. Not a foot beyond the cave mouth, where the stones crop up like sharp teeth, am I permitted. But what I see from here is quite more than one might at first assume. Like a reflecting pool, images fill the cavern entrance, and the occurrences of the world are delivered like strange yet familiar dreams. And they are such exquisitely painful dreams, the dreams of the living. They make me ache and stretch out my hands, unwittingly grasping after what has been taken from me.

There is no fiercer punishment than being shown what you desire but cannot possess.

❤

"WE'RE ALIKE, YOU and I."

Those were the first words I can recall him saying to me. Clearly they could not be the very first words he had ever said to me, though, because how would he have known we were alike if we had never spoken? But my memory of the other William Wilson before this particular statement is vague. What I remember is that we were in the same school, that our principal was the Reverend Dr. Bransby, who ruled with a draconian bent in the classrooms yet spoke the language of angels during his Sunday sermons. And I remember how William Wilson was one of the more intelligent among my classmates. He had always attracted attention, had always been lauded by our teachers and our classmates for his quick and cutting tongue, had always received more accolades and applause than I, who could barely raise my voice above the level of a whisper, had ever known.

He had dark eyes with dark circles beneath them, hair that curled around his temples like a crown of black ivy, the lips of a cherub, carved and smooth as stone.

When he leaned across the space between our desks that day to whisper, "We're alike, you and I," and I felt his lips brush against the curve of my ear, it was as if he'd blown life into me, and I awoke, right then, right there, into a room full of young men paying attention to their lesson, as if I was the other William Wilson's own creation, an eidolon he had dreamed into being, and when I turned to face him, I found him staring at me with the most delicious grin.

"How?" I said, even softer than normal, and my word drifted across the space between us like the seed of a dandelion.

Before he could answer, though, our teacher slammed a book upon his lectern. "Mr. Wilson," he shouted, "what is it that you think you are doing?"

We both turned to face him, not knowing which of us he meant, or if he meant both. In the end, though, it was my Other who spoke.

"Nothing, sir," he said, shaking his head innocently, that delicious grin wiped clean off his face. "I was just encouraging Wilson here to speak up when he answers your questions. He's quite brilliant, sir, don't you think?"

Our teacher neither smiled nor dignified the question with an answer. His white brows furrowed, and his forehead wrinkled like a washboard. I could see his lips held tight together, trembling to unleash a tumult of outrage, yet he did not lash out at my Other as he might have done so easily. Instead, he told us to resume our attention, and then he returned to speaking in the monotone voice for which he was known and about which the students joked after returning to our sleeping quarters in the evenings.

I sat quiet and attentive in my seat, still anxious that I would be associated with trouble due to my Other's instigations, but as our teacher returned to his lecture, I turned to find my Other staring at me once more with that delicious smile curling to reveal his teeth.

"Tonight," he mouthed silently, and though he did not make a sound, I heard the word in my ear as if his lips were still there, still brushing against me.

⁺⁺

I SPENT THE rest of that day in the long narrow room in which all of our studies were conducted, where high Gothic arched windows reached to the ceiling, and light filtered down through the panes of glass, illuminating the dust in the air. I did not break and take fresh air with the others that afternoon, but continued to sit at my desk, riddled as it was with the carved names of long forgotten students and the vague images of grotesqueries that I could never comprehend, no matter how long I stared at their overlapping lines and strangely bulbous proportions. I worked at a mathematics problem we'd been given earlier.

Ordinarily I would go outside, where the youngest of the students, the ten year olds, chased after one another as if they were still children, and where the oldest, the fifteen year olds, coolly went off in packs, or walked round the grounds two-by-two with a favorite friend. That day, though, I could not join the others. Not after what my Other had said aloud about my inability to speak above the sound of a whisper. It was the one thing, the very one thing, that I had no control over, and about which I wanted no attention. Yet he had brought attention to it, making me hate him a little, even as I trembled at the touch of his breath on my skin. That feeling of being stirred into being, that feeling of having been awakened into the dream of life for the first time, made me look at him as if it were the first I had ever seen him.

It was a strange feeling for many reasons, but especially because my Other and I *had* known each other for several years already, since we first entered Dr. Bransby's school on the very same day and were found to be interesting by all because we shared the same birthday and because we shared the same name. Our features, too, were remarkably similar, and sometimes, because of our shared name, scholars in the upper forms wondered if we were related. We both took any opportunity to assure them that we held no connexions beyond the queer coincidence of our names and birthdates and our similarly timed entrances to Dr. Bransby's school, but it was the other William Wilson who took particular delight in clarifying any misconception about our relationship whenever the occasion arose. "*Him*?" I once heard him say in response to an older student. "Never. No. We may share a name, and that name is unfortunately, pathetically common, I admit, but I am not common like *that one.*"

He spoke so loudly during this exchange that I knew he meant to shame me publicly, to sever any potential associations others might perceive.

So when he leaned across the space between us that morning to tell me we were alike, I could not comprehend his motives. Was it another cruel joke at my expense? Was it a way for him to bring our teacher's attention to us only so he could mention my weak voice while he had the attention of every boy in our form?

By the time I heard footsteps creaking across the floorboards behind my desk, I had worked myself into such a state of paranoia that when I felt a hand land upon my shoulder, I jumped from my seat and nearly spun in place, my fear had grown so outsized, the way a shadow thrown against a wall is sometimes larger than its owner.

It was only our teacher, though, returning. "Mr. Wilson," he said. "Why do you not join the others?"

I blinked, not knowing what to say, as I could not tell him the truth of the matter. Eventually, though, I found my inner resources and replied, "I was studying my mathematics." I then looked down at the desk where my work was displayed.

"You must give your mind time to rest," my teacher said. "Otherwise you will exhaust it. Go outside now. Join the others."

He nodded toward the high arched windows, and I turned to see a scene of boys mingling out in the chill of an autumn day, leaves swirling like bright stars between them. I gathered my coat and left the halls of the mansion for the cold air of the school grounds, where I did not join the others but instead walked the perimeter of the stone walls that surrounded the school, pausing when I reached the wrought-iron front gates that sealed us in, as though we were prisoners, to peer through the black bars at the outside world.

How like life my death is. Walled in by stone. But here in my cavern below the world, I am not as confined as I had been by Dr. Bransby's walls and wrought iron. I cannot only see the aboveworld from my cavern entrance, I can also reach out into the occurrences swirling before me, and sometimes I can grasp hold of the life that's been denied me, the way one can reach into the recesses of the mind, fumbling in the depths of dark water, only to find the form of a submerged memory and pull it ashore like the body of a drowned person.

❈

I WAS NOT made to wait much longer to understand what my Other truly wanted. He had mouthed the word *tonight*, and indeed that night he appeared to me as a white face suddenly hovering over my own as I lay in bed, surfacing from sleep, and I opened my mouth to gasp for breath that would not come due to the shock of his sudden appearance.

"Shhh," he said, placing one rough-skinned finger against my lips. "You mustn't make a sound, William."

It was possibly the first time he had ever called me by our given name without referencing our surname. It was, at least, the first time I ever took notice. Perhaps it was the way the moonlight fell through the window beside my bed and lay across his features like a sheer veil, illuminating his pale skin, darkening his dark eyes and dark hair, that made me want to comply with his order, because I did as instructed and did not make a sound beyond the gentle intake of breath that flew from my body as he pulled back my covers and slipped in beside me, pulling them up again, pulling them over us, so that we were encased in them, floating in the dark beneath them, where no moonlight could reach us.

In that darkness, his hands roamed across the bridge of my nose, the crevasse of my lips, the hollow of my neck, where he eventually lowered his mouth to kiss me. Then across my chest and down to my stomach, where his hands lingered, his fingertips softly drawing circles through the downy hair that grew there.

"It's much better like this." His voice was soft as he lowered his hand further, caressing me.

"How?" I whispered, as I had that morning.

"In the dark," he said, "when I cannot see you, it is like you are myself, only you are another. Another me. You are my other."

Then his fingers slipped even further and I was gasping again. Gasping even as he stroked me and held me close with his other arm and pulled at the skin of my neck with his teeth.

⊷⊱

THE NEXT DAY I found him in the dining hall eating breakfast, just as I would have on any other morning, but as I sat across the long table from him and met his eyes, he did not reveal any subtle indication, did not share an intimate look that only I would comprehend, to acknowledge what had passed between us. Instead, he looked at me as if it had been a long night of perpetual rain, and the worms had been washed out of the earth and onto the flagstones, wriggling beneath his dreadful notice.

"What are you looking at?" he muttered. His voice was acid thrown upon me, and I withered, my mouth gaping open without reply. "Oh, Wilson," he said, cringing at the mention of our shared name. "Do not be so petulant. It does not become *you*, of all people."

Other scholars were scraping back chairs now, joining us at the table, and I closed my mouth but could not refrain from frowning. *How?* I wanted to ask. *How can you treat me in this cold manner, after everything you said? After everything you did to me?*

He did not give me attention throughout that dismal meal, nor later, when we sat through our lectures. He did not lean across the space between us to whisper into my ear no matter how I wished him to do so. I thought I might force my will into his body, like a hand into a glove, and puppet him through the motions I wanted, which were only a repetition of what he had already said and done the night before.

But it was my Other who was the puppeteer, and I his stringed instrument, jangling at the twitch of his fingers.

He would come to me again despite the coldness he directed at me, like a blast of winter wind, in the days that followed his nighttime visitations. Again and again, he would appear at the foot of my bed during the midnight hour, staring down at my pale body in the moonlight, which I would display for him each time he came, as if I were placing myself on an altar.

Take me. Let me feel our lips together, our hands entwined, let me feel you press against my thigh.

150

I trembled at his touch, unable to muster any of the anger he evoked in the days that came after our secret meetings, when he would look right through me, as if I were merely the ghost of his own shadow thrown against the wall.

I hated him. I loved him. I wanted to pinch out the flame of his life between my thumb and forefinger.

But it was he who accomplished the snuffing out, it was he who anticipated my wild emotions, which had, over the months of our secret nights together, admittedly grown into raucous and rapidly shifting forms. Now I was calm, now I was furious. Now I was sober, now obsessively curious. I began to do things even I had not anticipated in my character, as if there were another me hiding within my body, aching to enter the world, to do the work I could not bring myself to do in daylight.

He caught me in his room one day in late autumn. I was going through the drawers of his dressing table, examining the remnants of his existence as though they might provide me with a substitute for him during the periods when he would absent himself from my bed. "What are you doing in here, Wilson?" he said, his voice as firm as Dr. Bransby's whenever he punished a student who had provided him with a case for severe disappointment. His silhouette crowded the doorway.

I pushed shut the drawer I'd been searching through before I turned to face him, and for a moment I could say nothing, could only feel the heat of my shame rise up through my body and burn me. And then, quite unexpectedly, even to myself, I said a dangerous thing.

"I love you."

My Other, though, simply sneered at this admission. Then, shaking his head, he crossed the room and slapped me once, hard, across my face. "Wake up," he said, as if he himself had not been the one to awaken me in the night, as if he were not the one who had awakened me into these feelings. "Get out of my room. Get out this instant."

I crept like an insect to his doorway, but looked back over my shoulder to utter yet another dangerous thing before leaving.

"I will tell," I whispered to the other William Wilson. "I will tell all of them what you have done. I will tell everyone what we have done together."

I remained for no more than a moment to enjoy the fear that passed across his face like wind rippling the still waters of a lake, and then I fled as though I were going to carry out my threat that very minute.

It took my Other mere seconds to catch up to me in the hallway. Breathlessly, he turned me around to face him. His hands gripping my forearms, he said, "Do not tell, William. There is no need to destroy what is between us. I am sorry for my ill treatment. Would you forgive me? Please? I beg you."

These words, they sang in my ears and lifted my heart and cleansed me of any poisonous feelings.

"Yes," I said, and nearly put my arms around him there, where anyone might have seen us. "All is forgiven," I told him.

"Good." He smiled, his dark eyes lit with a gleam. "I will come to you tonight then," he said, and I nodded. He was going to give himself to me, as I had given myself to him, over and over.

+ +

I WAITED IN my room for him to come that night, anticipating the meeting of our conjoined souls, and when eventually, hours later, my door creaked open, I sat up in bed and parted the curtains for him to enter.

No moon hung in my window that night, but my Other carried a lamp with him. Normally he would leave the lamp with a shade upon it outside, as he had always enjoyed the loss of self that darkness provided. Now, though, he crossed my floor with lamp in hand to stand above me, the curtain pulled aside, and gazed down upon my body with eyes that might devour me. When finally he placed a shade over the lamp and darkness fell like a mantle throughout the room, I held my breath, waiting to feel his body slip in beside me; and when he did join me, and I felt his hand on my hip, I sighed.

My Other began to stroke first my shoulder, then my cheek with just one finger, then my throat. I yearned for the burn of his feverish hands to mark me, but before I realized what, exactly, he wanted that night, it was too late. His touch in the dark had deceived me, as his words deceived any he encountered, and what had been just a single finger against my shoulder, what had been just the back of his hand rolling across my cheek, suddenly became a vice around my throat as he pressed me down with one hand and found a pillow with the other, which he placed over me, pressing down hard, then harder.

Even if I might have screamed, no one would have heard me. My voice — my voice that could not rise above the sound of a whisper — would have never reached them in that labyrinthine mansion.

+ +

WITH MY FINAL breath squeezed from me, I awoke in the land of shades, and stumbled my way through the caverns that led down to the heart of the underworld, where, when I reached its center, I found my lady greeting her newest subjects from a throne of broken bones. Her face was white as a powdered wig, her lips red as blood, her hair, black and writhing like the snakes of Medusa. There were so many shades gathered around her, so many lost souls wandering her hollowed-out kingdom, but when I approached to kneel, she raised her hand and said, "You are not a shadow, young one. Will still clings to your mind. Tell me, how did you come to me in this way, with so much life left in you?"

I told her my story, which I could see she could not help but enjoy from the wicked grin that lifted her cheeks at the various turnings in its telling. And as her pleasure became apparent to her subjects, they began to take an interest as well: murmuring their dissent when I told them of the other William Wilson's deception, raising their voices into a frenzy of outrage as I closed the story with the other William Wilson's hand closing upon my neck as he pressed a pillow to me.

When finally I fell silent, Lady Death lifted her strong chin and said, "You, my young one, have been wronged," and her shadow minions threw their fists above their heads, demanding justice. But when Lady Death scanned the room, they fell silent again. She turned to me then, her hair coiling about her face, and said, "If you could set your death right, would you?"

Without hesitation I spoke. "Yes," I told her. And for the first time ever, my voice was not a whisper, but loud as it tolled and echoed through my lady's caverns, growing louder and broader as it swept away from me.

Then the shades and lost souls threw their fists into the air again and cheered.

Lady Death looks kindly upon the world's victims. "Here," she said, and tied a black silken mask to my face as a wife might arrange a corsage in her husband's buttonhole. "You are bound to this place, but so long as you wear this, you may pass among the living as one of them on occasion. Go now. Claim your vengeance. For yourself and for your new queen."

Up the shaft of the cavern I went after receiving the mask. Up that steep incline I traveled until I reached the cavern entrance where I had been born into darkness. And there, for the first time since my exit from the world, in the mists that filled the entrance, I saw my Other continuing to live and breath, his existence as serene as still water.

He had left school not long after my death and returned to his family —
shocked, his father explained to the reverend Dr. Bransby, by the loss of his
friend who had died so suddenly and mysteriously in his sleep — and would
eventually be sent on to school in Eton, where he could start over properly.

If only everyone were given such new beginnings, the world would be a
fairer place. As it stands, though, only the ruthless, like my Other, enjoy such
grace, and only because they take what they want by any means: through
deception, theft, and rape.

✥

THROUGH THE MISTS of the cavern entrance I watched him, waiting
for my memory to grow cold and stiff in the recesses of his mind, biding
my endless time while he continued to drink himself into stupors, gamble
away his fortune, steal from his classmates at Eton who did not yet suspect
the evil among them — until I felt my lips rise on either side, and was quite
certain that I had come upon the perfect moment in which I could begin my
vindication.

On a night when William Wilson and his friends were carousing, drinking
and throwing cards upon the table of his room, I fixed Lady Death's mask
upon my face and stepped through the mists of my cavern entrance, only
to find myself in the outer hall of my Other's chambers, where his servant
asked for my name. "I am an old friend," I told the servant. "If you would
permit me, I would like to surprise him."

The servant had grown used to my Other's strange and profligate behavior,
so my wish was not so out of the ordinary, and he opened the chamber door
and announced the presence of a guest waiting for his master in the outer
vestibule.

From within the chamber, the sounds of raucous laughter rolled out into
the hallway. "Who could it be? Who could it be, knocking upon my door so
late in the evening?" I heard my Other ask his guests in a theatrical manner.
But as he crossed the threshold of his rooms and saw me standing in the
vestibule, wearing the same clothing he himself wore, thanks to the illusion
my mask conjured, his face twisted in a most delightfully frightening manner, and he stood frozen.

Before he could turn back and close his door upon me, I left the vestibule
and rushed to him. Placing my hands upon his forearms, the way he had held
my own that day several years ago, when he had lied in the form of an apol-

ogy and begged for forgiveness, I leaned in closer to him, thrust my finger toward his eyes, and hissed the words he most dreaded.

"William Wilson."

So frightened by my apparition was my Other than he nearly fainted in my arms. He stumbled against the wall in a weak attempt to escape, and by the time he gathered his disordered wits, I had retreated to the vestibule and returned through the morning mist to my cavern.

Gone. I had disappeared into the mist as if *I* were the mist, as if I had been a figure of his imagination sprung to life for no more than an instant.

✛

HE RAN FROM that moment, as he had run from Dr. Bransby's school after taking my life. He believed he could outrun the truth of his existence — that he was a liar who took pleasure in ruining the lives of others — and so he went on to Oxford, where his family provided him with an establishment so great he was able to appear as the noblest of commoners among those whose hereditary fortunes made them into giants.

When I next intruded on him, he was cheating a young nobleman out of his family fortune in a game of spades. The nobleman was a good sort. I could tell by the way he and his friends got along in decent fashion, liberally making gentle jests at each others expense, and I could tell by the way he grew flushed by his liquor much earlier than any other in the room, and how his words began to slur sooner than the others' as well. His hair was the color of sand, but it draped around his face like silk, and his skin was as delicate and white as a porcelain doll. I wanted to lean out of the cavern entrance, to brush a finger against that ivory cheek, and almost succeeded in convincing myself that I might use my mask's illusions to carry out other unfulfilled desires, but was stopped from indulging when I heard my Other offer to pour more wine for the table. Never before had I heard him offer to do something for others unless it was somehow to his own advantage.

By then, late into the night, the party members were already leaning one way or another in their chairs, or were holding themselves up by placing an arm across the fireplace mantel. My Other, though, appeared in good health as he stood from his chair and made his way to the next bottle, which he opened with a flourish while making a jest over his shoulder at someone else's inability to drink any longer. As he turned back to pouring the wine into their glasses, though, I saw him slip a small vial from his sleeve, which he uncapped and, from it, poured a powder into my porcelain nobleman's glass. This, I realized, was how he had gotten the young man so much more confused by his wine than any other person that evening. And it was but one of his strategies for cheating the boy out of his fortune.

I, too, was drunk that evening. Watching the young nobleman, I sipped at his beauty and felt a flicker of life course through my dead flesh for the first time since I had come to the land of shades. I wanted him. Not the other William Wilson but the young nobleman, who seemed kind and good, and whose features reminded me of seraphim. I wanted to wrap my arms around his back and press my face against his smooth chest, a portion of which appeared after he had grown hot and unbuttoned the top three holes. So when I noticed my Other subtly preparing to destroy him, I stepped out of the cavern as if it were my own life I were protecting, and burst through the doors of my nobleman's chambers, extinguishing the candles in the room with the force of my entrance. And within that dimly lit, smoke-filled room, I exposed my Other.

"Please to examine," I told those startled young men, "at your leisure, the inner linings of the cuff of this man's left sleeve, and the several little packages which may be found in the somewhat capacious pockets of his embroidered morning wrapper."

Immediately the young men took him into their many hands and divested him of his deceitful instruments — the black court cards he had placed up his sleeves that allowed him to keep winning — and my young nobleman who had nearly lost his fortune proved the greatness of his nobility by warning my Other to quit Oxford on the morrow, no more and no less.

And so the other William Wilson, cloak in hand, freed from punishment by the nobility of others, ran once again.

I remained after he had exited, lingering behind my young nobleman's figure by the window as he watched my Other flee across the lawn. I wanted to lean into him, to put my hands upon his large shoulders, to place a kiss upon his neck, to see him turn to me and feel the fall of his warm breath on my face before he pulled me to him. But it was impossible. With my Other gone, I was no more than a shadow. My young nobleman could no longer see me. Lady Death's mask was a gift for only one purpose.

So I left my young nobleman and my desires behind, and returned to the mists, where I began to look once again for the fleeing William Wilson. Wherever he ran to, I would find him. From the mists of the cavern entrance, I would go forth and come to haunt his days. In Paris, in Berlin, in Rome, in

Vienna. In Moscow and Naples, even in Egypt. Wherever he went, there I was, his shadow, brushing my lips against the curve of his ear, whispering his own name, the name he hated with the dread one reserves for the sight of a spectre.

⊷⊶

"WHY IS IT that you wait, young one?"

The question came as a surprise, as I had been incessantly watching the mist, and my Other within it, grinding out his days. I turned to find Lady Death standing in the shadows, where the cavern began its decline into the underworld. No smile lit her gray face though. No fire surged in the black furnaces of her eyes. When I looked down at my own feet without an answer for her, she came forward, put the tip of her finger beneath my chin, and lifted my face.

"We think we know why you wait," my lady said softly.

I had no reply, though this time I was forced to look into the cold and cobwebbed sockets of her eyes.

"It is because of our gift to you," she said, touching the silken black mask that had grown to be such a part of my own face that I had nearly forgotten it. "You've fallen in love with the illusions it provides. Though remember, young one, the illusions are meant to aid you in the taking of your vengeance, not to comfort you with a fantasy that you yet live. Death is where you dwell now, and Death is where you will remain, however much the mask allows you to partake in life again, if only for brief moments. You cannot remain in this in-between place forever, parting these mists for your own pleasure. You owe us fealty. Carry out your desire, or we shall be forced to retract our gift and that, unfortunately, would be most unsatisfying for both of us, as we and our shadows do so love retribution."

"I am sorry, my lady," I said, nodding, and she removed the tip of her finger from my chin.

"Good," she said, and then she began to walk backward, slowly at first, then quicker and quicker, as if it were the most natural direction, and I stood there watching, as any loyal subject should, until her face melted into darkness and she was gone.

⊷⊶

IT WAS IN Rome, during the Carnival of 18__, at a masquerade thrown in the palazzo of an old and enfeebled Neapolitan duke, where I next found my Other lifting more glasses from the wine table than any other guest. The affair was a large one, made even larger by the grandiosity of the guests' costumes and masks, some of which seemed like the wings of a black butterflies, flitting about the room, alighting here on one person's and then another's shoulder. Laughter shot up through the room like fountains, and music from the duke's ensemble wove between the loud and raucous voices like water through rock.

Taking a last swallow of wine from his glass, my Other began to weave his way among the crowd, though it was clear by the sweat on his brow and the strain on his face that he had little patience in him. And with good reason, as it was his mistress to whom he was making his way; and after having so freely imbibed so much of the wine table's contents, he wanted to reach her as soon as possible, to quench the fire he'd built within himself so early in the evening.

His mistress was the wife of the old duke, a younger bride who was kind to the old doter, but who arranged for other, more passionate relationships at her leisure. She had informed the other William Wilson about her costume choices a day prior, in a note sent in secrecy, or what she had thought was secrecy, so that he could find her and take her to a small antechamber adjoining the ballroom to have their way. This was the time. I knew as soon as I saw the note pass from her servant's hand to my Other's. This was the time for my final revenge upon my murderer.

He had just glimpsed her between the heads and shoulders of the crowded room, and was about to cross the floor to meet her, when I placed my gloved hand upon his shoulder and leaned down to whisper in his ear.

"William Wilson," I whispered, and immediately he spun around to seize me roughly by my collar.

"Scoundrel!" he said through gritted teeth. "Who are you? How do you come to haunt me? How do you come to *seem* like me, to wear my very own costume?"

Before I could answer, though, he pushed me through a door of one of the surrounding antechambers, where he had intended to consummate the affair with his mistress, and thrust the door shut behind him.

"You *shall not* dog me forever, impostor!" he shouted, and drew his sword.

"I am no impostor." I drew my own sword, laying my edge against his.

The wine he had so freely taken slowed him, and so his wits were not only dull but also frantic from the heat of his temper. He came at me again and again, thrusting his sword wildly, attempting to push me against the wainscoting; but, tripping over his own feet, he fell to the floor, where I finally plunged my sword into his bosom once, twice, thrice, until his clothes were stained with blossoms of blood as it left him.

As his will, defeated, began to leave him, I knelt next to him, and heard him murmuring these words: "You have conquered, and I yield. Yet, henceforward art thou also dead — dead to the World, to Heaven and Hope! In me didst thou exist — and, in my death, see by this image, which is thine own, how utterly thou hast murdered thyself."

Ravings. Ravings of a mind that had always been turned inward. Never once had he seen me standing before him, now or in the past, not even in my own bed during his midnight visitations. Only a reflection of himself could he behold, wherever he cast his eyes. Even now, as he began to rehearse his dying breath, his perceptions twisted and curled through the room like a thorny vine.

I could not abide it, for what vengeance would I accomplish if he could not see his own murderer truly.

So I lowered my lips to his ear for one last time.

"Self-deceiver," I said. "That sword you believe you have placed into your own gut, that blood that comes flowing from the cut: that is not your hand, nor your own self-imposed justice for your wrong-doings. It is my own sweet vengeance, and the hand that twists the blade, that hand upon the hilt, is my own and no other's."

From behind me, I heard first the slow and solemn clapping of Lady Death's hands coming together from where she sat upon her throne of broken bones below, watching, as she is always watching — me, you, everyone — and then the mask she had gifted me dropped away like an autumn leaf, its life expended.

I turned then, stood, and raised my hands above me, awash in the applause that the shadows rained upon me.

BY THAT SWEET
WORD ALONE

Heather Lojo

Every day was the same in the mausoleum:
wandering up and down your self-indulgent
hallways, thinking of castles —
I, Tristan, and she, Iseult. Or I, the Devil,
and she, Dahut, and the waters rising to drown us.

Of course my parents liked you. We had things in common:
You hated me for not being her, too blonde and earthy;
I hated you for a reason something like that.
So when I left you nursing a hot laudanum toddy
like a scarf against the chill,
and went reading and walking
and missing her all through your hallways,
and thought I felt a lifting of the loneliness — well,
it was precious, and mine alone.
I thought it was some inner condition of spirit,
that I could only reach when I walked away from you.
I had not been hungry for anything
in some time, so I treasured that feeling, and fed it.

I don't know why it sounds like I'm trying to apologize when I hate you,
    and love her.

I didn't think much when the curtains started moving.
Or when shadows fell without a light. I was in shadow there,
eating, sleeping with you in shadow.
My hair grew dusty and she twined it in her fingers
and wanted me, and I realized:

You cannot drink her alive again,
but I can.

TWO MEN IN A BEDCHAMBER,

AS OBSERVED BY THE GHOST OF THE GIRL
IN THE OVAL PORTRAIT

Terra LeMay

M Y château had been quiet for weeks and my own small room uninhabited and untended for a time quite longer, when one evening my attention was drawn by the sound of a violent crack, distant but terrible, and I suspected someone had broken through the front door. I remained trapped in the meanest suite, tucked away in one tower, ignored by the château's absent seasonal residents, who never knew that these chambers once contained beautiful and expensive appointments: tapestries, other paintings like my own, and trophy heads. All now ruined, decayed. I would tell myself the reason for such neglect was the tower rooms were too time-consuming to clean, what with all the strange nooks and crannies built to accommodate the château's unique architecture. In truth, the maids probably avoided my apartment simply because of my presence. I'd have done the same when I was alive and faced with the prospect of tending to a room containing a haunted painting, though unlike the dreaded ghosts of storytellers, I was limited to the occasional odd creak, unexplained moan, or cold draft of air.

I let out a scream, most shrill, channeling my many years of isolation and loneliness into it. I felt rather proud of the result, which echoed all through the château — bone-chilling to my own ears. Such a scream had brought many a housekeeper scurrying to stand before me. Some would threaten to burn my portrait or throw a chamber pot at the canvas, but none dared for fear that I might be loosed to haunt their person.

How I wanted to be free of this painting, of these rooms. My prison…

I listened to see if my call had drawn whomever had come to the château. Their quiet murmurs turned to footfalls in an adjacent hall. I made a great effort and turned the lock and pushed the chamber door ajar. The exertion left me weak.

I retreated back into my painting to recover my vigor.

Long minutes later came my reward: two men entered and peered around. They were not wearing the coarse clothing of thieves but rather dressed as a gentleman and his valet.

"What a bizarre suite of rooms," said the gentleman as he moved gingerly with one arm tight to his side. He inspected a particularly degraded elk's head, which hung on the wall opposite my own little nook. "Why do you suppose it has so many odd-shaped alcoves?"

"I couldn't say, sir," replied the valet. "Mayhap it's to do with the shape of the building, sir."

I took a fancy to the idea that the valet was admiring his master's figure whenever the man had his attention directed at my room's many decorations.

"Of course, Pedro, you must be right," said the gentleman. "What point to hiding the underlying architecture when you could make use of it instead? Well, so we shall. This room's as good as any other. Better, in fact, that it's remote. If the occupants return before the sunrise we should have plenty of warning. Close the shutters, please. And light some candles."

Pedro did as he was told. And all the while as he did, I took notice of how his master watched him move. I was reminded of how a man of wealth might study a handsome horse with admiration. Certainly Pedro snorted as he heaved at the shutters, heavy and without the benefit of oil. Or when he dealt with the dust on the bed's velvet canopy and linens.

When I was alive, my family would say I was poor at discerning the difference between reality and reverie. I suspect some blamed this fault for my eventual demise. But I was sure that something unspoken, some fraught romance, hung about these two men. Imagine…between two men…

Pedro then discovered the catalog left on the bed. A book describing all the portraits his master had turned to examine. He went to his master and handed it over with a quiet word. Their fingers touched during the exchange, their gazes met a moment.

The gentleman paged through the book. He paused at one illustration. I hoped it was my own.

Pedro helped his master undress and took care of his clothing, just a servant tending his employer. They spoke softly concerning the state of the gentleman's injury, which I could not rightly see from where I was in my painting. I was still too fatigued from my earlier exertions to venture out of the frame again so soon, but I could listen well enough, and from their conversation I learned Pedro's master was in very poor condition indeed, and that the terrible wound had been their reason for breaking into the château to take shelter from the cold and wind. I was unable to glean any insight into what had caused the man's injury. My imagination, honed by ages of isolation, fancied a duel. Yes. Or perhaps he had cause to protect his devoted valet from danger. Pedro himself seemed to be working hard at not looking at his master.

With aid and care, the gentleman settled into bed — half-sitting up with the catalog to read and the coverlet tucked in around him. Pedro's looks of concern for his master left me wanting to weep, but that was one more expression death had stolen from me.

I knew better than any the consequences of depriving oneself of desire. My greatest love had been the man who'd painted me into my portrait, and had I but acted on my love for him — had he but set his paintbrush aside long enough that we might fully embrace our feelings for one another — then the painting might never have been completed. I might've lived. Instead, I tried to take pleasure in my painter's company from the other side of the easel, believing there would be time yet for us once the painting was finished. In the end, it was not so. I died too soon. These two men, Pedro and his wounded master, restrained by class, by mores — I longed to shake them by their shoulders, rail at them to give over to their desires while there was still time. Where could be a better place than my château, abandoned for the season?

In my own ghastly, soundless voice, I beseeched the gentleman to take some initiative and kiss the man who now stretched out on the floor beside the bed. Did he hear me? He repositioned the candelabrum so he might see the entire room. He spent many long minutes gazing at my portrait. But no, he did not invite his servant to share the sheets with him.

At length, the candles burned down and I regained some measure of strength. Pedro snored. The gentleman did not stray from his reading. I, who died within arm's length of my beloved after so much wasted time, refused to permit this pair any taste of my fate.

I screamed again as I had before, putting more of my unbeating heart into my spirit this time. Both men sat up, startled, and looked toward the niche where my painting hung.

"Did you hear something?" asked the gentleman.

Pedro bunched the blankets nervously between his fingers. "I don't like the look of that painting, sir. She's staring at us. Those eyes could pry secrets from a man."

The gentleman gave a cough as if startled by the idea, then laughed. "Secrets? What secrets could you possibly have that a painting could know? As for myself, I certainly haven't any."

I screamed again, a wail like a banshee's. Anything less and they'd hear nothing at all. Though the effort caused me the first real pain felt in decades, as if the act shredded bit by bit what lingered of my soul.

"I'd rather you not ask, sir," replied Pedro. "I'm beholden to you. I would have to answer truthfully...and in your current state..."

The gentleman looked taken aback by this rebuke. Then he began to read from the catalog, telling Pedro about me. Hearing my account, that I'd lived for years only steps away from the man I loved, but had never kissed him, renewed my despair for this pair.

Then the gentleman said, "Her gaze *is* unnerving. As if she judges us from within her gilded frame."

"But we've done nothing, sir."

I had little spirit left; I could feel myself dissipating to nothing. Even my power to spy upon them was slipping, growing murky. All sounds came as if from a distance.

I heard the gentleman's voice: "Too right we have done nothing. Inaction damned her. Look, my good man, there's no need for you to tell me the secrets of your heart, if you'd rather not. Nevertheless, I should like to tell you mine. That painting has put me of a mind to it."

I feared I'd not be privy to Pedro's answer; the solemn sleep of the dead called me.

His master blew out the bedside candles; the room fell into darkness.

Pedro said, "Yes, sir." So faint, it might've been my own wishful thinking, except he added, "I would like that."

What came after that, I heard and saw not. I went to wherever the dead keep peace and knew nothing more until much later, when the sound of a distant, slammed door disturbed me.

My room was empty, the bed made and the shutters open, the catalog lying on the pillow as it had been. The previous night might've been nothing more than a dream, except I heard sounds at the door again…and familiar voices.

Were the men trying to fix shut the door they'd broken?

Able to step from the frame, I went to the window and pressed my face to the dirty glass. In the brilliant morning light I could see the road, which passed around the estate in view of my window. The pair walked below but the sight sank my heart for several steps separated them, the servant always behind his master. Nothing had changed. I had inspired nothing.

Then, the gentleman stumbled, fell to one knee. Pedro dropped the meager possessions he carried and rushed to the man's side and helped him stand. His reward was a gesture I have always ached to feel, to know, to possess. A kiss, lips and then bodies pressed together.

If I could breathe I would have gasped with envy and delight.

MIDNIGHT
AT THE FEET OF THE
CARYATIDES

Cory Skerry

FEETMEAT scurried up the cool stone bricks of the Teeth Tower, his toes splayed out over stone fruit and leaves, his fingers digging into the spaces between gargoyles' teeth.

Everyone agreed Teeth Tower was the tallest, though Feetmeat wasn't sure how they'd know. The towers reached so high that no one in recorded history had ever visited the attics. Every expedition, even using the indoor staircases, had turned back when they ran out of supplies.

Teeth Tower was also the easiest to climb on the outside — for fifteen stories, until the baroque style was replaced by austere Greek columns. The vandals who called themselves the Court consistently marked their territory below that line, unable to scale smoother stones the way Feetmeat could.

And the Court's vandalism was why he was headed for the ninth-story classroom window, where they'd left their latest painted gift. He reveled in how the climb stretched his muscles and the wind tested his grip. He fancied the building knew he was there to clean off the obscenities, that it welcomed his visit.

Even with that imagined benevolence, the ascent had its perils. He edged past a row of spikes placed on the cornice long ago to prevent pigeons from nesting. It worked, but it also attracted raptors from the desert to the east

169

and the sea to the west, swooping in with fish or rabbits and dropping them onto the spikes.

When he reached the ninth-story ledge, he rested for a few moments, his back against a gargoyle. Its claws had been sculpted so that they dug into the cornice; if upon each of Feetmeat's visits the gargoyle's grip seemed to have changed, or if sometimes there were gnawed bones lying on the ledge, it was no business of Feetmeat's.

The school and its Towers held many secrets, and Feetmeat reasoned that he didn't want to know most of them.

After all, there were plenty of daylight atrocities. Every student was a blue-blooded heir to varying degrees of fortune, and some of them seemed poisoned by it rather than blessed.

Feetmeat couldn't help but wonder if things would have been different with money, with a powerful family. His face was handsome enough, he thought; he had eyes as green and slanted as a cat's, a gentle hill of a nose, smooth skin the color of the desert to the east. His arms were nearly the size of other men his age, muscled from trips up and down the towers. But the chest that anchored them was the size of a pubescent child's, and his short legs each bowed inward so severely that if he stood up straight, he must walk upon the sides of his feet.

Most of the school only ignored and avoided him, but four of the richest and vilest students had made it their mission to torment him whenever they could catch him. He was sure it was only his knowledge of the best ways to climb that had convinced these four, the Court, to spare him so far. Otherwise, they might have already beaten him as they did with select students, or even killed him, as they had done with too-friendly cats.

Last night, the Court had scrawled a lewd act on the window in crimson paint: a woman with a crown being used as a conduit between two men, one of whom had a large hat, the other with tiny dashes for eyes. The students didn't fraternize with Feetmeat, even though they were his age, so the caricatures meant nothing to him, but he had a feeling their identities were clear to everyone else.

He slipped out his flask — not whiskey, but turpentine — and wetted an old sock. The paint came off the glass reluctantly, revealing a Lector in the classroom beyond, flapping her mouth soundlessly. Before her, seated at desks arrayed in a half-moon, the students scratched black wounds into paper with sharp quills and cold fingers. Their disinterest in Feetmeat's arrival was to be expected — to most of them, he was of no more consequence than the school's many ghosts.

The door opened, beyond the Lector, and there was a flash of yellow. Feetmeat paused, pressing his face so close that his eyes and sinuses stung from the turpentine fumes, but he couldn't let the overcast sky's reflection get in the way.

It was *his* library aide, the boy with the halo of black curls. The aide handed the Lector a stack of books, as confidently as if he approached an equal. Feetmeat's heart beat a fierce rhythm, like the drums in the caravan where he'd lived before the school. The aides rarely left the libraries in the Scroll Tower, and he'd never seen the object of his affections venture out before.

If he finished this quickly, he could climb down and…. Well, he was too shy to approach the aide, but the idea of seeing him without glass between them would be euphoric.

Feetmeat scrubbed at the graffiti with reckless fury, as if it was intentionally obstructing him. The vandals had used long-handled brushes this time, and Feetmeat had to climb onto a gargoyle to reach the highest daubs of paint. He strained, because if he had to climb another story and dangle on a rope, he would never make it down in time to see the aide.

His toes slipped off the gargoyle's pate, and he fell toward the spikes below.

He grasped at the ledge, catching it with both hands. The impact stung his palms, and his fingers slid off.

His descent stopped with a sudden yank, his rope belt digging into his gut. He breathed hard through his nose. Below him, past bare feet that were too warped to fit into any shoes, the spikes waited.

He reached up and grabbed at the gargoyle; his belt had caught on its curled tail. The muscles in Feetmeat's arms burned as he clambered up the statue and back onto the ledge. If he'd been an average-sized man, he wouldn't have had the strength to lift himself. It was a thought he held gingerly, because it felt strange in his mind.

His sides prickled with fear-sweat, the sour odor stronger even than the paint thinner. He picked up the sock where it had fallen and began scrubbing again. His cheeks burned, even though no students had come to the window to witness his struggle.

A ghost had. She looked just like all the other phantoms trapped in the school's towers: pale, hole-eyed wisps of young men and women whose hands ended before their fingertips and whose mouths held no teeth or tongues, as if in death they had forgotten some of what they were.

There was no way to tell how she had died, whether it had been inflicted by a cruel classmate or a bad decision. He knew she hadn't jumped or fallen: no one ever died that way on school grounds. There were dark rumors of past students and even Lectors who had tried, each of them saved by a sudden wind. Saved from death — but not necessarily from paralysis.

When the window was clean enough to reflect the dark shadow of his face and the silver sea behind him, Feetmeat scuttled down the side of the Teeth Tower. Below, he saw a flash of yellow through the trees, moving back toward the Scroll Tower through the connecting garden. He might not be too late.

He hobbled along the path, now angry at his tiny body, as if he hadn't been glad of it minutes before. Maybe he was light enough to climb well, but his stride fell far short of the aide's, and the rough gravel abraded his deformed feet.

As he neared the last garden, he heard the Court ahead.

He stopped behind a hedge, one gate away from running into the four psychotics. They'd smell the turpentine, know that he'd just come back from ruining their night's work. He wished it was anyone else between him and his aide, but there was no mistaking the distinctive honk of Bestra and Bulgar's laughter.

He would have to turn back and look for a place to hide. Silently. The Court had cat ears that listened for the sounds of hiding and retreating, and they had jackal hearts, their greatest joy derived from the hunt and its grisly end.

"Where's the key, fussy little mouse?" called another familiar voice, like a badly-played violin. Genevieve.

"We want to *improve* on those dusty old books," Bestra sneered.

Feetmeat froze as he realized they weren't talking to one another, but to a victim. Someone who had a connection to books.

The library aide.

A shriek cut the air, followed by the wet meat noises of impact-tested flesh.

Feetmeat knew he should flee, but instead, he crept up to the gate. Through the iron filigree, he watched the Court brace themselves on their strong, fit legs as they pummeled a blur of brown and yellow.

The aide. *His* library aide, with the beautiful brown eyes and curly black hair and huge, plush lips. His robes had always looked bright and noble through the windows, but now, in the apathetic daylight, the cloth seemed as dingy as weathered bones.

"Give us your key," demanded Ansimus King, the leader of the delinquent Court. Even the other spoiled nobles who attended class in the Towers avoided angering King. Whether he was telling a joke or breaking someone's fingers, he rarely changed expression, like a statue carved from a block of cold hatred.

The aide reached into his pocket — and just as quickly, pressed a glinting piece of metal into his mouth. His throat flexed. He looked up at his captors, smiling a gallows smile.

The Court cackled, as if it was a funny enough prank to get him to swallow a key, except for King.

"We'll have that back," he said.

Bulgar punched the aide in his stomach, but he only moaned — nothing came up.

"Not that way. It's between classes — no one to see if we do a bit of *excavation*. Hold him," King said, and he flicked out a blade. Genevieve slipped the scarf from her neck and worked it into the aide's mouth, drawing back on it like reins so he could only choke instead of cry out.

King sliced away the aide's robe, baring a smooth brown belly.

"You'll get blood all over you, and they'll catch us," Bestra said. She sounded frightened, and for a moment, Feetmeat had hope.

"I've done it before. If you cut slow enough, it all bleeds down instead of out," King said, and crouched in front of the squirming aide. If the others had qualms, they were too afraid of King with a knife in his hands to mention them aloud.

Feetmeat gripped the ironwork of the garden gate with his fingers and rattled it as noisily as he could. When he turned the handle, the gate swung open, with him riding it at an average man's height.

The other three turned to stare at Feetmeat, and King stuck the blade in just enough to squeeze out a few beads of blood. The aide stopped struggling, held himself motionless, but quivered with the effort.

"We're busy, Feetmeat," King said, as if he was only carving a holiday gourd.

"I have something that might interest you," Feetmeat called.

More than once, he'd traded a secret climbing route for mercy. He hoped they hadn't tired of his bargains.

"You going to tattle on us to the Administration, Monkey-man?" called Genevieve. She had the same dark brown skin as the aide, but where his was silken, her flaccid cheeks and short forehead held a sheen of grease. Her overbite was so pronounced she couldn't close her mouth all the way, and in consequence, her own damp breath kept her lower lip and chin slick and shiny. Feetmeat wondered how she could laugh at the way he walked, how she thought his fish-hook-shaped legs were any worse than her shark mouth.

"Leave him," Feetmeat said, "and I'll show you a better place to make your marks."

"We're bored of your places," said King. "We want somewhere new, and he's got it. The inside of the library can't be cleaned with turpentine."

"This place," Feetmeat said, spacing his words out to emphasize each, "is both familiar and unknown. Why paint the books, where only a few scribes will see, when you could paint a place everyone can see, from every class-room in Teeth Tower?"

They dropped the library aide. Bestra and Bulgar stared with dry red eyes while King stepped closer.

"You mean the library windows, the ones held up by those statues who've each got one titty hanging out," he said. He seemed close to genuine reverence.

"Yes. I can take you to the caryatides, but I'm too short to reach what you paint, and no one can climb higher than the windows, not even me, so your marks will remain, even long after you've left the school."

King regained his feet. He commanded the others from the peak of wealth, the peak of cruelty, and the peak of beauty. King had a square jaw with a dust of early stubble, dark-lashed blue eyes, and strangely small but perfectly aligned white teeth. Feetmeat had thought him handsome, the first time he saw him, but a few minutes in King's company and that changed forever.

"Usually if we want help, we have to catch you," King challenged, his voice low and soft.

Feetmeat's story poured out with all the bitterness he would have felt if it had actually happened. "I asked to live in the dorms, with warmth and the other youths, and they said never, not even in the worst blizzard, not even if wolves stalk the grounds and the ocean chews at the front steps."

"And a good thing," Genevieve said.

King's eyes glistened, unfocused as he no doubt imagined desecrating the Scroll Tower, the center tower, which could be seen from nearly everywhere on the school grounds. In all the years the Towers had been a school, no other student had ever managed to paint so high or prominent a place.

In the ensuing silence, Feetmeat thought only of ghosts pressing their spongy noses against the windows, scratching with their stumps. He would never ask to live inside. It seemed absurd that the Court and their ilk, who made the ghosts directly with their hands and indirectly with their words, would believe anyone wanted to trap themselves inside that world.

But though Feetmeat clung to the gate like a frog on a wall in summer, ready to snatch insects that ventured too close to the door lamps, they saw only that he was small — not that he was hungry. To them he was only fragile bones and bumbling steps, a child-sized tragedy.

"We'll need more paint," declared King. "We'll meet you here, four days hence. Veneris, at dusk?"

"Yes, Veneris," Feetmeat said. "Bring old clothes that we can blacken, and climbing harnesses with the longest ropes."

"If you're not here, we'll break the neck of every cat we see and tell the Administration we saw you do it," Genevieve said.

"I'll be here," Feetmeat said. He tried not to think of the cats who sheltered in the toolshed where he lived, their purring silenced by cruel hands. He remained on the gate, swinging slightly with the breeze, until they dropped the library aide and passed out of sight.

The boy's soft halo of curly black hair was mashed with mud and stuck all over with twigs and thorns. Normally there was a quill tucked behind his ear on either side, but those tiny wings were missing now. The corners of his mouth bled where Genevieve's scarf had abraded him.

Sometimes, when Feetmeat washed the library windows on the first seven floors, he would see this aide sneaking short reads as he reshelved books. His long, fine fingers splayed over the lines of text with such grace that Feetmeat had imagined those hands fluttering over his skin, reading him with the same fierce curiosity that drove them to turn pages. He knew that wished-for lust was impossible, that everyone saw him as an animal or a monster, or if he was lucky, as a child.

"Thank you," the aide rasped. They must have hit him in the throat. "They were going to…like a *fish* — "

175

"I know," Feetmeat said. He reached out a hand, intending to help the aide to his feet, and realized only too late that his gallant gesture was laughable. The aide did smile, but he held out his hand as well, and shook it once in greeting. His fingers were gentle and cold.

"Felipe," the aide wheezed.

Feetmeat was silent.

"Do you have a name, heroic window-washer?"

Feetmeat had come here as the barely-tolerated freak in a visiting caravan, and when their negotiations with the Administration of the school hadn't gone well, they'd decided Feetmeat was the cause of all their bad luck. They'd tried to burn him. A long-dead janitor had saved him, but the man wasn't much more sensitive than the caravan folk. "Feetmeat" was what the janitor called him, and in time, so did everyone else.

He couldn't bear to say this memory-tarnished name aloud.

"Not yet," he said.

Felipe struggled to his feet and headed through a side gate shrouded in foliage. Felipe walked slowly; whether from pain or to allow Feetmeat to keep pace, it wasn't clear. They wended through the garden, wet and fragrant with rose blossoms and mint, until they passed through one of the western gates onto the cliffs that held back the roiling sea.

Feetmeat's dread grew with each of Felipe's steps.

When Felipe neared the eroded edge, Feetmeat cried, "Don't!" and hobbled forward as fast as he could. He flung out a hand, intending to snag the scraps of robe as Felipe tumbled over the edge. Instead, Felipe's hand swept down and landed in his with the precision of a bird.

"I'm not going to jump," Felipe said. His laugh turned into a cough. They gazed down the jagged slope at the rocks below, where the sea thrashed and foamed. Felipe's one exposed nipple protested the bitter wind, as hard as Feetmeat's cock.

No one had ever held him with such charity — once a doctor, for money, and once a crowd, in the attempt to burn him. This warm touch, made all the more intense by the cold air, was like petting a fallen star. He was afraid his callused grip would extinguish its light, but he clung tightly nonetheless.

Felipe's injured voice frayed in the wind, but the connection of their palms seemed to amplify the words.

"Thank you. You saved me, but also my books. I wanted to work in the Scroll Tower since I was first admitted to the school. It's the only place I belong."

Feetmeat belonged on the outside of the towers, with the birds and the carvings, but he couldn't trust his voice. He squeezed slightly to show he understood.

Felipe let go, and cold wind filled Feetmeat's palm. "But I should jump. They'll find me again, and they'll take my key. The Administration would rather lose me or a roomful of rare books than anger those monsters and their influential families."

He didn't move. The wind made flags of his tattered garments, and his crown of muddy hair blew straight back from his face as he stared at the furious ocean.

"I care about...the books," Feetmeat said, and again he squeezed Felipe's hand.

"You're fierce," Felipe said. "All *books* should be so lucky, to have a strong gargoyle like you."

He smiled without joy.

Feetmeat's chest tightened, and tears burned his eyes as he thought of the gnarled stone creatures with their snaggle-teeth and bulging eyes. He should have known better than to let himself hope. He turned, because he would rather leave Felipe now, before he saw him cry.

Felipe suddenly went to one knee, so they were eye to eye. He grabbed Feetmeat's hand again, with both his own, and held him in place. "You misunderstand me," he said. "You know why the gargoyles are there?"

To scare away pigeons and rats, Feetmeat thought, but he only shook his head.

"Historically, gargoyles are placed as guardians. They chase away evil. You did that, today, and if I heard right, you've done it before. So yes, maybe you're not shaped as men expect to see; but every part of you is only mismatched so that you're the size and shape you need to be who you are. Behind those beautiful green eyes, you are as tough as stone."

Felipe smiled and pulled one hand away, revealing Feetmeat's callused palm. "Tough as stone doesn't mean it can't be a beautiful sculpture."

For long seconds, Feetmeat tried to enjoy this moment. Instead he panicked, knowing that somehow this would end. Nothing good lasted — not for long. Not for Feetmeat.

He remembered the ghost in the attic of the Shadow Tower, the only one of the school's five towers which was short enough that he had been able to climb all the way to the roof. This dead girl had been blonde, with prevalent freckles made even darker by death. Her ghost hadn't looked out the window, but had instead gazed at her desiccated body, curled like a spider in the corner where she'd slit her wrists. Her cavernous eyes swallowed the sorrow of her own death for such a long time that Feetmeat had fallen asleep against the glass as he watched her.

He thought of Felipe with hole eyes, with his long graceful fingers frayed into smoke at the first knuckles, staring at his own open chest cavity on a forgotten landing in a disused stairwell — or of his body smashed against the rocks below, his ghost flown away so that Feetmeat couldn't even have that much of him. Felipe was right. The Court would get to him, one way or the other.

They were the thing that would ruin this moment, that could flay the dedicated grip on his hand, that could dim these brown eyes so they no longer glowed with admiration.

"I would like to borrow your key," Feetmeat said. "I'll use it to save the books again. This time, forever."

"I owe you a favor. If it's my key, so be it," Felipe said.

"I may need more from you," Feetmeat admitted. "We may need to sacrifice the Scroll Tower's clock."

Felipe shrugged. "The worst — and only — noise in the library is the clock upon the hour."

✢✢

EACH OF THE next four nights, Feetmeat climbed the Scroll Tower in a different way, carrying a heavy coil of chain in his haversack.

The Scroll Tower's twenty-seventh story was a giant clock, floating about the twenty-sixth story, which was a solid ring of giant windows, impossible to climb. This glass level was held aloft by a circle of languid, willowy caryatides on the twenty-fifth story. Each of them held a vase, lyre, or switch in one hand, the other above her head to support the windows.

Feetmeat wired the chains among the feet of the caryatides into a safety net wide enough to support all of the Court. If anyone noticed the chains during the day, no matter — they wouldn't be there long.

On Jovis, the night before he was to guide the Court up to the ring of caryatides, he used Felipe's key and climbed the stairs inside the tower. After hours of wrestling with steps built for a different shape of legs, lugging a sackful of tools pilfered from the gardener's shed, he finally emerged inside the giant clock. It faced north, toward the Teeth Tower, where the lectures were attended.

He finished just before dawn.

When the clock next struck midnight, the hour hand would wind up the last of the rope, and the rope would pull the holding pin, and The Court would be cinched into a net of chains. Feetmeat didn't look forward to what he had to do — in fact, he wasn't entirely sure he could do it — because taking care of evil was an evil in itself.

But he knew what was required of a protector, and if he was also caught in the net, he was prepared to burn himself as well.

✠

WHEN FEETMEAT THUMPED down onto the roof of the toolshed where he lived, he barely had the strength to swing into the loft window and land on his bed. He still had work to do, however. When his hands regained their strength, he penned a note to Felipe. He stuck the key to it with grey wax, made from stolen candle ends.

"Yours in flesh and heart," he signed, and below that, in lieu of a name, he wrote simply, "Not Yet."

He crept into the vestibule of the dormitory and placed the missive in Felipe's box. Now that he knew his love's name, if he survived, he could write more letters.

Maybe he would write entire books.

✠

KING, GENEVIEVE, BESTRA and Bulgar arrived late, nearly an hour past dusk.

"We must hurry," Feetmeat whispered. "If we're to climb all the way to the great windows, we'll need time."

"Relax, Feetmeat," said King. "We're faster than you think. After all, we can use our legs." Genevieve tittered. Bestra and Bulgar waited for orders from King, as always. And the clock on the Scroll Tower struck nine.

Feetmeat began dragging supplies from the bushes. Pails with tin lids, brushes and palm-sized sacks of powder. He gestured to their clothing.

"The moonlight is already against us — tar your clothes, that we might pass the sentinels in peace."

"Sentinels?" King scoffed. "What sentinels?"

"I said I would take you where you'd never gone," Feetmeat said, his heart thumping. Tar was more flammable than their clothes. "If you want to reach the caryatides, and paint the windows they hold, you'll find it takes more cunning than throwing a rope around a gargoyle's horns and scrabbling up."

"I'll do no such thing. The Admins are all asleep anyway, and even if they woke up, who cares if they see us?" King said.

Feetmeat still had a flask of turpentine to pour on them, once they were trussed into the chains, and that would have to be enough. Perhaps it was best that they delay no longer — they still had several gardens to traverse before they reached the foot of the tower.

"Fine, then let's hurry," Feetmeat urged.

"Bulgar, he's right," said King. "Carry our twisted little friend that we might make better time."

Feetmeat protested, but Bulgar leaned down and scooped him up, holding him like a babe. He didn't struggle, lest Bulgar accidentally snap his bones. The boy's breath smelled like wine and wet dog.

"Where are your stencils?" Feetmeat asked, afraid they had left them and would need to go back.

King chuckled and pointed to Genevieve. "Tonight, we need only words, and Genna has a fine hand."

"Words, to go on the library," Bestra said, as if she was explaining something profound that a mere window washer might not understand. Genevieve pinched her, and she was quiet.

Feetmeat endured the journey in silence, sick with second thoughts. They were wicked, but perhaps not evil, not enough for the cruel example he planned to make of them.

When they reached the base of the Scroll Tower, Bulgar flipped him around like a doll, one arm crossing over Feetmeat's chest and arms, the other reaching between Feetmeat's legs and roughly palpating his privates. "What would you need all this for? Seems a waste."

Feetmeat kicked as the others howled with laughter, but he couldn't get free.

"Book boys, is what he needs 'em for," Genevieve added. "Maybe they'll make little babies, little butthole babies!" Her giggles took flight like bats, shrieking up the side of the tower.

"Let me go," Feetmeat snarled.

"You couldn't keep up with us, not on the stairs," said King, and he held up something that glinted in the moonlight. A key. "Turns out another book-boy was more agreeable. So we changed our minds."

He unlocked a small side-door, and the Court filed in after him, Bulgar last.

Feetmeat's chest seized. He thought of the note he'd left Felipe that morning:

> *Your regard for me is more than I could have ever hoped, even if only as a protector. I fear the price of being a gargoyle, however, is that one must also be a monster. Perhaps you can be my friend even after I become what I must; perhaps not. We shall see what you make of me, if you meet me at the library's northern window at midnight.*

He'd intended to wave through the glass, to deal with evil the way they had in the caravan, to see if Felipe could still look at him the same afterward. Now, Felipe would walk right into the library as the Court was destroying it, and there was no doubt they would be happy to vandalize his body along with his beloved books.

Feetmeat struggled, but Bulgar wrestled him sideways, one arm still gripping his chest, pinning his hands to his sides, and one arm around his legs, so he could no longer kick.

The dark stairwell coiled like a snake. As they passed the dormitory doors on the first three floors, Feetmeat thought about screaming for help, but he knew they'd toss him down the stairs and say that's why he'd yelled. They'd make sure his neck was broken before an Administrator got close.

If he didn't come up with a plan, he would end up broken anyway. He stared at the dark wall as it passed, his stomach clenched as he bounced with Bulgar's footfalls and eternally leaned to the right as they followed the steps. He was too small, too weak.

Every four turns, a window poured harsh moonlight into the stairwell, and then they marched back into darkness. The fifth window they passed illuminated a drab ghost, her white skin clay-like in the harsh moonlight. She looked out the window, her posture haughty, uninterested in the living. The Court had no use for a dead victim when they still had a live one, so they ignored her as well. As Bulgar passed her, Feetmeat's face went through her shoulders.

Cold air burned his eyes, stung the inside of his nose, raked over his brain like a cat's claws. Her memories settled into his brain like leaves sinking into a pond. His despair grew heavier, and he tried not to think about what they might do to him, even as he remembered what some other long-ago bullies had done to her.

She'd been proud, though. She refused to give in, had thought it meant something that she never cried or begged. She endured, and then she poisoned herself.

Feetmeat would rather be alive than be proud.

He counted ten more windows, just to be sure they couldn't go down the stairs quickly. On the fifteenth floor, he pissed all over Bulgar, who predictably dropped him with a shriek of rage. Feetmeat swung out the window faster than they could grab him, trusting the tower to save him. He caught himself on a stone vine, his fingers cupped over the slick leaves, and then he climbed faster than he had in his life.

Their hooks and harnesses clacked against the stone near him as they tried to snag him. He climbed up, so it would be harder for them to swing their equipment toward him. Once they gave up and retreated to the stairs, he would climb down and wait by the fourth-story window to warn Felipe. To tattle on the Court to the Administration would be suicide — they would force Feetmeat to swallow every key they could find and then cut them all out with separate holes — but he could at least prevent them from having a human victim to go with the library.

When they disappeared back into the stairwell, their whispered curses still skittering like insects in the night air, he began his descent, only to seize in horror.

There was a small glow by one of the library windows far above him, like that of a single candle.

✠

FEETMEAT CLIMBED AT speeds he usually didn't dare. He stopped just short of true recklessness — some voice in his head reminded him that he couldn't warn Felipe if he was motionless on the ground below — but he barely paused to wipe the sweat from his hands or mentally map his hand- and foot-holds.

However fast he climbed, there was the risk that the Court would have climbed the stairs quicker.

When he arrived at the feet of the caryatides, slicked in sweat and breathing hard, he still couldn't see who was behind the glow.

He grasped the stone tunic of the nearest caryatid. The folds were smooth and he didn't have the best purchase, but it was the only way to reach the window on this side — the chain he'd left dangling from the clock was on the north face, and the stairwell went up the west, the side that faced no other buildings, only the sea.

When he reached the window, his stomach sank. He'd hoped it was a cranky Administrator who'd fallen asleep at a window desk, but of course it was Felipe, who jumped when Feetmeat knocked on the glass.

"The Court is coming," he said. Felipe shook his head, and Feetmeat said it louder. Screamed.

The glass from the windows was too thick.

Shaking, Feetmeat slipped his small knife from his belt and held it in his teeth so he could slice the pad of his index finger. Using his blood as paint, he wrote *Hide* backwards across the glass.

Recognition dawned on Felipe's features, but it was too late. He jerked his head, drawn by some commotion Feetmeat couldn't hear, and dashed off into the stacks.

"The candle!" Feetmeat yelled, but moments later, King appeared. He saw the candle first, then the message in blood on the window, then Feetmeat's face.

King's blank face stretched into its first smile. He walked off the way Felipe had gone.

Feetmeat clung to the caryatid's arm like a bug on a branch, motionless even with the predators behind glass. He could never wake an Administrator before it was too late. If he climbed his way down to the stair window and back inside, it might still be too late. Besides, he was barely four feet tall. There wasn't much he could do.

The Court punctuated his failure by returning with Felipe squirming in their midst. Bulgar and King pressed him onto the desk while Genevieve snatched up the candle. She singed his hair.

Something cool touched Feetmeat's leg, and he glanced down to find a pale hand offering him a stone jug. The caryatid looked at him with eyes as blank as King's, and though Feetmeat should have been afraid, her stone face was gentler than King's flesh.

Feetmeat grasped the jug by the handle, and she released it, placing her free hand out to form a second foot-hold. Feetmeat looked down at the other caryatides. Their faces were all turned toward him, and below them, all down the building, the gargoyles faced his direction as well, baring their teeth. One flexed its wings; another lashed its tail. They seemed to guess he was about to destroy part of their home.

"I'm sorry," he said. "If it helps, I won't last long after I do it. But the tower can be fixed, and Felipe can't."

He swung the jug and smashed it into the glass window. That drew the attention of the Court for a moment, but King narrowed his eyes and shrugged.

Feetmeat imagined King's foot connecting with his chin, knocking him out into the air, just as he knew King was imagining it. It didn't matter. He wouldn't sit here and do nothing, and he wouldn't retreat. Felipe was going to die either way; he deserved to know someone cared enough to go with him.

The stone jug shattered the window on the fourth hit. Feetmeat used it to knock aside the largest shards. Bestra, who was closest to the window, was still shaking off her shirt when Feetmeat stepped onto the shard-strewn carpet.

He swung the jug into her left knee, and the sound was quieter than the breaking window, but loud enough to hear. That one moment of triumph blossomed: if Feetmeat could just injure each of them, just slow them down, Felipe could carry him down the stairs in time to get away.

His fantasy lasted less than second before Genevieve hit him in the head with a book and dragged him across the glass by the back of his shirt. She rolled him off the sill.

The caryatid reached out with the arm that didn't hold the window, tried to catch him, but the impact was too much, and her arm snapped off. Feet-meat plummeted toward the garden below, struggling to catch himself on something. He needed to get back, to distract the Court from Felipe.

His belt yanked tight around his waist. He almost vomited from the sudden squeeze, and then he was falling sideways. He opened his eyes, amazed to see tiny bits of glass falling like snow from his hair and clothes, sparkling in the moonlight.

Two stone paws hung in front of his head, their talons curled back toward him. The gargoyle that clutched his belt swung around, gently sweeping its way toward the ground.

"No," Feetmeat gasped. "Back to the window. I don't care if they kill me. I'm not leaving him."

He wasn't sure if it understood. Maybe it didn't care, and would rather have someone to clean pigeon shit from its feathers than some human it had never seen.

But after a moment of flapping in place, it banked right, then began to rise. When it swooped toward the window, Feetmeat spotted Bestra curled on the floor, clutching her knee. As soon as the gargoyle's shadow flickered over them, the others glanced out.

It swept in, its great stone wings knocking more glass from the frame, and gently placed Feetmeat on top of a standalone bookshelf. It grabbed Bestra in its hind claws and leapt off into the sky, her scream echoing back as it flew off to its perch.

Bulgar bellowed, like the camels in the caravan. He and King both let go of Felipe. Bulgar thundered toward Feetmeat, his fingers hooked like claws. Feetmeat tossed a book at him, but he didn't even notice. A dark shadow flitted across the moonlit floor once more, and this time, King grabbed the stone jug from the floor where Feetmeat had dropped it.

When the gargoyle flew in, King swung the jug, snapping off some of its feathers. It whirled on him in silent fury, even as more gargoyles crawled and flew in through the window. One by one, the Court were dragged screaming from the room.

The last gargoyle looked closely at Felipe, where he crouched motionless on the table.

"Please," Feetmeat said hoarsely. "He's my friend."

The gargoyle turned and took wing. It dipped down below the window sill.

Feetmeat clambered down off the bookshelf, suddenly aware of every place where glass had lodged in his skin. Felipe, who wore slippers, hurried off of the desk and over to Feetmeat, who sagged against the books.

"I'm sorry. Bleeding all over. And the window…. If it rains, the books will get wet," Feetmeat said, his voice as hoarse as if he'd swallowed the glass. He didn't know what else to say.

Felipe wrapped Feetmeat in his strong arms.

"How did you do that," he whispered. It didn't sound like a question.

Feetmeat shook his head. "I'm sure if the books could have, they would have defended you. It just turns out the place I belong has more teeth."

Felipe laughed, all relief and little humor. After a moment, he released Feetmeat. "Thank you," he said, but instead of getting up and leaving, he leaned toward Feetmeat once more. This time he pressed his swollen, bleeding lips against Feetmeat's. Soft but unyielding, he kissed Feetmeat until neither of their mouths tasted of blood.

"Now, whose lips are these?" Felipe asked, outlining Feetmeat's mouth with one gentle finger.

Feetmeat thought of what he'd done, of the burden he'd taken upon himself, of the friends he hadn't known he had, and most of all, the caryatides watching his combined sins and heroism with their implacable stone gaze.

"Telamon," he said. "That is my name."

READING POE

SURROUNDED
BY DEATH

Ronna Magy

I WAS brought into this life surrounded by death…a great part of my existence lived upstairs in that room. The signs were all around me: markings
on the walls from those who'd lived there before. Their names and insig-
nias etched in the stone…circles and crosses, stars and initials. Fragments of
poems. Trails they'd carved grooved like rivulets running through the floor.
Papers they'd written on, pages half-filled with writing I only later understood. Piles of notes, some neatly stacked, some folded, and some thrown
askew. All of them connected somewhere in the mind by science or illusion,
alchemy or dreams. Some spiral notebooks were there, and binders labeled
on each tab subject-by-subject: life, the afterlife, suicide, murder, poison,
torture, suffocation, drowning, and sin. Faded brown accordion folders with
sheets organized in one order or another, and piles of books. Books in boxes,
hardback books, paperbacks, all about what happens when someone dies.
And some odd stones, several bricks, scraps of brass and iron, tins of plaster,
pieces of glass, and tools strewn in a corner. Dusty chains shadowing the
ceiling.

On days when the afternoon light filtered through the windows of my
room and the sun's rays reflected on the raised letters of blue or gold in the
titles, my young, fascinated mind was drawn into the books. My mother

often read them to me — stories about the mysteries at the end of life just before death. And sometimes she'd recite a writer's last known words.

I wasn't confined there, but all my life seems to have been lived upstairs in that room. Everything I needed was there. Mom brought me meals between those walls, taught me to read there, and explained that death was what a person experienced when the body ceased to breathe and the spirit passed on. A home where the soul lived when the body departed and was put in the ground. A place of limbo where the soul remained after leaving its earthly form.

Sometimes children came to visit me there, like a friend I had for a while, Susan. We used to talk and play together up there in my room. Child talk of fairies and witches, ghosts and goblins, princesses and kings. What we wanted to be when we grew up. Fantasy dreams of life after death. We'd play together amongst the bricks and stones. Building them into castle towers and walls. But then, Susan stopped coming, I never saw her again. I don't know why. She seemed to somehow just disappear. One day I asked mom where Susan went and when she'd come back. Perhaps you know where she is now? My mother told me she'd just gone away.

I lived in that room surrounded by death.

In that room, mom and I read through the scary passages of *Hansel and Gretel*, who fought off being eaten by the witch of the forest, *The Count of Monte Cristo*, where prisoners trapped in a dungeon inscribed their words in the stone, and *Lord of the Flies*, where boys killed each other off. Mom taught me the ways of life and the endings in death. She explained the ways of the mind and the ways of the flesh. What happens when people are abandoned and lost. The savageries of people trapped and confined.

Poe's *The Casque of Amontillado* was one of my mother's favorite stories. Here it is, open beside me as I tell you this. Page 216 of *Godey's Lady's Book*. Mom hasn't been on this side of the wall for a day or two now. At first, there were the soft noises of her tapping on the wall. I can't hear those sounds much anymore. Every once in awhile I hear something like a knock. I hid her behind the stone wall I made a few days ago, like Poe did in his story. Perhaps she'll come back. What do you think? I gave her a tablet to write on, a pen, and a few pebbles.

She may want to make notes on the pages, carve inscriptions on that side of the wall, or groove her initials deep in the floor. One never knows the trails made by the dead.

THE BELLS

Chip Livingston

this was it   logic presenting itself
eleventh grade Mrs. Wills' English class
Poe's perfect path   my entrepreneurial thought

a transfer student with muscles of Olympian divers
rite's passage and a lighthouse vow
"best friends digest rare conditions"

including this eclipse-brought revelation
the Baptist bodybuilder at sixteen iridescent
our homework excuse a pep rally party

one of us would have to stay over
rattling a nervous mother   suspicious
of the rhythmic thumps against the paneled walls

of the light within light   of the bells
bells bells bells bells

THE DEMON
AND THE DOVE

Collin Kelley

I F you say *Annabel Lee* three times while looking in a mirror, the maiden herself appears, reanimated dust and bone with seaweed hair, called forth from her sepulcher to drown you in your bathroom. The demon fills your lungs with saltwater until you're flopping like a fish on the tiles.

I wished this on many a kid as they recited Poe's final poem by heart for a prize. From the wings, I minced and mimicked, silently flipped them off, cursing Edgar for bequeathing this simpering, sorta-ballad on the world. There's no middle ground with Annabel — she's either a monotone dirge or overwrought declaration. It should be stricken off, banned from future butchery. Quoth the emcee…nevermore!

Then another fair lady whirls out of the darkness, a raven of skirts and shawls — the spotlight catches her tambourine. Her red lips part, a husky voice sings…*for the moon never beams without bringing me dreams.* O, Stevie Nicks, you white-winged dove, you Welsh witch, you sprinkler of faerie dust. You, and only you, could rescue Annabel Lee. You wrote music for the poem at seventeen, sitting in a pink bedroom, besotted with longing and romance. Before the waitress gigs, before cleaning offices, before Lindsey told you to go your own way. You record it forty years later for an album called *In Your*

Dreams, which is where the possibility of me ever loving Annabel Lee again resided for many a year it seems.

Now, whenever a kid approaches the mic — stuttering and bespeckled or overconfident overachiever — and begins to recite the old warhorse, I hear Stevie in my head, picture her tottering on platform boots, know that she is far wiser than me. She has worked her magic, and I find myself, once again, in love with the beautiful Annabel Lee.

THE DEATH OF BEAUTIFUL MEN

Jeff Mann

For years I've sought you, fellow Virginian,
literary kin, in places you once knew,
historic spaces memorializing your name:

your mother's grave in St. John's churchyard;
West Range Number Thirteen, the room
assigned to you during that brief stint

as a student at UVA, where you broke up
and burnt your furniture for warmth; your statue atop
Richmond's Capitol Hill; the Old Stone House

Poe Museum, prized relics of your walking
stick and a snipped lock of hair; Hiram
Haines' Coffee House in Petersburg,

where you and Virginia Clemm spent your honey-
moon; and finally, in Baltimore, that ornate
tomb set over your soil-shrouded corpse,

the sculpture's every niche wedged with coins
left by the superstitious and the admiring.
I designate Beauty as the province of the poem,

you proclaimed, and Melancholy *the most*
legitimate of all the poetical tones.
How lovely they were to you, those emaciate maidens,

hyacinthine Ligeia wasting away,
pallid Madeline Usher too early entombed.
You mourned by the vault of Ulalume when the leaves

were ashen and sere; you lay down by the side of your bride
Annabel Lee in her sepulchre there by the sounding
sea; you sought surcease of sorrow for the lost

Lenore, by a black-plumed demon denied
nepenthe. *The death, then, of a beautiful woman is,*
unquestionably, the most poetical topic

in the world, you conclude. I fear, darksome brother,
against this aesthetic definition I must
demur. Who knows what god or Weird decides

where or when a man finds beauty?
For you, those fragile ladies — neurasthenic,
consumptive, most bewitching in their vanishing.

For myself, the virile, heroic, manly. Here,
the death of beautiful men.
                                   Magnificent
Hector, stabbed through the neck, slumps and gasps.

Dying, he knows all he loves will fall
through his failure. Dead, his body's dragged
across the plain, sprawling useless in the dust.

Blood stains the unmoving swell of his chest,
the sticky thicket of his beard. Here, the scruffy
King of the Jews, roped to a pillar and flogged,

bare and sweaty flank spear-pierced,
left to sag upon the killing tree.
Here, Ashby, leading Confederate cavalry,

musket-shot through the heart, scarlet welling
from his tautly muscled torso like hot springs
through hirsute grass. Or your hometown, Richmond,

whose fall you were spared by early death. Sixteen
years after they found you dying on the streets
of Baltimore, the city writhed in flame, the Yanks

ripped down from the Capitol the Stars and Bars,
hoisted up the Stars and Stripes. Here's
one of the South's last defenders — a dark-

bearded soldier of twenty, belly slit
at Petersburg by a Northern bullet only
a week before four years of war

are fated to end — panting pained breaths
in Chimborazo's musty hospital ward.
No one knows his name, no one loves him

here but I. The boy's baby-faced,
eyes lustrous with delirium. I brush mussed
bangs from his fever-hot brow, tip

a cup of water to his lips. He's shirtless,
thick black chest hair glistening
with sweat. Resting a hand upon his breast,

I mark how his heart's elegiac tide recedes.

I stroke his cheek, clasp his callused hand,
lie by his side, easing him into merciful sleep.

Tomorrow's prayer and shoveled soil. Poe,
we know the poet's perverse fate and cost —
our love's most ardent for what's irretrievably lost.

EUREKA!

Nick Mamatas

※

A DAM hadn't worn the crushed velvet blouse in his hands for a long time. It was from his goth phase, twenty pounds and twenty years prior. He shuddered at the thought of it distending around his spare tire these days, but he couldn't bring himself to put it in the box he'd set aside for Out of the Closet either. And not only because it would be embarrassing if anyone saw it.

There were memories in the wrinkles of the velvet — well, not memories exactly. Half-memories, images and glimpses and smells. Two decades of gimlets and bad decisions and a few teeth and a trio of cross-country moves. What was the place? It was Huggy Bear's on Thursdays, when they played disco for a majority black clientele, but on most nights it was just The Bank. A real bank, in the sepia-toned days when great-grandma worked in an Orchard Street sweatshop, a goth/darkwave club now.

No, not now. *Then*. Then Adam was just another baby bat, because eyeliner and bad music is what nerds thought cool was. And everyone in New York's goth scene was at least bi, or at least self-identified as bi despite never sucking a cock or doing more than kissing another girl on the dance floor. So it was something to do.

Was it New Year's Eve? Couldn't have been…no, it *must* have been. What was his name? Adam remembered everything about the man from Poe's house, how he kissed with his eyes wide open and searching, his snickering during the long subway trip up to the Bronx, how his breath somehow didn't steam out of his mouth on the walk through the park, but what the hell was his name? Something old. Maybe Josef with an *f* but it's not like Adam asked for an ID or saw a pile of junk mail for the park ranger on the old cottage's stoop.

"I need your assistance," Josef — that was good enough a guess for now — had said. He was tall and dark and thin and shined somehow under the lights of the nightclub, like a crane that had pulled itself out of an oil spill.

"Hmm," Adam said, his lip still on the rim of his glass.

Josef leaned in and shouted into Adam's ear to be heard over the music. "I've seen you here before. I want you come home with me. I've met many people in my time in this city. To put it delicately, I've seen the inside of many tastefully decorated apartments." His breath smelled of cloves, which Adam liked then, and still liked now. Now, in the present, he brought the shirt to his face and hunted for a whiff. Nothing but dust and the scent of cardboard.

That night, Adam felt sweaty, very suddenly, and itchy. But he stood on his toes and, for a moment concerned about his own breath, shouted back, "You sound like a serial killer. It's not as enticing as you think!"

Josef laughed, and Adam was relieved that it was a human laugh, complete with a smile you might see on television. So many goths were so affected that you never got to meet the fleshy little man pulling the levers in the brain of the giant bombazine-enrobed homunculus.

Josef shouted back, "It gets better. I'm a park ranger!" He held up a long finger and dug into his pocket for his wallet, then flashed his work ID. Adam snatched the whole wallet from Josef's hand and waited for one of the stage lights to spiral around to the edge of the bar where he and Josef stood. The light flashed and in those two seconds, the NYC identification card sure looked authentic.

Of course, the ID! Adam thought as he struggled with a packing-tape gun. But he was only sure for a moment. *I didn't ask, he offered it! Was that the name on the ID, or did I put it on the ID now, myself, through the act of trying to remember…?* He sealed the box of cast-off clothes shut.

Adam handed the wallet back. "You don't look like a park ranger," he said.

"I wear black leather knee-shorts in the summer, and a velvet kerchief," Josef said. That jack-o-lantern smile again.

In the now, Adam turned to his bureau and to the small hand mirror balanced between its top and the wall. He tried to mimic Josef's smile. Nope, still too fat. Christ, did he get old, just over the last few days it felt like.

Josef was a very special park ranger. He said he was the sort of park ranger he knew Adam would like. Josef was in charge of the Poe house, in Poe Park.

"And with what do you need my assistance?" Adam asked. He pressed his arm against Josef's arm. This was all so easy. A Christmas miracle, a week after the fact?

"Two things. The band that goes on at midnight — Creature Feature?" Josef began.

"Yes?"

"They're *terrible!*"

"I know," Adam said. "Everything is dark and terrible." He shifted away from Josef's gaze, took what he hoped was a sophisticated sip of his drink, and then added, "but those guys are truly awful. So what's the second thing?"

"I've been with many men," Josef said. "Many women. But never where I live. I've always been to their apartments, or just cruised around."

"You're back in serial killer mode!"

Josef pushed his lips against Adam's ear, so Adam could feel the words on his flesh. "I live in the Poe house."

There was packing to do. So much packing. And unpacking. Adam snorted — a flashback within a flashback? Why not? Why was he folding clothes to give away? Adam was nervous, he needed to keep his hands busy. He couldn't smoke anymore; nobody smoked anymore. So, even further back, into the era from which he had kept no clothes. High school Adam was just another suburban brat in Dockers and polo shirts. He didn't read, he let MTV choose his music — and this was before Nirvana, when *120 Minutes* was on too late to watch regularly. But Poe, in tenth grade, changed everything. Weird little stories that barely seemed to be in English, and in them anything could happen. A slow and careful murder with no hero to save the day. A detective that solves a crime, but with no sense of justice. "You can't send an ape to prison, and even if you could it wouldn't mean much more to the ape than a zoo" — Adam actually wrote that on the essay exam for "The Murders in the Rue Morgue" and enjoyed a rare 99+ from Mr. Goldstein.

And that was that. Adam would be a writer, though he knew better than to tell anyone, or to even engage in any writing. Even diaries could be discovered. Adam would keep it all in his head. He'd be an English teacher, and he'd study in the city, at Eugene Lang, to get away from his parents and experience a little bit of life during the week before taking the Metro North back up to Danbury with a load of laundry. Then he found the goth scene, and made a point of keeping his stranger garments back in the dorm, stuffed under the bunk.

It would have been too perfect for the old Poe paperback to be at the bottom of Adam's closet now, as he packed his little room on a sunny North Beach day. The complete works, which he never made it through, were on his smartphone anyway. Came bundled with the e-reader. The towel Adam has been using as a curtain was already packed, and it was hard to read off the phone screen with the sun's rays coming through the window unimpeded. Only a few more boxes left.

Adam was a naïf back then — he had heard of the Poe House that NYU owned, and figured that the subway ride from the Lower East Side to the border of the West Village would be short and convenient in the snowy night. Clearly, Josef was somehow responsible for Washington Square Park. Cleaning up the syringes, or polishing the cement chessboard tables or something. City work, union work. It's all supposed to be money for nothing. But at West 4th, Josef led him on to the D train.

"Now you'll discover my problem," Josef said, snickering. The train was packed with drunks. Mostly lots of Long Island girls with high hair and wobbly heels and their fat Italian boyfriends with rings the size of human eyes yelping and guffawing their way to Times Square, but there were a selection of quieter locals lolling about in the seats. Josef hugged one of the poles for straphangers and shouted in Adam's ear. "The Poe Cottage is in the Bronx." All the blood left Adam's face that moment and Josef smiled. "That's right," he said.

"I...don't mind," Adam shouted back. He tried to smile, but his lips felt blue and dead. He'd never been to the Bronx. Had never met anyone from the Bronx. It was a strange little island — no, it was the only part of New York City that *wasn't* an island, the Bronx really was part of mainland America — that so far as Adam knew was comprised of one hundred percent raging crack addicts and black street gangs who breakdanced on flattened cardboard boxes all day and mugged old ladies at night.

Adam sucked on his teeth now, thinking of his old idiocy. College and moving to the West Coast had beaten most of the casual racism out of him, and that was a good thing. "But all I got in exchange was guilt," he said, aloud, to himself. Then he huffed and returned to sorting the socks with holes in them from the socks without holes in them.

"What's your favorite Poe?" Adam had asked Josef that night. He almost said, *Mine's "The Masque of the Red Death,"* but didn't want to sound stupid and obvious, so he said nothing more.

"*Eureka!*" Josef yelled, but nobody turned. "I design to speak of the Physical, Metaphysical and Mathematical," he said, each adjective louder than the last. "Of the Material and Spiritual Universe: — of its Essence, its Origin, its Creation, its Present Condition and its Destiny."

"Oh," Adam said.

Josef smiled and leaned down and brushed his lips against Adam's. Adam waited for someone to scream *Fags!* or just for a knife in the kidney, but neither was forthcoming.

"It's okay; it's not on the usual syllabi," Josef said, keeping his mouth close and voice down. The train had stopped at 42nd Street, and let out a bunch of confused bridge and tunnelers who didn't know how far Times Square was from Bryant Park, so the car was a bit quieter now.

"Poe called it a prose poem, but it's not really poetic. It's essentially a lecture about the creation of the universe. He basically predicted the Big Bang theory."

"Okay," Adam said. He wanted to get off the train and go home. *And do what?* This was his first time staying in the city instead of watching the ball drop on TV with his grandmother.

"Let us conceive the Particle, then, to be only not totally exhausted by diffusion into Space. From the one Particle, as a centre, let us suppose to be irradiated spherically — in all directions — to immeasurable but still to definite distances in the previously vacant space — a certain inexpressibly great yet limited number of unimaginably yet not infinitely minute atoms," Josef recited, smiling and pleased. He drew himself up to his full height, leaving Adam to contemplate the nipples visible through his black mesh. Those would need to be warmed up later, Adam decided, with his very own tongue.

"Previously vacant space," Adam repeated. "That doesn't really sound like the Big Bang theory to me." Josef frowned, so Adam quickly added, "But not bad for a poet from the 1840s. Sheer literary insight, and he almost got it right."

"No," Josef said. "He got it all right. It's the modern world that's got it all wrong. You'll see."

Adam wasn't quite sure at what stop it happened, but at some point he and Josef became the only two white people in the train car. They'd passed through some sort of racist mesh, a geographical sieve. He hoped he would see everything Josef had to offer. It had better be worth it.

It was nearly two a.m. when Josef led Adam up to Kingsbridge and the Grand Concourse. Adam heard the voice of his old grandmother saying how nice everything in the city used to be before *those* people started moving in. It was depressing now, but not dangerous. Just dead. Everyone had watched the ball drop on their shitty little televisions, then turned off the lights and went to bed. Josef walked quickly, with determination, a prize tropical bird again.

"Do you like Public Enemy?" Josef said, seemingly out of nowhere. Adam walked through a puff of his own steaming breath, to catch up.

"What?"

"You know. 'Fight the Power.' Chuck D and Flavor Flav? I saw them a couple of years ago, with Sisters of Mercy."

"Oh, no," Adam said. He'd been in high school a couple of years ago, and only knew what little Sisters of Mercy MTV played. "I missed that show."

"It was great. Gang of Four opened — old school punk, that is. And nobody came; Radio City was practically empty, just like the streets up here are tonight. That's what reminded me," Josef said. He wrapped his arms around himself and shivered, finally playing human again for a moment. "I got a great t-shirt. It says, IT'S A BLACK THING. YOU WOULDN'T UNDERSTAND. I should have worn it tonight. I'm freezing my tits off." Josef ran his palm over Adam's velvet top. "You're a smart lad," he said.

Adam was smart enough not to ask how Josef actually lived in a tourist attraction. Did he stow everything in a closet, or have to take all his meals out? Poe Park was small, but bright thanks to the blanket of diamond snow on the ground. A stone tablet on the walkway read EUREKA! and went without snow. There was probably something with the relative temperature of the tablet versus the modern concrete Adam thought, then he realized that everything he'd been thinking — the fear, the trivia, had all been to put aside his wonder and craving for the taste of Josef's cock.

The cottage itself was a small little two-story number with a porch. It wouldn't have been out of place in Danbury, with some old cat lady or poor family with seven kids stuffed into it. Josef trotted ahead again and waved Adam around the corner. "The digs are in the basement. You can see my problem, yes? I made a New Year's resolution to have sex in my own bed, in my own place, sometime this year."

"Well, it's already next year," Adam said. He flashed a crooked smile and pointed to his watch. "See?"

"Oh, in that case you'd better just get back on the train and go home." Josef stood straight as a rod and waited. Adam puffed out a breath and smiled. Then Josef smiled back. They tumbled joyfully down the concrete steps and into the cramped studio.

Josef's hair was long and chaotically spiked. One of the wayward points practically scraped against the low ceiling. There were milk crates stuffed with books and CDs along one wall, a futon on the other, and a laptop blinking away in the corner. No real kitchen, but there was a sink and a hot plate and a microwave and a coffee maker. Not much closet space either, if the puddles of black clothing on the floor were anything to go by. It smelled a little moldy, a little tangy, like old sex.

Even now, Adam can taste the next morning's coffee on his tongue. Part of why he had moved to North Beach was that one of the little Italian dives served coffee that almost tasted like Josef's.

Josef ran his hand along one of the walls. "The cottage was originally down the block," he explained, suddenly professional. "It was moved here when the subway came in. This basement is modern, and serves as the foundation for the cottage in its new location right over our heads. Had it been a nineteenth century basement, the walls likely would have been of hewn stone, plastered over..." He trailed off, seemingly unsure of what to do next.

Adam walked right up to him. "You're a park ranger, not a serial killer. I believe you. Kiss me, stupid," he said, and Josef did indeed kiss him stupid, sucking on Adam's tongue softly, like it was a half-hard cock.

The basement was cold, and the boys were cold too—their limbs were more like a quartet of icicles looking to melt than anything else. The winter had never left Adam's bones, not even after fifteen years in California. He shivered in the middle of his empty room, only now realizing how closely he had arranged its layout to match Josef's basement studio. Back in 1993, belts slid off, knees all pointy and white rose up, and Adam buried himself in Josef's lap, mouth open wide.

Josef leaned back and muttered something. First it was the usual — *good boy, my little facecunt, more more.*

Then, something odd. "Especially attractive Adam…"

No. *Especially attractive atom.*

Then some more muttering Adam didn't catch, as he was busy trying not to use his hands on Josef's cock, but just his mouth and lips and tongue and jaw. "I propose," Josef said turned on to his side, his fingers seeking out the crack of Adam's ass as he said the words.

Adam jerked upright. "Wait, what?" He smacked Josef's hand away. "What?"

If I propose to ascertain the influence of one mote in a sunbeam upon its neighboring mote, I cannot accomplish my purpose without first counting and weighing all the atoms in the Universe and defining the precise positions of all at one particular moment. If I venture to displace, by even the billionth part of an inch, the microscopical speck of dust which lies now upon the point of my finger, what is the character of that act upon which I have adventured?

Adam looked at the boxes on the floor of his bedsit. Seven to keep, three to donate, one just to fling out the window, but he didn't have the balls for that. San Francisco wasn't that kind of place anymore. The Imp of the Perverse had left the world, it seemed. It was a small life he had. That was the character of the act upon which he had adventured, Adam realized.

Josef was stronger than he looked. He had a wiry strength to him, arms like rebar. But his face was suddenly soft, so soft, like a child. Like Poe's little virgin wife, Adam thought, dying of consumption. "Please don't tell me to stop," Josef said, practically whimpering. "Please don't." He kissed Adam's shoulder, took his cock in one hand and pumped a finger into Adam's ass with another. "Please don't tell me to stop."

Adam didn't say anything. It was dark in the basement — everything was black on black, and when he turned his head he couldn't even see the little green light from Josef's computer. He couldn't see the white knuckles wrapped around his dick, or the edge of the wall, or anything. The world fell away from Adam, and the dark grew ever longer in every direction.

The futon was gone.

No. Adam's legs were gone, his thighs were. The world was gone. Adam was a point, floating in infinite black space.

No. Not space either. *The previous vacancy.* Adam was terrified — the little ripple in the velvet of the night that he was quivered, and the universe shook with him. Then he sensed them. The other men. The men that Josef had brought down here. The man that had brought Josef down here for the first time to suck and fuck, years prior. Decades of men, with thick hands and huge round shoulders. Little men, willowy like girls, their fingers tracing at what were once the borders of his body. Toothless grins and soft soft gums around his cock. Terrible bloodshot eyes, the pressure of blood pushing through the capillaries. Then the man himself, with his head huge like a white pumpkins, scrounging for winter roots in the field across from his home, and finding only the previous vacancy in the dirt between his desperate fingers. Adam could eat that agony, feed off it for years. And before Poe, men in wigs, then breeches. Brown men with smooth chests and nipples like chestnuts. And before them, men of vintages of yet unknown, or types that could never be forced to fit into the taxonomies of the species. Adam didn't see them, he wore them like a snake slithering back into a strange discarded skin.

Thus, according to the schools, I prove nothing.

Adam gulped something older than air. But he could feel his tongue again, his teeth, and Josef's as well.

There is no mathematical demonstration which Could bring the least additional True proof of the great Truth which I have advanced — the truth of Original Unity as the source — as the principle of the Universal Phaenomena.

Somewhere, miles and eons south of his brain, Adam felt his body experiencing an orgasm. It was distant and remote, like listening to a tinny radio through a closed door.

I am not so sure that my heart beats and that my soul lives: — of the rising of to-morrow's sun

And he was cold again. Bare feet on concrete and scraps of cloth.

I do not pretend to be one thousandth part as sure — as I am of the irretrievably by-gone Fact that All Things and All Thoughts of Things, with all their ineffable Multiplicity of Relation, sprang at once into being from the primordial and irrelative One.

"Do you see?" Josef said. "Did you see it?" Only now was steam coming from his mouth as he spoke. He nestled closer to Adam and asked again, and again. "It's us. It's the whole world. Created from one, not two. Just one. We are all that we ever need, see? Did you see?"

Adam said the worst kind of truth — the literal sort of truth that burns hotter than the worst of lies. "I didn't see anything."

Josef pulled himself away, sticky crotch peeling from sticky crotch, and hugged himself on the far side of the futon. "I'm not sure I believe you, but I know what you mean," he said. "Well, think about it."

Adam did, all night, not sleeping, trying to listen for Josef's breathing, trying to hear the sunrise and the morning frost melt in the grasses over his head. When Josef finally woke up, he was reasonably chatty in the way a goth boy would be. He asked after Adam's dreams and if they had been twisted and nightmarish. Adam had none he remembered. Josef then made coffee, followed by apologies for having no cream for it.

He smoked a clove cigarette — the smell filled the little room instantly — and nudged at his clothing with a precise and subtle foot when trying to decide what to wear for the day. "New Year's Day. The cottage is closed, so I can wear black on the outside." Adam wanted those toes jammed down his mouth. "The way I feel on the inside!" Josef finished, then guffawed loudly at himself like a cartoon donkey. Adam drank his coffee and realized that he didn't have to make excuses for an early exit. The cup in his hands was a farewell.

One of the local homeless guys hooted as Adam shouldered the last of his boxes into the hatch of his Zip Car.

"Yo, they rent out your room yet?" he asked.

"Of course they did!" Adam said, louder and angrier than he wanted, but he didn't turn around. "It's the Bay Area."

"Where you going off too?"

"Storage warehouse in Oakland."

"And after that?"

Adam did turn around at that question. He didn't even recognize the guy, and he thought he knew all the homeless guys and all the SRO bottom-feeders on the block. North Beach was no Castro, not with the families grazing at the restaurants and the straight strip joints, but the neighborhood was still *pretty* cruisy. "The airport," he said. "One way trip, for the time being at least."

"Going to New York or somethin'? You sound like a New Yorker?" the guy said. He scratched at his balls absently through his ruined jeans. "Stawrije wear-haus" he said. "That's Noo Yawk."

No, that's not it. Never New York. Never ever. Adam walked around the car, got in, started the ignition, rolled down the window, pulled out of the parking lot, looked at the homeless guy — whose hand was still on his own crotch — and said, "Connecticut, sorry. My mother is getting old. I have to care for her."

"You *are* sorry," the homeless guy said. He smiled, planted his free hand on the car door, and showed off three teeth.

"I am sorry," Adam said. He thought about swinging the door open hard and getting rid of the guy that way. But he didn't do anything.

"I know you is," the guy said. "Just remember..." He stopped to chew on his furry bottom lip. "Uh...that the sense of individual identity will be gradually merged in the general consciousness."

"*What!*"

The homeless guy opened his mouth again, his voice loud and strange. "That Man, for example, ceasing imperceptibly to feel himself Man, will at length attain that awfully triumphant epoch when he shall recognize his existence as that of Jehovah!"

Adam stared at the homeless guy, his eyes wide. The homeless man was as surprised as anyone else. Behind them, someone impatiently honked their car horn, so Adam revved the engine and when the homeless guy lifted his hand Adam slid the car easily into traffic. It didn't even occur to him until an hour later, when he was standing in the security line at Oakland International, that he could have said something to that homeless guy. Something like, *I bet you say that to all the boys.*

SEVEN DAYS OF POE

Richard Bowes

MONDAY

*I had been passing alone on horseback, through a singularly dreary tract
of land and at length found myself as the shades of the evening drew on,
within view of the melancholy House of Usher.*

I READ those lines for the first time in the stacks of the Boston Public
Library on a summer day in 1960 when I was sixteen. Sunlight came
through skylights and I sat cross legged in what someone would later tell
me was a yoga pose.

The book was *Terror by Poe*, a slim popular paperback at a time when even
straight boys still read stuff like this and Poe was kind of hip. I had seen the
movie *Usher* with Vincent Price lisping madly.

Life for a gay kid fifty-plus years ago was a series of half open doors, whispered secrets, stories you had to find within the stories everyone else told
each other.

Edgar Allan Poe was part of this. Price's campy performance introduced
me to the suspicion that Poe spoke to queers. And a narrator going to visit a
childhood friend of whom he says, "*Although as boys we had been even intimate
associates...*" had to be talking about something beyond friendship.

So involved was I in the tale that a voice whispering in my ear, "We have put her living in the tomb!" made me drop the book and half jump to my feet. I'd just read those words!

It was Charlie Gains, the stacks supervisor; tall, queer, dressed in sneakers and chinos like he was one of us stacks kids but old, twenty-seven he'd told me.

"Richie, your break is long over. There are trucks of books waiting down in Sorting." Gentle reminders: Charlie never ordered anyone around.

My trips to the Sorting Room always included a detour out of the stacks and into the public areas of the Copley Square Library. The building was a classic Italian palazzo, an ornate, impractical anomaly way more alien in that northern city than the House of Usher in its bleak landscape.

Down the marble stairs I trotted. Overhead lighted glass chandeliers shone. High on the walls were John Singer Sargent murals.

I loved the grandiosity, imagined myself booted and spurred, with hair in ringlets to my shoulders and a sword at my hip. A cavalier with a secret both exciting and dangerous.

In fact, because leather shoes were too noisy, stacks kids had to wear sneakers, which were entirely unhip back then. And I was spending my summer in a short crewcut because I'd flunked French.

These were the visible aspects of my lack of cool. But this city at this time held no place for gay kids, even ones like me who somehow thought we were kind of straight. Either we got shoved into niches where we didn't quite fit or we tried to carve out ones of our own.

The nice, polite boy making deliveries for the local drugstore, the high school hall monitor, the kid who sang in the church choir, the tame-looking teen hitting the bottom of the marble library stairs in his black PF Flyer Hi-Tops and slipping through a door marked "Personnel Only," were each trying to find a way to make sense of his life in the fierce hetero world.

And any one of us could also be the kid who went by the bus station to use the men's room even when he didn't need to. And maybe that boy made it a point to walk at night past the nameless bar to try and glimpse through the darkened windows the guys he'd seen slipping in the door.

The back areas of the library were dim and dingy places. I swung down the small circular metal stairs that were like something from a submarine movie and went past the basement men's room.

The Poe book in my back pocket was pulsing against my ass. This had started a couple of days before after I'd read "The Telltale Heart," with an obsessed narrator and the corpse he murdered and concealed

True! — nervous — very dreadfully nervous I had been and am; but why will you say that I am mad?

I crossed the hall and opened a door into a large, badly lighted region. The Sorting Room lay a bit ahead, a light in the dark. Otherwise to the left and right all was black recesses — the boiler room, storage vaults. I saw nothing moving. This wasn't always so. The shadows were a meeting place.

The door of the men's room opened and closed behind me. I heard that as I took a slow, deliberate step into the dark. Then I jumped as a pair of hands had my shoulders. I turned enough to see a guy, old, grey haired but big. I nodded and found myself propelled through the door and into the dark.

Last September just after I started in the library I had seen a pair of guys disappear into the dark. In the previous couple of years I'd had enough encounters like that to know what I saw and what it meant for me. Several times since then I'd let guys lead me into these shadows.

Mostly, though, I did this at night when nobody much was around. And the guys who picked me up were nervous and jumpy. The ones that wanted kids who still looked like they were thirteen usually were. With them I could be a bit removed like this was a movie or play I was in. And I had some control over the action.

This one kept his hands on my shoulders and guided me into the darkest corner. He stuck a bill in my shirt pocket before I could even say, "Five bucks." Taking money meant you weren't queer. Everyone knew that.

I started to unzip my fly, wanting not to be too exposed. But he yanked my belt open, hauled my pants and jockeys all the way down. I heard the paperback fall on the floor. Then he had my shirt unbuttoned like he could see in the dark.

In seconds I was half naked, vulnerable if anyone really looked and the guy crouched down, grabbed my ass with both hands and pulled me towards him.

Usually I stayed mostly clothed and managed to imagine I was with some kid I'd seen on American Bandstand or some rookie just brought up by the Red Sox.

With this guy working me, all I felt was him, me in his mouth, his hands pushing me into him. The danger excited me. I was panting loudly and when I came I heard myself cry out.

As he stood he smacked my ass hard with each hand like he was spanking me. He spat into a corner and went out the door as I pulled my clothes back together in the dark.

Then I had to walk into the Sorting Room. There Eddie and Hal, two older full-time workers, straight and fat, worked without shirts in the stifling cellar, took books out of dumb waiters, off a conveyer belt, sorted and slammed them onto old wooden library trucks.

They saw me, said nothing, pointed at two loaded carts. They stared like I disgusted them. Understanding they'd heard what had happened outside and knew it had to be me, I got out of there fast.

Pushing one heavy cart, pulling the other one, I left the Sorting Room and went into the dark. I must have remembered to pick the Poe book up because I felt it beating against my butt like a pulse and thought of the line from the story:

What you mistake for madness is but over-acuteness of the senses.

Moving the trucks onto an elevator was a struggle. I wasn't a big kid. The books were for the reading rooms — the large lending library within the reference library.

Charlie was there when I hauled the trucks into this public area which had lots of people around. My shirt was out of my pants and my expression, I guess, was dazed.

Shaking his head he got me into a quiet corner and made me pull my clothes together. "Had a bit of a dizzy spell did we?" he asked in a cockney accent. "Bit of oopsy-daisy, was it?"

I caught his amusement and was horrified to realize that any queer or even any straight who knew anything could guess what I'd been up to.

But Charlie sent me up to a quiet balcony that ran around the main reading room. I straightened books, sat with my head in my hands, recovered from getting raped.

When I felt a little better I looked down and saw some of the other kids shelving and Charley standing at the information desk talking to Mrs. Lord, the boss, and a couple of the other librarians.

Charlie knew a lot for a guy who'd never quite connected with college, had never really got past being a stacks kid. The librarians were always telling him, begging him really, to go back to school. He'd just shake his head like they were asking too much, or he had something better to do.

That seemed to be what was going on. It didn't occur to me that I was the subject of conversation. When it was over, he spotted me, beckoned and I joined him in a corner.

"Feeling better?" I nodded. "Okay, I want this truck shelved before you leave." Then he said, quietly but very seriously, "No more fun in the building, understand? The vice squad has that men's room targeted. Stop squirming and looking so embarrassed; anyone seeing us is going to think I'm propositioning you."

When I signed out, instead of taking the subway home to Dorchester, I made a little detour, walked up Boylston and past the Common. I looked up and down Arlington Street to see if I could spot my friend, a kid named Ty.

I even looked into the Greyhound terminal at Park Square, taking a bit of a risk by going there. But he was nowhere to be seen and I didn't have a lot of time.

At moments like this when I couldn't find him, Ty seemed more an imaginary friend than a real one. We were Boston Irish kids, a bit undersized, looking cuter than we were, with the same brown hair and blue eyes. We seemed enough alike that I sometimes thought he was me but me without parents or school, a scary life but a tempting one.

When I finally hit the subway, I was already late. A couple of tough kids stared at me like there was going to be trouble. But they got off at Broadway in South Boston. I played a game of looking and not looking with this old guy who had combed-over hair. But I was careful after what had just happened.

Mostly I finished "The Fall of the House of Usher," read about Lady Madeline's interment, saw her with the blood on her robes, heard her brother's shrieking, "*Do I not distinguish that heavy and horrible beating of her heart?*"

Reading about the destruction of Usher, I pictured the Public Library falling down and getting sucked into the ground. Imagined standing in a suddenly desolate Copley Square.

In my neighborhood, guys my age gathered in the playground and around street corners. I'd drifted apart from them in the last couple of years. I came across not quite as a sissy but as someone whose parents ran his life too much.

The neighborhood had its sissies, boys who giggled and wore short pants to church well into their teens because their mothers insisted. I made it a point not to be seen with them.

When I got home my parents wanted to know where I'd been and why I wasn't back in time for dinner. They weren't happy with me but it seemed like they never were. They said I couldn't leave the house that night. I had no place to go.

My little brothers and sisters watched TV while I read "The Masque of the Red Death" and sympathized with Prince Prospero defying the plague, imagined myself as a reveler in the colored rooms. Then Red Death appeared at the end, "*And darkness and decay and the Red Death held illimitable dominion over all,*" and I identified with the specter and had to read it all again.

Getting undressed, I remembered to take the five dollar bill out of my shortsleeve shirt before that went in the hamper, and stick it in the book.

⊹⊹
TUESDAY

TUESDAY WAS A late day at the library. I went to work at four in the afternoon and stayed till eight. I'd told my parents that I worked until ten. In the morning I went to summer school, took French, and learned to type.

Then I came home. To please my mother I wore short pants around the house but nowhere else. To keep my tan that's all I wore as I mowed the backyard and trimmed the hedges. Then I lay in the sun reading and dreaming. Not quite a sissy.

Afterwards, I got dressed again, put on my sneakers (like T-shirts worn as outer clothing and jeans, these were forbidden in school) and went to work.

The library was full of odd legends and odder people. One of the librarians sent me on an errand and going up the main stairs I imagined myself as Prince Prospero in his palace. In a perfect coincidence I then saw the one Charlie called Red Death.

A queen with outlandish long scarlet-dyed hair, penciled eyebrows, thick makeup, given to shawls, parasols and flowing pants that could almost be dresses, he was someone with whom every man gay or straight was afraid to be seen.

And as I saw Red Death, he saw me. He'd spoken to me once before, affixed me with his bloodshot eyes, asked my name and age. One of the librarians had shooed him away.

Now he stood right in my path. "There's a legend of kidnapped children in this place," he told me. "They take boys like you, ones that can't grow up, and keep them here forever."

"It's what happened in my case," a voice said behind me. It was Charlie.

Red Death smiled. "Saving him for yourself?" he murmured. "That's *adorable*! It's his little friend I want. Or is that other one your brother?" he asked me. "A tough boy, not a fairy." Red Death must have seen me with Ty.

Charlie guided me away, shaking his head. "Sooner or later Red Death comes to each of us!" he said. Then he asked, "What friend was he talking about?"

"Just someone I know."

I shelved books, talked to one of the girl shelvers who was going to college in the fall, did odd jobs for the librarians.

Just before eight o'clock I looked up and Ty was there. Ty was a smart, cool kid who knew lots of stuff. His hair was how I wanted mine to be: combed back like a greaser but with strands flopping over his forehead. His T-shirt, pants and tie-shoes were all black.

Maybe we were similar but I was the clueless twin. I looked to make sure Red Death didn't see us as we left and walked up Boylston Street. It was sunset and lights were on in the stores.

I told him about the guy in the cellar getting rough. "You gotta carry a knife or something," he told me. "Otherwise they're gonna get you where first you do it for free and pretty soon you're doing them and you're a fucking fag."

Ty had done a stint in a halfway house and a couple of months in reform school. I still got hit at home and had been punched around a few times in gym. Ty had gone through much worse stuff.

I bought us both ice cream cones since I had that five bucks and had to spend it where my parents wouldn't see. Ty just gobbled his down and asked me for another one. His parents weren't dead but they weren't around. He was staying with some relatives. But that was it. Staying. They didn't feed him.

He mentioned wanting to get dexies and said, "First we need some money. I gotta see the Collector." I liked doing speed.

He wouldn't tell me anything about where we were going, took me to the other side of Beacon Hill near the hospital where it wasn't so nice. It was an apartment house where you had to buzz to get in.

A voice said, "Yes?"

Ty said, "It's Tom." He shrugged when I looked at him.

"Oh, Tommy!" and the buzzer sounded.

The Collector was right on the first floor at the back of the building. He was a thin guy with a grey mustache, seeming not really creepy.

Until we went in his place and all I saw was underpants. Some boxers but mostly ones like I wore and most kids did. White briefs were displayed on top of cabinets, laid out on bookshelves, hung on the walls like paintings.

"Amazing isn't it?" the collector said. "I have the shorts of half the teenage boys in Boston. What do you have for me?"

I shook my head but Ty said, "I want to sell," and pulled down his pants. He was wearing red boxers. Old guy clothes, big and flowing around him like he was wading up to his waist in blood.

The Collector looked offended. "Those aren't yours."

"I'm wearing them. What more do you want?"

"I'll only buy those if you get your friend to sell me his. Five for both of them together."

This was super creepy. "My mother may notice if they're gone." The Collector found this wonderful, I could tell.

But Ty kicked off his shoes, dropped his pants and the shorts. His t-shirt didn't cover him. I looked at his dick. He noticed and flicked it. Here we were different in a couple of ways; his was more impressive and he'd been circumcised.

He said, "Come on, do it. We got places to go."

If my mother noticed I was going to have to say I must have left them in the gym locker or something and get in trouble. I sighed deeply, untied my sneakers, kind of trembled as I pulled off my khaki chinos. You had to do this in front of the Collector.

"Oh, nice and white!" he said when he saw my undershorts, "Your mother buys Sears and Roebuck briefs. Size sixteen, boys, I'll bet." So it turned out to be when I handed them over. He gave Ty/Tom the fiver as I got dressed.

"Mine's bigger," Ty said when we were outside heading away, "even though part of mine got cut off. You need to ditch those faggot shorts. Hustlers don't use underwear. Sell them to the Collector."

"Where did you get the ones you had?" I asked, like I hadn't noticed his prick or seen him looking at mine. My balls and cock bounced around inside my pants and I kept checking to make sure my fly was zipped. Until now I hadn't been much interested in guys my own age. Mostly sex was just older guys interested in me. Now I spent a lot of time imagining myself as Ty with his hair and clothes.

"They're my aunt's boyfriend's. He's too fat and dumb to notice," he said. "Guys like you got it easy. Mother to take care of you."

We stopped and we got hamburgers at a diner, ate as we walked, shoved it in our mouths as fast as we could.

My time was running out and Ty hadn't found any dexies. We headed for the bus terminal.

At school there had been a kid in the year ahead of me who sometimes had Benzedrine. He'd gone in the navy. But over the last couple of years I'd gotten in the habit of doing speed when I could find any, which wasn't often enough. Like sex, it got me around bad days and boring adults.

And looking for drugs and sex gave me the tang of danger which was part of the excitement. Being in the bus terminal was part of that. Looking around I didn't see anyone who seemed like a cop. Ty was a step ahead of me and he saw nothing either.

The light in the restroom and in the waiting room made the people slumped on benches look like hopeless plague victims awaiting Red Death.

A bus was leaving for Worcester and the few people kind of stumbling towards it reminded me of refugees fleeing. There was one dark guy, Italian maybe, standing near the big entrance. He was there for some bad reason but not speed. Ty saw him and shook his head.

We left fast because it wasn't wise for either of us to hang around. This was where we'd met maybe a month before:

We were both loitering on a Saturday when I didn't have to work but had told my parents I did.

In vain I'd visited my usual spots for getting picked up, the Y, the far side of the Public Gardens, the bad stretch of Washington Street. Then I came here and spotted Ty.

He caught sight of me out of the corner of his eye, I could tell. Each of us, I think, recognized in the other the good-looking Boston Irish boy with the nice smile when he chose to use it.

Then I noticed a guy who spotted Ty and moved toward him grinning. As he did, Ty broke and ran out the terminal door. I was so stupid I stood staring and the vice cop turned and grabbed me. Did it very quietly and walked me out back to a parking lot.

He asked me what I was doing there. Said he could run me in. I was going to tell him I had an uncle on the force which legend had it would stop them arresting you. But he slapped me and said not to let him see me there again.

Walking away, I was scared, relieved. Looking real young was a pain sometimes if you were a kid trying to grow up but an asset at moments like this. My face stung where I'd been hit. I wondered if I should go home.

Then I saw the other kid across Arlington Street. He saw me, stood blank faced. When I stopped and looked his way he made a little gesture. I crossed the street. We introduced ourselves, told our names, where we lived. He was Charlestown, which meant hard; I was Dorchester, which was boring. Immediately I thought his hair was great, his clothes cool.

When I told him some of what had just happened Ty said, "I can't believe we're the exact same age — you're like a retard. Why didn't you run when I did?"

I couldn't stop staring at him. We were about the same height. We could have been brothers. That first time Ty and I walked together around the Common and he told me, "I'm on my last chance. One more bust and I'm going away for good."

On the night a month into our friendship, I needed to head for the subway and home. We walked down a side street past a place I'd seen before, the bar with darkened windows and shadowy guys you could glimpse slipping in the door.

It had nothing on the neon sign but the word BAR. "Queer bar," Ty said when he saw me staring.

"Guys call it the Sugar Bowl. Queens go there. We could get in, I bet. And someone will have speed."

I'd been in a queer coffee shop over on Washington Street. Kid hustlers hung out there. I was curious but I needed to get home.

Two figures crossed the street, a tall guy and what I thought at first was a woman. I looked again and saw it was a guy in a pink shirt, loose pants and sandals. He had short hair. But something about his walk, the way he leaned towards the man with him, was feminine.

The other guy was a bigger shock. I didn't know if Charlie Gains had seen me. But I saw him go in the door of the Sugar Bowl.

It was late when I waved goodnight to Ty, wanted to touch him, to hold him. "See you Thursday," he said. "We're gonna sell all your shorts."

And I went down the subway stairs at Washington Street and caught a half-empty train to Dorchester. That night, though, I paid no attention to the passengers, to the talk around me or to the lights playing on the water when we came out from under the ground at Columbia Station.

I was reading "The Cask of Amontillado" imagining myself in a red cape, black velvet doublet and hose and knee-high boots, my hair like Ty's, smiling a smile only I could see as Fortunato ran his ridiculous schemes.

When I got home it wasn't real late and I said I'd already eaten so things weren't that bad. I remembered to throw a pair of clean briefs from my drawer into the hamper.

⁜

WEDNESDAY

I SAT CROSS-LEGGED in the library stacks. aware of my cock loose in my pants, re-reading the "The Cask of Amontillado" as a succession of guys, the vice cop from the bus terminal, the man who assaulted me in the dark, assholes who'd pushed me around in the high school gym, my father, Eddie and Hal from the Sorting Room, pleaded naked and in tears, "*For God's sake, Montresor!*" And I walled them in.

Right then Charlie appeared. "Break's over, lover boy: the Lord has summoned us." I knew the Lord was Mrs. Lord, head of Public Service. But as I stood I looked at Charlie like the first part made no sense. He was smiling the same way he'd done when he saw me after I got mauled by that guy.

"Spotted you and your friend last night," he said.

"Just a kid I know. What about your friend?"

"Larry/AKA Lauren? My *roommate*?" he said turning the word over a little bit. What's your friend's name?" I told him. We descended circular metal back stairs, reached the basement and went along a dark corridor. The Sorting Room was down another passageway.

The whole place reminded me of Castle Island. Just that day I'd learned that Boston, like most East Coast cities, had a Poe connection. In this case it was the old fort on Castle Island in South Boston. Poe served there when he was in the army.

Learning this struck me as a major coincidence. I'd been inside that fort. A causeway connected the island to the mainland now. Picnic tables were set up on the grass. But the dark grey building itself, all stone and mortar, was sealed.

When I was maybe ten, I was there on a family picnic. A bunch of guys, government surveyors and engineers, had pried open one of the entrances to the fort.

I was curious and in the slaphappy way of that time and place I got to follow them and their flashlights through dark passages inside the walls. Doors were jammed closed. Rooms smelled of stale water and decay. It was scary and I was glad the guys made sure they didn't lose me.

Now in memory it felt like Usher, and Montresor's wine cellar and the basement that held a Telltale Heart all at once. And the stairs and passageways where Charlie and I had just walked could have been in Castle Island.

Ahead of us light came from a room. Mrs. Lord stood in the doorway with an expression of mild disgust. She turned, "Charles, go up and get discard tickets from Preparations — lots of them, if you would. And pens."

Charlie hesitated but went. I wondered why she hadn't sent me. Mrs. Lord didn't come up to my shoulders. She wore a dark blue jacket and skirt and a ruffled blouse. She had grey hair and in this stifling heat did not break a sweat.

She looked not at all like anyone's idea of a librarian. Mrs. Lord's husband had died long ago. He'd been the mayor's lawyer and the library job was said to be a political plum. Nobody had ever seen her read a book.

She indicated the room and its shelves crammed with volumes. "These need to be weeded out: damaged books, duplicates, things not read in twenty years, must go. Charles will show you what to do.

"He suggested you as his assistant on this project. I've seen you about and you seem a good worker. Do you plan on going to college?"

"Yes, ma'am."

She looked me in the eye. "Keep to that plan. For boys of a certain kind libraries become a trap. They lose their ambition, fall in with the wrong companions and fail to grow up."

She nodded her head in the direction of the Sorting Room. "I loathe accusations with no proof. But if someone is accused too often I must act. Understand?"

A chill ran through me. I'd been reported. "Yes, ma'am."

We heard Charlie returning. "Very good. This should take you today and tomorrow." She walked past Charlie with barely a nod.

He asked, "Did she talk to you?" I hung my head.

"I guess so." He sounded amused. "And did she tell you to go on to college — like I didn't?"

I nodded, glad to change the subject. "Why didn't you?"

"I found other things. Like Larry." I thought that over. He showed me how to make out a discard ticket, stuck it in a book and put the book on a truck.

It was hot and stuffy and there were thousands of books. He took off his shirt. "Better do this," he said. "Otherwise it'll be a stinking mess at the end of the day." He had body hair and was better built than I would have guessed.

Everyone wanted to get my clothes off me. I made a face. "I'll turn my back," he said and did. We worked on opposite sides of the room. I looked at him each time I put a book on my truck.

I had almost no body hair but I had somewhat of a tan from sunbathing and the beach. His skin was white. I started to sweat and took my shirt off.

We both turned to put books on a truck at the same time and I asked. "Why do you call him Lauren?"

He said, "I'll have to show you. Bring your boyfriend by. I'll give you the address."

Hearing Ty called my boyfriend made me feel exposed. I covered my chest with my arms like I was cold. But after a while I asked, "Why is Red Death the way he is, scary and everything?"

"When you're a queer kid and everyone hates you for stuff you can't help, you can either die or make them afraid."

Somehow being shirtless and our not looking directly at each other made it easier for me to talk. Charlie told me how Larry, his boyfriend, sang at the Sugar Bowl and how the bar's management paid off the cops.

I talked about guys who gave me money, the first time I ever told anybody. It made me feel less alone. I wished Charlie had been my big brother or older cousin or something.

At the end of the day the job was more than half done. We washed up in the restroom and got dressed. Charlie said, "I meant it about you and Ty visiting us."

++

THURSDAY
Had the routine of our life at this place been known to the world, we should have been regarded as madmen...

I'D READ "THE Murders in the Rue Morgue" before I saw Charlie and Larry/Lauren's apartment and not thought much about it. After being there, I realized the story wasn't about murder, detection, Paris and weird apes, it was about two strange men living together.

Charlie and Larry even blotted out the sunlight like Poe's narrator and the French detective had.

Made a counterfeit night until the real thing came along.

Then we sallied forth into the streets, arm and arm, continuing the topics of the day or roaming far and wide until a late hour...

Charlie and Larry lived on a shabby street near the Back Bay. Their place had drawings up on the walls of naked guys with their dicks displayed, and clothes piled on the chairs and the half-made bed. On a bookshelf was a row of wigs on stands.

Larry wore a dressing gown and selected a wig. He'd just washed his hair and I guessed he was being Lauren right then. He and she changed back and forth.

Lauren started singing "Right from the Very Start," like some night club singer. But my two musical beacons at the moment were Sam Cooke for his voice and his smile and Beethoven for the heart-thumping rhythm, so I was a little removed.

"I'm in a bad mood," Lauren said. "I need some happiness pills if I'm to perform Saturday."

Looking at Ty she said, "And I'll bet you know how to make that magic happen."

Ty smiled like he knew how.

I'd thought Larry/Lauren was going to wear the wig. Instead he leaned forward and put it on my head. It was so sudden I didn't know what had happened. Charlie stared and smiled. I put up my hands to take it off.

Larry grabbed them and was stronger than I'd imagined. "Stand up and take a look," he said.

Ty with a half grin nodded that I should do this. Charlie opened a closet door and revealed a full-length mirror. In it I saw a figure wearing my clothes. But the face framed with blond hair and looking out at me was a young girl's.

I took the wig off and no one stopped me. The kid in the mirror became a crewcut boy. But I couldn't stop seeing the girl.

It was as if Ty couldn't either. Outside, he kept looking at me like he'd never seen me before. I had to get home, was already late. We walked through the Common and when we got to the subway he said, "Meet me here, tomorrow at six. We got some business to do." He'd agreed to cop speed for Larry/Lauren. I waved, watched him turn and walk away.

A line kept popping into my head.

"Have I not indeed been living in a dream?"

I needed to sit down and read and think. I'd found out the library was Usher, discovered a book that could beat like a buried heart, a crazed queen who was Red Death, Montresor's Vault in Boston, and Charlie and Larry in the Rue Morgue.

Now I'd found Ty and me in a Poe story.

That evening, after Charlie and I finished working in the cellar, before going to his and Larry's place, I'd started to read "William Wilson." It's a story about a man haunted by his double. The difference was Wilson hates his double. I had a crush on mine so big it frightened me.

I thought about that as I walked from the subway station, thought how Ty was part of a world I could never show my family.

⊹⊹

FRIDAY

IN THE BACK of French class in summer school, on my breaks at work, I reread "William Wilson." I stood with the narrator as he looked down on his sleeping double: *"The same name! the same contour of person! the same day of arrival at the academy!"* And wondered why Wilson wanted to kill him.

At six p.m. I came out the library doors and there he was. "Hey, thought maybe you'd be wearing a dress."

"No," I said, "Just pants and no shorts the same as you."

Ty was amused. "The Collector's gonna be sad."

I'd just been paid so we got something to eat and he said over burgers and cokes, "I need you to front me ten bucks for dexies that Lauren wants. You'll get it back."

Ten dollars was a big deal in those days and would be a big chunk of the paycheck I was saving to go to college. But because it was him and because it was speed, I did it. We went to some place near Washington Street.

It was this narrow old building with kind of rickety stairs. This guy up on the third floor, real thin with intense, staring eyes, let us in.

Ralph was his name and I noticed he called Ty "Ted." "Who's this, your cousin?" he asked and looked again. "A brother?"

The place was kind of empty, a table and chairs and a bed in the next room. Not much else except that completely filling one window was this great big ancient iron birdcage with all these little sparrows chirping away inside. They had birdseed and a nest and everything.

The cage rested on the windowsill and the window was open but the cage blocked birds from flying into the room. There was this little round hole on the outer side and as I watched a sparrow flew in. They were all chattering and I saw eggs in the nest.

Ralph saw me looking at this and said, "I spend hours watching them." His voice sounded creaky like he needed to be oiled or something.

It took them a little while negotiating, but Ty (or Ted) got twenty pills for ten dollars. As that was happening, this seagull appeared in the sunset light, floated in front of the cage not able to get in.

"I had a hawk outside a couple of weeks ago. My birds all went crazy," Ralph said from behind me. All of a sudden there was one hand on the back of my neck then down my back, another touching my ass.

I jumped out of the way because you didn't let guys do that. "You should come by and watch the birds," Ralph said.

Ty told me when we were back outside, "He's talking about seeing a hawk and he's a chicken hawk! He goes for you, he'll give you speed. But the thing is you gotta go down on him. Of course, then we could sell the pills."

He gave me a couple of dexies. I put them in a pocket. Speed was better than booze, undetectable by parents. They thought I was just in a good mood when I took it. It even made it easier to study. I'd have taken it all the time if I could.

"Is Ty your real name?" I asked.

"Sure," he said and I wondered if that was true.

I took one of the pills. The other I saved for Saturday. On the train home which became this intense ride with blazing subway lights, I reread the story. The narrator wondered about his own alter ego.

Who is he? — whence came he? — and what are his objects?

I wondered the same stuff about the kid who obsessed me. That night at home there was a baby sitter who was an old family friend. She wasn't going to report me for showing up late and didn't think I needed to get told to go to bed like my brothers and sisters.

When my parents returned I pretended to be asleep. When all was quiet I looked again at the end of "William Wilson" where the narrator thinks he's killing his doppelgänger but actually kills himself.

"You have conquered, and I yield...see by this image which is thine own, how utterly thou has murdered thyself," said the bleeding double in the mirror. And I fell into the kind of red-tinged doze that passes for sleep with speed.

⁺⁺

SATURDAY

S ATURDAY WAS A day off from school, from the library. I was awake and alert and busy convincing my parents that I was going to a Boston Pops concert on the Esplanade (they were playing Beethoven's Seventh — I'd checked that out in the *Globe*) with school friends and said I'd be back before twelve.

My parents were so busy wanting me back before ten that they didn't even remember I had no school friends.

That evening I wore my best tight black chinos, my blue polo shirt with matching blue socks and dress-up loafers with taps on the heels. I took the second pill before I got on the subway.

Ty was late and I stood for a while in the evening light on Park Street with crowds walking by, guys noticing me. Dexedrine made me good at spotting that.

When I saw Ty he was on the other side of the street and I knew he'd been watching me. When he crossed, he said, "Decided to go as a guy, huh?" But I was getting tired of being reminded of how I'd worn a wig for two minutes.

Like magic, Dexies let me take long remote looks into others. The opposite of William Wilson, I stared at my double and saw ways he wasn't me. Caught the furtive look of a stray and how it seemed like maybe he'd slept in his clothes.

When we stopped so he could get something to eat, I asked for another pill and he was very reluctant. "I gotta save these for Lauren. We need to go back to the Hawk tomorrow and you need to be nice to him."

He was looking for my reaction and I knew he thought I was as queer as Larry and Red Death. And that I'd go down for dexies.

Then it was after dark and we were headed for the Sugar Bowl. I'd never been in a bar, let alone a queer one.

"I don't think we can get in."

"They'll let us in but they won't serve us," he said. "Don't worry. They'll want to see you."

As we approached, I saw guys walk down the street and suddenly turn toward the dark windows and door. A big man with a bald head stood inside the doorway. He shook his head when he saw us.

Ty told him, "Lauren said we should see her." The guy turned and shouted something. Charlie appeared, smiled at the sight of us, nodded and the guy waved us past.

It was bigger inside than I'd thought, a long bar with dim lights behind it, a jukebox playing Sinatra, some tables, a low platform at the back with a mike and a piano.

Walking behind Charlie and Ty, I felt eyes on me like every guy in the place was staring at me. I couldn't raise my eyes to look back at them.

"I said they'd like you," Ty told me.

In the back room Lauren wore the gold wig. She had big breasts and wore a red sparkling dress and gold high heels.

"I need an empty stomach to do drag," she said in a hoarse, sexy voice to a guy who turned out to be the pianist. "It is most trying. Drink just makes me dizzy. But these cherubs have brought me relief."

She went into the bathroom with Ty. Charlie put his arm around me, gave me a hug, "So glad to see you." He took me back outside. On the jukebox a woman sang "The Man That Got Away" and guys sang along.

"Friendlier than the library," Charlie said. He brought me a beer and I knew it would be on my breath unless I chewed a lot of gum but I used it to wash down the pill. This made my blood pulse and the lights brighten to pinpoints. Someone pinched my ass.

"Don't worry about it," Charlie said. "It's time you got to see all this!" Time and Space began to slip. And when Ty came back, I thought it was me sitting down. He handed me a couple of bucks and, "One last pill. We need to see the Hawk tomorrow."

"You said you'd return my money when she paid you."

He looked like he couldn't hear me. Then he handed me another dollar and said, "This is all I got." I didn't want to think of what lay in store for me at home.

The place filled up. At some point the jukebox went off and the pianist sat on stage playing.

Lauren came out and there was applause, some whistling. She started singing "Right from the Very Start" again. Charlie looked at her like he was in a dream.

"So many men here I'd *love* to start with!" Lauren said when she finished, and a couple of guys stamped and cheered. I drank the rest of the beer and washed down the pill. She sang "Moaning Low" in this weird woman's voice.

The room rotated around me. All I could see were guys' faces in the dark. Charlie had disappeared so I moved close to Ty. But he was so busy pretending not to see a guy in a suit who was staring at him that he didn't see me either.

Finally, between songs I told him, "Let's get out." And he ignored me.

My mind raced and it seemed everyone in the place was staring at us. I realized I was chanting under my breath, "Want to get out; want to get out." But somehow I couldn't leave without Ty.

Lauren was ending her act, singing pieces of songs one after another. "Dear Marlene," she'd say, and sing "See What the Boys in the Back Room Will Have." Then it was "my older sister Bette Davis," and some other song.

Right in the middle of the applause, I heard something cold and scary outside. Sirens, shouting. "*Raid!*" someone yelled and then someone else.

Charlie jumped up on stage and escorted Lauren off and into the back room. Ty moved fast. I was right behind him. We ran across the platform and into a corridor. The bathroom was on one side, the dressing room on the other.

Lauren was tearing off her dress and wig. Charlie handed her Larry's pants and shirt. A back door was open, light came in, people were pushing me from behind, someone spilled beer on my clothes, someone else shoved me aside. Cop voices were yelling and someone was screaming back in the bar.

Ty yanked me through the door. We were in an alley, light came from the street and noise, police radios. He grabbed my arm, tried to hand me a few pills. "They won't search you," he said. I didn't take them.

Then the cops were there. One of them in plain clothes had Ty by the front of his shirt and smacked him up against a wall, asked his name and address.

Another had me, a uniformed cop. "What's your name? How old are you? What were you doing in there?"

I gave my name and age and said, "Just looking. I didn't know." My cop slapped me so hard across the face that my head spun. I tasted blood in my mouth.

I heard Ty give his name as Timothy Connors. The cop who had him was holding the pills he'd tried to palm off on me and yelling, *"Where did you get these?"*

When Ty just shook his head he got punched in the stomach. He doubled over. "A guy," he said. "What guy? Where?"

The cop who held me went through my pockets, found the book and tossed it away. Took out my wallet, used his knee in my stomach to hold me still and looked at my name and address. I got the wallet back.

"I'm running you in," he said.

"Please no." I started to cry. "My uncle's a cop," I said and gave his name and precinct and my aunt's name when he asked for that to make sure.

Larry, half naked, and Charlie in handcuffs were shoved down the alley to the street. Ty was in cuffs too. "You're going to Juvie," the cop who held him said.

"You know that one?" the cop holding me asked. I shook my head and he slapped me again and hauled me down the alley.

On the street outside the Sugar Bowl, the cop cars had their lights and sirens on and there were lights on the top of a truck. Photographers from the papers were there and a TV crew.

They all caught Larry's face smeared with make-up. Charlie leaned over and kissed him. Ty was shoved in the back seat of a squad car. His eyes glistened with tears and his jaw was clenched. It was like I saw myself get arrested.

My nose was bleeding. I thought I was joining them in the light and that my life was over. But the cop said, "I'll tell your uncle about this and let him decide what he wants to do," and pushed me into the dark. "Run," he said.

‡

SUNDAY

I MOVED AS fast as I could, ran through the streets, guessing I'd never see Ty or Charlie again. Way after midnight I got the last subway train to Dorchester. People stared at my bloody nose and red eyes and torn shirt, smelled the stink of beer on me. Home was the last place I wanted to go but the only place left for me to go.

I felt the book in my back pocket and was too strung out to be surprised. I remembered a line.

"I was sick, sick unto death, with that long agony..."

The first story I'd read in the Poe book was "The Pit and Pendulum." Memories of the dark, the rats, the bottomless pit, the blade swinging ever closer had held me. That, I now realized, in the horrible clarity of a speed crash, was my special tale.

My picture wouldn't be in the paper or on TV but the story would be everywhere. Would my parents, once they'd seen me, draw the obvious conclusion? Would the cop contact my uncle? Poe's Inquisition seemed like nothing compared to what was in store for me, the humiliations and ass whipping I'd suffer, the rights I'd lose.

Like prophecy, I knew there'd be no more Charlie to talk to and protect me at the library. No more Ty waiting for me. My first adult friend and my first love both wiped out.

Off the train, walking through the sleeping neighborhood, I tossed the book in a trash can. I wanted to lie down in the street and let a car run over me. But I knew I wouldn't.

In the story, at the last moment the French army storms the prison and saves the narrator. *"An outstretched arm caught my own."*

Nothing like that was going to happen for me. My parents would make me do whatever they wanted. I turned the corner onto my street and saw the lights still on at home. I felt the book pulsing in my back pocket as I went to meet my fate.

THE CHICKEN FARMER AND HIS BOY:

A METAPHYSICAL HISTORY

John Mantooth

THE boy who walks with me is young, innocent to the ways of the world. Normally, I wouldn't make the effort, but this is my son, and I want him to understand despite the unusual nature of our relationship that I am here for him, that I intend to love him like any father would love any son. Better, actually, though my intentions will ultimately bump against the constraints of this place.

You can call me anything; it does not matter because my real name would burn your lips if you tried to say it. I'm not evil as many think. I take no delight in being here, watching over this place. I am simply a man — twisted and deformed by my own regret — condemned to watch over the tormented, the lost, the people swallowed by their failures. The best way to explain it is that I'm a keeper of sorts. I keep the ones who stumble like the dead but live on despite their better yearnings.

There's a place in your town, I tell my son (but I'm telling you too), woods or open fields or maybe even swampland where no one ever goes. This is the shadow world, and though there are many entrances, it's all one to me, a vast forest that misdirects the sun or blots it out completely. It's where the lost walk without progress, where they speak without making a sound. Maybe you're thinking, calculating where such a wilderness place might be in your town, as if you want to verify my knowledge of such things. Understandable, I suppose, as you people on that side know so little about the way the world works. Science and physics, perhaps, but your easy dismissal of the meta-physical, the spiritual is a glaring weakness that in some ways is responsible for this very place where we walk now.

The boy looks at me. He's my son, but I choose not to know his name. Cruel? Perhaps, but the distance is essential. The love I spoke of will have to come from afar, as this may be the only time we will be able to communicate directly. He's confused. Understandably. All who come here are confused. At first. Then, enlightenment dawns, and I release them to find their own way out of the mist, though many, nay most, never do.

The mist, the boy says. Tell me about the mist.

I nod and wave my hand through it as we walk. It clears for a second and then reforms, perhaps thicker than it was before I agitated it.

Do you know what a metaphor is? I ask him.

He nods, uncertainly. I think he does not, or he knows without being able to explain it, which is the best way to know anything, I think.

A metaphor is like a story except it's a story within a story, I tell him.

He cocks his head and looks at me. But the mist?

It's a metaphor for something, temporary blindness, think of it, which all suffer from time to time. Or maybe it signifies the blotting out of the sun, the confusion where many find themselves.

Up ahead, I see the chicken farmer and his boy. They are the most recent victims of this blindness, the ones I came to show my own son. The people that come here often bring objects from the physical world with them — a toy or piece of jewelry. Dozens of cars cruise through these woods, floating, disembodied except to their owners. These two — the chicken farmer and his boy — have brought a bedroom, or maybe the bedroom brought them. Doesn't matter. Somehow, the weight of silence between the two caused it to fall right off the back of their house and they are trapped together inside it, together until they untie the knot that anchors their silence. The boy sits at the window of the moving room, the walls still jagged from the separation from the house, writing something, perhaps his life story, perhaps it's a note to his father, the man sleeping in the bed.

These two, I tell him, gesturing with my longish fingers, have a story. It's a specific story but also a universal story.

How they got here? the boy asks.

Indeed. And how they got here can be answered on two levels.

Metaphor?

Yes.

A story within a story?

Yes, a story within a story.

Can you tell me both of them?

I nod. They're inextricable.

Inex — what?

They're like a knot tied with two strings. They make one thing. Only when they are unraveled can we really understand that they are different, and even then you might drop them on the ground and not remember which is which because they serve the same purpose, at least here.

Here?

My boy, you do know you're in the shadow world, the in-between place, a kind of paradox of shadow and light, an inversion if you will, the place where problems are not solved, they just coalesce into a knot so tight, not even my slender fingers can work it out.

You use a lot of big words.

Ah, I apologize. Let me use a simple one. This place is the slip.

The slip?

The place where people go when there is nowhere else, when their lives have reached impasse. Perhaps you've heard someone speak of Hell?

He nods.

This is it, at least after a fashion.

But —

You expected fire? Or maybe you expected gnashing of teeth?

I don't know. Are these people dead?

No. They live on, tortured by the misery they have created.

Are you...?

I wave my hand again, scattering the mist. Never mind that. Names are not important. I'll tell you their story. Hold my hand, and listen closely.

＋＋

THE BOY, IT'S his story, really. His name is Tucker or Tuck and his father is the most-liked man in Shelbourne County, which is a small, insignificant place in the grand scheme of places, but that's no matter. Significance is in the eye of the beholder, just as beauty is.

In Shelbourne County, Tucker's father was a chicken farmer, which really means he owned some land and some chicken houses and paid Hispanic men to tend to the chickens. He's a rather — hmmn…perhaps I'll just let you decide.

He's a rather what?

Never mind. I was going to tell you something about him, but I think the story will work better if you decide that for yourself.

You're always wanting me to decide things.

I look at him, perhaps surprised.

He shrugs. You told me when I followed you here that I could decide if I liked you myself.

And?

He shrugs. Let me hear the story.

Fair enough.

So I begin again, this time in earnest. This time, I focus on something specific. The day his father met Pedro. The day the boy, Tucker, understood that his father had a power he did not.

⊬

"SON," THE FATHER said. "Come down with me this morning."

Tucker sat up, disoriented and sad. Sleep was always such a refuge for him, a way to silence the war inside his mind. Despite the wave of grief he felt upon waking, he smiled good-naturedly at his father. Tucker was nothing if not an actor, showing the things he imagined and hiding the things he felt until they were like dry kindling to the fire that burned inside him.

"It's your birthday," Tucker said.

"Fifty," the father said. He didn't look fifty. He looked thirty-eight, maybe forty if the light was right. Tucker was eleven, and already in a desperate place.

I'm eleven, the boy — my boy — says, interrupting.

That you are, but Tucker was eleven going on twenty.

What does that mean?

It means his innocence, his childhood was being stolen from him.

Who stole it?

I shrug. It's a good question. I don't know the answer, but if pressed, I might say that his father did. But the boy doesn't press me. He wants the story.

So, on his father's fiftieth birthday, Tucker went with him down to the chicken houses. In the chicken houses, they called him *el gran jefe*, which means "the big boss." They called Tucker nothing because the workers sensed what the father pretended not to. Tucker was different than *el gran jefe*. He would never walk among them and make them tremble and adore him in equal measure. His destiny lay elsewhere. They saw this instinctively, and this is only one of the great mysteries of this story I've yet to work out.

The men all stopped their work and smiled and waved and called out warm birthday greetings to the father. They loved him and they feared him, and Tucker sensed this, had sensed it for a long time, but on this day, he not only was aware of it, he was in awe of his father's easy power. It was like a code that didn't use numbers but gestures, movement, sounds, presence. Yes, presence, Tucker decided. That was what made his father so strong. That and the knowing. In every situation, he knew, as if by instinct, the right thing to do, the right thing to say.

One of the men, Esteban, came over, smiling broadly. He was the foreman when the father was away, which was increasingly more and more during those days, as he was a beloved man in their small town and he was deeply involved with the issues and controversies that trouble all such small towns.

Esteban whistled sharply and a small boy hustled over to his side. Esteban's son was dark-eyed and shy, but in a deferential way that the father liked.

Esteban's English was broken, but it was clear he wanted to say something, and he wanted to say it in English. "Sir," he began, "I wish to you a happy birthday. You are good to me. My family. My son." He smiled again, patting his boy on the head. "Good worker, my son. One day, he will take my place. He'll be working for you. Maybe even your boy."

Tucker felt a tremor of shock at this idea. His father had always talked of the day when Tucker would take over for him, and when he spoke of it there was no question, just that easy confidence he exuded in every aspect of his life. And maybe because of the forgone way in which his father spoke of it, the prospect of running the chicken farm himself had never seemed real to Tucker, but it did then. It felt real and surreal at once, and even though his father draped an arm over Tucker's shoulder warmly, and laughed, Tucker felt colder than he had ever felt.

His father ruffled his hair and leaned over to speak to Esteban's son. "Do you have a name?"

The boy nodded, clearly intimidated in the presence of the *jefe*.

"Well?"

Esteban nudged him. "Shy boy."

Tucker's father seemed pleased by this, but also was waiting. He expected an answer.

The boy shuffled his feet. "Pedro."

The father beamed. "Well, Pedro, do you work as hard as your father?"

Pedro nodded.

"Good. The world is a good place to those that will work hard. Don't lose that." He put a hand on Pedro's shoulder. "And listen to your daddy. He's a good man."

"I tell him he be *presidente* one day!" Esteban said proudly.

Tucker's father wasn't listening. He had turned to Tucker and was squeezing his arm like he did when he checked for biceps muscles playfully sometimes. "One day, your boy will work for my boy. Maybe he'll be the foreman just like his daddy."

Esteban's smile disappeared, but Tucker's father didn't seem to notice. He knelt down to look at Pedro.

"You keep working hard, and one day you'll be just like your father."

Pedro started to say something, maybe about how he didn't want to be like his father, but *el jefe* cut him off. "Run along now. Work to be done."

Obediently, Pedro turned and headed back to the eggs he'd been collecting, but not before sharing a meaningful glance with Tucker. It seemed to be sympathetic and angry all at once, and Tucker never forgot it as long as he lived.

It was the first time Tucker felt the conflicting emotions about his father that would dominate the reminder of his life on that side.

⁜

THAT SIDE?

Well, your side. Remember, where we walk now is shadow.

My son nods, and I'm proud of his alertness, his repose in the face of such strangeness. His mother was like that too, which of course is one of the reasons we were able to get along. When I reveal myself to people, as I often desire to, they are taken aback by my appearance. The time spent in the shadows has made my appearance disturbing, inhuman — the tiny nubs for ears, the longish neck, and downturned, pale lips, the freakishly long fingers, the slumped shoulders because of my extreme height. Of course my tendency to stare unabashedly at what interests me does not help either.

Has anyone ever gotten back?

You mean from here, from the slip?

Yes.

I think about it. My answer surprises me: Not totally. The slip always stays with you. Edgar Allan Poe was here, once. He returned, but if you've learned about him in school, he never truly returned. First you enter the slip. Then the slip enters you.

That's sad.

Is it? I don't know. I suppose in some cases it is. But I also believe that it's important for a man like Poe to glimpse this place, to write about it, and therefore help others who might find themselves on the same road.

Is that why you wanted me to come?

Again his alertness, his intuition surprise me. Yes, I say. That's why I wanted you to come.

My son shrugs. Can you finish the story?

Of course. You have much to learn about Tucker and his father.

⊹⊹

TUCKER HAD ALWAYS been aware that he was different. Even standing across from Pedro that morning, eye to eye, trying to imagine a day in which he might be the boy's boss, he'd felt different. It was hard to define for him though. It was just a feeling, and he wanted more than anything else to hide that feeling from his father.

In truth, the only person Tucker had ever shared these feelings with had disappeared from his life. Something he didn't quite understand had happened between his parents when he was eight. Some disagreement that had sent her away. There had been the day in court when the judge asked him questions about his mother. His father made him promise to answer honestly, and he had. He thought his mother would have been angry at him, but she only seemed sad. Afterwards, she'd found him and his father in the lobby of the courthouse. The father held up a hand. "Mary, you know you can't do this."

"I know I'm not supposed to do this, but I'm going to do it anyway." She took Tucker's hands then and pulled him away from his father. Tucker could feel the anger radiating off his father because he was a man used to getting his way, but he was also a gentlemen, and Tucker knew he wouldn't cause a scene. Perhaps his mother knew this too and that's why she acted so boldly. Of course, Tucker's mother was a bold woman, and the father still loved her fiercely, even as he hated her and wanted her to leave them alone.

She knelt before him and looked in his eye. "I've got to go away."

Tucker nodded, trying very hard not to cry.

"I love you, Tucker. As you grow up you'll hear things about me, and I suppose you'll make your own decision. The only thing I want you to remember is this. Everything I did was for you. Everything I did was because I truly, truly believed it was the right thing to do. Sometimes right things have very bad consequences, but not doing them will always be worse. So I did them. And now look at this terrible consequence. I'll worry for the rest of my life if maybe this was the time I should have just let it go."

Tucker nodded again, but he wasn't following her very well. He only wanted her to hug him hard and hold him and tell him that she wasn't really going anywhere.

He reached for her, but she stood, tears streaking her face, and turned away. It was the last time he ever saw her.

⊹

HOW CAN YOU love someone and hate them at the same time? the boy asks.

It takes me a second to realize he's asking about the father. About how I said he loved her, but hated her too.

I slow down, run my hand across one of the old oaks. The trees are the only things that retain their form here, the one concession that was granted to me when I was sent to oversee this place. I always liked trees, especially the kind that spread out their limbs and reach skyward. Those are the ones that inspire me. To be rooted and to still reach up toward the warmth of the sun, the paradox that is life.

How? the boy asks again.

How can you not? I reply.

⊹

TUCKER DISCOVERED THAT he was different in a number of ways, but there was only one way that he could never accept, and that was because it was the only one his father couldn't accept. He didn't like sports or hunting or pickup trucks. His father often shrugged these oddities off, draping that heavy arm around his son, kissing his head. "You're my boy," he'd say. "No matter what you like."

These assurances only made Tucker feel a little better because he had other memories too, one in particular that haunted him even if he couldn't say exactly why. Once, he'd lain awake in his bed, the window open on a cool spring night, listening to his father and one of his friends, talking and drinking on the front porch.

At first, they were quiet, but as they drank more and the night grew longer and the breeze turned to wind to blasts from the oncoming storm, Tucker heard them laughing. As if marking time, they crushed each empty can underfoot and began another story.

Tucker listened, transfixed, soaking it all in, this world of men that he understood was his inheritance. There was comfort there, lying secretly awake and eavesdropping on them, but there was also apprehension, that vague feeling again that when his time came to be a man, he would fail somehow.

Then it happened. The conversation turned somber. Just like that. The rain started lightly on the roof, and lightning flashed out over the chicken houses.

The father's friend — his name was Rodney — spoke, his voice stilted, more sober than seemed possible: "My boy's back from Nam."

Tucker's father grunted, popped another can of Stroh's. "He's a good boy."

Rodney laughed the kind of laugh that felt like a knife to the gut. It was sharp and jagged and it hit a secret place inside Tucker he had thought was safe.

"He ain't as good as you think."

Tucker's father didn't say anything. Tucker imagined him turning back to the Stroh's, draining it. As if in confirmation, he heard the can crunch underfoot on the wood planks.

"What do you mean?"

"He ain't been the same since he come back."

"Well, I don't reckon anybody would — "

"It ain't what you think."

"Well shell shock ain't nothing to scoff at. I saw boys come back from the big one, wasn't never quite the same, but that didn't make them no — "

"Ain't shell shock, T.D."

"Well, what the hell is it?"

Later Tucker would think about this moment, this silence between the question his father asked and the answer Rodney seemed unable to give. The silence seemed to mirror the silence that would later invade his life when he needed to speak the truth most of all. But this first silence was part of the reason why he could never break his own, because he learned then there is a certain level of safety inside the vast windless house of no words, and if he never said the words that burned him on the inside, maybe that could keep them from being true.

When Rodney finally did speak, the silence was diffused, but Tucker never forgot that moment, and in fact, remained trapped there for most of his later years.

"It's the whiskey. The boy's strung out on it night and day. Says it's the only way he can face the day. He's done been fired twice since coming back. It's embarrassing to have a boy that can't hold a job."

Tucker's father laughed then. It was low and happy, and for some reason, the scariest laugh Tucker had ever heard. "Damn, Rodney, is that all? I thought you was about to tell me your son was queer."

Rodney laughed too, but it was a nervous laugh. "Come on, T.D. This is serious."

"Hell, a queer is a damned sight more serious than one that can't hold a job. If I ever found out my boy was queer, I don't know what I'd do."

Another silence, but Tucker found no solace in this one.

Thunder broke the quiet. The sound of a can crumpling underfoot. Tucker turned over and faced the wall.

"He's pretty screwed up. The other day he never left his room. I tried to clean out the liquor, but he's got it hid all over the house."

"Listen. I want you to know I'm here for you and the boy. I'll come by the house tomorrow. See if I can't talk some sense into him. I'll offer him a job here, working for me. Go light on him at first, till he gets his feet under him."

"Now, you don't have to do that, T.D. That ain't why I brought it up."

"I know. You brought it up because we're friends. I'm doing it because we're friends. He'll have to pull his weight. Eventually. But, you know, I got a boy too. He'll miss this war, but the next one might get him, and who knows what might happen to him. It's the least I can do."

"Jesus, T.D., I appreciate it."

"Don't get all sappy now. Lord, like a woman." He hesitated, and Tucker heard him drain his beer. "Or a damned queer." The can hit the porch. Crush. Both men laughed, and the sound rose into the sky, blending with the thunder.

When they stopped, the rain was coming down really hard, but Tucker could still make out what his father said next.

"At least he ain't queer. There's always that."

"I guess that'll teach me to count my blessings," Rodney said.

"Me and you both. My own boy ain't perfect. He'll get caught up in a book quick as you can cut a fart, but he's a good boy anyway. He turned out right, you know? God knows what I'd'a done if he hadn't."

"Probably shot the poor bastard," Rodney said, giggling.

His father giggled too. "I reckon so. In the pecker."

"Lord," Rodney said. "What is this world coming to?"

After that the subject changed to whiskey and cars and the crops.

Tucker cried as silently as he could, though he couldn't say exactly what he'd heard that made him so sad. That silence. He kept coming back to that. It was safe, it wasn't risky. In that silence his father would love him. Did love him.

But what was he being silent about?

It was the first time Tucker remembered wishing he had been born differently, that he could have been born better.

⋇

HE WAS OFTEN afraid at night, afraid of the silliest things, he later realized, like the house crumbling in the middle of the night or his father getting up in his sleep, and walking zombie-like through the house, hands extended, looking for Tucker's neck, looking to squeeze the life right out of him. His father must have been exasperated with him, but he always welcomed him into his bedroom on the top floor in the back of the house, the one that overlooked the vast woods, and made the stars seem as close as frost on the other side of the windows.

He'd always tell Tucker the same thing on these kinds of nights. "There's no bad guy or ghost or nightmare that your daddy can't handle, Tuck. You're safe with me." Tucker never could tell him that in the nightmare, his father *was* the bad guy. Still, he was comforted beside him, and the version in his dream would fade, and sometimes, when Tucker was almost asleep, safe, secure in his father's love, he'd hear just a little more. "One day, son, you'll be the same. One day, you won't be afraid of nothing."

It took Tucker many more years before he realized what a lie that had been.

⋇

TUCKER REMEMBERED THE last time he'd gone to his father's bed, the final time before he felt too awkward and embarrassed to do it. His father had been slow to wake that night, and Tucker kept marveling at how his father

243

could sleep through such a violent storm. The bright flashes of lightning alone could wake the dead, he'd thought. Tucker was twelve, nearly thirteen, and he was on the cusp of his life changing forever, on the cusp of taking the barely traveled road to the shadow world. He was slipping already.

Eventually, the father woke, grumbling at first, but then understanding it was his boy, his son. He sat up, kissing Tucker's forehead. "It's just a storm," he said. "Storms don't scare me. I once walked four miles in one worse than this. Been struck by lightning in another one. Lived to be right here with you, Tuck. One day, you'll laugh at storms too. One day, you'll wake up and realize you're a man, and you'll be the best kind of man, I know because you're my boy."

The words formed on Tucker's lips almost before he knew what they were. "What if — ?"

The father patted his arm. "Go on. No secrets between us, Tucker."

Tucker nodded. "What if I don't become a man?"

The father laughter. He laughed hard. "Hell, son, I thought you were worried about something. You'll become a man, sure thing."

"How do you know?"

"I just know. It's as natural as the birds and the bees. Natural as anything."

"But what if I don't."

"You will." Tucker thought he sensed just the slightest edge in his father's voice now. "Now what's this all about?"

Tucker shrugged and the lightning flashed again, and somewhere outside in the woods, a pine cracked open and burst into flames. "It's just that you always say I'll be like you. What if I'm not? What if I'm different?"

The father was silent for a while, but Tucker couldn't help but sense that the tension, so present in the room just moments before, was leaking away. "You be your own man," he said. "That's how you'll be like me, Tucker. Now let's get some sleep. In the morning, we'll go eat pancakes."

Tucker smiled and closed his eyes, but when he did, the afterimage of the last flash of lightning remained, and it illuminated shapes on the underside of his eyelids that seemed like people, dozens of them, shambling and lost.

⊹

TUCKER DISCOVERED ONE more way he was different when he was sixteen. It had been lying dormant inside him since he could remember, but dormant things are easy to ignore until you stumble over them.

It took a girl to make him stumble. Her name was Roxanne Chambers, and she was the "it" girl when he was in the tenth grade. Largely because of his money, his father's status in the town, and his face that girls found "cute," Tucker was the "it" boy in the tenth grade too. This was before the other boys turned mean, before they made fun of him for not knowing how to fit in, before he found their presence made him feel like an outsider more and more.

It started with a note dropped on his desk during fifth period. The note smelled like perfume. He waited until after school, when he thought he was alone in the parking lot, to open it. He read it twice, dreading what he felt like he had to do.

He'd tell her no. She wasn't his type. He'd heard some of the other boys say this about certain girls, and no one really questioned them. He'd been about to stuff the note in his pocket when Cedric Turner snatched the note out of his hand, smelled it, and then read it, his eyes getting wider with each word.

"Holy shit, man. How lucky are you? Roxanne Chambers asked *you* out. Holy, holy shit. And did you smell this?"

Tucker nodded. He had. Would it still work to say she wasn't his type? Or was Roxanne a girl who was everyone's type? He really didn't know, so he shrugged, playing it off.

"Dude, you are going to call her, right?"

"Maybe."

Cedric started to laugh. "Wait, let me get this straight. Roxanne Chambers gives you a note all but begging you to ask her out and your response is 'maybe'? Dude, are you gay?"

He said it as a joke because this was small-town Alabama and *gay* was an abstraction, something weird people in the north engaged in, but not a real possibility, especially for the son of the most-loved chicken farmer in the county.

"No. Look, just don't get in my business. I'll think about it."

"You'll think about it? Well, if you don't, I will." Cedric started repeating the phone number, in order to memorize it.

"Stop that. I'm going to call her."

It was a decision made in a second, and he didn't regret it. His thinking at the time was that he'd just be straight. Easy enough. She was hot. He'd think of her that way. They'd go out and have fun. It wasn't like they had to have sex.

❋

ROXANNE CHAMBERS WAS born in the wrong place, or perhaps she was born exactly in the right place. It's hard to tell. Certainly, she was a needed firebrand in a community stuck so far in the past as to be practically medieval. It didn't hurt that she was beautiful and bold, and spoke to people with a frankness that was disarming. Still, it seems a shame to think of her mingling with the backward and the progressively challenged.

She'd had her eye on Tucker for a while. No secret, she thought he was cute, but she also found him refreshing. Many of the other boys couldn't really talk to her. Of course, she found that cute too, but in a different, more irritating way. She could find a boy who would wilt before her easily enough. Those had stopped being fun a while back. She wanted a boy who could look her in the eye and have a conversation without being intimidated. That, more than anything else, turned her on.

Tucker seemed to fit that bill perfectly. They'd only talked a few times, but he looked at her directly, and his eyes never drifted to her body. He laughed easily, and made her laugh too, and the confidence was not practiced, but natural. She looked forward to their first date, very much.

Meanwhile, Tucker was cautiously optimistic. News had spread around school quickly thanks to Cedric. Upperclassmen Tucker didn't even really know were high-fiving him in the hallways. One of them, a nice-looking football player, pulled him aside and forced a condom into his hand. "She puts out. You definitely want to wear this. At least at the end." Tucker took the condom. That afternoon, he pulled it out of his pocket to look at it. He had no idea how to even put it on. He was turning it over in his hands when his father walked in, kicking off his work boots, heading for the kitchen sink where he'd rinse out his coffee mug and fill it with cold water.

Tucker slipped the condom back into his pocket.

But it was too late, his father had already seen it. He tossed his coffee in the sink, but didn't bother rinsing the cup. Instead, he pulled a chair away from the table and turned it to face Tucker. He sat down. Grinning.

When he grinned like that, Tucker felt something inside him lift. It was a grin made out of pride.

"I heard a rumor that you've got a date tonight." He crossed his legs like he did when he was settling in, ready to talk. Tucker had seen him do that with his friends, men he respected.

"Yes, sir."

"Roxanne Chambers, right?"

Tucker blushed. "Yeah."

"I bet you didn't know her mother and me dated, did you? I mean way back before me and your mother started hot and heavy. Her name was Diana Lillard. She had three sisters, and they were all the kind of girls you couldn't hardly be around without stretching your pants, you follow?"

Tucker did follow, and he felt suddenly uncomfortable with where this was going. Yet he couldn't help but remind himself this was a chance to cement his sexuality in his father's mind.

"I hear Roxanne takes after her mother and her aunts. Hell, I more than hear it. I've seen it with my own eyes." He didn't wait for Tucker to respond. Instead, he pressed on, still relaxed, at ease, totally confident. "I also saw you slipping that condom back into your blue jeans when I came in. That's smart. Real smart. I knew some boys who had to marry young because they got girls pregnant. It may not feel as good, but think of it this way, you'll get to dip your pecker in a lot more pussy if you just cover it up. The one time you don't, you better make damn sure that the pussy is special because it might be last pussy you'll ever get."

Tucker could tell his father was excited that this sort of moment had finally come, but he couldn't bear any more of it. He left the room without saying another word. He closed his bedroom door, but not before he heard his father howling with laughter, and saying, "Well, I done went and embarrassed the boy."

⁋⁋

THE DATE WENT so well, Tucker had half-convinced himself he liked girls after all. During dinner, they'd laughed so much, that they'd drawn nasty looks from some of the older patrons. Later, at the theater, they did not watch the movie; instead, they talked and laughed until an usher asked them to leave. He didn't seem angry though. In fact, he seemed, well, Tucker thought he seemed in awe. Clearly, he believed Tucker possessed something akin to supernatural powers in order to land a girl like Roxanne.

During the movie, she'd touched him a few times, playfully, but intimately enough to put him on edge. He found himself wishing she wouldn't invade his space, but he tried to push those feelings back and just ride the wave of their good vibe together.

Back in the car, he asked her where they should go, and she told him it was a surprise. "Head out Highway Seven. Up the mountain."

She took his hand, and he found he didn't mind this so much.

They talked about school and teachers and the silliness of having a dress code.

She directed him up the mountain and onto an old gravel road that twisted around and around, until the road fell away and they were left with a spectacular view of the night sky and the lights of the town below them.

"It's nice he — " His words were swallowed inside Roxanne's mouth as she pressed her lips hard against his, her tongue probing. Tucker recoiled — not physically, but certainly emotionally. He knew he was supposed to reciprocate, so he tried to push his own tongue against hers, matching her urgency, but it didn't feel right, and he pulled it back, pulled himself away from Roxanne. She reached for his zipper, her hand patting for something that wasn't there.

At first she was pissed. Later, Roxanne would wonder how she could have been fooled so easily, but she realized that she'd wanted to be fooled, that she'd wanted very badly to find a boy that she could talk to *and* have sex with. After the initial shock wore off, she understood. She understood it, and wondered why it had taken her so long.

"Oh my God," she said. "You don't like girls."

"What?" Tucker tried to seem offended. "It's not that. You're just not my type." It even sounded lame to him, so he said, "Let's try again. I think it'll go better."

"Wait, you haven't even admitted it to yourself, have you?"

"I don't know what you mean?"

"You don't know what I mean? Come on, Tucker? Do you want to fuck me?"

"I — "

"Tell the truth. The absolute truth."

"I think I just need some more experience."

"It doesn't work like that, Tucker." She took his hands in hers. She looked straight into his eyes. "You're gay."

Tucker felt his throat tighten up, and for a moment he believed he would suffocate beneath the weight of that truth. His head swam, and he couldn't focus on anything except the words inside his brain, which would not stop.

I'm gay. I'm gay. I'm gay.

On and on, and it was almost a relief, like he was a dam that had been holding back so much water for so long, and somebody had come along and said, it's okay, just let it go. He was letting it go when he thought of his father, and then he tried to pull it all back, to do the impossible and seal every crack that had formed from all the years of holding on.

⁘

MY BOY IS a good listener. He doesn't interrupt, not even when I say the bad words that I know his mother doesn't let him say. If anything, he urges me to continue with his silence, and when I stop to let a young woman pass by. She's carrying a dog in her arms and it barks at everything, including me. The bark, like all things here is impotent, soundless, a ghost of a bark, and the woman's eyes are haunted by it. Another story within a story, but our time is too short to tell more than one.

My boy reaches for my hand and squeezes it. Tell me the rest, he says.

Okay. I need to backtrack a little.

I want to know what happens next, though. Does he tell his father?

Soon, but stories are not about what happens next. They are about what happens. The truest stories — like this one — do not conform to time, they happen all at once, the past, the present, and the future flowing together like a river, if you'll forgive the trite metaphor.

The boy squeezes my hand again. I won't forgive you unless you tell me the rest.

So I do, though I wish I had a better ending to tell.

⁘

AT SOME POINT around the same time Tucker realized he was gay, he began to learn more about his mother. It wasn't a purposeful seeking of information about her, but rather a purposeful receiving. He decided to listen, to contemplate, to truly understand the stories that had been circulating about her for years.

He heard most of them from his father's sisters, his aunts. They were all different, but sometimes if you get enough differing takes you can put them together into something like the truth. Tucker tried very hard to do this, and came up with another story, one that made him very sad.

It seems his mother and father were once as madly in love as two people have ever been, but even madly in love, they were pulling apart because they were so different, so fundamentally opposed to the other about the way the world worked, about how to make your way through it. His mother, he gathered, was something of a firebrand in their small town, frequently questioning doctrine at the Baptist church they attended, arguing that women were not paid enough, and even going as far as to openly state that she had doubts about God. The father was nothing if not measured, and he tolerated these sort of indiscretions with great magnanimity. Everybody said so.

The first real test came in the late sixties, when Tucker was just a very small boy. There were some black people who wanted to join the local country club. His mother joined the group, to match in the street, holding signs, demanding equality. His father took that in stride, smiling at her when the local news caught her outside the club shouting with the others. Meanwhile, he sat on the board of the country club, and led the other members in drafting a new policy that did not mention African Americans specifically, but made it clear the club would stand by its previous decision to not allow any members who weren't white.

According to his aunts, this one ended quietly enough. "Your father was always such a gentleman, she couldn't even get him to fight. Until that man came to town."

"That man" was Billy Waters. According to aunts, he was devil's spawn, and he came for the sole reason of corrupting a "good, God-fearing place."

Tucker had found a photo of him once underneath the couch, a year or so after his mother had left them. He was a black man, holding a sign near the side of Highway Seven — Tucker recognized it because First Baptist was in the background. The sign said, *God Loves You No Matter What.* He seemed happy because he was smiling in a really pure kind of way.

On the back of the photo, his mother had written *Reverend Waters.*

According to his aunts though, calling Billy Waters a reverend was nothing short of blasphemy.

"He lived with a another man, up on the mountain. Folks always said they were just friends, but I didn't fall for that," Aunt Wanda said. "Then he started all that roadside shouting — some folks call it preaching, but I call it shouting — saying God didn't care if you loved men or women. God just wanted you to love."

Aunt Viola picked up from there. "People started bringing signs to him, marching in front of where he was shouting. Their signs had scripture on them. The Lord sayeth homosexuality is an abomination."

"Sodomy," Aunt Brenda said, as if this were the only word necessary to sum up Billy Waters and the sad state of affairs the world was in.

"It's a wonder he didn't get struck down by lightning for being so blasphemous," Viola said.

"And then that woman…" Aunt Brenda said.

"I still can't believe she did that," Aunt Wanda said.

The other two aunts shook their heads, tut-tutting his mother's foolishness.

"What exactly did she do?" Tucker finally asked.

"She helped him. She stood beside him on the side of the road while he preached at the rest of us," Aunt Viola said.

"She never was saved," Aunt Wanda said.

"It's not like she wasn't presented the Gospel," Aunt Brenda said.

"Some folks would reject God even when they're in hell burning," Aunt Viola said.

They went on, though Tucker pretty well guessed the rest.

This time, Tucker's father couldn't just let his wife's behavior go. He called her on it, quoting scripture to her about the abominations the Good Book speaks of. She came right back with her own quotes, and told him the real reason he didn't want to support Billy was that he wasn't secure in his own manhood. She also told him he was afraid of someone who actually wanted to use the Bible for something other than a bludgeon.

"Let me tell you, Tuck," Aunt Brenda said. "That was when I knew she had lost her mind. Your father is as straight as an arrow, and she ought to know that better than anybody."

It ended with divorce, of course, but the aunts also made it clear that the whole ordeal was an embarrassment for Tucker's father. The divorce proceedings were the one thing his aunts seemed reluctant to talk about, but he gathered his father made sure she would never see Tucker again. The reason? She was unstable. The proof? Her support of Billy Waters.

✤✤

WHERE ARE THEY? my boy asks me.

Where are who?

Tucker's mother and Billy Waters.

I'm not sure I understand the question.

I want to see them. Here, in the mist. They seem like the kind of people who would end up here.

I nod, understanding. No, actually, they're the kind of people that tend to avoid this place. While they were both tormented during their lives, they were true to their selves, they were never conflicted, never tormented from the inside. It's no better, actually, to be tormented by others than to torment yourself. Just different. No, Billy was murdered some years ago, but he was smiling when the bullet entered the back of his head. The man that shot him…well, he's not made it here yet, but I do have tabs on him already. He's made strides, but he still has a long way to go.

And Tucker's mother?

She walks a different path. Her life aches from the inside out because she feels what others feel, a gift and a curse. She misses her son, and keeps her regrets balled tightly in the spaces around her heart.

So, what's the next part?

The next part is the rift and the slipping.

❋

SEE, SOME PEOPLE deny either the truth or themselves for so long, a rift is created. This causes them to slip. All of the people here, all of them walking soundless and unable to communicate. It's the worst possible way in which to be alone.

Poe wrote about it in one of his stories, "MS. Found in a Bottle." Read it, and when you do, pay attention to the end, when the narrator lands on the second ship. That was Poe's description, his metaphor for where we are right now. He even had enough sense to end it with the second ship going down through the whirlpool.

There are many ways to get here, but they all come down to living a lie, to fear, to regret stuffed deep down inside you. Most people here are holding on to it; they wouldn't let it go even if they knew it would save them.

The rift started for Tucker and his father when Tucker was eighteen and working in the chicken houses. His father had been grooming him to take over, oblivious to Tucker's reluctance.

Tucker wasn't supposed to be a part of what happened. He was inside one of the chicken houses when the foreman came in. Esteban had died a few years back — worked himself to death, actually — and the new man was just as hard a worker as Esteban but he was cruel and the men did not like him. Tucker wasn't sure if his father knew this or not. Sometimes he thought there were certain things his father chose not to know.

On this day, he was gathering eggs when he heard shouts in Spanish coming from outside. This wasn't unusual; the men often shouted — sometimes playfully, sometimes in anger — but in this case, the tone was particularly harsh and hateful. The person shouting was Pedro.

Tucker hadn't kept up with Pedro very well. Honestly, there were very few of the workers he had personal relationships with. It was another way he realized he'd never be like his father, another failing he tried to hide, and whenever his father was around, Tucker smiled brightly and spoke to them, calling the ones by name that he could recall. The men weren't fooled; many of them seemed to sense his secret instinctively. Not that he was gay, necessarily, but that he was a pretender.

Despite this, Tucker knew Pedro had withdrawn in his own way since his father's death. It was easy to see, he had been devastated by first his mother and then his father dying, but until that morning, Tucker hadn't realized that he was unhappy working the chicken houses, that like himself Pedro was incapable of following in his father's footsteps. Like Tucker, Pedro kept getting too tangled up in the shadow his father cast to make any progress on his own.

On this morning, Pedro had flatly refused to clean a particularly filthy cage. He was shouting *el agua, el agua* over and over again, and Tucker knew that Ángel had demanded he go inside the cage and clean it with a rag instead of using the pressure washer.

This was a common punishment for insubordination, one of Ángel's new tactics to keep the men in line.

Tucker stepped outside the chicken house, where the cages were lined up, waiting to be cleaned. Ángel was yelling at Pedro now, his index finger poking into Pedro's face. Pedro stepped back, shaking his head — he'd been shaking his head over and over since Tucker came out, and he understood: Pedro was refusing to clean the cage. Ángel seemed to take offense at this and shoved Pedro hard. He fell on top of one of the cages, and his body twisted off, the metal stubs scraping long lashes across his bare arms. He wiped blood off his biceps and stood again, but Ángel shoved him a second time, and Tucker realized this was about more than the cage. Ángel was fighting Esteban, not Pedro. Many of the workers complained that Ángel wasn't as good as the previous foreman, and Ángel seemed all too aware that he was not loved. He must have seen Pedro as a threat. And now he meant to beat him down in front of all the men.

Pedro's face was bleeding — his nose wrecked — by the time the father showed up. The men saw him first, walking casually around the corner of the chicken house. They shouted *gran jefe, gran jefe* and Ángel, who had wrapped Pedro's sweaty shirt in his fist and was holding him up now while he pounded on him, released him and let him fall into the dirt.

"What's happening here?" Dad said, and Tucker was amazed by the way the men — just moments ago so feral and bloodthirsty — parted for him in respectful deference. Everyone was silent. Everyone except Pedro. He pulled himself up. "He doesn't want hit me, but wants hit my father." He shook the dirt off his pants, straightened his shirt, and wiped the blood flowing freely from his nose with a grime-covered hand. "I am not my father."

Tucker's father nodded slowly, the corners of his otherwise flat lips playing at a smile. "Pedro speaks truly. He's not his father." He stepped forward, and the lips did smile now, though it was a cruel thing, and Tucker wondered if this was the real man, the one who held his prejudices quietly and without open disdain, but still held them just as deep as the raving bigot, maybe more deeply, the man he'd heard that night on the porch with Rodney. Tucker wondered, most of all, if his father even knew he was there. He decided he did not.

"See, that's the problem we have here. We have a boy who owes everything to his father, a boy whose father literally worked so hard that his heart just couldn't beat one more day. And how does he repay him? He works like a pig with a bad attitude and poor workmanship. He tries to live off his legacy, but when asked to work he tells anyone who is listening, 'I am not my father.' Of course, you are not your father, Pedro. You are your own man, and a pitiful man that is." Tucker's father dug his boot heel into the dirt and seemed to think. "I'm done with you. Your father was a good man. He gave you everything, but you're nothing like him." He looked at Ángel. "Just don't make me call an ambulance."

Ángel suppressed a grin and said, "Yes, sir."

El jefe turned and walked back up to the house.

Tucker stood by, horrified as the men took turns punching, kicking, and spitting on Pedro. When they saw he could take no more, Ángel ordered them to put him in the back of the pickup truck and get him out of there. Tucker didn't know where the men took him, but he never saw Pedro again. In fact, he rarely ever thought of him again, but he did think about those words his father had said. He thought about them often.

He gave you everything, but you're nothing like him.

WHAT ABOUT PEDRO?

Pedro is angry.

Will he come here?

No, but he is very angry, and sometimes that is just as bad.

Can you help him?

No, I cannot help anyone except for you, and I am not even supposed to be doing that.

But you are.

Because I love you.

He nods thoughtfully. I don't love you yet, but maybe if you come around more, I will.

I can say nothing to this because the truth neither requires nor permits any answer.

✢

TUCKER AND ROXANNE became best friends, and she was good for him. She encouraged him to accept who he really was, all while helping to shield his secret from the people who wouldn't understand. For a while, she even told lies about the things they had done together, and some of these lies made wide sweeps around the town, until even Tucker's father heard them and thought of his son proudly, and even with a twinge of jealousy, but that's not unusual. Speaking from personal experience, it's hard to not be a little jealous of your son, the potential he represents, the years he has before him that you will never see again.

Roxanne couldn't keep up the lies though. Like many of the best people, she was allergic to them. Even when she knew why she was telling one, and that it would make a difference for her friend, she felt miserable afterward because lies twist the world and distort reality, and for some people — the liars among us — this is a good thing, but for the rest of the people, the ones that have managed to carve out a niche within the world without lying to themselves, lies are abhorrent, vomit-inducing things, that burn like bile in the back of their throats.

So she stopped, and even confided in some of her friends that all of it had been lies, and some of Roxanne's friend's were as allergic to silence as Roxanne was to lying, and soon these words swept the small town, and when his father heard this, he found himself stunned and worried.

He approached Tucker on the back deck, while his son was reading a Poe story for his Humanities class at the community college. Reading was something Tucker's father had never fully understood. It seemed like a waste of the day, to sit and do nothing, to stare at words that didn't even tell anything true. Still, a part of him admired his son for understanding the secret to this puzzling activity when he could not.

He sat down beside his boy, trying to see him in the way people were suggesting. It didn't seem possible, but then again he'd thought the same thing when the boy's mother had pulled all that foolishness with the queer so long ago. He took a deep breath, ready for just about anything, though he couldn't say how he'd react if it was true. He felt like there was a bomb in him, and if it went off it could blow up both of their lives.

"Whatever happened to you and that Roxanne girl?"

"We broke up. No big deal."

"What, you cheat on her or something?"

Tucker was surprised. He put his book down. "No, why?"

"No reason. Just thinking. She was a hell of a catch."

Tucker felt himself beginning to sweat. Where was his father going with this?

"You ain't found nobody else that strikes your fancy like her, huh?"

He decided to lie. Remember what I said about liars, how they are trying to straighten their crooked world? "A few, but nothing too serious. Just, you know..."

His father cocked his head. "What? Just like one night stands?"

"Well, I wasn't going to say that, but yeah."

His dad came over and patted Tucker on the shoulder. "You ain't got to worry. I understand. I'm a man too. Bring the next one around, though, give an old man a look." He grinned and walked back inside. Tucker, flushed red, picked up the Poe collection and continued to read.

❉

HE DIDN'T GET angry at Roxanne. Tucker understood. Lying was tough for her. Besides, he had dodged the bullet with his father. That was what mattered. Roxanne only wanted the truth, and she wanted to lay it out in the open for everybody to see, which was probably why she did what she did.

It was after class one day at the community college. She asked him to ride with her to Birmingham for coffee.

"That's a long way for coffee."

"Just say yes."

"Yes. Heck, my father has a lot of friends up there. Maybe one of them will see us together and give him a report that will make him proud."

256

"You're smiling, so it makes me think you are trying to be funny. I don't find it funny at all."

"Wait. What? It's just a joke."

"A joke? It's pitiful. Have you even considered coming out to your father?"

"Every minute of every day since before I knew I was gay, Roxanne. Don't talk to me about something you don't understand. Besides, it's not really any of your business."

"It's not? Wow, and here I thought we were friends. My friend is living a lie, a miserable, soul-destroying lie and it's none of my business?"

"You think this is soul destroying? You're right, but telling him would be worse."

"Nothing can be worse than living a lie, Tucker."

He said nothing in response. He feared she was right, and most of all, he feared he was too afraid to do anything about it.

"Come on. We'll talk more over coffee. I'm driving."

⁌⁍

THEY'D BEEN SITTING in companionable silence for a few minutes when she said, "I want you to meet somebody."

Tucker was caught off guard. Not so much by what she said, but by the way she said it. She sounded too happy, the way people sound when they're playing matchmaker.

"Okay…"

"Oh! Here he comes now."

Tucker followed her gaze to the door. A tall, bearded dream of a man stood there, surveying the café. He was conservatively dressed, but wore two earrings, a dead giveaway in 1970's Alabama. Immediately, Tucker felt exhilarated and exhausted. He couldn't do this. He just wouldn't.

But when the man spotted them and smiled, Tucker felt something turning inside; he began to think that maybe this time he'd just be who he was meant to be.

The man came over and stood awkwardly beside their table. "Tucker," Roxanne said, drawing his name out the way people do when they are happy about two other people meeting and the possibility of being the architect of a great romance. "This is Jeff. Jeff, meet Tucker. We go way back."

Tucker stood and extended his hand. Jeff reached for it, and right as he did, the door opened, and in stepped one of Tucker's father's best friends, another chicken farmer named Pete Staley. Mr. Staley was his dad made over except

257

he was the type of guy who wore every emotion he'd ever had on his sleeve. He looked right at Tucker, and his face seemed to light up. Like most people, he liked Tucker a lot because he saw him as an extension of his father.

Panic seized Tucker. What if Mr. Staley saw him? Wouldn't he wonder why Tucker was hanging out with someone like Jeff, someone so clearly different?

So he did the unthinkable. He let his hand drop to his side, leaving Jeff hanging. Jeff's expression went from slightly confused to offended.

"Tucker," Roxanne said harshly.

Tucker smirked, just like he'd seen his father do when that show came on television where the men dressed up like women in order to live in a women's dorm.

"Nice earrings," Tucker said viciously.

Jeff literally stepped back as if hit. "This your friend?" he asked Roxanne.

She looked at Tucker, shaking her head. "Not anymore."

"You think I'm queer?" Tucker said. "Jesus Christ. I ain't no queer."

But Roxanne was done. She took Jeff's arm and pulled him away to the next table, whispering apologies. Tucker looked over at Mr. Staley. He was seated at a window table, looking at the newspaper. Was it possible he'd never even seen him? That was the moment Tucker felt it inside. Some deep subfloor cracked; something in him — call it the heart, soul, mind, whatever — splintered.

He was a fool.

✦✦

THAT AFTERNOON, TUCKER found his father on the floor of his bedroom, one knee bleeding from where it had cracked open against the wall. His father explained that he'd tripped. The rug, he said. Nothing to worry about. He smiled, said he was fine, but Tucker could tell he wasn't fine, that he was in fact shaken.

Later, when his father was icing his knee in the kitchen, Tucker went back to his father's room to investigate something that had caught his eye earlier. The hardwood floor seemed to have buckled, as floors do when wet.

Tucker knew this meant something, but he didn't know what that something was. He noticed one more thing before leaving the room. There was a gap — only about an inch or so — in the floor near the doorjamb. Had that been there before? Surely not. If it had, his father would have certainly fixed it by now.

That night, Tucker dreamed of the same people he saw illuminated on the back of his eyelids so long ago. Now, he recognized them as the voiceless, lost denizens of a Poe short story. He woke up in the middle of the night, shaking with fear, wishing he was still a little boy, wishing he could crawl into bed with his father, wishing there was some grand gesture he could make to heal the both of them.

⁓⁓

A MONTH LATER, there was no denying something was happening to the house — specifically something was happening to his father's room. It was separating from the rest of the structure. It should have been alarming, even frightening, but another more urgent issue had arisen. His father was sick. He had cancer, and the treatments were the first thing Tucker had ever seen that seemed to knock his father flat on his back. Cracks in the house didn't matter. Tucker pushed it all aside, except for the lie he was living. That could never be pushed aside. It had begun to haunt him like ghost, a vengeful spirit, living inside him.

⁓⁓

SO THE ROOM fell off the back of the house?

Here's where the literal and the figurative get tangled up.

The metaphor.

Yes. See, if you went to visit the house, the room would still be there. But that doesn't matter because the spirit of the room is here.

So wait...what about Tucker and his father? Are they here in body or spirit?

After a while, the spirit weighs the body down. I know it's not an answer, but we are coming near the end of our walk, and such things will only serve to confuse him.

We've come to the final betrayal, I say.

This gets his mind off the question.

Final betrayal? he asks.

Yes, as I alluded to earlier, the soul can only be sold down the river so many times before it becomes a useless thing.

A useless thing?

Yes, I wish there were a better way to put it, but there's not.

I understand.

I hope you do. We are almost finished now.

⁓⁓

TUCKER RAN INTO Jeff walking across campus one afternoon after his Poe class. More and more, Tucker had become enamored with Poe. He was the quintessential outsider, a man driven to write about the places in the world where the shadows walk and metaphor becomes reality. Tucker had read "The Tell-tale Heart," "The Black Cat," "The Fall of the House of Usher," all the classics, but his favorite was still "MS. Found in a Bottle." He sensed somehow that he was on the same journey, and he read and reread the story for some clue of how to stop it.

When he saw Jeff, he thought he might have found it. Tucker wanted to tell Jeff he was sorry. That was all.

He had to follow him, no, it was more like *chase* him across campus. When Tucker finally caught up to him, Jeff wheeled around, a hateful smile on his face. "Come to call me a faggot? Come to make fun of the way I walk like a queer?"

"No," Tucker said, trying to make his voice low and sincere, to sound like the person he really was inside, the boy that had been locked away a long time ago.

"You're a piece of shit," Jeff said. "What kind of person does what you did? Roxanne told me you're gay too. It's...I don't know. Unbelievable. I feel sorry for you."

"I'm lost," Tucker said. The words just sort of came out. He didn't know where they originated. It was the first time he'd ever thought them, but as soon as he said them, he knew they were true. Lost, just like Poe's narrator in "MS. Found in a Bottle." Lost at sea. When would he capsize and find himself among the shadow people? Soon, he knew in that instant, if he didn't do something about it.

What he did surprised him. It thrilled him. Deep inside, he will hold the memory like a treasure — stepping out from his father's great shadow, feeling the sun, the moment he grew and his lungs expanded and his skin glowed and his blood thrummed with energy unlike anything he'd ever felt. He leaned in and kissed Jeff hard.

At first, Jeff resisted, but not for long. Soon, he was returning the kiss, equaling Tucker's passion, his urgency.

And for those few seconds, Tucker didn't care who saw them because he'd felt the sun, and the shadows were far away.

Too bad moments never last.

⊬

WHY DON'T THEY?

I stop walking. The room with the father and Tucker in it has been on our right for most of the journey. I gesture to them now.

Moments, by definition, are fleeting. What's inside you is eternal. Don't ever mistake what you feel in a moment as being something that will last forever. You have to do more than feel it, you have to live it with every fiber of your being. Forever and ever.

My son says nothing for a while. Instead, he gazes at the room, Tucker sitting by the window, fretting, the father in a deep sleep. I don't know what he's thinking. This may surprise you, but it's a choice I made. To know someone's thoughts is to know them too well.

I hope he is thinking about the importance of not only knowing something deep inside, but living it too.

I wish the story could have ended with the kiss, he says.

Alas…

Maybe we should leave it there.

If it were just a story we could, but this is a story within a story. It has to be told to the end or its power is lost.

He nods. I think I know the ending.

Go ahead.

Tucker and Jeff fall in love. It has to happen.

How do you know?

Look at him. He's so sad. He's sad because he cheated himself and somebody else out of happiness.

Maybe even his father, too, I suggest lightly.

The boy considers this. Maybe. But I'm not as sympathetic.

Why?

Because he lived a lie too.

And that was?

Pretending to be perfect, pretending to be a good man, a brave man. He fooled a lot of people, maybe even his son half the time, but he couldn't fool himself.

I treasure this moment. I know my time with him is coming to a close. I know he will think of this one day as if it were a dream, and I know he might even convince himself that I don't exist at all, but in this moment we are one. I glow with pride for him, and yes, envy too. For he is so young to have figured out so much. I'd give much to have his understanding and his youth, to fix my own mistakes, to make the world a place worth living in, and myself a person capable of loving the truth like a tree loves the sun.

They fell in love, he continues, and I'll bet the rift healed itself a little. Maybe even the father's cancer, I can't be sure how that fits in. But I'm betting Jeff wasn't satisfied with secrecy. I'm betting he demanded to meet Tucker's father.

Loves does demand things, I say.

He looks at me funny then. It demands pain sometimes, doesn't it?

I nod. Sometimes.

I think I'll feel that when you're gone.

Only for a while.

What happened to you, Father?

It is a different story, but the same. All who come here live different stories, but they live the same story too. The denial, the lies, the rift. There's a say-ing: *You are not punished for your anger, but by your anger.* Man creates his own shadow according to where he moves. The sun only shines.

I see him thinking, and again, I feel the swell of pride. He's smart, thought-ful, and courageous. He'll be okay. It's me that will continue to suffer.

Can I finish? he says.

Of course.

Jeff demands to meet his father, but eventually Tucker tells him no. When he does, it's a betrayal of himself and of Jeff. There is only so much the soul can take. One day he comes home to find his father in the bed, the room splitting from the house.

He shrugs because there is nothing more to say.

I nod, pleased that the trip has not been wasted. It was no small feat to bring the boy here, just as it was no small feat to bring his mother here so many years before. Nothing important is small. Everything important can kill you, and some of the most important things can cause fates worse than death. I think this is what I want to tell my boy most of all.

But our time is coming to a close here. I'll have to take it on faith that he's learned enough, that this story within a story has not been wasted. The mist parts in the distance, and very soon my boy will walk away without me, out into a world where the truth matters, where every action and inaction has an equal and opposite one here in the shadow land, where the sun still shines, waiting for someone to reach up their arms toward it, straight and true.

When he leaves, I will say but one prayer, and it will be that I should never see him here again.

A PORTRAIT
IN INDIA INK
BY HARRY CLARKE

Alex Jeffers

to Elizabeth Bowen and Edgar Allan Poe,
Harry Clarke and Molly Keane, strange bedfellows

CO. WATERFORD, IRELAND, 1968

FREDDIE knew he shouldn't try to read through a migraine so he only looked at the pictures, just glancing at the titles to remind himself of stories he'd already read: every student in the Baltimore schools read Poe. He didn't live in Baltimore anymore and barely remembered the outlines of the famous tales. "The Cask of Amontillado" — a frightened man in carnival motley chained at the waist in a dark cellar, its walls deformed by dripping stalactites. "The Pit and the Pendulum" — a cadaverous fellow bound by black ribbons, which piles of rats appeared to be gnawing apart while the razor-sharp pendulum descended. "The Murders in the Rue Morgue" — a huge vicious ape (it looked more like a chimpanzee than the orangutan Freddie thought he remembered) attacked a desperate woman with a straight razor while the corpse of another woman stared in the background.

Freddie knew his father had bought the fifty-year-old book for him on account of the illustrations. Allan Bowes was more impressed by his son's drawings than Freddie was. This Harry Clarke was *good.* Freddie recognized the influence of Beardsley in the unbalanced compositions, but where the drama in Beardsley was trumpeted by contrast between flat black and stark white, Clarke's drawings were…textured. Pattern upon pattern laid down in precise India ink like overlapping Oriental rugs, none of it merely decorative. White faces exploded out of the ornamentation like bombs of tortured emotion.

Maybe that was the migraine. Freddie couldn't trust his vision. Dim floating motes and trails clung to the edges of black lines when he concentrated, a faint aurora borealis troubled the periphery, rustling and crackling. Freddie flipped through the pages.

Roaring down over the Comeraghs, the sudden winter storm that had brought on the migraine battered Ladytown. Freddie's room was at the front of the house but he could hear the wind's bashes and buffets at the back and roof even with his door closed. Lifting his head, he glanced across the room. The tall windows were black and the panes seemed to ripple. Migraine? No — he remembered a daytime summer downpour. A broken gutter or something sent floods sheeting down the glass. He ought to fetch a towel before the window-seat cushion was soaked through. He turned back to Harry Clarke.

These faces weren't tortured. He saw the woman first, supine across the bottom of the page, her profile carved from ice, severe and serene, surrounded by unearthly blossoms. Then the heavily ringed left hand of the man above her in the picture plane. Harry Clarke's rendering of hands was peculiar. Nobody had fingers that long, tapered, pointy — anybody's fingers crooked at the knuckles if left to themselves. Freddie tried to make his own hand assume the posture. It was an effort, uncomfortable.

On the facing page, the title was "Morella." The name — of the sleeping or dead woman? — rang no bells. Freddie turned back to the drawing.

To the man's face. Stylized in a less unnatural manner than the hand, it reminded Freddie of one of his younger teachers, though Mr Palmer didn't have a beard. The expression more than the fine features: lecturing, Mr Palmer now and then would become distracted and turn up his eyes to gaze into nothingness like the man in the drawing. Mr Palmer wasn't as good looking, though, with his short nose and prim small mouth, thin eyebrows invisible in the wrong light, a plumpness about his cheeks that promised jowls.

Freddie blinked when a translucent, prismatic veil wafted across the page, painting the drawn man's features and elaborate costume with uncanny vividness, and then a horrible squeal made him jump and yelp. Swallowing hard, he dropped the heavy book and staggered across the room to the window seat. The wind must have reached an arm around the house to scrape a broken limb of Virginia creeper across the glass. Must have. Migraine flickers at the edges of his vision sparked and flared.

He was still trembling when a rap at his door made him jump again. "Who is it?" Freddie bleated.

"Herself sent up tea, Master Freddie."

"Barry?" Dropping the blanket, Freddie hurried across the room — paused a breath. There was nothing to be done about pyjamas and bathrobe. He pushed his hair out of his eyes and pulled the door open.

Unexpectedly, handsome Barry with the tray from downstairs looked right into Freddie's eyes. For an instant. Had Freddie always known Barry's eyes were that lustrous brown-almost-black, like broken anthracite?

Handsome Barry focussed on the small teapot and plate of digestive biscuits on the linen-covered tray. "Herself said you'd the headache. I brought aspirin."

"Thank you. It's the storm, I think." Aspirin would do nothing for migraine but it was a kind thought. Freddie dared another look at the handsome face before realizing why Barry hadn't entered the room. "Oh — " Flustered, Freddie stepped aside, out of the way.

Tea tray deposited on the table, Barry straightened up. He was never as tall as Freddie remembered — tall enough, bigger than Freddie, but not like a movie star on the big screen. Glancing at the streaming window, he said, "'Tis a great gale indeed."

"Shouldn't — How will you get home through this, Barry?" Freddie knew it was two miles from Ladytown to Barry's father's farm. His own father had pointed the place out once, driving Freddie back to school in Waterford city. He knew Barry cycled those two miles every morning before Freddie got up, back again in the late afternoon. "Helen should have let you go before it came on."

Barry shrugged. "It was terrible sudden, Master Freddie, there was no warning."

"I wish you wouldn't call me *Master*. I've asked you before."

Anthracite eyes glanced at Freddie, away. "I forget while you're away at school. I'm sorry...Freddie." Did handsome Barry's lips twitch toward a smile?

"That's better. How will you get home?"

"Mr Bowes offered to drive me. 'Tis fearsome weather for the roads, though."

"You could — " Freddie swallowed. Shining light outlined the figure of handsome Barry and his black eyes gleamed but that was just the migraine. "You should stay the night. There's plenty of empty beds." Ladytown had been built for a much larger family than Freddie Bowes and his dad and stepmother. A bigger family with frequent weekend guests and live-in staff, although Freddie wouldn't stand for Barry's being exiled to the maids' attic. The room next to his was empty. "Where's Helen? I'll tell her."

"Don't trouble yourself about me, Master Freddie. Your head — "

"*Freddie*," said Freddie firmly. "Don't trouble yourself about my head. Come on." He turned toward the door. "Where is she?" He didn't wait for an answer. His stepmother would be on the ground floor somewhere.

The long white corridor, poorly lit as it was, hurt his eyes. Hurrying down the quarter circle of the grand staircase made him dizzy. At the bottom, fighting nausea, he clutched the newel post for a moment's support. "Are you well, Freddie?" asked Barry, thumping down behind him.

"Where. Is. Helen?" said Freddie, not looking back. He had a mission.

"Herself was in the drawing room. Drinks before dinner with your father."

The closest door. Good. He made it across the hall without stumbling or puking.

"Fred?" said his stepmother when one leaf of the double door flew open. Helen believed a young man of sixteen needed a grown-up name.

"Freddie, you look terrible!" exclaimed Allan Bowes, rising from the sofa in a rush, dropping his *Irish Times*. "What are you doing out of bed?"

"Dad," said Freddie, "I don't want you driving in this storm. You can't remember which side of the road to stay on in good weather. Barry can stay the night here — he can have the room beside mine. He'll call his family so they won't worry and stay here."

The tall Palladian windows above the great lawn rattled and Freddie had an instant to wonder why the curtains weren't drawn before they exploded with unbearable white light. He was on the Persian rug before the boom of thunder rocked Ladytown and Helen shrieked. He was blind. "Freddie!" roared his dad.

"I've got him, Mr Bowes."

"I'm — " mewled Freddie as careful hands rolled him onto his back. Barry's elbow under his neck started to lift his head. "I'm going to throw up."

He heard Helen wail, "Not on the carpet!" but her strident Ballmer tones were abruptly receding. Freddie was flying. Strong arms under his knees and shoulders supported him and he was flying through the roaring dark. Just as suddenly, he was on his knees and the hands were helping him discover the chill open bowl of a toilet. He was still blind. "I'm sorry," handsome Barry muttered near his ear. "I couldn't think where to find a basin quickly enough." Freddie with a half-drowned whimper began to vomit.

After the first acid retch it was just slime and spit, sour and burning, but his stomach continued convulsing. At a great distance, Allan Bowes said, "Thank you, Barry. I'll get water for him to rinse his mouth." The water in Ladytown's pipes wasn't potable. Their drinking water came from a well half a mile away — Barry fetched it in every morning.

"Be careful in the dark, Mr Bowes."

"Dark?" asked Freddie in a pause between gripes. "I thought...I thought I went blind."

"No more blind than any of us. Electricity failed with the lightning. Struck a pole, I expect. Are you well, Freddie?"

"Not very. But done puking."

Barry helped him sit back against his chest, reached around to lower the seat and lid. "Can't reach the flush," Barry grunted. "Why would you think you'd gone blind?"

"The migraine. It's happened before." Freddie felt comfortable, comforted, in Barry's embrace. "It only lasts a little while but it's frightening."

He heard leather soles smacking the slate floor of the hall. When he moved in Barry's arms and looked toward the downstairs loo's half-open door, he saw a fluttery orange glow that brightened as his father approached. Relieved he wasn't blind, self conscious, he meant to pull away, try to stand, but Barry held him. "You're weak yet, boyo," Barry murmured. "Don't attempt standing on your own." Barry's breath was warm and sweet on his cheek.

"Freddie?" asked Allan Bowes, pushing the door wide. Candle flame fluttered, candlelight licked and flickered at his face, making him look monstrous.

"I'm okay, Dad."

"No, you're not." Allan looked around for a place to put the candlestick — there wasn't one. "You're going straight back to bed." He crouched to set it on the floor and held out the tall glass of glimmering water. "Here. You haven't had a migraine so bad it made you fall down and throw up since we came to Ireland."

Barry's steady hand reached the glass before Freddie gathered the strength to try. He held it to Freddie's lips and Freddie took a sip, swished it around his mouth. He didn't want to swallow it, polluted by bile and acid. Reading his mind, Barry opened the toilet again, supported him as he leaned to spit. The stench of his vomit in the bowl made him light headed again but he held it down for another rinse and spit, then reached for the chain himself and flushed.

He had suffered migraines as bad in Ireland — worse. At school. A stern, kind woman, Matron had learned the best she could do was lead the American boy to the curtained bed in the dimmest, quietest corner of the dispensary and give him a warm compress to cover his eyes, leave a basin nearby. They must not have told his dad — his dad must not have asked.

"Barry," said his dad when the rush of water from the tank slowed, "would you help Freddie upstairs, please? Mrs Bowes is afraid of thunder and lightning — I'd better check on her. We haven't lost power before."

"Certainly, sir," Barry said, while Allan went on: "You'll stay the night, of course. I shouldn't leave Freddie and Helen alone. I'll call your family. If the phone's still working. Take the candle. Freddie, I'll be up in a bit." He was gone.

With Barry's help, Freddie got to his feet. He trembled when Barry bent for the candlestick on the floor but didn't fall. Barry regarded him shrewdly. "Will I carry you, lad?"

"You can't carry me and the candle," Freddie retorted.

"True enough, I suppose. Lean on me, then."

They started into the hall, toward the stairs. The gale still roared outside Ladytown. "I'm not a lad," said Freddie, fretful. "I'm sixteen. How old are you?"

Barry grunted, a sound of amusement. "My brother is your age — he's but a lad. I'm going on nineteen myself."

Passing the open drawing-room door, Freddie heard Helen whimpering, his dad comforting her, saw the shivering glow of many candles, but he didn't want to know. At the foot of the staircase climbing into gloom, he hesitated.

"Will I carry you?" Barry asked again. "With you pickaback, I expect I could manage the candle as well."

"No." Freddie lifted one foot to the first step, holding onto Barry's sturdy arm on one side, the polished bannister on the other. They took the stairs slowly, like halt old men. Halfway up the quarter circle, beneath a ten-foot-tall painting of a noble eighteenth-century horse too big for the previous owners to take away, Barry said, "It's not simply a fierce headache, then, the migraine?"

"My head hardly hurts at all. Yet. It will later, probably. It's my eyes, my vision, even when I don't go blind. I see…things. That aren't real. Lights, floating lights — glowing auras, haloes, around people and things. They make me dizzy and sick. Hallucinations sometimes, things that aren't there, couldn't be there, but they scare me. My house was on fire once, I was sure of it, back — back in Baltimore. Scarier things."

"That sounds dreadful."

"Then the headache. That's — that'll be bad. If…Barry, if you hear me whimpering or moaning in the night, ignore it. I mean it. There's nothing you can do that won't make it worse."

Barry stumbled on the top step. The candle swooped and drops of liquid wax splatted on the polished floor. Freddie nearly lost his footing as well but he still had a hand on the bannister and prevented Barry from falling. "I'm sorry!" Barry blurted, recovering. "Is — Can a doctor not give you some-thing?"

"Nothing that helps. Barry, I should lie down."

"Yes. Of course."

Barry supported him down the long corridor. Candle flame painted white-grey walls in shifting blushes of rose and gold. Inside the bedroom door, Freddie loosed his limpet hold on Barry's arm and tottered to the bed. After a clenched-lids moment, lights blooming and fading and revolving through red-tinged black infinities, he opened his eyes to Barry's shadowy face above him. It was nearly the same expression as the "Morella" illustration, except Barry was looking at him, not at nothing. *Seeing* him. Stars smoldered in brown-black irises, flames burned at the margins of tousled blue-black hair. Freddie wanted to lift a balky hand, caress the closely shaved cheek and chin, run the tip of his index finger down the long, straight nose, touch full lips meant to be smiling, not compressed in concern. "Your dressing gown?" asked Barry.

"Never mind."

"Your slippers?"

"I suppose."

Barry removed them gently, set them aside. "You should be under the blankets, boyo. There's a chill."

"I'm…hot."

"Fever? Your feet were cold." A cool palm came to rest on Freddie's brow. "No, you're icy."

"I'm not." Freddie didn't want Barry's hand to move.

"What's this?" Barry pulled the heavy old book from among Freddie's pillows. "*Tales of Mystery and Imagination*," he read aloud, "by Edgar Allan Poe. I read some Poe at school. 'The Tell-Tale Heart'? It didn't frighten me as it wanted to. My grandda tells properly scary stories. I can't sleep some nights."

"I'm not so interested in the stories myself," Freddie said dreamily, gazing at Barry's handsome face instead of the book in his hand. "Dad brought that back from London for me. Because of the illustrations. I like to draw, you know."

"I did not. Harry Clarke?" Barry asked, peering at the second name on the cover.

"He's Irish. Was Irish, I think he's dead. The drawings…there's so much in them, it's frightening. Beautiful and fascinating but frightening."

Barry wasn't interested, only a minor disappointment. He set the book aside. "I doubt you should be looking at drawings in your condition, boyo. Tell me now, Freddie, how may I help you? Tea? I expect it's stewed and cool but I could fetch a kettle of hot water."

"Don't leave me!"

"Hush, laddy." Moving Freddie's arm out of the way, Barry sat by his head. "Hush, now. I'll not be going." His fingers glanced at Freddie's hair, then gave in, stroking, combing. "A poor friend I'd be to leave you in misery."

Freddie listened — listened the way Pluto, his old cat, had listened, long ago in Roland Park, wanting to understand the words but content to recognize the tone. Through half-closed eyes, he gazed up. Barry stroked his hair as if he, Freddie, were a beloved pet, taking comfort in the action as much as giving it. Motes and glowing filaments danced slowly about Barry's head without obscuring his handsomeness. Freddie thought he knew what he wished Barry to do, how Barry might help him, but he didn't know the proper language, the words Barry would understand. He wanted, like a cat, to lick Barry's thumb, his small, slightly protruding ear, his chin. He wanted to butt his head into Barry's belly. Barry's black eyebrows, as he stroked Freddie's hair, were frowning, but not his black eyes.

Barry started at the knock on the door. Freddie swallowed, blinked away darkness and light, said, "Dad?"

Before the door swung open, Barry was across the room, peering at the storm or his reflection in the window. Allan Bowes ignored or didn't see him, going to the bed. "How are you feeling, Freddie?"

Freddie sat up on his elbows. "How's Helen, Dad?"

His father set his candlestick on the bedside table, leaned over Freddie. Gathering quickly, the migraine lights made a mystery of his expression. "She'll be fine. You know and I know. It's nothing but nerves. She's in front of the fire with another drink and blazes of candles. She'll be fine. How's your head?"

"I'll be fine."

"Frederick."

"It's not hurting yet. Not much." Giving up, Freddie lay back in the pillows. "My eyes are funny."

"Your tummy?"

"Sixteen year olds don't have *tummies*, Dad. It's okay."

Allan sighed, lights congregating in his eyes. "You're *my* sixteen year old, Freddie. I hate to see you hurting. Your mother — "

"Yes." Freddie closed his eyes. "I know. That's how you knew."

"There's nothing I can do, is there?"

"Wait it out. Like I do."

Freddie's father knuckled his cheek. "There should be something, though. What's a dad for?" Another sigh. "Thank you for helping my son, Barry," he said, pitching his voice away.

Across the room, Barry's voice fought with the noise of the storm. "It's no trouble, Mr Bowes. As you said, 'tis a terrible thing to watch and do nothing useful."

Freddie wanted to protest but didn't.

"I spoke to your father," Allan went on. "He seemed relieved you wouldn't be out in the storm. Their power's out as well. The room next door's clean, I expect, but I doubt the bed's made up."

"I know where to find sheets."

"Yes, of course. Well. Freddie." Another invisible touch to the cheek. "You send Barry to find me if…if you want me."

"G'night, Dad." Freddie kept his eyes shut. "I hope Helen feels better."

"I hope *you* do."

The door closed carefully. Freddie opened his eyes. With only one candle burning, the ceiling billowed and danced like racing cloud. The green stripes of the wallpaper looked like prison bars, closing in. The wind and the rain clamored outside.

"I'll not be using the other room." Barry's shadow wavered across the ceiling, then his face appeared, blobby and monstrous for a moment before it resolved into fineness. "I'll not leave you lonely in your misery." He sat again beside Freddie. "I'll curl up on the window seat if need be. Are you well, Freddie?"

"No." Acutely grateful, Freddie moved. Throwing his arm over Barry's legs, he pushed his face into the solid corduroy thigh. "No, I am not."

Comforting fingers combed Freddie's hair, traced the whorl of his ear. "There, now. There, now. I'm here, lad. Will we talk? Would that help at all?"

"May I — may I lean on you?"

Barry was already moving. "Of course you will, boyo." He plumped up pillows against the headboard, pulled his legs onto the bed, helped Freddie sit up and nestle at his side.

When they were settled, Freddie realized he had nothing to say. He wanted to know everything about Barry but now, really, all he wanted was to have him there. "Why did you come work for us, Barry?" he asked at last.

"It's no story at all," said Barry comfortably, his arm warm around Freddie's shoulders. "Da's farm was Ladytown land back in the English days. His aunties and great-aunties always worked in the house, his da and uncles in the fields. *My* auntie cooked for the new owner when I was a wee lad. Mam was poorly so Auntie Mag would bring me with her to take a burden off, so I knew the place upside and down. When Mr Bowes bought Ladytown, his agent looked about for a girl to come in but I've no sisters and the other girls around wanting to work in town shops to meet town boys, not in a lonely old house in the country. Your da didn't mind I was a lunk of a boy instead of a lass and I was right happy to return to Ladytown. I love the house, you know. And I'm a poor farmer, too. Young Leary's a better hand in the fields."

"I'm glad you're here, Barry. I'm glad it's you."

"Ah, 'tis a kindness for you to say so."

"No, I mean it."

"I know you do, Freddie. Ladytown's a brighter place when you're home from school at the weekend and the holidays."

"Not tonight."

"Without the electricity, no." Barry seemed to search the gloomy corners of the room. "With the tempest blowing and your poor head."

"You make me feel safe."

Barry's arm tightened. "Glad I am I can do that little thing."

They were silent some while. Maybe Barry had no ready topics of conversation either.

The storm was not silent. No thunder again but the wind thundered. Freddie wondered about his stepmother: he had not known she was afraid of thunder. He knew she didn't like him much, afraid he came before her in his father's eyes, foolishly jealous of the migraines that now and again put Freddie first, that Freddie shared with the first Mrs Bowes.

He wondered how to get closer to Barry — if Barry could ever wish to be closer. Hardly moving his head, he regarded the young man's profile, distinct against flickering candlelight and migraine light. Handsome Barry. The long nose, the lips parted. The things Freddie wanted — the things he wanted to do. He didn't believe they were horrible, evil, his thoughts.

"Will you tell me, Freddie, why it was you came to live at Ladytown, so far from America?"

Freddie's thoughts had to shift around. He wasn't certain what question he wanted Barry asking but that wasn't it. He had to look away. "Well, we're Irish, the Boweses, a long time ago. Two Bowes brothers went over on the ship that founded Baltimore. My mother's family, too, not quite so long ago. She visited as a child and always wanted to come back, but then she died." It was years ago, Freddie was over it, but he heard the catch in his voice.

Barry heard it too. Drawing Freddie still closer, he leaned his cheek against the boy's skull.

"I was ten. She was going to have another baby. My sister. They both died."

"'Tis a sorrowful thing to lose your mam before you're grown."

"Then Dad married Helen. It wasn't...comfortable where we lived."

"She's not your sort," Barry observed, his voice cynical.

"How did you know?"

"The three of you all from the same town but herself's way of speaking isn't yours and Mr Bowes's."

"It doesn't matter to Dad, it doesn't matter to me, but it mattered to people. And she's so much younger. And then she was ill, the same way my mother was ill, but Helen only lost the baby, she didn't die, and my mother's family held it against her. So it was uncomfortable. Helen's family's from Galway, forty years ago, but Dad didn't find a house he liked there. He liked Lady-town. I like Ladytown." Freddie meant, *I like you.* Meant it so hard Barry should have known.

Barry's hand moved up Freddie's arm, rubbing the fabric against his skin in a way that could only be better if there were no fabric at all. In the dormitory at school where Freddie was a weekly boarder, it was a known thing that certain boys were special friends. Freddie had ideas about what happened between them when one slipped into the other's bed after lights out but no boy at school was special to him. He'd wished one might be, but not now. Barry's fingertips grazed over the crumpled pyjama collar onto his bare neck, strangely warm and cool at once, and Freddie sighed.

"Sleepy? Will I leave you room to stretch out?"

"No — please, no, don't go."

"Would you sleep on my shoulder then?"

Nestling closer, Freddie didn't know how to say he didn't expect to sleep. The migraine wouldn't permit it. "I'll try." When he shifted his cheek against the solid comfort of Barry's arm, coarse woollen tweed scratched. He had never seen Barry without his jacket. Peering the length of the bed through half-closed eyes, he saw his own legs stretched out across the green coverlet — claret-red winter bathrobe to the knees, navy-blue pyjamas, bare white feet — but Barry's leg was angled off the bed, booted foot projecting into the air. "You can't be comfortable," Freddie protested.

"Nor will you be comfortable, lad," said Barry, "if you don't climb under the blankets. Sharp now." He was off the bed before Freddie could protest. "I'll put out the candle."

Thrilled somehow by Barry's command, Freddie wrestled off his bathrobe, pushed it aside. As he wormed himself up to wriggle under the covers, the candle flame went away into darkness with an audible hiss, as if Barry had spat on thumb and forefinger and pinched the wick. Freddie was blind. Again.

Falsely blind. Blind in the way of migraine. Motes and auroras, lightning bugs and contrails and the subsiding sparks of pyrotechnics zoomed through the black, dispersing and immediately coalescing.

Less blind than Barry, who stumbled getting his boot off. Freddie turned toward the noise. Gathering willingly, the lights formed a dim flickering curtain behind the young man so Freddie could make out black flashes of his silhouette. Giving in, Barry found his way to the window seat and sat with a thump before attempting the second boot. The stormy glass of the window flooded with migraine lights.

Barry was taking off more than boots. Freddie kept his breath quiet. He was certain of jacket and jumper, but more came off the top and he didn't know how many layers Barry might wear. Then Barry stood. He seemed to fumble at belt and fly buttons. His trousers fell. After shaking them off his ankles, he took a moment to pick them up and place them with the other discarded garments on the window seat.

"That might flood," Freddie said. "I meant to get a towel. Put them on the chair."

"Or I'll be miserable and damp come morn?"

"Not if you sleep in...a bed, and move your clothes."

Barry had already tossed the clothes into Freddie's wing chair. "How is it you know what I'm doing, Freddie? Can you see in the dark? Speak for me now, let me follow your voice."

"I don't know. I think I'm guessing."

"You never intended me to sleep there."

"Helen would have put you in a maids' room in the attic."

"I'm here," Barry said. Freddie already knew it. "'Tis a terrible liberty to take."

"Get in." Freddie was too worried Barry wouldn't not to make it an order. "You'll get cold." He lifted the covers aside.

The mattress dipped when Barry sat. Uncertain, Freddie didn't permit himself to roll against him — discover how unclothed Barry was. But Barry drew his legs in and extended them under the covers, one foot tracing the length of Freddie's leg until it reached a bare ankle. Barry wore socks. His foot was warm. "Will we sit up or are you ready to recline?"

Pulling himself a little higher against the pillows, Freddie edged closer. Without resistance, Barry held him, pulled the bedclothes up with his free hand. He was probably wearing some sort of undershirt, some sort of undershorts — swaddled in pyjamas, Freddie couldn't tell. "It's nice to have someone — to have *you* here. We don't need to talk."

"Ah, laddy. Freddie. 'Tis a fearsome liberty I'm taking." Turning his face as if he could see in the dark, Barry squeezed harder, bent his head to kiss Freddie's brow.

"Please," said Freddie.

Barry sighed surrender. The warm tip of his tongue dabbed the length of Freddie's nose. When it reached his lips, Freddie sighed as well, breathed longing into Barry's lungs. He had never imagined how a kiss would feel. It felt like the storm outside bottled down to fit inside him. It felt like a lightning strike on the surface of the sun. It felt like a hot needle stitching acid through the back of his left eye. It felt like all the pain in the world. Freddie mewled into Barry's mouth.

"Freddie?" Barry's breath tasted sweet, fresh, warm, like summer meadows. "Are you well?"

Freddie was a cat, a small black cat in the warmth and darkness of a bed safe from tempest and anguish, a creature of dumb instinct without words. No words for wanting, only wanting — no words for pain. His long-dead cat in Roland Park had never understood words, not even the name Freddie's mother had given him without explanation, only intonation. "You are a beast of monstrous evil" had meant the same to Pluto as "I love you I love you never leave me." Kissing Barry's lips, the tip of his nose, the hard wedge of his chin, Freddie mewled and pawed at Barry's underclothes.

"Ah, Freddie," Barry murmured. "Sweet lad. Sweet sad laddy. If it's what you want — "

Barry *wanted* too. Freddie's clumsy hand discovered the wanting, big and stiff in Barry's undershorts. Barry groaned, groaned again as Freddie wriggled it free, and then Barry's bigger hand got a grip on Freddie. "There it is," he muttered against Freddie's neck, his voice low and nearly ugly. "Your little man." He fished it out of Freddie's pyjamas. "Not so little as all that." His fingers were knowing, brutally gentle. "I'm wishing I could see it, Freddie," he said, but then his lips were hungry on Freddie's mouth again and so many sensations flooded through Freddie like sleet and thunder and outrage that he needed to close his eyes against the darkness. "No, don't stop," Barry said, not stopping himself, his voice rough. "Don't stop."

Freddie couldn't understand how to stop. In his hand, Barry was hard and needy, animal, demanding. He'd never felt anything so alive. "Ah," said Barry. "Wicked boy. Wise, wicked boy. But not yet. Not so soon."

He moved. With a shudder and a jerk his girthy hardness slipped stickily from Freddie's fingers. As Barry pushed him over onto his shoulders and back, Freddie whimpered. "We're not done yet, boyo, far from done," Barry murmured, opening the buttons over Freddie's chest, brushing fingertips through the fine hair that made Freddie self conscious when he undressed with the other boys at school for games. "Who's a little man then." It seemed Barry liked it, stroking, patting, as if it were a cat's pelt, and then licking, nipping, his mouth hot. He'd released the part of Freddie that most wanted but all of Freddie wanted. The lips dabbling down his chest only made him want more, so that he trembled and whined and the pinpricks in his eye almost felt good, right.

"Here we are." Barry's breath purled gustily against Freddie's belly, coiled airy fingers around the…thing Freddie didn't have a name for. *Down there.* His little man. His other self, reaching, longing. He wanted to touch it himself — Barry brushed his hand away. Barry's breath was torture. "Pretty thing. I needn't see it, Freddie, to know it's pretty. Here, let's find out." A knuckle ran up its nervy underside. "I expect it's tasty."

"What?" said Freddy, frightened. "It's dirty."

"Why would it be? I know you wash. Have you never thought? I would not try, Freddie, if I didn't wish to."

The soft, wet, definite lap of Barry's tongue on his flesh made Freddie cry out.

"Not so terrible, now, was it? And quite clean enough but not too clean. Not soapy. Salty. Will I try again, Freddie lad? Will I do more? I feel I might be powerfully fond of the flavor."

Freddie couldn't speak. There was no room for words in his mind. Barry's tongue did not pause for permission, lapping, dabbing. Barry's fingers lifted the thing taller, held it still for his mouth's ministrations. He licked its monstrously sensitive length, bottom to top. His lips closed over the tip, drawing Freddie in.

Commotion licked through Freddie, burning. How he could feel so much he didn't understand. The files rasping at his eyeball grew adamantine claws and tolling chimes. Ribbons of briar bound his skull beneath the skin — his hair was afire. Down there — down there, Barry sank nails of thrilling ice into his thighs and Barry's lips were like animals, slavering dogs or savage cats, his mouth a cavern of conflagration. Freddie opened his eyes.

He could see. The room remained dark, night dark, storm dark, but Freddie saw. Everything was black on ivory — not like a photograph but a drawing, India ink scribed and stippled with the sharpest steel nib on fine-grained paper. Flowers filled his eyes, millions upon millions of unnatural monochrome flowers embroidered on every surface, brocaded into the air. Faceted jewels, diamonds and lustrous jet, and gleaming tears of pearl. Figured velvets and bolts of sequinned silks and rich Oriental carpets strewn, piles of glossy pelts, mink, ermine, sable.

He looked down his own torso. It appeared intolerably long, intolerably naked though inked with roses and peonies and poppies. Where his thighs joined was Barry's face, mouth stuffed full, bearded and mustached by the curly hair between Freddie's legs. It was different seeing it than feeling it, more terrible. Barry's paper and India ink face was the face of the man Harry Clarke had drawn to illustrate Poe's "Morella."

"Ah," said Freddie. The air was thick with fumes of church incense and potpourri, with bells and pouring rain.

As if he too could see in the darkness, Barry peered toward Freddie's faraway face, dark irises glistening under heavy lashes and brows. His nostrils flared wide as he suckled on Freddie's blood-hard flesh, his cheeks hollowed and filled. A kind of gentle cannibal or vampire, he nursed. The sensations were unbearably real. Freddie had touched himself down there, played with himself, any boy who said he didn't was a liar — Barry had touched him, handled him, moments ago. This, himself between Barry's lips, prodding his warm pliant tongue, was not the same. More awful, more strange. Not fleeting and effortful and filthy.

"Ah," he said, reaching. His fingers threaded into Barry's hair as if the hair were heavy rings of gold and tarnished silver and black glass. It seemed more of him might fit into Barry's mouth. The way grew stranger and more strait. Barry hunched his shoulders and lowered his eyes, bending his brow to Freddie's beating belly. Threads of spittle like fine silver chain trailed from the corners of lips stretched wide and thin, depositing a treasure of lace across sable fur. Barry made a noise, a constricted choking noise that grated through Freddie's nerves like iron filings, and began to lift his head, dragging tight lips and blunted teeth after him.

"Ah," said Freddie. There was so much of him, so much still hidden, so much to be revealed.

"Big little man," said Barry when flesh like an iron bar fell clamoring from his lips to Freddie's belly. Ducking like a cat, he licked its length again, then raised his eyes. Tears made the white parts around anthracite irises glimmer like opals. Cheeks and brow were bleach pale. "Will you spend for me, Freddie? Spend in my mouth? I should like that."

"I — " said Freddie, his tongue and head thick.

"You will of course. I'll see to it."

Barry's mouth returned to its task. Freddie moaned. Barry's face was the face of the man in Harry Clarke's drawing again, buried in blossoms. Freddie was remembering he had read "Morella," Poe's story.

The supine woman in the illustration, Morella, was the man's wife, who awed him with her knowledge and wisdom, oppressed him with her theories of the perfection of death, the immortality and grim persistence of souls, so that he came to long for her to die — to break free of her morbid obsessions. And so she did, but in dying gave birth to a daughter of perfect beauty and uncanny intellect, memento mori of the mother she could not know. Enraptured yet terrified, the unnamed narrator refused to name his daughter but taught her the secrets Morella had imparted to him. As she grew, coming more and more to resemble her mother, in beauty, in wisdom, so the father's conviction grew of the dire influence of the dead on the living. At last he resolved his daughter could be saved to live her own life only if she were baptized with her own name. But when he took her to the church built over his ancient family vaults and the priest asked what name to bestow, the father in a moment of madness spoke the mother's name: Morella. "I am here!" cried the child in a dead woman's voice and died herself in wondrous agony. Carrying the child's corpse to lay it beside the mother's, the father was strangely unsurprised to find the tomb empty, for the two Morellas were the same.

"Ah!" said Freddie, distraught. Was he his own dead mother who had suffered migraine like himself — his dead sister? Who was he? Between his legs, Barry raised his beautiful eyes: the haunted black eyes of Poe's morbid lover-father. What he was doing with his lips and tongue and throat was unbearable to Freddie. What Freddie felt in his own head, the crashing, ascending, unending pain, was unbearable. They were the same, the impossible sensations, the same, like the two Morellas. He was going to die. He didn't want to die — he had barely lived. He was dying. It was horrible, bigger than himself, death, too big to be contained.

In the hush that followed death, Barry choked again. Dead Freddie still saw, still felt. Felt the exquisite largeness of himself overfilling Barry's mouth — saw the phosphorescent pearls dribbling from Barry's lips, drooling down the length of the turgid spear as Barry slowly freed himself from its impalement. The thing broke loose with a slurp, slapped down on Freddie's belly with a startling thump, a thrill.

Barry wiped his lips with the back of his hand and smiled. "My little man," he said from between Freddie's thighs, his voice thick with satisfaction. "Now, wasn't that splendid."

"I — " said Freddie. "My head — " he said as darkness like India ink flooded his eyes, hiding Barry again.

"Your head — " Barry's voice broke raggedly and he seemed to surge up and forward like a black wave. "I'm so sorry, Freddie. I forgot your head. Is it bad? Are you well, my dear?" Full length, he stretched himself upon supine Freddie, a sweaty weight like sodden blankets, like life.

"I — " Freddie said. His head rang like an empty bell with no clapper. "It... doesn't hurt anymore."

Gentle fingertips mapped his face. "Truly?"

"Not at all. When I — when you...it got very very bad, but then it stopped."

Lips bitter and salty kissed Freddie's mouth. Breathless, ravenous, he tasted the pearls on Barry's tongue, drank them down. He clasped his arms around Barry's broad back. Invigorated, impossibly strong, he rolled Barry over, lay atop him. "I'm well, Barry. Truly, I'm well."

Barry kissed him again. His mouth tasted like itself. "I shall consider myself the sovereign cure for all that ails you, lad. My mouth, at any rate. I shall become conceited."

Freddie stopped his mouth. Beneath him, he felt all of Barry, substantial, fleshy, alive. "But you," he said. "Your...little man."

"Don't trouble yourself about that, Freddie. I am well content."

"I *want* to. I want to." Lifting himself to his knees between Barry's legs, he groped for it: steel hard, velvet soft, leaky about the crown. He bent.

His hand made Barry sigh, but when the older boy felt his tongue Barry pushed Freddie's head away. "Not — not your first time, Freddie."

"I want to please you," Freddie blurted, hurt.

"You please me utterly. But it's a skill and a trouble and I am too near to guide you. Another time you can practice. Your hand will do now."

"Another time? I want to see it — see you. Do you promise?"

"Precious lad, I am in your hands so long as you live at Ladytown and we continue to please each other."

For a moment, only a moment, the wonder of Barry's words stilled the hands he was in. Freddie drew a picture in his mind with India ink: Handsome Barry, perched at the sunlit window, gazing at him with the calm rapture of the man in the "Morella" illustration — first clothed and then…not. "And my dad doesn't find out." Freddie would need to get in the habit of locking his bedroom door.

"'Twould be wise to keep it from him, yes."

"Barry?"

"Yes, Freddie? That feels marvellous. Keep…it up, if you would."

"I liked the taste of you."

Barry's reply was noise, a bleat, a moan. In Freddie's hand, his little man swelled harder with the hot pulse of blood and jerked again and again. Freddie seemed to feel the pearly fluid rush to expulsion. Quick, unthinking, he bent to take a splash of the heated stuff on his cheek: a baptism. He felt the warmth of his own breath radiate back from the quaking surface of Barry's belly. A drop trickled down his cheek into his mouth, as salty-bitter as his own, as real as tears. He was crying.

"Ah, Freddie, Freddie." Barry's fond voice came from far away. "Easy now. Let loose, it's tender for a bit, and come to me."

Weeping silently, Freddie climbed the slippery length of his lover, into his comforting arms, and two boys slept away the last of the storm together.

LACUNA

Matthew Cheney

I heard this story from an acquaintance of mine a few years ago, and he claimed to have heard it from his grandfather, who heard it from the daughter of the man whose story it was. I have filled in gaps with my own best guesses for how certain events might have happened; as an amateur historian of nineteenth-century New York City, I was able to draw on a significant amount of information accumulated over a lifetime of study. Nonetheless, I am painfully aware of how unlikely it is that everything happened as I tell it here.

I tried many times to write this story in as straightforward and objective a manner as possible, but repeatedly failed. There are too many lacunae. Therefore, I am taking the liberty of writing this story from the point of view of the person who is its main character. I have never written fiction before — its conventions are anathema to me — but I hope readers will forgive any awkwardness, for I do believe this is the only way I could accurately preserve what is, I hope you'll agree, a most remarkable history.

A TALE OF THE CITY

LET me call myself, for the present, Adam Wilson. My true name is
not well known outside certain circles, but within those circles it is
known too well, and the knowledge associated with it is more hearsay
and fantasy than truth. Perhaps after my death the truth of my life can be
aligned with the truth of my name, but I do not believe such an event is possible while I am alive.

As a young man, I was passionate and indiscreet. I had been raised on a
farm in northern New York, and had no knowledge of the world until I
had nearly reached the age of maturity. My parents were taciturn country
people, God-fearing and serious, the descendants of Puritans who escaped
England and helped found the colonies that became our Republic. Ours was
a singularly unimaginative race of people, but stubborn and loyal. My childhood was not what I would deem a happy one, yet neither was it painful or
oppressive; instead, it was a childhood of rules and routines, most of them
determined by the sun and moon, the weather, and the little church at the
center of the town three miles south of our farm, the church we traveled to
for every Sabbath, holiday, festivity, and funeral.

As I advanced in years, I became aware of desires within myself to learn
more about a world beyond the narrow realm of my upbringing. Ours was
not a family given to frequent newspaper reading, but I had read enough to
know that the life I lived was not the only possible life. I dreamed of cobble-
stone streets, tall buildings, and crowds of people. Now I know mine was a
common dream, but when I was the dreamer I thought my dream must be
unique in the force of its import and portent. My fate was, I was certain, a
great one.

With only the hope of my naïve yearnings to sustain me, I borrowed a
few dollars from my parents and rode in the carts of merchants taking their
wares toward Manhattan. I don't remember how many days it took to wind
a serpentine way to the isle of my dreams. My memory of that time is obscured by all that befell me, for within a day of arriving I had been most
violently shown the enormity of the chasm between my imagined city and
the one to which I had brought myself. Desperate and hungry, I found what
work I could, but I knew no one and could rely on only the barest charity.
Huddled by night in shadowy corners, trembling from cold and starvation
and fear, I gave thought to returning home, of settling down to the simple

life that seemed to have been predestined for me, but the very idea filled me with a nausea of defeat, for I would have rather thrown myself into the river's muddy torrent than retrace my journey. An evil luck brought me into acquaintance with a certain group of young men who showed me a way to profit from certain men's dark desires, and soon I did not have to hide myself on the streets for I could afford a small room in a ramshackle building among the most disreputable of the city's inhabitants. It was here I lived and here I sold the only good that I possessed: myself.

After I had worked for a time in this most shameful of all employments, one of the men I provided services to asked me if I would like an opportunity to work in pleasanter surroundings, for a better class of customers and certainly more income than I might otherwise make in my debased and impoverished conditions. I was wary at first, having, after bitter experience, become something of a cynic, but this was a man who had been particularly kind to me, his tendency always toward gentleness, and I knew from his attire and mode of travelling that he was a man of means. Habit kept me obmutescent at first, but he persisted every time he saw me in saying how suited I was to the work, given my fair and feminine features, and I believed he was sincere when he said it pained him to see me in such low circumstances as then composed my life. Therefore, one Sunday morning late in the spring of 184_, after we dined together in my room, I accepted his offer and he provided me with an address at which I was to present myself two weeks hence.

During the time between that Sunday and the later night, I imagined countless and baroque possibilities for what this place might be. It was an address near Thompson Street, an area I knew well enough, though I did not frequent it, my haunts being more to the east, and in the fortnight between receiving the address and going to my appointment there, I carefully avoided the vicinity, for I have always been a superstitious man, and I feared some ill might punish my curiosity. The closer the moment came to present myself at the address, the longer the time stretched out and the more excited grew my imagination. I slept fitfully, my dreams alternately haunted by visions of great pleasure and nightmares of grotesque, delirious pain. Entire lifetimes seemed to pour themselves into the last hours before I set out from my gloomy little room.

Eventually, the waiting time dissipated and I found myself walking almost without awareness from street to street at dusk on the appointed day, the scrap of paper on which the address was written clasped in my hand, for, though the address itself had long ago lodged in my memory, I conceived the paper on which it was scrawled to be a fetish, a charm against forces I could neither predict nor apprehend.

I arrived at the address as twilight gathered darkly and more darkly through the city streets. Though I had prepared myself to expect nearly anything, I was not expecting the address to lead to a few small, crude steps descending to a weathered grey door. Not knowing what else to do, I knocked.

‡‡

This is one of the things I most dislike about fiction: the need to set a scene. Certainly, when writing a historical narrative there is context that has to be established, but it's not the same — here what we have is brazen lying. I know nothing about what the exterior of this building looked like. I don't even know that it was on or near Thompson Street. It was somewhere on the island of Manhattan, I do know that, but to be more realistic, I probably should have put it at one of the more remote areas — maybe up north in the twelfth ward somewhere. I chose the location I did because, once you move too far out of the city as it was in the 1840s, you get away from the sorts of buildings that could house the events that are central to the story. Honestly, I expect it all actually happened in Brooklyn, but the person who told me the story specifically said it took place in Manhattan, and so I am sticking to that.

My mood is bleak today, and it's affecting my writing. Adam came over to pick up some of his stuff, and inevitably we had to have a Conversation (I yearn for the days when our conversations were lower-cased). It ended when he asked me how I was doing and I told him it was none of his fucking business. I regretted it immediately, but regret is a useless emotion. He walked out. Just walked. Didn't storm out, didn't slam the door, didn't break windows or anything like that. Walked out. Again. Without a word.

Words. That's part of my problem: I'm trying to capture at least some of the diction of this character, and spending hours with the OED, looking up the histories of one word after another to make sure it's historically accurate, or to find others that are more appropriate. It took me all afternoon to write one paragraph. It's stilting the voice. I can't go on like that. I just need to write and not worry about the historical veracity of the vocabulary and syntax.

I'll never forget Adam unless I write this. The nights when we drank cheap wine and played word games, the delirious night when we fell into each other's arms screaming our various pronunciations of "Ulalume" and "Angoulême," and the one glorious night when silence was enough. I loved his blue eyes, his wild blond hair, his crooked tooth. ("My own little Aryan," I called him.) We told each other stories of our pasts, and his were always full of adventure and excitement — because they were never true, and I knew it, and I loved him for it, and he told me I should loosen up and let go of myself and let my imagination play. I never could, and never dared try, and I hated him for it.

He accused me of being a slave to the facts, and later on, in the nightmare days, I accused him of writing potboilers. The worst nights were when he did more drinking than writing. "Great writers have written stories like mine," he said after half a bottle of Jack one night. I laughed at him and said, "Keep telling yourself that. Crappy writers always think they're great. And drunken assholes figure if they drink like Poe, maybe they'll write like him." He took a swig from the bottle and then spat it in my face. I can hardly blame him. I knew the nerve I was hitting. Still, I was angry. "You're a fucking hack," I said, "and your stories are pathetic and disgusting. They wouldn't scare a child." At the time, I thought it was the beginning of the end, but really, it was the middle. The truth is, I'd never liked his stories, even when we first started dating.

Anyway...

⊱⊰

THE DOOR OPENED, no more slowly or quickly than any other door might, and a small man wearing the most ordinary clothes imaginable stood there in front of me. I showed him the slip of paper I had brought with me, but he didn't look at it. Somehow, he knew I belonged here. He gestured to his side — his right, my left — and I followed his gesture through a nondescript room and perfectly ordinary, if narrow, hallway, to another, and unmemorable, door. I knocked, but there was no answer, and so I turned the knob and opened the door, revealing a set of carpeted stairs leading down. I descended. The air grew musty and cold, the stairway became grey and then dark, and I felt my feet hit stone. I looked down, thinking I had reached some sort of bottom, but in the greyness I could make out more steps, now made of stone. Granite. Descending.

Eventually, light slipped through the darkness from candles set on shelves at the bottom of the stairs. I know now that the stairs were not miles long, but that is the impression they gave during that descent. Certainly, the caverns they led to were deep, and the edifice as a whole a marvel of architecture and engineering, but there was nothing supernatural about the place, at least in its design.

What the stairs led to was a series of small rooms with rock walls. Within moments of my arrival, a dark-skinned young man dressed as a servant brought me to one of the other rooms, a place filled with piles of women's clothing. In the dim light, the clothing looked expensive and impressive, but soon the young man held some pieces out to me and instructed me on how to wear them, and touching the fabric I saw that it was tattered, torn, and stained. I should say here that I had not worn women's clothing before, nor had much cause to examine it closely — a fact that had purely been a matter of chance, given how many of my compatriots were instructed at one time or another to unsex themselves for their men — and so I was awkward and required much assistance from the young man. His touch was gentle and soothing, as if he expected me to be frightened or disgusted, but given the circumstances of my hiring and the strangeness of the setting, I felt little surprise at the necessary attire. "What is your name?" I asked him. His smile was unforced and uncertain, as if it was the strangest query he'd encountered in many days.

"You don't need to know me," he said, averting his eyes.

I shifted my gaze to grasp his again, then took his hand in mine. "Necessity is the least interesting force in the universe," I said, parroting an aphorism once uttered by a priest who insisted on philosophizing whilst I pleasured him.

"My name is Charles," he said. "But please forget me. They'll call you to the stage in a moment, and you need to be ready."

"Will we meet again, Charles?"

I pulled him closer to me, but released his hand when I saw tears in his eyes.

Hands gripped my shoulders, spun me around, pushed me forward into light. Whiteness enveloped me, blinded me. I stumbled forward, knocking my foot against an obstacle. I heard chattering voices, the rumblings of impatient conversation. My eyes adjusted slowly, bringing shapes and colors into focus, and then I saw where I stood: a living room with a long couch, three chairs, and a low table. No — as my eyes accustomed to the light, I saw beyond it, beyond what I had taken to be walls and windows — beyond the whirlwind of lamps, mirrors, crystals, and smoke that obscured the view — I saw faces stacked in a small and narrow amphitheatre: the leering, lusting faces of men.

Breathless, my knees trembling with infirmity, I staggered to the couch and fell upon it. At that moment, a figure appeared from somewhere behind me. A man in a swallow-tailed black coat — his visage concealed by a black silk mask, his hands protected by white gloves — moved forward and presented himself to the audience. The men applauded vigorously.

I sat up on the couch and whispered, "Who are you?"

The masked figure rushed to me, his hand struck my face, and I fell back onto the couch. My cheek burned, my forehead ached, blood crossed my tongue. Ringing filled my ears, but then I heard the audience through the noise: their laughter, their rallying cries. His hands pulled me up, turned me to face him. The fabric of his mask was wet at the mouth and nose; his breathing made the silk pulse like a sail in a storm. Again his hand hit my face, and then the other hand, and then again, again — and all the while, the audience applauded, their claps in sympathy with each slap across my skin.

My abraded cheeks bled, my nose and lips bled, blood filled my mouth, I coughed. His hands grasped my throat and pushed me back onto the couch. Men whistled and stomped their feet. He tore the dress at the shoulder, snapping its seams. He wrenched it down. I pushed at him feebly, my arms and muscles moving by instinct, but he was stronger than I and easily held me back against the couch. His fists hit my stomach, my kidneys, then the bones of my ribs, knocking sense and breath from me. I keeled forward, and again he pushed me back, slapped my face, grabbed my hair. My eyes saw swirls of colors more than shapes, but soon I discerned that he stood over me and was pulling back his mask. I expected any face except the one I should have known would be there: The face of the man who had so gently implored me to come to this place. His eyes, which I had once, briefly, thought displayed a kind of love for me, now burned with contempt.

My recognition fired his fury. He rained more punishment upon me, and then, as I lay on the couch, my body throbbing, my eyes blurred with tears, he lowered his face to my chest, and the familiar tenderness there found its parody in his nuzzling kisses. The audience grew silent, their attention rapt, and yet soon there were stirrings — they became restless.

My tormenter paused. He now prepared the *pièce de résistance* of his performance. Holding me under the arms, he pulled me up to stand. The dress I wore sagged around my hips. He wrapped his right arm around my neck and with his left arm pulled — slowly but fiercely — the dress and all my underclothing down toward my knees. He could not hold my neck and further undress me, and so he pushed me forward — I braced myself with my arms, but fell hard on the floor, cracking a bone — and then felt myself hoisted backward as he ripped the shredding dress and all the rest from me until I was entirely naked in the hot fire of the lights and the hateful glare of all the men.

He retrieved his mask from where it had fallen beside the couch. He covered his face with it, sat on the couch, and removed his shoes. His feet bare, he walked toward me, then slowly, gently, took off each piece of clothing until only his mask remained. I glanced at him, not letting my gaze linger, for the pains coursing through my body demanded most attention for themselves. A quick look was enough for me, though, for I knew his strong, supple body well, and the sight of it above me now filled me with terror — the engorgement of his desire offered no thrill for me — rather, he seemed entirely grotesque, a demon, a force of unimaginable agony.

Even now, decades after the events, I cannot describe his actions without bringing myself to tears and raising aching memories across my skin.

I do not have the words to describe his final abuses, nor do I want to remember all he did to me or to remember the wild joys of the crowd.

⁓

I don't remember writing the scene I just wrote. I would never write such an absurd phrase as "the engorgement of his desire." It's disgusting and ridiculous. Those are not words I would choose. I should erase them now, I should get rid of this whole thing. And yet I know I won't. I've written those words there — "I should erase them now, I should get rid of this whole thing" — to let myself off the hook. I had no intention of erasing any of this. I've enjoyed writing it. I've gotten out of myself, away from the shitstorm with Adam. I don't believe a word of what I wrote above about responsibility. That's not true, either, though. I believe in the idea of it. But it has no visceral meaning for me. Because I really am writing this for myself. Really. It's an escape, a bit of fun. Meaningless. Really. I don't need you to read this. I don't need you.

⊹

(THE MEMORIES REST as jagged shards, sharp and ready to freshen wounds.)

The light burns and stings its smoke into my eyes. My body moves, pulled over the wooden stage, splinters pricking my knees and legs. Darkness, then soft candlelight. Fingers trawl my skin. Cold water washes me. Charles won't meet my gaze. I realize why he had tears in his eyes. He knew. There are many words I would like to say to him, but my tongue is thick and my mouth dry. He dresses me carefully in the clothes I arrived in. Shadows shift in the room and take hold of me and drag me up the stairs and outside into early morning air, and I am carried around corners and dropped in an alley onto soggy newspapers and chicken bones and scattering rats. They toss coins at me.

I do not move. Movement is pain. I barely breathe.

(The subsequent memories are more dreamlike, less present, and they do not wound.)

The sun rose somewhere above me and distant voices fell and echoed through the air. A rat bit my leg. I coughed and yearned for water or, better, gin. I swept the coins from my chest and hid them away in my pants. My employer had been correct that this was more lucrative work for me — these were good coins, more than I would earn in a month usually — but the cost was too much.

I leaned against a brick wall and inched my way toward the street. Somewhere in this Herculean effort, I met my savior. He was a thin man, disheveled, and his attire making it seem that he, too, might have been dropped in an alley, but he sported no wounds to his bones and skin, just sunken, bloodshot eyes and an unsteady step.

I do not remember what conversation we had. I drifted from awareness to a kind of half-sleep where I was awake but uncomprehending. Somehow I told him the address of my room, and somehow he took me there. My first thought was fear: did he intend to add to my abuses? He seemed afraid to touch me, though, and so I did not long fear him. My second thought was embarrassment: at the squalor of my tiny room, at the weakness of myself. I had little reason for such feelings, though, for soon he had lain himself down on the floor and fallen asleep.

I woke in the night when he opened the door.

"Who are you?" I called, fearing I would never see him again, never see him when I was healthy enough to thank him for his tremendous kindness.

"A man who needs to piss," he said, and walked out. He returned some time later.

"I have a chamber pot," I said.

"I know," he said. "But you didn't have this." He held up a small bottle of whiskey.

"I have gin."

"I saw your gin. Indeed, I smelled it." He sat on the one chair in the room, a small wooden chair I had built myself from scraps I'd found near the docks. He opened his bottle of whiskey. "What you call gin is a fast road to blindness. I might consider using it to remove stains from my clothing, but I am afraid it would remove the cloth along with the stains."

"I wanted to thank you," I said, "for —"

"No need for thanks. My motives were entirely mercenary, and you still should receive the attention of doctors, especially given what looks to me like a broken bone in your arm. I have not called a doctor, however. I must leave that for you to do yourself. You were a useful excuse for me at a difficult moment. I needed to disappear from the vision of certain people for a few hours while they sought me out for debts I most surely do not owe them, and since you are a stranger to me, and we have no previous connection, it is unlikely anyone will think to look for me here. I trust you are sufficiently healthy to avoid immediate death, however, as I have no skill as a nurse. Also, I expect I will become insensibly inebriated within the next hour. I have been an advocate of temperance recently, and I intend to return to advocating temperance in the future, but in the present I desire nothing so much as the soft obliteration bestowed by this bottle." He drank deeply from it.

"I am still grateful to you. There is no telling what could have become of me."

After many more minutes and many more drinks, the man said, "How *did* you end up in this state, if you'll pardon my curiosity?"

"I hardly know myself. A poet might say I fell into a vortex of vice and infamy."

"A villainous vortex of vice. Or, perhaps, a villainous veritable vortex of vice. No, a vortex of villainy, a veritable vice of..." He sighed and swayed a bit on the chair. He emptied the bottle into his mouth, then carefully slid from the chair to the floor, his care undermined by his drunkenness, causing him to end up on hands and knees with little comprehension of how he got there. Eventually, he rolled onto his side and stared at me.

"Are you a thief?" he muttered.

"What?"

"You live in a thieves' establishment."

"No, there are no thieves here. We are people of business."

He chuckled. "And what business is your business?"

I looked into his hazed and glassy eyes. "You won't remember anything I say in the morning."

He coughed fiercely, but somehow avoided vomiting.

"Men pay me money," I said. "And for that money, I pleasure them. I kiss them. I undress them. They kiss me and undress me. We pretend at love. Their tastes are, shall we say, Hellenistic. Some of them are strong men whose pleasure comes from dominating a weaker man. Some of them are weak men who fancy themselves women at heart. If they pay enough, I can give them any pleasure they desire."

"Do you enjoy…" he began, his words fading into gibberish.

"Sometimes, yes, I enjoy it," I said. "A shallow enjoyment, briefly real. I learned early to survive by trying to fall in love with them all. They pay better when I am convincing. They return. My best men seek my body's spirit, and they pay me for it, so I must…deliver it unto them."

He chuckled again, weakly, as he slipped away from consciousness.

In the morning, his body was so consumed with nausea and pain that the doctor I summoned to attend to my wounds spent as much time with him as with me. A few of my friends and regular customers paid a visit during the day, and while most of them assumed the man sprawled on the floor was an especially satiated customer, one of my favorite men, a lovely brute with mischievous eyes and a lady's lips who worked among newspapermen, said he had seen my visitor around his own haunts and knew him to be disreputable and irresponsible, often a danger to himself but generally harmless otherwise, though he was said to have an acid tongue.

By evening, he had recovered sufficiently to depart, offering to return with provisions should I need them, but by that time my friends and colleagues had determined a schedule by which they fulfilled my needs in shifts, for though we may be lowly in our employment and circumstances, lowliness inspires fierce comradeship: my fate was one all my peers could envision for themselves, and though I knew of none whose experiences were as decorated with grotesque mystery as mine, few had escaped bruises, broken bones, and alley trash heaps during their careers.

And so my savior departed, and I thanked him, and he seemed to remember nothing of our conversation, and I set my sails toward healing and forgetting.

I sent my customers away with apologies — the doctor had informed me that my body needed significant rest and tenderness, and my broken arm was going to be a problem for months. A few men offered me a penny or two for food and medicine, though most simply gave me a wary smile or hasty kiss before closing the door behind themselves. Many would never look at me with the same lust in their eyes as before, and most would pay someone else for their pleasures.

As the months passed and my body healed, if ever the terrible night left my mind my dreams brought it back in monstrous nightmares. Shadow creatures tore all the skin from my face and chest and arms and legs — massive hands pulverized my bones — wild, full, liquid eyes flashed with red light across all my visions — and endless applause echoed through the maelström.

Many months later, as I undressed in darkness for a customer who sprawled naked across my bed, a shaft of moonlight illuminated my face more fully than he had seen it before, and he gasped and covered himself with the sheets. I knew then what I had first suspected when I saw him: This was Charles, the attendant to my nightmares. His face had grown more sallow, his body more angular, but this was he.

I jumped atop him and held him to the bed. (In the moonlight, we perhaps resembled a strange etching of midnight wrestlers.) My muscles flexed with fury, and I wanted nothing so much as to tear him apart with my hands, not because he had himself abused me — he had been nothing but gentle and sympathetic — but because here, for the first time since that ghastly night, I held in my hands some physical representation of the misery that still terrorized my mind.

Leaning down close, I spat his name into his ear, enunciating it as a vicious noise, an accusation and condemnation, a curse. I held him firm, but gave him everything he had paid me for, and more than that — for though I always made sure to keep him pressed to the bed to prevent his escape, my every caress was soft, careful, loving. Malnourishment and maltreatment had faded his previous beauty, but its shadow remained, and it was the shadow I sought, the shadow I held in my imagination. This was a greater torture to him than any I could have inflicted with fists or whips or the manifold tools of so many Inquisitions. Once I recovered from my terrible night, I took to keeping my room quite dark, for certain scars and bruises never left my skin, and only a minority of customers are excited by damaged goods, so Charles had not been able to discern my features and had not known whom he was buying — his intent was as innocent as any such attempt could be.

After, as he lay nearly comatose from exhaustion and shame, I retrieved some rope from a corner of the room and bound him with it. He fought listlessly against me. I hauled him to the floor and dragged him up against the wall. And then I waited.

Though first he resisted and pleaded ignorance, then wept over the consequences his words would bring himself and his family, by mid-day, he had told me everything I hoped to know. He did not know names, or at least not useful ones (the names he knew were descriptive: "The Sailor," "The Old Swede," "The Painter," "Doctors D and F") but he knew times, locations, and passwords. Though he wailed that he was certain things had changed since he had been unceremoniously relieved of his duties (for reasons he knew not), I thanked him and removed the ropes that bound him. I had brought a bucket of water into the room, and I cleaned him with it, and as I did so his tears subsided and his weeping gave way to stoic impassivity. I dried him with a small towel, then dressed him as if he were an invalid. I kissed him, but he did not respond. In the years since that moment, I have imagined many words that must have passed through his mind, but the truth is that he did not speak — he lifted his head high and walked away, a new force of will, or a newly willed force, propelling him from the room.

He had given me the address at which the malevolent club would meet, for they moved their meetings according to a strict plan, and he said it was always the third Thursday of the month, and that the revels began precisely at eleven minutes past eleven in the evening. That gave me one month to prepare, for Charles had visited me on the night of the third Thursday.

I spent the month perfecting my scheme and collecting the various items I would need to effect it. This required much cleverness and a certain amount of daring, for I had not nearly enough money to purchase all the items, particularly the clothing, and so I had to insinuate myself into places where such things could be acquired. My greatest luck came when a friend of a friend introduced me to an expensive card game in a building near Gramercy Place, and my experience with far less trusting competitors in far more compli-cated games allowed me to leave not only with what was, for me at that time, a small fortune in cash, but with what I had really come for: a fine hat, cape, and walking stick. (The other players were so amused by my encouraging them to wager their clothing that they insisted I return again in the future, as indeed I did many times, making the associations that would, in fact, send me toward the far more reputable sort of life I lead today.)

Thus it was that I was able to dress myself as a man of considerable means, and to secrete on my person two pistols obtained for me by a faithful cus-tomer who was also an officer in the Navy, and who provided me with, in ad-dition to the pistols, ammunition and numerous small sacks of gunpowder.

⊷⊷

I began writing this as a way to, I thought — or I told myself — exorcise Adam. But that's not it.

Words are magic. That's what he said to me when we started dating. I loved his words, and I told him so, and he smiled and he said, "Well, words are magic." It's only when you're first in love with somebody that such banal and empty ideas seem profound. I should know better, but those first, rushing, blinding moments of love make everything seem profound, unique, consequential. I should know better. I've got a master's degree, I've studied philosophy and literature and art and history — and yes, my daily life is not glamorous, I work as a shipping and receiving manager at a warehouse, yes, I know I am not, as he said, living up to my potential (whatever that is!), but you don't think I'm as aware of that as anybody else? I've spent a lifetime being told how much potential I have, how brilliant and talented I am, what a fine mind I have. At the warehouse they call me "Professor" and "Einstein," but that's nothing compared to what people say to me when I get into a conversation with them about, for instance, the building of the Croton Water Aqueduct or the history of the Tombs and then they ask me if I've written a book or if I work at a university and I mumble and I shuffle my feet and I cough nervously and eventually, if they're persistent, I tell them, "Actually, I work at a warehouse." You should see their faces. You have seen their faces. And I've seen your face when you've seen their faces. It's not just that you think I haven't lived up to my potential, no — you're ashamed of me. At your book parties, at your conventions and conferences. You were always happy to be around anybody other than me. Remember the party where, after at least a couple of bottles of wine, you grabbed me and groped me and people gathered around, laughing nervously, and you yelled to them all, "Look, friends, at my Hop-frog!" I should have grabbed a torch and hurled it at you and set you all aflame.

Words are magic.

No they aren't. I keep writing this, thinking of you, wondering what you would make of it, wondering if it would, somehow, be enough. Enough what? Enough magic.

Words are not magic. Words are echoes, shadows, ashes.

We tell stories because what else is there to do? This is a story. I am telling it. Summoning voices to keep me company through the night.

✛

THE ENTERTAINMENT THAT month occurred in a palatial private residence far north, at 52nd Street and Fifth Avenue. My card winnings easily paid for a fine carriage to carry me to the location, and, though I had feared the password system Charles taught me would have been changed, it was not, for I was admitted without a second glance from the masked and muscled men who guarded the inside of the door. From there, a very small man — a dwarf, really — dressed in an expensive (and miniature) butler's uniform led me through a corridor and up two flights of stairs to a kind of recital hall. It was a circular room, very lofty, and received the light of the moon only through a single window at top. A few dozen chairs stood in rows in front of a small stage, at the center of which had been placed a settee, and above which hung an immense chandelier dripping wax from its countless candles. Most of the seats in the audience were filled by well-attired men, and none of us looked at each other or spoke.

Within minutes, the man in the world whom I most loathed, the man who had first enticed me to participate in one of these performances and then scarred and humiliated me so brutally, so publicly — this man now stood on the stage, directly in front of the settee, his face unmasked. His words echo through my ears as if I heard them mere minutes ago:

299

"Hello, my friends. Tonight's revelry is a singular one for us. It has been arranged to honor one of our most devoted members, a man who has been a friend to these festivities for longer than most, and who has provided us all with much continued pleasure through the imaginative chronicling of the emotional forces that are unleashed here every month. His is our true voice, his words the metaphors of our reality, his dreams the ones we share. He has, alas, fallen on hard times, as can happen to any man, and to lighten the burden of his days, I asked him what spectacle he would most like to see, and so tonight's pantomime is one that we should consider authored by our dear friend."

With that, the man gestured to a figure sitting in the front row, a figure who stood and acknowledged us — and it was at that moment that I nearly gave myself away, for I could barely stifle a gasp of shock and revulsion on seeing the face of my savior, the man who had rescued me after I had been subjected to such evil, the man who guided me home and stayed with me on the first night of my recovery.

I hardly had time to absorb the fact of his face before most of the lights in the room were extinguished, save for the chandelier above the stage, and a young girl stumbled forward, golden braids bouncing over her face. She looked confused and stunned. Before she could gain her bearings, the malevolent host strode forward and grasped her in his arms. She screamed, and a few men in the audience responded with laughs. The host lifted the girl onto the settee and then his hands performed a terrible dance upon her body. As her screams grew more desperate, the laughter in the room rose, and so, too, did sounds of encouragement and goading. I felt a psychic hunger course through the audience as the host held a dagger in his hand and, with great precision, sliced the girl's dress open slowly and methodically, then, after excruciating minutes of this, pulled the dress from her trembling body. It was then that we all saw that this was not, in fact, a young girl, but a young boy — and the men in the audience screamed their approval as the host slit and removed the last garments from the unfortunate boy's frame and then held him aloft like a prize calf. He held the boy before the man in the front row, who nodded his approval without touching the chaste, white, shivering body.

I was about to enact the climax of my plan when two men wearing masks of the *commedia dell'arte* style appeared, carried a small ivory casket onto the stage, and opened it. I stayed my hand because of a moment's fascination. The host then placed the naked and whimpering boy into the casket and closed it. The casket had been fitted with locks, and the cover was thick enough to muffle the boy's terrified screams. The host gestured to the audience to enjoy the screams. It was what they had assembled for — not merely the sight of the boy being degraded and abused, but for the pleasure of his terror.

I couldn't keep watching. I stood, withdrew a pistol, and shot the host in the chest. The audience thought this was part of the entertainment, and they applauded and cheered. Only the man in the front row seemed to understand that something was wrong, and he stood up. I moved forward, keeping the pistol aimed at his head. "Do you know me?" I said. "Do you?"

He stared at me, and then recognition dawned across his face.

The pistol now pressed against his forehead, I repeated, "Do you know me?"

"Yes."

The shot would have cracked his skull open, but at the last moment my hand wavered and I merely fired past his ear — the shock and noise enough to make him fall to the ground, thick red blood oozing from inside his ear, but very much alive.

The men who had guarded the front doors rushed into the room, and the audience had now figured out that something was amiss, but they were paralyzed by shock and confusion.

I pushed the bleeding body of the host away from the casket, its ivory now decorated with blood. I sprung the locks, opened the lid, pulled the terrified boy out, and wrapped him in my cloak. "Hold onto my hand," I told him. "Don't let go."

As the guardsmen and the audience approached, I tossed bags of gunpowder toward the candles in front of them, bringing loud, acrid explosions that blinded them and robbed them of breath. I whisked the boy out of the room, down the corridor and stairs, and then outside, where my carriage waited around a corner. I attempted to hasten him into the carriage, but his terror gave him new strength, and he was unable to distinguish my care from the abuses of the men in the mansion, and so he struggled and fought until he was free of my grip and my cloak, and he ran, naked and screaming, into the night. I knew that the noise of my guns, perhaps, and the boy's screams, almost certainly, would alert neighbors and elicit eyes at windows, so I gave the boy no more thought and jumped into my carriage and we hurried away.

I learned much later that, shortly after I proved unable to shoot him in the head, the man I had previously thought of as my savior showed up drunk and sick in Baltimore, where he died. His literary work gained fame and notoriety in the following years, but I have always refused to read a word of it.

As I alluded above, I was able to make a new life for myself thanks to my own cleverness and determination, and to acquire something of a reputation as a philanthropist and an advocate for the preservation of Saxon strength through careful, deliberate habits of breeding — I am pleased that my pedagogical historical narrative *Hengst and Horsa, or, The Saxon Men* sold extremely well some years ago under one of my *noms de plume*. But I am an old and ailing man, now, and my time is limited, and as I have always devoted my life to the truth, I feel I must pen this manuscript, for fear that I will disappear otherwise into the vortex of time without having expressed the truths of my life — truths which, for all their apparent wonder and horror, I trust will speak their veracity to you, dear reader.

> *"In me didst thou exist — and, in my death, see by this image, which is thine own, how utterly thou hast murdered thyself."*
> — EDGAR ALLAN POE, "WILLIAM WILSON"

⁓

It is not the ending I intended. I had been struggling with it for a week or so, failing to create the tone I wanted, trying out a bunch of things to give it both a sense of verisimilitude and drama, never achieving it — and then three days ago got a call from Ginny with the news that Adam is dead.

I was going to try to revise the ending, but why bother now? I secretly hoped he would read the story and like it, or even hate it but be amused. I thought he would see that I understood how hard he worked, how talented he was, the worth of stories and storytelling. Or something. I don't know. Maybe my intentions were less noble or naïve. I don't know.

What I know is that now there is no point. Words are not magic. If there is truth, it lurks between the lines, unreachable, silent, lost like the truth of whatever happened to Poe in the last week of September 1849. Lost. We can imagine stories, but that is all they are: imagined.

I was writing this story for myself, I thought, but really I was writing it for him, and so I wrote it for nothing. It is here now, it exists, like me, alone, unfinished, a testament to nothing but itself.

I've read so many interviews with writers and artists who say they create to have a sense of immortality, of leaving something behind after they go. Adam said that sometimes. His stories, he said, were his children, his legacy, his history, his immortality. Even if he wasn't rich and famous, at least he had books on shelves and maybe one day in the future somebody would stumble on one in a library or a bookstore and his words would live in their mind. His work would live on. But what good is posterity? You're still dead.

Words are not magic. Stories are not truth; they are evasions, misdirections.

He took a couple Valium, drank most of a bottle of vodka, loaded his father's old Colt 1911 pistol, put it in his mouth, and pulled the trigger.

Those are the facts. End of story.

Contributors

CHRISTOPHER BARZAK grew up in rural Ohio, went to university in a decaying post-industrial city in Ohio, and has lived in a Southern California beach town, the capital of Michigan, and in the suburbs of Tokyo, Japan, where he taught English in rural elementary and middle schools. His stories have appeared in a many venues, including *Nerve*, *The Year's Best Fantasy and Horror*, *Teeth*, *Asimov's*, and *Lady Churchill's Rosebud Wristlet*. His first novel, *One for Sorrow*, won the Crawford Award. His second book, *The Love We Share Without Knowing*, is a novel-in-stories set in a magical-realist modern Japan, and was a finalist for the Nebula Award for Best Novel and the James Tiptree, Jr. Award. His most recent release is a short story collection, *Before and Afterlives*. He lives in Youngstown, Ohio, where he teaches fiction writing in the Northeast Ohio MFA program at Youngstown State University.

RICHARD BOWES has won two World Fantasy, an International Horror Guild and Million Writer Awards. His new novel, *Dust Devil on a Quiet Street*, will appear in 2013 from Lethe Press, which has also recently republished his Lambda Award winning novel *Minions of the Moon*. Recent and forthcoming appearances include: *F&SF*, *Icarus*, *Lightspeed* and the anthologies *After*, *Wilde Stories 2013*, *Bloody Fabulous*, *Ghosts: Recent Hauntings*, and the forthcoming *Handsome Devil*.

SATYROS PHIL BRUCATO is an American writer, journalist, editor and game designer. Based in Seattle, WA, he is best known for his work with White Wolf, Inc. — including role-playing games such as *Mage: The Ascension*, *Werewolf: The Apocalypse*, and *Mage: The Sorcerer's Crusade* — and BBI Media, for which he has written articles and columns for *newWitch* and *Witches & Pagans* magazines. He has sold several macabre short works of fiction.

Seth Cadin is from New York and now lives in California. More of his short stories can be found in the Prime anthologies *Bewere the Night* and *Bandersnatch*, in the anthologies *Willful Impropriety* and *Brave New Love* from Running Press, *Suffered from the Night* from Lethe Press and in Issue V of the annual *Three-Lobed Burning Eye* anthology. He has one partner, one daughter, and many pet mice.

Máiréad Casey hails from a little spot of the Irish countryside named Lough Gur. She graduated Trinity College Dublin with an M.Phil in Popular Literature. She has been published in *The Attic* and *Fullstop Literary Magazine* but this is her first professional publication.

Matthew Cheney's stories have appeared in *Icarus*, *One Story*, *Weird Tales*, *Lady Churchill's Rosebud Wristlet*, *Interfictions*, *Logorrhea*, and elsewhere. He is the former series editor of the *Best American Fantasy* anthologies, and his blog, *The Mumpsimus*, was nominated for a World Fantasy Award. He has worked as a high school teacher, college teacher, and gun dealer.

Ray Cluley has been published several times in the TTA Press publication *Black Static*. One of these stories as selected by Ellen Datlow for *The Best Horror of the Year*, Volume 3, and another was republished as a French translation in the annual anthology *Ténébres 2011*. He has also been published in *Interzone*. His non-fiction has been published in the British Fantasy Society's journal but generally he prefers to make stuff up. You can find out more at probablymonsters.wordpress.com.

Peter Dubé is the author of four works of fiction: *Hovering World*, *At the Bottom of the Sky*, *Subtle Bodies*, which was a finalist for the Shirley Jackson Award, and, most recently, *The City's Gates*. He is also the editor of the anthologies *Madder Love: Queer Men and the Precincts of Surrealism* and *Best Gay Stories 2011* and *2012*. A collection of prose poems entitled *Conjure* is forthcoming from Rebel Satori Press. Peter lives and works in Montreal and his website is peterdube.com.

L.A. Fields has a long fascination with gay boys who are both troubled and in trouble. Her first novel, *Maladaptation*, was chosen by the Insight-Out Book Club, as was her latest book, *My Dear Watson*, a clever historical volume that explores the relationship of Holmes and Watson discovered by the latter's second wife. She is suffering through the banalities of earning an M.F.A.

ALEX JEFFERS lived in a Georgian big house in Co. Waterford for some impressionable years in the 1960s but now for far too long in New England. Migraine and he are ancient companions. He wishes he could draw like Harry Clarke. His latest book is *Deprivation; or, Benedetto furioso: an oneiromancy* and his latest stories appear at GigaNotoSaurus.org and in *Bad Seeds: Evil Progeny* and *Zombies: Shambling through the Ages* (both Prime Books).

KYLE S. JOHNSON has appeared in the anthologies *The World is Dead*, *Dark Faith*, *Dark Faith: Invocations*, and can be found in the upcoming anthology *Vampires Don't Sparkle* and a future episode of *Pseudopod*. He currently works and resides in Namyangju, a city in Gyeonggi Province, South Korea.

COLLIN KELLEY is the author of the novels *Conquering Venus* and *Remain In Light*, a 2012 finalist for the Townsend Prize for Fiction, and the short story collection *Kiss Shot*. His poetry collections include *Better To Travel*, the spoken-word album *HalfLife Crisis*, *Slow To Burn*, *After the Poison* and *Render*. A recipient of the Georgia Author the Year Award, Deep South Festival of Writers Award and Goodreads Poetry Award, Kelley has published poetry, essays, interviews and reviews in magazines and journals around the world.

TERRA LEMAY was born on top of a volcano (in Hawaii). She tamed a wild mustang before she turned sixteen, and before twenty-five had traveled through most of the U.S. and to parts of Europe and Mexico. She has also held some unusual jobs, like training llamas and modeling high-heeled shoes (though not at the same time!). Her short fiction has appeared in a number of fine magazines and anthologies, both online and in print. Find out more at terralemay.com.

CHIP LIVINGSTON is the author of two poetry collections, *Crow-Blue, Crow-Black* and *Museum of False Starts*. His fiction and non-fiction are also widely published, in journals including *Ploughshares*, *Cincinnati Review*, *Potomac Review*, *Court Green*, *Subtropics*, *Crazyhorse* and *New American Writing*, and in anthologies such as *I Was Indian*, *SING: Poetry from the Indigenous Americas*,

Sovereign Erotics, and *Who's Yer Daddy? Gay Writers Celebrate Their Mentors and Forerunners*. Chip has received writing awards from Wordcraft Circle of Native Writers, Native Writers' Circle of the Americas, and the AABB Foundation. He has spent a number of years teaching writing in Uruguay but has returned to the United States of America recently.

HEATHER LOJO has published poetry in *Cicada* and *Electric Velocipede* and fiction in *Fantasy Magazine*, with honorable mentions in the Datlow and Link & Grant Year's *Best Horror and Fantasy*.

CLARE LONDON took the pen name based on the city where she lives, loves, and writes. A lone, brave female in a frenetic, testosterone-fuelled family home, she juggles her writing with the weekly wash, waiting for the far distant day when she can afford to give up her day job as an accountant. She's written in many genres and across many settings, with novels and short stories published both online and in print. She says she likes variety in her writing while friends say she's just fickle, but as long as both theories spawn good fiction, she's happy. Most of her work features gay romance and drama with a healthy serving of physical passion, as she enjoys both reading and writing about strong, sympathetic and sexy characters.

ED MADDEN is the author of two books of poetry, *Signals*, which won the 2007 South Carolina Poetry Book Prize, and *Prodigal: Variations*. A third book, *Nest*, is forthcoming from Salmon Press in Ireland. His work is also included in *Best New Poets 2007*, *Best Gay Poetry 2008*, *Collective Brightness*, and in the Notre Dame collection *The Book of Irish American Poetry*. Madden is an associate professor of English and director of the Women's & Gender Studies Program at the University of South Carolina.

RONNA MAGY came onto the planet as the colors of World War II were fading from Detroit's skyline and Sputnik orbited the skies. She is a member of QueerWise, a collective of LGBT elders doing spoken-word performances in Los Angeles. Ronna's recent work has appeared in: *Southern Women's Review*; *Trivia: Voices of Feminism*; *Lady Business: A Celebration Of Lesbian Poetry*; *My Life is Poetry*; and *Sinister Wisdom*. She is the author of several English as a Second Language textbooks.

NICK MAMATAS has given up writing speculative fiction for stories of crime and avant-garde fiction. Is "Eureka!" one such tale? It doesn't matter if this story is one of his older and fantastical tales finally seeing the light of day (though he wrote the story in one day at my behest, so I think I'll consider it quite experimental). He resides in California, where all new ideas are born and all old trends go to die.

JEFF MANN grew up in Covington, Virginia, and Hinton, West Virginia. His poetry, fiction, and essays have appeared in many publications, including *Arts and Letters, Prairie Schooner, Shenandoah, Willow Springs, The Gay and Lesbian Review Worldwide, Crab Orchard Review,* and *Appalachian Heritage.* He has published three award-winning poetry chapbooks, *Bliss, Mountain Fireflies,* and *Flint Shards from Sussex;* four full-length books of poetry, *Bones Washed with Wine, On the Tongue, Ash: Poems from Norse Mythology* and *A Romantic Mann;* two collections of personal essays, *Edge: Travels of an Appalachian Leather Bear* and *Binding the God: Ursine Essays from the Mountain South;* two novels, *Fog: A Novel of Desire and Reprisal,* which won the Pauline Réage Novel Award, and *Purgatory: A Novel of the Civil War,* which won a Rainbow Award; a book of poetry and memoir, *Loving Mountains, Loving Men;* and two volumes of short fiction, *Desire and Devour: Stories of Blood and Sweat* and *A History of Barbed Wire,* which won a Lambda Literary Award. He teaches creative writing at Virginia Tech in Blacksburg, Virginia.

JOHN MANTOOTH is an award-winning author, middle school teacher, former school bus driver, and basketball junkie. His first novel, *The Year of the Storm,* was published by Berkley in 2013, and his collection *Shoebox Train Wreck* was published in 2012. He lives in Alabama with his wife and children.

SILVIA MORENO-GARCIA's fiction appears in a number of places, including *Imaginarium 2012: The Best Canadian Speculative Writing.* Her stories are collected in *Shedding Her Own Skin.* She owns a micro-press, Innsmouth Free Press, and has edited anthologies such as *Dead North* and *Fungi.* She lives in Vancouver.

TANSY RAYNER ROBERTS is the award-winning author of the *Creature Court* trilogy (*Power and Majesty, The Shattered City* and *Reign of Beasts*) and the short story collection *Love and Romanpunk.* You can find her at her blog (http://tansyrr.com/), on Twitter @tansyrr and on the Hugo-nominated podcast Galactic Suburbia (http://galactisuburbia.podbean.com/). Tansy lives in Tasmania, Australia with a Silent Producer and two superhero daughters.

CORY SKERRY lives in the Northwest U.S. in a spooky old house that he doesn't like to admit is haunted. When he's not peddling (or meddling with) art supplies, he's writing, reading submissions, or off exploring with his sweet, goofy pit bulls. When his current meatshell begins to fall apart, he'd like science to put his brain into a giant killer octopus body, with which he'll be very responsible and not even slightly shipwrecky. He promises. For more stories, visit coryskerry.net.

DANIEL NATHAN TERRY, a former landscaper and horticulturist, is the author of *Waxwings, Capturing the Dead*, which won the Stevens Prize, and a chapbook, *Days of Dark Miracles*. His writing has appeared, or is forthcoming, in many journals and anthologies, including *Cimarron Review, New South, Poet Lore, Assaracus, Hypertext, Jonathan, Chautauqua,* and *Collective Brightness*. He serves on the advisory board of One Pause Poetry and teaches at the University of North Carolina in Wilmington, where he lives with his husband, painter and printmaker, Benjamin Billingsley.

Editor

Editor of numerous anthologies, most of which deal with queer themes and speculative fiction, **STEVE BERMAN** tried to participate in the Goth subsculture but discovered he was not a fan of black or purple or crimson. He prefers earth tones. Perhaps orange since you can't have an authentic pumpkin without the color. Still, he has a dark sense of humor and a collection of macabre toys. He has never tasted Amontillado, has never attended a masque, or found a message in a bottle. But tomorrow night he will dream something eerie might happen.